TERMINUS 3

EDITED BY
MILTON J. DAVIS

MVmedia, LLC
Fayetteville, GA

MVmedia, LLC
PO Box 143052
Fayetteville, GA 30214
www.mvmediaatl.ocm

Publisher's Note: This is a work of fiction. Names, characters, places, and incidents are a product of the author's imagination. Locales and public names are sometimes used for atmospheric purposes. Any resemblance to actual people, living or dead, or to businesses, companies, events, institutions, or locales is completely coincidental.

Cover art by Marcellus Shane Jackson

Ordering Information:
Quantity sales. Special discounts are available on quantity purchases by corporations, associations, and others. For details, contact the "Special Sales Department" at the address above.

Terminus 3/ Various Authors. -- 1st ed.
ISBN no.: 979-8-9905121-2-2

Contents

Just another day in the A.

—Unknown

WONDER ISLAND
BY
BERNETTE SHERMAN

Day One

Minutes ago, I fell out of some tube-like chamber into a shallow pool of tacky liquid that smelled like antibiotics. The pool drains, leaving me curled up, shivering. A clear warm liquid falls, rinsing off the sticky residue. Drops of water cling to the skin I am experiencing for the first time.

Blank white walls stare back at me and glass I can't see through with my new eyes mock me before adjusting to the reflection.

A pretty older woman with chestnut brown skin and thick tightly curled black hair with gray roots appears from behind what must've been an invisible door on the wall. It reminds me of the pictures I'd seen and of someone I once knew but can't place. Someone close to me. *Programming*. That's the only way I can describe it. She smiles as she wraps a towel large enough for both of us around my chest and helps me out of the small puddles gathered around my legs.

"Welcome to Wonder Island," she says, allowing my new ears to hear words for the first time. "We've been waiting for you."

Day Two

Memories and information from the programming combined with fragments from somewhere else, flutter into my mind. Perhaps due to spending most of the first day resting.

The woman who brought the towel is in the room with me. They've moved me to a suite. It's bare and empty of anything that might give a clue about where I am.

Lying in the soft bed under an oversized white comforter, I open my eyes enough to see out without alerting her that I'm awake. It's all familiar. I grimace from the moan that accidentally escapes my lips. My body is sore from being stiff in the chamber for so long, and unfortunately, she knows I'm up.

Her heels clack on the hardwood floors towards my full-size bed. I keep my eyes closed, wanting to sink back into the softness of the mattress.

"You're awake. You had quite the trip. I hope you're feeling rested. We have a lot to go over and I know you have plenty of questions."

I do have questions. Many. I'm supposed to be here but can't remember why.

"I'll let Nurse Helena help you get ready and bring you to my office. Welcome back."

Welcome back?

A thick woman with a shock of poorly colored red hair walks into the room. Her light brown eyes have an air of kindness. As she helps me stand, I feel a little safer.

"I'm Helena and I will be helping you until you get used to doing these things yourself again. It won't be but a few days. You're smart." Small crow's feet underline her eyes as she smiles, looking long past her prime.

"Thank you, Helena." My voice cracks with weakness.

"It should come back. Don't worry."

"How do you know me?" I ask, but she smiles and steps back, looking at something on the paper in her hand.

I stand in the shower and let the water run over me. I don't mind the sting against my skin and the blood rises to the surface. I need time to think and clear my head of the fog. *Helena.* I have a vision of Helena checking my temperature and blood pressure. She finishes and touches my cheek before placing a mask over my mouth and nose. Then she's gone.

The rush of water pouring over me stops, as I contemplate being here, in this strange place with these people who seem familiar.

Welcome back? The words echo in my mind. My mind. The idea of that bothers me. *Wonder Island?* I've just been dumped out of a chamber. I press my palms against the shower walls and the water drips from my body. A light knock on the door forces me to move.

Outside of the shower door is the towel Helena left on a large knob. I wrap the soft fabric around me before wiping the moisture from the mirror. My dark curly hair is the perfect complement to my rich brown smooth skin. I'm probably nineteen or twenty. Still, who am I? Where am I and why? Helena interrupts my exploration of my body by rapping against the door much more firmly.

I tighten the towel around my chest and open the heavy metal door. No lock.

"Feeling nice and fresh and clean?" she beams.

"Yes."

I scoot around her large frame to return to the bedroom.

"Do I have something to wear?"

She points at a chair by the bed. "You can put that on. Slippers are on the floor. I'll meet you outside the door in a few minutes. You look great, by the way."

She leaves and I pull on the blue pants and shirt that look like scrubs.

I will get answers soon.

***

My hands shake on the doorknob as it turns slowly beneath my long fingers. Helena stands to the side, looking over those papers again.

"Okay. Doctor Wattley is waiting for you in her office. I can see you're nervous, but you'll understand everything soon enough."

Helena stops in front of a frosted glass door with gold letters that read, 'Dr. Victoria L. Wattley', and knocks. She turns back to me and tries to give me a comforting smile, but it can't shake the rolling in my stomach from angst and possible hunger.

The door swings open and a chipper Doctor Wattley smiles. Her eyes trace me from my hair to the slippers on my feet. She's the first person I'd seen yesterday.

"Come in. Thanks, Helena. Can you do the general rounds? Let me know if there are any issues."

Helena nods and closes the door behind her.

I stand nervously under her studious gaze waiting for whatever is coming next.

"Please have a seat." She points to a beautiful white upholstered leather sofa with floral stitching.

I sit, my back erect at the edge of the seat, repeating the questions I'd planned in my head.

"Are you comfortable? Can I pour you some cucumber water?" she asks.

The vase with fresh green cucumbers floating around in it looks refreshing, but I won't take any gifts from her until I know what's going on.

"No. I want to know who I am, where I am, why I'm here, and what's going on." The words tumble out.

She pours the water anyway, placing the glass in front of me.

"Of course. Although you want to know who you are, that is a tricky question without understanding first why you're here and how you got here. Let's start with that."

Doctor Wattley stands and paces around her spacious office, toned in white with accents of gray and lavender.

"This is Wonder Island. Our founder named it that because she believes the work we do here is filled with wonder – wonderful. It's an island because we're secluded and exclusive, outside the city of Atlanta, a few miles from the Centers for Disease Control and Prevention in Atlanta. Plenty of nature and privacy outside."

The wooded view through the window behind her doesn't allow me to see anything else.

Doctor Wattley nods as if she understands my confusion. "We've made our own island of wonder, pressing through the limits of science in the sphere of aging and death. It will be easier to understand once we complete the day two processing." Her passion is palpable.

"Processing?"

"Yes. Right now, you're still missing what will make you feel like yourself again, the return of your memories."

"Will this processing help this all make sense?"

"That's the idea. Come with me."

The hallway, bright with fluorescent lights that line the ceiling in neat rows, casts an otherworldly glow as I cautiously follow the doctor. Along each side are doors, all white, with silver knobs. The only thing telling them apart is numbers posted in black on the wall to the left of each.

I glance behind me before following Doctor Wattley to the room where they'll examine me. Helena's eyes move along with me. She quickly turns, raising the clipboard and marking something with her red pen.

"This way," Doctor Wattley calls back. I pick up my pace and try to ignore the creeping feeling beneath my unfamiliar skin.

At the end of the hallway is another door, but unlike the others, it's a striking violet color. It's as out of place as I am.

She pulls a set of keys from her white lab coat and goes through each, checking the labels until she finds the one she's looking for. Her gaze returns to me momentarily and then down the empty hallway before sliding the key into the lock. According to Doctor Wattley, the answers to my questions wait just behind this door.

Day Three

Light filters into the room where the curtains gape a couple of inches. The prior day is a blur. There's no difference between what was real and the parts I might have imagined. Like the day before, I awake in a sterile room on the most comfortable bed I can remember ever sleeping on.

Doctor Wattley's hushed discussion with someone in the hall comes through the door. It's probably what woke me. The light peaks in as if it's still morning.

They won't control my schedule today. I swing my feet from beneath the covers. Small red dots line my legs from the ankle all the way to my thighs, up both sides.

I tiptoe to the bathroom for a better look. The dots travel up my hips, sides, and up my arms. They're spaced about four inches apart. There's one on each side of my neck and one last set where my temples meet my hairline.

The day before is like fog but I recall the room with the purple door. I sit on the small dressing chair in the bathroom, searching for memories that elude me. Walking behind Doctor Wattley and her asking me to sit in a chair surrounded by equipment. Preparing for a procedure to help me get my memories back and feel more comfortable in my body.

I sat in the large leather chair with a headrest and Helena strapped me in. *Why didn't I struggle?* She then stuck a long needle in my arm and after that everything is a haze.

Frustrated, I get up and snap the shower on. Whoever is out in the hall will hear it, but I don't care. She can't tell me to shower if I'm already doing it. What happened yesterday? I step into the tepid shower. Maybe the cool shock of water will jar me somehow.

People. Exchange. Death. Me. Seventeen. I let the water beat against my back as I feel the tiny welts that run the length of my body. I was strapped down, in and out of consciousness, and I have no idea for how long. People. Exchange. Death. Me. Seventeen.

Someone, maybe Doctor Wattley, had spoken those words and now they're part of the puzzle filled with missing pieces that create my existence. I'm here because I chose to be. All this is possible because of me. That's what she said. Who am I to make whatever this is, possible?

Yesterday was supposed to fix that, but I'm as cloudy as before. When we talked in her office before going into the room for processing, she said it might take several days to work.

I'd asked, "What needed to work?"

Doctor Wattley had turned and looked at me as if trying to see something past me. She then leaned in and said, "This is your work. We will make sure it works. We have done everything right. It will work. Don't worry."

Today, I'm getting out of the room without them seeing me so I can find out what Wonder Island is, really.

There's a sharp knock on the bathroom door. *Do these people not know what privacy is?*

"Good morning. When you're done, please get dressed and come right out. Your clothes for the day are on the chair," Helena speaks loudly through the closed door and over the sound of water.

Damn. It won't be today.

"Okay," I call back.

If I'm going to find out where I am and who I am it means shaking my shadows.

With a reluctant flip of my wrist the shower's off and I grab the fresh towel hanging by the shower door. It's day three of being alive in this body and hopefully my memories start coming back.

Helena has laid out a crisp turquoise cotton shirt and pants on the freshly made bed. Scrubs. Again. I slide them on and step into the slippers on the side of the bed. I walk to the door, pausing a moment to take a deep breath before opening it.

"Good morning. Doctor Wattley wants to see you in her office. I trust you rested well?" Helena smiles.

"Yes. I wish I could remember yesterday. It's all a blur."

I smile in hopes she'll spare me a clue about what happened.

"That's normal after day two processing. Today's the real test."

Her answer holds no commitment as we walk to Doctor Wattley's office.

"Here you go." Helena knocks on the door and steps back.

The clack of heels comes through the other side of the door.

"Good luck." Helena lightly touches my arm before the door opens.

"Hi there. You look rested. Thanks, Helena. And Helena, please pull the reports for one and two. I need to make sure we're on schedule. Thank you."

Doctor Wattley stands back to let me in and then promptly closes the door.

"We're excited about the initial results. The merge seems to have taken this time. I know you don't fully understand, but it'll come back to you soon. All our data suggests that within the next twenty-four to forty-eight hours you'll remember who you are. By extension, you'll also remember what we're doing." She doesn't try to hide her excitement.

"What if I don't remember? What if I'm just some college girl?" I asked, hoping for a clue.

"Connections are already firing and no matter what, you'll be more than that. At the very least we were successful in bringing you to the state you're in. It may not seem like much, but this is a generation of work, your work, realized. You are proof that what you dreamed of is possible."

"That I can be dumped out of a tube without a memory?" I ask snarkily.

She smiles, as if dealing with someone below her intellect. I'd seen it before, somewhere, in one of those elusive memories. I try to shake the odd feeling, but it lingers.

"Cucumber water?"

I shrug. She'll give it to me anyway.

"Today, I'll show you one of the labs. We've had success with the primates, but you're the first human we've had success with. It's fitting that it's you."

My mind flashes to my body in a chair, leaning back. Nodules are placed all over my head as I watch myself from the outside. In the memory, there's a tag on my wrist. 'Zari H'. Before anything else registers my eyes closed in front of me.

"Who's Zari H?" I ask Doctor Wattley.

She nearly spits out her water with a look of shock.

"Excuse me?"

"Zari H. That was on a wristband I had on."

"Oh. It's just an identification."

"That's obvious. It was on my wrist. I saw it there before falling asleep. Or being put to sleep. I had nodules on my head. There were needles and tubes. And…and…you were there. I remember. I didn't like what was happening."

"You're beginning to remember. That's good. Right now, what you're seeing can be confusing since it's not the whole story."

"I was drugged," I whisper. "Someone wheeled me out of the room. How could I see myself if I was asleep?" I ask, standing up from where I sat perched on the edge of the seat.

"You're agitated. Try to calm down and relax so we can talk."

"We're talking right now, Doctor Wattley. Who else was in that room?"

"Well Helena and I were there."

"I can see someone else, like I see you right now."

"Let's go see the primates. It will explain a lot."

Doctor Wattley stands and tries to take my arm to lead me to the door but I yank away.

She walks ahead and opens the door so I can walk out. The halls are eerily empty and quiet. A door closes somewhere down on the right, but there isn't a person anywhere.

"This way." Doctor Wattley walks to the left.

"Down that way is where we were yesterday. Where you all did something to me."

"We brought you your memories."

Her heels are irritatingly sharp against the floor. Her pace is quick but she glances back every few steps. In front of a door labeled 'Primates' she stops and scans her card. *No key this time.*

"After you." She holds the door open.

Inside are thick clear containment cells with chimpanzees. Two on each side. The two on my left sit with their backs against the bars, barely glancing up as we enter.

"What's wrong with them?" I point at the two docile chimps.

"They're old. Dying. But over here are young healthy chimps."

"I can see that. Is that what you wanted me to see?"

"What if these old chimpanzees didn't have to die? They are some of the brightest ones we have, even if their bodies can't keep up with their brains. The experiences they've had makes them special and would take a lifetime for these younger chimps to gain."

"Well that would be great if they didn't have to die, but that's part of life, right?" I laugh. "I mean did you discover the fountain of youth? Are the two over here what these old chimps will be like after you give them the same treatment?"

She's smiling condescendingly, again.

"Not exactly. We have discovered our own fountain of youth here, but as with everything, there is some sacrifice."

She walks through the rest of the room to another door and scans it with her card before putting her finger up for a second scan. I can't help but roll my eyes.

"In this room, is our first primate success. We call her Ruthi."

"You get CDC or NIH funding support? Private?"

"We have many wealthy Atlanta donors to support this science. And after this it'll be global."

Doctor Wattley turns up the dimmed lights, slowly revealing a young chimpanzee. The chimp looks up at Doctor Wattley, a knowing look in her eyes and then pans to me. She looks back at the doctor again before returning to the blocks she's stacking and sorting, pushing them down.

"What's so special about her?" I ask. *My younger brother could do that.*

As soon as I have the thought, I realize I do have a younger brother. Much younger. And parents. Something happened to them. We'd been separated. The memory stops, replaced by another. I see myself lying on a gurney, oxygen mask over my face. Someone is taking my pulse.

I see my eyes open. Something is wrong. I'm seeing from two angles at once. I see myself and I see everything else from where I lie. Everyone is masked. I see myself going in and out of consciousness. I'm in an ambulance. Then I'm being rolled out and put on a helicopter.

"Hurry. We need her fresh. We need to get her back to 'we'." The voice called out from a place that felt like me.

"Are you okay?" Doctor Wattley asks.

"What's 'we'?"

"I was just saying that Ruthi had a successful transfer, like yours. We transferred the memories and what made Ruthi who she was into the healthy young chimp you see before you. It's been effective. She can do a lot more than this but doesn't like strangers much."

"Wait. What about the chimpanzee that was in this young body first?"

"They weren't hurt. We removed all existing memories first so that it would be done on a fresh slate. Ruthi is her old self but with a new lease on life. We give an initial foundation of memories to build on from Ruthi and then add the rest when we know the process is successful."

I let her explanation sink in, wishing I didn't understand. I look down at my hands and touch my thighs and then my breasts. Everything is youthful.

"What's 'we'?" I ask again.

"What?"

"What is 'we'?"

"Well, it's the collective of you and I."

"No. I remember someone saying we need to get back to 'we'."

She nods. "W.I. Wonder Island. Your memories are coming back. Right on time."

"I think so. Getting pretty drained, really. Can I go back to my room?"

"You do need time to rest and let your brain and body process everything and get in sync. I'll walk you back."

"I can find my way."

"It's no problem. I'm going that way."

She's lying. She's not leaving me alone. If what she showed me means what I think, they can't afford for anything to happen to me.

Day Four

"I did it. I did it," I whisper to myself.

Decades of research and trials to extend life. I was on the edge of running out of time and now I have an extension. It was the breakthrough Wonder Island needed. All the investment and time would finally pay off.

"Are you crazy?" a tiny voice says from somewhere inside.

I knew there might be some resistance, but the transfer had taken. My new body is taut and supple. I haven't felt this good in decades. My firm cheeks pull back in a smile. People will pay any amount for this. I'm going to be rich.

"I said, are you crazy?"

This girl is annoying. I might have to make some adjustments since I don't want to go through this again. This body is number seventeen. Each time before, the transfer had failed and the bodies had to be discarded. I like this body and we've gotten this far. It will work.

"Seventeen? So that's what that meant? You've done this sixteen times before?" the voice asks.

"Are you awake?" Helena asks as she knocks on the door.

Helena. Naïve and sweet, but strong and loyal. She's wrestled down her fair share of resistant subjects.

"Yes. Come in."

Helena walks in and eyes me curiously.

"Well don't just stare, get me some clothes. We have a busy day today. I need to get to the lab and make a few adjustments. Have Doctor Wattley meet me there. Thank you. You can leave the clothes on the bed. That's all."

"Doctor Cheetum? Doctor Alice Cheetum? Is that really you?"

"You bet it is, Helena. And I've got work to do."

"It worked? It worked!" she says, giddy.

She then looks down at herself and back at me. "Can I be next? My body is waiting and ready."

"You may have some competition. Doctor Wattley has been itching for a new body since she came here. Now, I need to get ready."

I look at my new form. I hand-picked it myself. Now I'm in it. Everything is in place. Youth is definitely wasted on the young. Not this time.

"But, it's not yours," the pesky voice returns.

"It's my body now. Go to sleep, why don't you?"

"But this is my body. Mine. I'm not an 'it'. I'm a person."

"You were."

The shower runs over my shoulders as the appreciation of my success washes over me. I have a full life ahead of me and next time the process will be even easier. We need to clean the slate better and when they come out of incubation, they need to go immediately to the lab for the transfer.

"Are you saying that yours didn't work right, Doctor Alice Cheetum?" the voice asks.

"Shut up."

"You don't like me in your head, do you, Alice?"

"You were a means to an end and whatever is left of you will be ending very soon. And it's Doctor Cheetum to you. We're not associates. Not even in the same league."

"Doesn't it bother you, Alice?"

"What? Being alive in this beautiful young body?"

"No. Stealing my body. My life. Taking me from my family. I have a little brother, you know. He's funny and silly."

"Why would that bother me?"

"You are a person, right? Somewhere in here you're more than a collection of ideas, thoughts, and memories. I mean do you still have a soul? If you died, if this body died, would you cease to exist, Alice?"

I scrub the shampoo through my curls and then rinse it from my curly hair, squeezing the water out. I'm in control now.

"That's not how you wash curly hair, Alice. You'll regret it when you're out of the shower and it dries. So, will you cease to exist?"

I consider her comment about my hair and then put conditioner in.

"Smart move. Conditioner. But you already scrubbed knots in it. That'll take you at least an hour to detangle. Are you ignoring me, Alice? I'm Zari by the way."

I crack the bathroom door. Good. Helena has laid out an outfit for me. Much more appropriate than the scrubs I've been wearing. She knows I love white. This damn girl remembers her name. Trouble.

I slip the pants on and zip them as I steal another look in the mirror. I can't wait to love again with this body. A lifetime of experience packaged in this form. Heartbreaker, for sure.

"Doctor Cheetum?" Helena calls out.

"Yes. I'll be out in just a moment. Is Doctor Wattley in the lab?"

"Yes, Doctor."

"Good. I want to make one stop before the lab. I'd like to see the other subjects. There may be a change required to the protocol."

"Yes, Doctor. They are both in suspension right now, waiting for their time."

"Perfect."

I walk out of the room in my white suit with a bright red blouse beneath. I've pinned the curls up into a bun. I'm not quite ready for the big hair, but I'm sure there'll be occasions for it.

The room holding the two subjects needs the card and finger-print like the room with the chimps. I feel my pockets for a card.

"Do you want to test it out, Doctor Cheetum?"

Helena hands me a badge with my current photo. *When had they taken it?* I can't remember having it done. I hold it against the scanner and then press my finger down. I smile as the door clicks open, letting me into one of my favorite spaces.

"We've added another level of security before you can access the chambers where the subjects are held. From here you can see them through the glass."

The two females are perfect. Their large suspension chambers provide their needs for now. Helena eyes the female to the right hungrily. She'd picked the specimen out for herself when we knew we were close. Doctor Wattley's new body was a delicious choice as well.

"Has Doctor Wattley been monitoring brain activity while they are in suspension?" I ask.

"Yes. Every couple of days she runs those tests. They're normal. In line with what your body experienced."

"You probably won't get away with this, you know that, don't you?" Zari says in an eerie whisper.

"I want to make sure that every part of them is completely gone. I don't want more than a fragment of what is required neurologically to receive the transfer. Anything more could be a nuisance and a waste of energy."

"I understand, Doctor Cheetum. Is there something wrong?" Helena asks, a look of concern coming over her face.

"Not at all. I am the first success. We learn from my experience and every future transfer will be even more successful. Prepare to be young and rich very soon."

Helena laughs. "I've been preparing for that moment since I joined you here, Doctor Cheetum."

We walk out of the room, but before closing the door, something makes me look back. They are great subjects. Near perfect human specimens in the prime of physical life. That's all. I shake my head. She is trying to get to me. They are just subjects and they wouldn't cease to exist. Their bodies will live on, and even better, they'll have the wisdom Helena and Doctor Wattley will bring with them.

"Those are someone's kids. Just like me," Zari says.

This time her voice isn't a whisper. It's calm. Confident.

"Go ahead of me, Helena. Tell Doctor Wattley to get everything prepped and I'll be right there."

Pressure builds behind my forehead. Within seconds it goes from twinges to a painful throbbing. Probably a side effect of the stress the body and mind have been under. Inhabiting a new form is bound to bring its share of discomfort.

"Painful, isn't it?"

I refuse to answer the needy girl.

"What you're doing is wrong. You know it."

"What I know is this is my body. There are people who've been on the list for years waiting for this breakthrough. In less than an hour you'll be out of your misery."

"What if you can't get rid of me? What you did the first time didn't work. I still exist inside of MY body. You're the intruder."

She's getting stronger. I lean against the wall, slouching, and shielding my eyes from the lights stabbing my forehead.

"You know what the body does when it experiences something foreign? It fights. Tries to expel it. Our bodies are programmed for survival. I saw it in Ruthi yesterday. There was something else in there with her, fighting."

"You don't know what you're talking about. Dumb girl."

"I wasn't a scientist, but I've had the flu before. My body was sick trying to get it out. Stayed in me for several days. And then, it was gone."

"That's a virus. I'm not a virus."

"Maybe you are. My brain might think so. In fact, I'm certain that's exactly what you are. A virus."

"Don't be foolish. You'd likely kill both of us if you try to get rid of me."

"Did you know the mind is the most powerful force we have to use? I once heard that you can do anything if you put your mind to it."

"Well, my mind is better."

"You might be smarter, in some ways. More experienced. Old in your thinking. I mean that was the point. To put your old ways and thinking into a new body?"

"Aaaaaa!" I shriek in pain. What is she doing?

I fall to my knees. They need to get her out. Now. I'll make it to the lab, even if I must crawl. But it isn't stopping. The searing pain blinds me. More than I've ever experienced. It shoots up the back of my legs, up my side, and around my head. It feels like someone is pricking me with a thousand needles.

I try to call out for Helena, but my voice catches in my throat. No sound escapes.

Focusing on my throat, I try again, but there is a full assault on my senses. I can't speak. I can't see. I search for the floor, only able to move an inch at a time, stopping with each move to bear the attack.

This Zari bitch is trying to bring me down.

"You won't succeed. Helena will come looking soon."

"She'll find you, you old hag."

I can't see anything in front of me. The only sounds are inside my own head. She's got me all alone.

"I told you – this is my body. And I want it back!"

With that, I feel a push against me that brings me to the floor, my head hits the wall and…

Where am I? Where am I going? Where is she taking me? To the lab. Why? Am I leading or being taken?

"Nothing in there can help you," I tell Zari.

"Hey, Helena, Doctor Wattley. Thank you for waiting and getting everything ready." Zari walks in and towards the computer.

"It's great to see you back, Doctor Cheetum."

"It's great to be back. The fact this worked is unbelievable."

"We did it."

"Yes. We did. And we're all getting our dues! I need to make adjustments. Helena should have told you what I wanted. Can I see what you have set up on here?"

"You didn't do anything," I scream at the girl trying to steal my success.

"Sure. Just go in here and you'll see the program we'll run to adjust any interference. You know, basically remove any remnants of the subject."

"I'm so sorry. You'll have to bear with me and forgive some of the gaps. That's why this is so important. How do I adjust it again?"

"Oh. No problem. It may be several days or even weeks before you're fully back to normal. You saw how much progress Ruthi's made in just a week. Be patient, Doctor Cheetum," Doctor Wattley smiles.

"When have I ever been that?" Zari smiles at Doctor Wattley.

"Very true," Doctor Wattley responds.

"You know nothing about me. What you're doing won't work!" I scream at the adolescent trying to steal my life. She ignores me.

Doctor Wattley walks around to the other side of the computer and shows her how to adjust the levels.

"What are you doing?" I scream again at the girl ruining my life's work. This isn't right. I'm not supposed to be the voice inside. I'm meant to be in control.

"And once this is done, the prior subject should be eliminated, correct? Permanently?" Zari asks.

"That's how it's designed. I understand you had some concerns with the other two subjects," Doctor Wattley answers.

"Yes. I want to eliminate the risk of internal resistance to the transfer. I am allowing myself to be the guinea pig and accept the risks so we can learn from them and bring this to market as soon as possible."

"Liar!" I scream. "You want to kill me. This is my research. Decades of my life. I'm the genius. You're just a pretty face. You won't even remember what to do. You stupid girl!"

"Can you set everything up over there for me, Doctor Wattley, while I study this a moment?" the lying wench says and then sits down in my seat.

"No problem. When you're ready just come over and lay back. This time it shouldn't be nearly as uncomfortable."

"Good. We need to make this as pleasant as possible for the two of you. And for our future clients, when the time comes."

"You'll mess this all up!" I yell. "No! Don't do that! You'll erase me! No! Please. What do you want? I'll give you a new body. I'll take a different one. I'll even let you stay in here with me. Just please...don't kill me."

I'm begging and Zari acts like nothing is happening. Two can play this game.

"Don't even think about it," she says to me inside where no one else can hear, before I can even consider how to attack her.

"I know my body. That's right, my body. I will win. And when you cease to exist, no one will mourn you. No one will see you go. No one will miss you."

"But I'm the one who made this possible. They'll know you aren't me."

"By the time they realize it, it'll be too late."

"I'm ready, you two. Everything is set."

"You won't get away with this," I snarl from somewhere deep inside. "They'll check the settings."

"You are smart. Thanks," Zari says back.

"Helena, would you mind getting me some cucumber water? I had a bit of cotton mouth last time."

"Sure thing, Doctor Cheetum."

"Doctor Wattley," she says, "You must catch me up on what's been going on with you. Last time we talked, you were getting serious with someone you'd met, right?"

"You remember? I didn't think you would. Yes. It's one of the reasons I'm so excited about my new body. She's smart, beautiful, young, and a great conversationalist. We haven't met yet. We've only talked online. I've been waiting for this." She waves her hand around the room.

"See? You'd deny her love? A chance to be with the woman of her dreams?"

"Not if it were done the right way. We all deserve a chance for love, but not by stealing life from someone," she shoots back. I haven't swayed her decision to go through with this.

"So, Helena will have some competition for who goes next."

"You bet your ass she will. We get you up and going and you can pull me out of this old body, put me in that tube, and prep my new body. I'm ready."

24

Doctor Wattley laughs. I can't believe she doesn't see right through this.

"Here you go, Doctor Cheetum." Helena hands the stupid girl the glass of water.

"Thanks, Helena."

"Let's check the settings and get started."

"See I told you. You'll be caught," I say with a smile in my voice.

"Oh, Helena, remember I told you that you'd have some competition being next?"

"Yeah. Oh, are you trying to get in already, Doctor Wattley?" Helena says half-jokingly.

"Yeah. I told you about the lady I met. I have to meet her, but I can't in this body."

"She seems lovely," Helena nods.

All the while they're attaching everything to me...to her. What's wrong with them? No. Come on, Doctor Wattley, she's an imposter. You press the button on your handheld and I'm through.

"Are you talking to yourself in there?" the smug girl asks.

"You can't do this. Please." I hate that I've resorted to begging. .

"I already have. And then, they'll get what they've asked for. Sorta. They'll get out of the bodies they don't want."

"You'd be killing them."

"You're right. That wouldn't be fair. I won't kill them. Don't worry."

"What about me?"

"I have to make a choice between you and me. I choose me. Like you did."

"Okay, Doctor Cheetum, you'll probably feel sleepy, so just let yourself go to sleep. You'll wake up feeling even better. Even more brand new." Helena takes my pulse.

"Is that even possible?" Zari smiles.

Day Five

I open my eyes, searching the room. Was it a dream? Did any of yesterday really happen? How much?

I sit up and something crunches under my hand. A note.

We flipped a coin. I get to go first! – Helena.

I re-read the note. She'd been kind of nice, even if she is an evil life-stealing demon.

I can't draw any unusual attention to myself. I need to follow the normal routine. I walk into the bathroom and start the shower. I need to wash off the contamination of Doctor Cheetum. But she's been inside where this water can't wash or rinse her away.

"Doctor Cheetum?" Helena calls from outside the door.

"Yes. Come in, Helena."

"Did you see my note?"

"I did. How many times did you all have to toss that for you to finally have Doctor Wattley concede?"

"Twenty-one times."

I smile. "Well, she doesn't need to worry. You'll both get what you've earned soon enough. When do you plan on doing it?"

"The specialist is on his way right now to Wonder Island to give you a thorough exam. Once you get the okay, I can go. Doctor Cheetum? Do you know what that means? I could be born tomorrow!"

I see the excitement in her face. It's sickening, but real. The idea of having the experience I'd had just days earlier thrills her. I'd been flushed out of a tube, disoriented and confused.

"I can tell you're excited. If you're excited, I'm excited for you. I need to take a shower though. After I see the specialist, I want to examine the chimps again before we do either of you. It'll only delay us a few hours at most, maybe not even."

"Should I get them prepped? Doctor Wattley and I would be happy to do that while you see the doctor. It'll speed things up," she says hurriedly.

"That would be great, Helena. I want to get them to the point of being in the chamber, ready for incubation and rebirth."

"We can do that. I'd love to help. Does it matter which one goes first?"

"No. Why don't you choose? Pick the one you like the most, in fact."

"Oh. Thank you, Doctor Cheetum. This is the best day of my life!"

Helena scurries out the room. The water temperature is perfect today. It rushes over me, reminding me of the day I'd been reborn as Doctor Cheetum. Most of my memories are gone, erased by the people at Wonder Island. I have little idea who I was before this, aside from fragments that remain like residue on a window after cleaning.

It means starting over. A new life, but not before I finish this one.

The outfit Helena laid out is nice but in no way comfortable. It looks like something my grandmother would wear, fashionable sure, but not for my age. Doctor Cheetum had been eighty-six years old and still hunting for the fountain of youth. She'd found it, taken a drink, and it ended her.

Slipping on my shoes, I think of the older chimps being prepped for transfer. Make the best of a bad situation. *Hmm. I think my father would say that.*

I stare at the laptop sitting on the desk that had been unused and open it. The badge clipped to my jacket says Janice Cheetum, MD, PhD. A new name. I put my finger on the reader and login. As far as the system knows, that's who I am. A relative of Alice Cheetum. A twenty-seven year old woman. I look great. Very accomplished for twenty-seven.

This is a nice facility. Under the right leadership, it can be used to do something good. I have nowhere else to be. I'll have to find Doctor Wattley and secure my files and identification before they go through their transfer. Talking to them afterwards will be impossible, at least until they can manage basic communication. And, they'll have to share space with some old chimps. I have a feeling those old chimps won't like the company.

I walk out the door and look back at the room where I've spent the past four nights. I feel reborn, again. It's time to return the favor. I'd promised Alice I wouldn't kill them, nothing more.

AN ECHO OF DREAMS
BY
TIARA JANTE'

Atlanta, 2064

The ground vibrated beneath my feet, a rhythmic thrumming sounding from ancestral drums echoing through the streets of a neighborhood where history and the horizon merge. Here amidst the transformative landscape of Atlanta's Castleberry Hill skyscrapers rose, their forms a testament to the fusion of past and future. These structures, once warehouses and galleries, now stretched impossibly tall, their surfaces alive with smart materials that glowed with digital murals celebrating the area's artistic heritage.

In an alcove, a sanctuary amidst the biotech gardens and the quiet hum of drones, a select group gathered. Shielded from the urban thoroughfare's hustle by green walls that whispered tales of a city reborn, their faces shimmered in the blue glow of a holo-projector. Around us, the air was charged with the potential of what was to come, the promise of a future that honored its roots while boldly embracing the new.

I took a deep breath. These weren't all strangers. Many were friends, mentors, supporters – my people. Yet, the weight of what I was about to reveal felt like a stone in my stomach. Surrounded by the echoes of a city that had mastered the art of blending the old with the new, I stood ready to unveil a digital world that offered a glimpse into what could have been—a world where our Ancestors' dreams were the foundation of our future.

"Obsidia Prime," I said, activating the projector. The room dimmed as a holographic simulation unfolded in the air before us.

The laughter and conversation died down. Eyes widened. Before us was a massive baobab tree, its roots and branches merging seamlessly with circuitry. Ethereal wildlife, both familiar and alien, grazed on digital savannahs. Floating market stalls were manned by merchants, their attire a blend of colorful fabrics and augmented reality interfaces.

"This," I breathed out, watching their reactions, "is where our past meets our future."

Ayesha, my old friend from college, stepped forward, her fingers almost touching a water spirit dancing in binary code. "It's... it's alive, Jonyé. Is this... magick?"

I smirked, "Magick and code, Ayesha. Magick and code."

Derek, one of my academic mentors, squinted as he inspected a futuristic version of the Great Pyramid, now a power hub. "The detail, Jonyé! How did you even...? This isn't just another VR world. This is... it's a marvel."

"It's home," I whispered, my voice barely audible over the hum of the pyramid's energy. "A home we've longed for. An Africa unburdened, unconquered, and unstoppable."

Gia, always the skeptic in our group, raised an eyebrow, her curiosity piqued. "But how, Jonyé? How did you make it feel so real?"

I smiled, turning to face her and the rest of the gathered media. "It's more than just advanced coding or immersive technology. Each element, from the sands of the Sahara to the waters of the Nile, is imbued with stories, with history. We consulted Elders, historians, artists, and scientists to ensure every detail was not only accurate but resonant with the spirit of the continent."

"And the people," another journalist chimed in, "they're so...lifelike. How?"

"That," I said, pausing for effect, "is thanks to a breakthrough in AI and machine learning. We didn't just program them; we taught them to learn, to evolve. They carry the essence of the cultures they represent, learning from each interaction, making Obsidia Prime a living, breathing world."

The group nodded, impressed. Derek stepped closer, his gaze still fixed on the pyramid. "And the energy it emanates?"

I followed his gaze, pride swelling in my chest. "Renewable sources power everything here. The pyramid, a symbol of our past, now stands as a beacon of sustainable future, harnessing solar power, wind, and more. It's a testament to what Africa can achieve, free from the constraints of history."

The air was thick with anticipation as the journalists recorded notes, their earlier skepticism melting away in the face of Obsidia Prime's undeniable majesty. As they ventured further, exploring, questioning, I knew they were seeing more than just a technological marvel; they were witnessing a dream made manifest, a vision of Africa that could inspire the world. As the group engaged with the sensory holo-projections, conversations erupted in pockets: amazement, technical inquiries, and deep philosophical debates about what this could mean for our people.

Sensing my introspection, Lena inched closer to me. "You've outdone yourself, baby," she murmured.

"Thanks, love. But I want everyone to know that this isn't just a program," I said, my voice thick with emotion. "This is a legacy. A world where every Black soul can find their place."

She nodded, her eyes glistening in the holographic glow. "Our Ancestors are so proud."

The air grew still as I opened a case revealing the medium for our journey — bodysuits woven from a fabric of shimmering nanofibers. Their design, sleek and form-fitting, was inspired by the bioluminescent beauty of deep-sea organisms, their exterior a mirror of the wonder within.

"We are going beyond sight and sound, my friends," I announced, holding up one of the suits. "This will engage all your senses. The feel of the wind, the taste of the air, the scent of the savannah. You'll feel it all as if you are truly there."

One by one, they donned the suits, their awe and anticipation palpable. I joined them, the fabric cool and inviting against my skin. For me, it was a familiar gateway to the world I'd built, but that night it felt different - less like a test and more like a journey shared. With a collective deep breath, I initiated the immersion sequence.

Reality folded around me, the relentless drone of city life abruptly giving way to the soft whisper of a breeze through fields of golden grass. The firm tile beneath my feet softened into the warm, grainy texture of earth. The urban environment that had cocooned us vanished, revealing the vast, panoramic expanse of Obsidia Prime. We arrived at the historic port of Ouidah, a place that had once marked the turning of destinies. Now, it was the gateway to our reclaimed world.

Bathed in the golden hue of the setting sun, the port buzzed with life. Vibrant markets sprawled around, the air thick with the scents of spices and echoing with languages from every corner of Africa. The sea, a serene mirror to the sky, gently kissed the docks where ships, their sails a vibrant patchwork of colors and patterns, bobbed peacefully.

I gathered my friends, "This is where our journey begins," I declared. "Ouidah, once a site of immeasurable sorrow, has been reborn as the beating heart of Obsidia Prime. It stands as a testament to our resilience, our collective strength to reclaim and transform our past into a source of unyielding power. From here, you can travel instantaneously to any location across the continent, exploring the boundless richness and diversity the continent has to offer."

Continuing, I felt a surge of pride swell within me. "When you're ready to explore, just envision your destination. This simulation is tuned to your very thoughts and can transport you there in the blink of an eye. Just keep in mind, our journey is tethered to a timer. Once it ends, no matter where you've ventured, you'll return here, to Ouidah, where we'll disengage from the immersion together."

As everyone ventured to their desired destinations, I headed to East London, one of my favorite places in Obsidia Prime. I needed to see, to understand the changes happening since I'd visited last. My steps led me through landscapes that were vividly alive, beyond anything I had programmed. The air was fresher here, carrying the scent of the sea mingled with wildflowers, an aroma that spoke of freedom and endless possibilities. The market I wandered through was a spectrum of colors and emotions, with my coded inhabitants displaying spontaneous expressions of joy and moments of sadness that I had not explicitly designed. It was unexpected, a testament to the complexity of life that had taken root in my digital world, unnerving yet utterly captivating.

Beyond the bustling life of the market, at the edge of a village under the expansive canopy of the Great Baobab Tree, stood Mama Nolwazi. This place, where the wild grass danced with the ocean's breeze and the horizon stretched infinitely, merging sea and sky, was her sanctuary. Her eyes held stories of a time long before ours, her wrinkles etched with wisdom. As I approached, she bowed, her voice trembling, "*uThixo wethu,* Jonyé; our God, Jonyé."

"No, just Jonyé," I replied, taken aback. "I'm no god. I... I was the one who designed this world, yes, but..."

"And you've given us life, Creator," she insisted, her eyes shining with conviction. "Your code, it didn't just create a playground. It gave birth to a world, to Us," she insisted.

"But the essence of life, the breath that animates our dreams and fears, isn't mine to give. I've merely provided a canvas," I countered, trying to ground her expectations in the reality of our creation.

"Yet, a canvas can inspire a revolution," she said softly, her gaze unwavering. "You've crafted more than a world; you've sparked hope. In Obsidia Prime, our histories are unbroken, our futures, limitless. Here, we reclaim what was lost and forge what never was."

I paused, her words resonating deeply. "It's one thing to imagine such a world, another to live in it. My hope is that this... this creation of ours serves as a bridge, a way to carry these reimagined truths back into our real lives."

"Then you've already succeeded, Creator. Because in dreaming of this world, you've awakened something in us all. A yearning not just for what could have been, but for what still can be. Your vision offers us a glimpse of our true potential, unbound by history's chains."

As we conversed, her words weighed heavily on me. Obsidia Prime was no longer just an echo of our dreams, it was a living, breathing entity, evolving beyond its original design. When I returned to my friends, their excitement was a stark contrast to the depth of my revelation. They shared tales of their encounters, their voices filled with glee and wonder. But all I managed was a nod and a cryptic smile as I considered the implications of my creation. I'd never set out to create a world so profound— I'd only wanted to create a safe space where we could experience our roots in a way that was authentic and untarnished by outsiders.

But I was beginning to realize that Obsidia Prime was evolving into more than I could imagine— and I couldn't help but wonder how the world outside would respond. In that moment, I felt less like the god Mama Nolwazi believed me to be, and more like an explorer on the edge of a vast, uncharted ocean.

***

The sharp chime of my comm-device jolted me from sleep. Groggily, I reached for it, rubbing my eyes to focus on the flashing notifications. News outlets, tech blogs, social media—every screen beamed with my face, and more importantly, with mesmerizing vistas of Obsidia Prime. The headlines were a blur: "The Dawn of New Reality", "Beyond Virtual: Obsidia Prime's Living World", "Jonyé: Architect of Life?"

A sudden rush of adrenaline coursed through me, dissipating any remnants of sleep. Taking a deep breath, I rose, pushing aside the curtains. The morning sun streamed in, though its brightness paled in comparison to the glaring media spotlight now fixated on me.

I stepped into the shower, letting the stream of water ground me. As droplets traced paths down my skin, I pondered over what lay ahead. There was no playbook for creating a new world, nor for dealing with the tidal wave of attention it would bring. How was I supposed to manage it all?

After dressing, I dialed one of two constants in my life—Grandma Ayana. As the call connected, her familiar, gentle face filled the screen. "Jonyé," she greeted, her eyes crinkling into a warm smile, "saw you on the news this morning, baby. Your parents would've been so proud."

Swallowing the lump in my throat, I replied, "Thank you, Grandma. It's all so overwhelming."

She nodded knowingly. "Your creation will touch souls, Jonyé. But, remember that all of this influence comes with a lot of responsibility."

Our conversation, as always, soothed me. Her wisdom, rooted in years of experience and understanding, provided the anchor I so desperately needed.

After our call, I shot off messages to my investors. Their excitement was palpable, even through the screen. The future of Obsidia Prime seemed brighter than ever.

As I scrolled down my timeline, a ping from my email drew my attention. Scanning the contents, my heart rate quickened. A request from Global Tech Spotlight, the top media network, beckoned me to Peachtree Skyscape for an exclusive interview. And, as if that wasn't enough, an invite followed for a closed-door meeting with Elara Tech-Ventures, helmed by the enigmatic tech magnate, Lucas Sterling.

Lucas Sterling's reputation preceded him. A visionary, but with a streak of ruthlessness that made even the most stalwart Peachtree Skyscape players tread carefully. His interest in Obsidia Prime was both an exciting and daunting proposition.

Taking another deep breath, I realized that this was no longer just about introducing a new tech marvel to the world. This was about steering the narrative, protecting my creation, and ensuring that Obsidia Prime remained a haven, not a commodity.

My fingers hesitated over the comm-device, then quickly typed out a message to Lena.

"Headed to Midtown Metro for an interview, then Peachtree Skyscape for a meeting with Lucas Sterling. Join me?"

Almost instantly, her reply flashed on screen: "Wouldn't miss it for the world. I'm in."

"Okay, get ready. I'll be there soon," I replied.

Grabbing my essentials, I locked my apartment and descended to the building's landing bay. My aeropod, the newest model of autonomous vehicles, awaited. Its silent propulsion system hummed to life as I set the coordinates to Lena's place. Arriving at her apartment complex, Lena emerged, looking chic in a travel-ready ensemble. The smile she wore did little to hide the seriousness in her eyes, a reflection of my own concerns. She quickly stowed her bag inside the aeropod and settled into the seat next to me, before leaning in for a quick kiss.

As we ascended, merging with the flow of traffic, Lena broke the silence, "So, this Sterling guy... what do you know about him?"

"Enough to be wary," I replied. "He's brilliant, no doubt. But he's also known to prioritize profit over ethics. I've heard stories..."

She pursed her lips, contemplating. "Obsidia Prime is more than just another tech innovation, Jonyé. It's a world. Our world. We can't let someone like Sterling turn it into a playground for the elite."

I nodded, running a hand through my locs. "That's my fear. How do I protect it?"

Lena leaned back, looking out at the sprawling city below. "We need a plan. A way to ensure that whatever happens, Obsidia Prime remains true to its essence, that it's not exploited or altered in ways you didn't intend."

She pondered in silence for a moment before she continued, "Why not set up a governing council? A group of trusted individuals who can oversee its evolution. Ensure that decisions made are in the best interest of the world and its inhabitants."

"That's a start," I conceded. "But the tech behind Obsidia Prime is still vulnerable. Sterling and his team could try to replicate it, modify it."

Lena smirked, a mischievous glint in her eyes. "You're the genius coder, right? Embed a failsafe, something that safeguards against un-authorized alterations."

I chuckled, "You mean a kill switch?"

"Exactly. If they try anything shady, pull the plug."

Our conversation continued, brainstorming ways to preserve the sanctity of Obsidia Prime. By the time we neared Midtown Metro, a plan had begun to form. Whatever challenges lay ahead, I took comfort in the fact that I wasn't facing them alone.

As the aeropod began its descent, the sprawling skyline unfurled beneath us. Landing softly on the designated pad, the pod's door slid open with a seamless swoosh.

Standing there, with the backdrop of Global Tech Spotlight's ultra-modern studio, was Janine. Her statuesque figure stood out even amidst Midtown Metro's buzz. Clad in a crisp white pantsuit that con-trasted beautifully with her rich, brown skin, her braids were styled into a chic updo, with a few strands playfully framing her face. Gold hoops dangled from her ears, catching the sun's rays and making them dance in the daylight.

Janine had always been the epitome of confidence and grace. Her unwavering assertiveness had paved the way for numerous successful media campaigns, and she had an uncanny ability to turn even the most challenging public relations situations into gold.

"Jonyé! Lena!" she exclaimed, approaching with outstretched arms. "You two look like you're gearing up for battle," she teased, her eyes twinkling.

Lena chuckled, "With the media circus surrounding Obsidia Prime, it feels like we are."

Janine's laugh, hearty and genuine, eased the tension in the air. "Don't you worry. That's what you have me for. This is our narrative. We control the message."

I smiled, grateful for her unwavering support. "It's not just the media, Janine. After this, we have a meeting with Lucas Sterling."

She raised an eyebrow, her playful demeanor shifting to one of keen interest. "The tech shark? I've heard... stories."

"Exactly," I replied, "and that's why we need to be prepared."

Janine nodded, her gaze sharpening. "First things first, the interview. Remember, Jonyé, the world wants to see the genius behind this groundbreaking creation. But they also need to see the heart, the passion. That's what will resonate."

She turned, leading the way. "Now, let's get you mic'd up."

As we followed, I couldn't help but appreciate the force of nature that was Janine. With her at the helm of my media front, I felt a tad more secure. In a world where perception often drove reality, having Janine by my side was more vital than ever.

***

The bright studio lights shone down, setting the stage apart from the shadowed audience beyond. At the center sat an elegant glass desk, behind which the interviewer, Patricia Kane, sat poised. Patricia was renowned in the industry, a veteran with sharp wit and an even sharper tongue. Her silver hair was pulled back into a tight bun, her blue eyes scrutinizing every detail. She had a reputation for asking hard-hitting, occasionally intrusive questions, making even seasoned celebrities and CEOs squirm.

Beside her, I took a deep breath, adjusting my posture. Janine had prepped me for this. "Stay calm, collected. Answer with your head, but also with your heart," her words echoed in my mind.

The camera lights blinked red. Live.

"Good evening, viewers. Tonight, we're joined by Jonyé, the prodigious mind behind the revolutionary virtual realm, Obsidia Prime," Patricia began, her voice cool and clinical. "Jonyé, your creation is unlike anything we've seen. A blend of ancestral magick and state-of-the-art tech. Why create such a world?"

Gathering my thoughts, I replied, "Obsidia Prime is more than just a digital construct, Patricia. It's a reimagination, a world untouched by colonization. It reflects a dream where technology and traditions coexist, where Black people can feel a deep sense of belonging."

Patricia's eyes sharpened, sensing an opportunity. "Some critics argue that it's escapist, a way to avoid dealing with our world's realities. Your response?"

"Escapism implies a temporary respite. Obsidia Prime is a permanent testament to what could've been. It's a space of exploration and education, a reminder of our roots. It's not an escape but a bridge to understanding."

There was a brief pause as Patricia processed my answer, clearly not expecting such a nuanced response. She shifted gears. "Your technology allows users to wear virtual skin, making the experience incredibly immersive. Don't you think that's...unnatural?"

I smiled, remembering Janine's training. "Every major technological advancement faced skepticism. Cars, phones, the internet. Virtual skin is no different. It's a tool to foster connection and genuine empathy, enabling users to truly walk in another's shoes."

She leaned forward, attempting another curveball. "You've made Africa a paradise. Isn't that a romanticized view? Perhaps even a dangerous one?"

This was a sensitive area, but I was ready. "Obsidia Prime is an ideal, yes. But ideals inspire. They encourage us to strive for better in our world. By experiencing this 'paradise', users can bring back lessons of unity, respect for nature, and the beauty of blending the old with the new."

The interview went on, Patricia firing question after question, but with each response, it became clear that she was no match for all that Janine prepared me for. As the segment wrapped up, Patricia, perhaps for the first time in her career, seemed at a loss for words.

"Thank you, Jonyé, for enlightening us," she managed, her professional facade slightly cracked.

As the camera lights dimmed, I exhaled, feeling a weight lifted. I had not only navigated Patricia's minefield but had perhaps changed a few perceptions along the way. Stepping off the stage, the studio lights now just a soft glow behind me, I made my way to the private backstage area. Lena and Janine stood waiting, their faces a mix of relief and pride.

"You nailed it," Janine declared, her eyes shining with approval. "Kane didn't know what hit her."

Lena grinned, playfully punching my arm. "I mean, I knew you were good, but damn... that was next level. Even Patricia Kane seemed...impressed."

Chuckling, I replied, "Thanks to Janine's rigorous prep sessions."

Janine waved a dismissive hand. "You had it in you. I just made sure you were ready." She checked her wrist comm-device. "You two should head to your meeting with Sterling. And remember," she added, locking eyes with me, "stay vigilant. Protect Obsidia Prime."

Lena and I nodded in understanding, and with that, we made our way to the aeropod. Buckling into our seats, we watched as the studio faded from view.

After a brief silence, Lena asked, "You think Sterling has ulterior motives?"

I sighed, "The man is a genius but also a business shark. Obsidia Prime is enticing, and he'll want a piece of it."

She looked thoughtful. "You ever consider making Obsidia Prime open source? If the world has access, there's no exclusivity for Sterling to exploit."

I pondered her suggestion. "It's risky, but it might be a way to protect its essence. Still, that's a massive decision."

Lena nodded, her gaze fixed on the horizon. "True, but sometimes, the best way to protect something is to set it free."

The aeropod began to lower into Peachtree Skyscape, signaling our arrival. Sterling's corporate headquarters, a gleaming tower of glass and steel, dominated the skyscape. We both took a deep breath, preparing for the negotiation of a lifetime.

The double doors to Sterling's penthouse office swung open, revealing an expanse of opulence. Floor-to-ceiling windows offered a panoramic view of the skyscape, punctuated by hovering aeropods and floating LED billboards. The setting sun bathed everything in streams of gold and crimson. High above the bustling streets of Midtown Metro, it felt like an entirely different world.

Lucas Sterling stood from behind his sleek obsidian desk, donned in a dark grey tailored suit. His silver hair, meticulously combed back, shimmered under the ambient lights. He wore a pair of augmented reality glasses, their glint betraying an air of arrogance. He was a tall man, his posture straight, every bit the tech magnate who had reshaped industries and toppled competitors. His piercing blue eyes appraised us, lips curling into a practiced, disarming smile.

"Jonyé... Lena, I presume?" Sterling greeted, his voice rich and deliberate. "Jonyé, I just saw your interview. Quite an impression you made on Patricia Kane."

"Thank you, Mr. Sterling," I replied, opting for formality.

"You know, in my years, I've seen countless innovations, many touted as 'game changers'. Most were mere flashes in the pan." Sterling paused, circling us like a hawk. "But Obsidia Prime? It's...revolutionary. You've built not just a product, but an experience. A dream."

Lena, always more forward, jumped in, "And what does that dream mean to you, Mr. Sterling?"

Sterling chuckled, the sound echoing around the spacious room. "Opportunity. Progress. Profit." He fixed his gaze on me. "You've changed the game, Jonyé. And I want in."

There it was, the proposition we both anticipated and dreaded.

"Name your price," Sterling continued, his tone bordering on predatory. "I can ensure Obsidia Prime reaches every corner of the globe. But more than that, I can make you wealthy beyond your wildest dreams."

Lena leaned forward, her voice firm. "At what cost?"

He chuckled again. "Simple. An exclusive license. I want total control over its distribution and monetization."

I felt a cold knot tighten in my stomach. It wasn't just about money. It was about the soul of Obsidia Prime.

"We've always envisioned Obsidia Prime as a space for everyone," I began cautiously, "not just a select few who can afford it."

Sterling's smile didn't waver. "That's the beauty of it, Jonyé. Everyone will want it. And they'll pay. The demand will be insatiable."

"And the essence of Obsidia Prime?" Lena interjected. "The message? The history? The cultural significance?"

He waved a hand dismissively. "Minor details. Those can be...adjusted for wider appeal."

Lena's face grew hard, her eyes flashing. "Those 'details' are the very heart of the project."

I placed a calming hand on Lena's arm. "Mr. Sterling, we appreci-ate your interest. Truly. But this is more than just business to us. It's a legacy."

Sterling looked between us, his façade of charm slipping instantly. "I advise you to consider my offer. Opportunities like this don't come often."

"I understand, Mr. Sterling. And I appreciate your interest, but I'm going to have to decline your offer... respectfully."

As we departed, the weight of Sterling's words pressed down on us. The path ahead was unclear, but our resolve was stronger than ever. The true worth of Obsidia Prime was beyond any monetary value Sterling could offer. We were determined to protect it, no matter the cost.

The view from above enveloped us as we navigated between Ster-ling's towering headquarters and my apartment. I gazed out of the window, the lights from the skyway now just specks against the vel-vety night sky. Beside me, Lena sat, her face contemplative.

It had been a rollercoaster of emotions over the past 24 hours – from the unveiling of Obsidia Prime, to the media frenzy, the intense interview, and then the unsettling meeting with Sterling. And through it all, Lena had been my anchor. I found my mind wandering back, not just to the day's events, but to our shared past.

Lena was radiant, not just in beauty, but in spirit. When she walked into a room, her presence was magnetic. Her skin, an illustrious shade of mahogany, always seemed to capture and reflect any light around. Her eyes were deep pools of onyx, always sharp, always seeing more than she let on. And those lips – soft, full and expressive, they re-vealed her moods even when she tried to hide them.

But what I truly adored was the fire in her – the unyielding passion for our shared cause, her intellect that rivaled anyone, and her deep-rooted sense of identity and culture. She wasn't just my partner in Ob-sidia Prime, but in life itself.

We had grown close, not just in shared ideals but in heart and soul. Romantic strolls through the city's historic sites, late-night brain-storming sessions over cups of Ethiopian coffee, debates, arguments, moments of vulnerability. They all painted a picture of a relationship that was both deep and nuanced.

"Do you ever feel," I started, breaking the silence, "like this is all too much?"

She turned, her eyes meeting mine. "Sometimes," she admitted softly. "But then I remember why we started all this."

I nodded. "It's just, everything has changed so quickly."

She reached out, her fingers intertwining with mine. The touch was reassuring, grounding. "It has, but *we* haven't. Remember that."

We continued the ride in a comforting silence. I felt a profound gratitude for her presence, knowing that as long as we stood together, we could face any challenge that came our way.

***

The soft drone of the apartment's air purifiers provided a gentle lullaby. In the dim ambient light, Lena's face was tranquil, her soft breaths rhythmic. I traced a gentle finger down her cheek, cherishing the warmth it radiated. But sleep eluded me. The weight of Sterling's proposal, his thinly veiled threats, our shared responsibility to protect Obsidia Prime — it all weighed on my mind.

I turned to face the wall, where a digital interface blinked softly. With a sigh, I sat up and donned the virtual skin. Its snug fit always amazed me, and the initial tingle as it activated and merged with my senses made me momentarily forget the world around. I decided to take a solo journey into Obsidia Prime to clear my thoughts.

But as I transitioned into the lush green savannahs, instead of the usual peace it brought, my senses were on high alert. The vibrant blues of the sky seemed to darken and the melodic songs of birds were replaced by eerie silence. Something was wrong.

A red flash in the peripheral of my vision signaled a system alert. My heart raced. Hackers. A breach in Obsidia Prime was something I hadn't anticipated. How was it possible? The security measures I'd set up were meticulous. Scanning the landscape, I initiated the in-built tracking system, which quickly led me to an unauthorized avatar — a figure clearly out of place in this world.

As I approached, I recognized the facial features — it was modeled after Sterling, but with a cold, emotionless demeanor. A spy.

"Heard a lot about you, Creator," the figure sneered.

"Who are you and what do you want?"

He chuckled. "I'm Sterling's insurance policy."

"It's illegal to breach private virtual worlds," I retorted.

"Legalities are for those who can't afford to shape them," he smirked.

I needed to get this intruder out and fast, but more importantly, find out what he'd learned or tampered with. "What have you done?"

The avatar laughed, "Taken a peek under the hood. You have something very special here, Jonyé. Sterling was right. And we're just getting started."

Before I could react, he executed a command, causing the world around us to flicker and distort. My heart pounded. The very fabric of Obsidia Prime was under threat.

Retrieving the spy's digital footprint would be key. I activated a series of firewalls, trying to contain him. As we engaged in a high-stakes digital chase, the landscape of Obsidia Prime shifted and morphed, reflecting our battle.

And then, suddenly, a light. From the horizon, a group of inhabitants, led by Mama Nolwazi, approached. They began chanting, their voices forming a protective barrier, slowing down the hacker's advance. The combination of their ancestral Magick and my coding skills managed to temporarily halt the spy's assault, allowing me to capture his digital essence, forcing him to disconnect, But the aftermath of the breach lingered.

I stood, exhausted amidst the digital chaos, Mama Nolwazi beside me.

"Your creation is powerful, Jonyé," she whispered, "but remember, power always attracts those who seek to control it."

I looked at the her— her wizened face holding tales of centuries, her eyes filled with wisdom, warmth, and a hint of sorrow. She reminded me so much of my grandmother, from the way she carried herself with grace and poise, to the gentle, measured cadence of her voice. The similarities were uncanny, almost as if I had subconsciously modeled her after my grandmother.

"Thank you for coming to my aid," I began, searching for words. "I didn't expect to face threats of this nature so soon."

Mama Nolwazi softly rested her hand on my arm, her touch calming and reassuring, much like how my grandmother would comfort me after a bad dream. "This realm you've birthed, it's an echo of our souls, our histories, our dreams. Such a creation will always face threats, from inside and out."

I nodded, the weight of her words sinking in. "But how do I protect it? The man behind this— Sterling— his reach is vast. If he's willing to send a spy here, there's no telling what else he's capable of."

Mama Nolwazi chuckled softly, her laughter reminiscent of wind chimes. "Power, Jonyé, isn't just in vast armies or great wealth. True power is in unity, in understanding, in love. This world is alive because of the people, their stories, and their beliefs. Protect them, nurture them, and they'll be your greatest defense."

I pondered her words, the weight of it all heavy on my shoulders. "But how can I ask them to fight for me? For this world? It's not their battle."

She looked deep into my eyes. "It's not your battle either. It's *ours*. This world is as much ours as it is yours. And remember, there's strength in numbers."

"I just... I fear for you all," I admitted, my voice barely a whisper. "I don't want my creation to become your prison."

Mama Nolwazi gently cupped my face, her touch filled with motherly warmth. "Fear is natural. But so is hope. And with hope, anything is possible."

She paused, letting the words sink in. "Now, go back to your world, young Creator. And remember, you're not alone in this fight."

With a final nod, I disengaged from Obsidia Prime, the Elder's wisdom echoing in my mind. The instant I returned to the waking world, I found Lena sitting up, her almond-shaped eyes clouded with concern.

"You were gone longer than usual," she remarked, her voice soft yet laced with worry.

Taking a deep breath, I responded, "There was an intruder."

Her eyes widened. "In Obsidia Prime?"

I nodded. "Sterling's doing. He sent a spy, someone who's learned a lot about our world. I managed to fend him off, but I don't think that'll be the last we see of him."

Lena exhaled slowly, pulling her knees close. "So, what do we do now?"

"I spoke with Mama Nolwazi," I began, sharing the depth of the conversation, how the elder's wisdom reminded me of my grandmother's, and the realization of the real-life essence of Obsidia Prime.

Lena listened intently, her fingers tracing patterns on the bedsheet. When I finished, she took a moment, then said, "If Obsidia Prime is a living entity, then maybe we need to treat it like one. Maybe it needs its own immune system, something that can recognize and fight off intruders."

I blinked, processing her idea. "You're suggesting we create a self-sustaining defense mechanism?"

She nodded. "Exactly. Like white blood cells in our bodies. If Sterling or anyone else tries to infiltrate again, Obsidia Prime's defenses would identify and neutralize the threat."

I felt a spark of inspiration. "And what if we combine that with the world's intrinsic Magick? Let the inhabitants contribute to its defense. It'll be an amalgamation of code and conjure."

Lena's eyes gleamed with excitement. "The users, the inhabitants, they could act as protectors. They'd be intertwined with the system, constantly evolving, learning from each threat."

"It won't be easy," I cautioned. "But it's the best shot we have."

She squeezed my hand. "We've faced bigger challenges before. And we've always come out on top."

"Alright, then. Let's fortify Obsidia Prime. And let Sterling know he's not dealing with anything ordinary."

***

Sunrays danced across the village as Lena and I arrived in Obsidia Prime. It was opening day, and the air was rich with the scent of blooming flowers and spiced food. Everywhere I looked, there was vibrant color – from the lively banners that waved in the wind to the traditional garments that the Obsidian people wore. Music resonated through the air, the beats of drums echoing as children ran about.

As Lena and I headed toward the central meeting area, Mama Nolwazi greeted us with a wide smile. "Jonyé, Lena," she began, her voice like a soft melody, "so good to see you."

We were led to a clearing where a sizable crowd had gathered, a circle of people holding hands, their voices rising and falling in harmony.

"As we welcome all to our world," Mama Nolwazi began, "we also share the story of its creation." She beckoned to an Elder, who stepped forward with a large, ornate book. The pages seemed ancient, filled with symbols that shimmered and danced.

The Elder narrated, his voice deep and resonant:

"In the heart of Obsidia Prime, pulsating beneath the fertile land and serene rivers, lie the Echostone. This monolith, with its iridescent glow and intricate patterns, is not of this world, nor any world known to mankind. It carries within it the essence of creation itself, a divine tool with the power to craft reality from the ether.

From the instant it touched the barren nothingness, it began to sing. A hymn that echoed through the void, reverberating with the potential of life. Terraforming the empty expanse, the Echostone weaved matter from its celestial energy. It painted the sky with hues of dawn and dusk, summoned the wind to caress the undulating grasslands, and whispered life into the forests, lakes, and mountains.

Yet, it wasn't an act of unguided spontaneity. The Echostone was not alone in its grand act of creation. Guiding its power was a deity from another realm, an architect of worlds, a maestro who orchestrated the melody of existence that the stone sang. This deity is known to us as Jonyé.

With each line of code that Jonyé etched in his world, the Echostone breathed it into being. Every creature, every tree, every ripple on the surface of the water was born from this harmony between the divine programmer and the celestial stone. It was a dance between technology and the universe, crafting a realm where the past and future converged.

Obsidia Prime, thus, stood not merely as a testament to Jonyé's skill as a master designer but as a manifestation of her spirit, an echo of her soul harmonizing with the song of the Echostone. It is more than just a virtual reality experience. This is a living, breathing world, sculpted by the union of divine intention and alien power. And for this gift, we are grateful."

I blinked in astonishment, trying to process his words.

"In an underground cavern, the Echostone stretches endlessly, its energy pulsing through every being, every blade of grass, every droplet of water. It's the lifeblood of Obsidia Prime."

Lena squeezed my hand, her eyes wide. "You created this world, Jonyé. Not just as a coder, but as a deity."

Mama Nolwazi stepped closer, placing a gentle hand on my shoulder. "Your spirit, Jonyé, is ancient, powerful. It has returned to us, and with it, the promise of hope."

Before I could respond, a sudden, deafening roar shattered the serenity. From the horizon, a dust storm approached, growing rapidly in size. As it neared, we could discern figures within – figures on mechanical beasts that looked like distorted versions of majestic African animals, their eyes glowing malevolently.

The leader, a tall figure with a sharp gaze and a haughty demeanor, stepped forward. His face, though obscured by the shadows of his helmet, was familiar to me. I remembered him from our previous encounter in Obsidia Prime. With slow, deliberate steps, he advanced, halting at the edge of the sacred grounds of the village.

"Ah, Jonyé," he began, a sardonic smile tugging at his lips, making his voice icy cold. "Did you really think you could play God in peace, crafting this vast world without anyone wanting a piece?"

My chest tightened, anger bubbling within. "What twisted game are you playing?" I shot back. "What have you done to Obsidia Prime?"

His chuckle was low and menacing. "Oh, we haven't harmed your precious world... yet. We simply... mirrored it." The glee in his eyes was unmistakable. "Using the DNA traces from your Obsidia Prime, and Sterling's unmatched technology, we crafted an identical realm. But here's the catch," he leaned in, his eyes glinting with mischief, "our world is entangled with yours. Dominance over our realm gives us the keys to yours."

Lena, always the fire to my calm, stepped forward, her voice strong and unwavering. "You may have replicated the structure, the visuals, but you can never capture its essence. Obsidia Prime thrives with life, history, and spirit. What you've made is nothing more than a cold, lifeless reflection."

His smirk, once filled with arrogance, faltered for a moment. His gaze hardened, and the air around us grew colder. "Our endgame, Jonyé," he declared, ignoring Lena, "is the Echostone. The heart and soul of your world. And rest assured, we will stop at nothing to possess its power."

The leader, seeing the doubt on my face, decided to elucidate. "You're wondering how, aren't you? Despite all your ingenious barriers and that intricate immune system you implemented?"

I clenched my fists but held my tongue, waiting.

"You see," he began, a hint of pride evident in his tone, "when I infiltrated Obsidia Prime the first time, I realized the defenses you placed were... prodigious. But every system, no matter how advanced, has its vulnerabilities. Especially when the human factor is involved."

His eyes flicked to my virtual skin, the access point. "You've made an impressive leap with these," he continued. "Such direct integration, merging the digital with the biological. But, in ensuring that the experience was seamless for the user, you overlooked one tiny detail."

My mind raced, trying to anticipate his revelation.

"The moment a user immerses, the skin maps their neuro-signature. To make this possible, the virtual skin temporarily stores fragments of the world's code – Obsidia Prime's DNA. All we needed was to obtain a discarded skin. Someone careless enough to dispose of it without proper protocol."

Lena's voice was razor-sharp. "And you found one?"

The leader's grin was predatory. "It wasn't that difficult. A gathering as vast as the immersive experience? Bound to have one or two attendees who aren't as meticulous."

A sinking feeling settled in my stomach. It was a vulnerability I hadn't considered, an error in judgment. But now, the consequences were unimaginable.

"The moment we had it," he continued, relishing in the revelation, "we extracted the necessary data. Sterling's tech did the rest. And now," he gestured expansively, "we have a world of our own, tethered to yours."

The leader leaned forward slightly on his mount, and his demeanor shifted. The arrogance in his posture subsided momentarily, replaced with a cold, business-like detachment. "But I come bearing a proposal," he started, his tone measured.

I met his gaze warily. "I'm listening."

"You've seen what we can do, what we have. Sterling's resources combined with our determination are formidable. But conflict is costly, even in a world like this. So, we're giving you twenty-four hours." He raised a single finger for emphasis. "One day. Reconsider Sterling's offer, accept his terms, and we will withdraw from Obsidia Prime, leaving it in peace."

Lena interjected, disbelief evident in her voice. "And if she refuses?"

The leader's predatory smile returned, chilling in its resolve. "Then, we will take over, assimilating every strand of your world's code into ours. Obsidia Prime will cease to exist as you know it. You won't just be losing a creation; you'll be forfeiting a world, its history, its soul."

The atmosphere grew dense with tension. I felt the weight of the invader's ultimatum pressing down on me, a noose of choices, each with their own set of consequences.

His steely gaze fixed on mine. "You have your window, Jonyé. Use it wisely."

The intruders turned their backs to us then, the cold glint of their tech armors dimming in the dimming light. As they retreated beyond the horizon, the unease they brought lingered, wrapping the village in a somber mood.

Mama Nolwazi, sensing my worry, took a few graceful steps toward me. Her age-worn hands clasped my own. "Jonyé, do not let fear write the story of this land."

"But they have a world that mirrors ours, Mama Nolwazi," I retorted, frustration evident in my voice. "They can control ours if they control theirs."

She chuckled softly, a sound that reminded me of wind rustling through the leaves. "Young Creator, they might replicate the land, the trees, and even the rivers, but they cannot replicate the spirit of Obsidia Prime, the magick. We are bound by Ancestors, by the very essence of life itself. That cannot be cloned."

Lena added, "Mama Nolwazi, they seem determined. And with Sterling's resources, who knows what they're capable of?"

The elder woman's eyes twinkled, "Remember, Creator, our magick is older than any tech they possess. And as for that offer," she tilted her head towards me, "trust in your spirit. The Ancestors are with you. Obsidia Prime is more than just code. It's an essence, a spirit, a song sung by the heart of the universe."

Lena and I exchanged a glance, both of us searching for answers, yet comforted by Mama Nolwazi 's unwavering faith.

Later, at my apartment, the skyline of our world shimmered through the glass windows. I sank into the sofa, my fingers drumming a restless beat on my lap. Lena, seeing my distress, sat beside me.

"Talk to me, baby."

I took a deep breath, gathering my thoughts. "Sterling's offer... it's a way out, Lena. If we accept, Obsidia Prime remains untouched... sort of."

"Yes, sort of... but at what cost, Jonyé?" Lena's eyes, usually so warm, were now clouded with concern. "You've created a world, breathed life into it. Giving Sterling the keys means sacrificing its essence, its freedom."

I ran a hand through my hair, stress pressing down on me. "I know, but what if they succeed? If they take control, everything we've built, everything we've dreamed, it'll all be for nothing."

She cupped my face in her hands, forcing me to meet her gaze. "We fight, Jonyé. We use the magick, the tech, everything at our disposal. We don't just hand Obsidia Prime over."

Closing my eyes, the memories of Obsidia Prime swirled in my mind - the vivid landscapes, the echoing laughter, the pulse of life that ran through it. "Lena, it's not just about Obsidia Prime anymore. It's about us, our future, the legacy we want to leave behind."

Her voice softened, "Whatever you decide, Jonyé, I'm with you. Always."

We sat in contemplative silence, the future uncertain, the challenges ahead daunting. As the city lights danced before us, the story of Obsidia Prime, of us, was just beginning. And the next chapter was yet to be written.

RIGGAMORO
BY
ALAN JONES

Cast:
   The Sentinel, Flap Jack, Hussle Man, Fool Fiona.
Date:
   Saturday Morning, Eight AM.

"Damn, another dead body," Hussle man lamented.

"So, what *we* gon do?," Flap Jack asked.

"*We*, ain't gonna do squat." The Sentinel, the block captain of our street, in our historic West End neighborhood, replied harshly. "At this point, I'm washing my hands of the lot of you."

"Really?" Hussle Man reacted.

"Really indeed, this is the third one this week, and worse yet, they dropped this one on the sidewalk right in front of my house!"

"Hmm, I get it, you being the HOA president and block captain." After taking a beat, Flap Jack consoled, "But it does appear that Lucky Larry, was definitely not so lucky, huh?"

The Sentinel acknowledged, "No, he was not, not today anyway. And if this keeps up, before long there won't be enough of us in the HOA to even form a quorum. If that happens everything will go to pot."

"So, what you gon do?" Flap Jack asked of the Sentinel.

"Well, I've already done what I'm going to do. I called the police, and once they take my statement, I'm done. Every other day somebody is coming up missing or dead from these six streets."

Hussle man took his eye off the body before him, just long enough to see Fool Fiona skipping down the street.

"What you doing over here?"

Fool Fiona, reached out her hand to pinch Hussle Man's cheek, then seeing the body on the sidewalk she gasped, "Oh wow, another body, huh?"

"No shit, sherlock," Hussle Man offered sarcastically.

"Why you always coming at me sideways, huh?" Fiona asked.

"Sorry Fiona, please let me try again. Dear Fiona, I hear what you're saying, and all of us find the loss of Lucky Larry to be a very sad thing. And might I add, regardless of what words might happen to come out of my mouth on any given day, I respect you and ask for your forgiveness and grace."

The Sentinel smiled and dapped up Hussle Man. "I see what you did there."

Hussle smiled, "Man, thanks for hipping me to that whole emotional intelligence vibe. Not only does it defuse situations and difficult conversations, it's also proving quite useful in the club with the ladies."

"You don't say. I'm gonna have to flex that, next time I'm in the spot."

"Bet." the Sentinel replied.

Standing over the body, Fiona asked, "So, how'd he die?"

Hussle Man, pointing at the victim declared to Fiona, "Oh, I think that meat cleaver sticking out of his head had something to do with his condition."

"Oh, I see your point, or the point as the case may be."

Switching subjects, Fool Fiona asked, Flap Jack, "Hmm, so Flap Jack, which one of these lovely West End homes are you *occupying* these days?"

"Unh, unh, you not crashing with me. No way in hell we doing that again!" Flap Jack declared for all to hear. "You get a little taste, and that other side of you, the demon spirit, comes out!"

"Other side? Child please, I'm as constant as the northern star." As her words passed through her lips, everyone else in the circle looked away, refusing to make eye contact with the madam.

"So, do you even know which way is north, Fiona?" the Sentinel asked.

"I don't know; and why you asking me?" Finona replied.

"Because, you said…" The Sentinel started.

"Apple Carts!" Fool Fiona yelled, interrupting everyone's train of thought. "Forget all that, we all know that at the end of the day, if I come knocking on your door tonight, you're letting me in."

At Fool Fiona's reply, each of the men looked at the ground, refusing to make eye contact with anyone else in our circle.

"Yeah, that's what I thought."

Flap Jack broke the silence. "Yeah, and that's exactly why I'm not telling you where I'm posted up right now. Plus, every time you come through, stuff comes up missing."

"That's the cost of doing business," Fiona laughed.

Flap Jack grunted, like he'd just eaten something not meant for human consumption.

Hussle Man stuck out his hand, as though he was protecting Fool Fiona, like an umpire calling time, for the batter to reenter the box., "Hold on y'all. Not that I support robbing and scamming folks, but if you live around here, and you're still fooling with Fiona, that's on you. So let's get back to the matter at hand. Block captain, I saw through your front window, that your bags are packed and ready to go in your foyer."

"So…? That's my house, I do as I like," The Sentinel smirked.

"Well, as the men of the community, shouldn't we handle this?" Flap Jack asked.

Fool Fiona coughed. "What?"

Flap Jack corrected himself. "As the men and *woman* of the community, we need to do something."

Flap Jack, the neighborhood squatter, wrapped up the point he was making in a side conversation with Hussle Man. "All I'm saying if I can be faithful in removing my garbage bin from the curb once a damn week, why can't everyone else?"

Everyone turned to Flap Jack with their own incredulous reaction. Sensing his neighbor's reaction, Flap Jack admitted, "Well, just because, it might not technically not my house, doesn't mean, I shouldn't try to be a good neighbor."

The Sentinel responded. "Well, you're half right. What's so hard about pulling our trash bins from the curb? And yes, I checked the tax records, and that's certainly not your house."

"Dude, you doing too much… all up in my business." Flap Jack grumbled under his breath. But as a guy who's worked for pretty much every security firm which does business in the hood, Flap Jack knew the weaknesses of all the security systems in use in our little world.

The Sentinel smiled. "Ah at last, the authorities are here." The Sentinel stepped over to the body as the two officers also converged there too. The Sentinel began, "Officers I'm glad you're here. We've been waiting for more than an hour for someone from the police department to get here."

"We?", the taller male officer, asked.

"Yes, me and my neighbors…" The Sentinel turned to see that each of his compatriots had unceremoniously dipped out on him, just as the officers pulled up to the curb. "Jive… never mind, anyway, I stepped out this morning to grab my morning paper to read with my morning coffee, and saw this fool sprawled out on the sidewalk.

The shorter female office offered, "Looks like somebody really, really didn't like this guy, huh? Was he in a gang?"

"A gang? Really? Look at all that gray hair on him. He was just a couple steps away from the other side before all of this popped off. Does he fit the profile?" The Sentinel asked. "Guys like Lucky Larry aren't in gangs. And that's his cane laying there in gutter. He played the numbers occasionally, when he was feeling lucky. But who doesn't? These kids do all that online crap. Personally, I find it amazing that these kids don't recognize a con when they see one. But not my business."

The older officer, stooped down to take a look at the hatchet impaled upon Lucky Larry's dome, before asking, "So, did he owe anyone money, or did he have a recent altercation which might have escalated?"

"No, not that I know of," the Sentinel answered for everyone, as most of the group stepped away, once the officers pulled up, for their own various reasons.

After the policewoman and her partner passed a look to one another, the larger of the pair of officers, offered, "So nobody knows nothing, right?"

"Nope," The Sentinel answered.

As the officers both shook their heads in disappointment, the Sentinel went added, "However, quiet as it's kept, no one who lives over here believes these killings are random. In fact, my years of living have taught me that something like this is far from random."

"No shit, Sherlock," the brown skinned officer offered with a chuckle.

"No, you're not following me, I mean there's a pattern. Every two days, there's another body. And not only that, there appears to be a pattern."

"Really?" the shorter officer asked.

"Yes, really, indeed." The Sentinel answered.

The old man went on. "Well, the first body was found on the southwest corner Peeples Street, and the second body was found right up there in front of the Catholic church on Ralph David Abernathy, cattycorner from the West End mall. The third body was dropped on the northwest corner of Peeples street up there near the Hammonds House. While at first sight, these murders appear to be fairly random, but not so much if you mark each location where a body was dropped. Then if you draw it out where these bodies were left, you're halfway to a…"

"Pentagram!" The female officer injected.

"Damn," the older officer offered, as he shook his head. "So, if the pattern continues, then the next body should be dropped in the southeast corner of this community, just west of MARTA station, down there near that new fancy retail space."

The pair of officers stepped a couple of steps away from us, as the older one called in via the radio on his shoulder, "Houston, we have a problem."

A voice came back through the officer's radio, "Sorry, we're full, we don't need anymore problems down here."

"Yes, neither do I, Sarge, but it is what it is."

"Feels like I'm going to regret picking up this call. Okay Roy, give it to me."

"First off Sarge, sorry to say, but you're gonna need a team out here."

"Damnit, we're full over here already."

The older police officer spoke into his radio again, "Looks like we have a serial killer on the prowl over here."

"Really?" the voice came back.

"Yes, sir. Visualize where the first three bodies were dropped. If the fourth one is dropped down by the park and brewhouse two days out, then yeah, we've got a problem, a really big problem. If the pattern continues, then the next murder will be in that area some time on Monday."

The Sargent on the other end of the call conceded at last. "Wow, I can see it in my head now. I'm going to need to cough up some overtime to get a few of the guys who worked this weekend, to patrol the area on Monday, regulars and plain clothes."

"Thanks, Sarge."

As the gang dared to approach the officers, Hussle Man dared to ask, "So what's the deal?

The Sentinel interjected, "it looks like we might have a serial killer on our hands."

"Officially, no. But," the officer waved his hands, as if he really didn't know. "The odds of that being the case are still pretty small when you think about. But then again, part of the problem way back with all those kids gone missing was that folks refused to acknowledge there was an issue. So we have to treat every case now, because it can and did happen here before."

The old man of the group, and block captain, and treasurer of the HOA, turned to walk back to his house to resume loading his bags into his SUV. "Sorry to say y'all, but I don't plan to be anywhere near here come Monday. But y'all do whatever the hell, y'all want to. I'm lights out."

Date: Monday Afternoon, Three PM., at the new eatery.

Flap Jack smiled when he saw Fool Fiona walk into the trendy brewery.

"Hi Fiona, I like the wig. I mean generally, blonde is not my thing, but it works with the old school sunglasses. It looks good on you. I thought for a minute that you weren't going to make it. I mean we said one-thirty. I thought that maybe you were still hot with me, for not telling you where I'm staying these days."

"Oh no, you don't think I'm that that sensitive, do you?" Fiona asked, laughing. "Come on, now."

"Good. I was waiting for you here, downing a couple of brews to past the time, but now I do need to step away to the men's room for a second. Be right back…"

"Oh, no worries. I'll be here."

Fool Fiona mumbled to herself, in a singsong voice. "A night in your place, wouldn't have cost you anything. My pocketing whatever happened to catch my eye, was, as I said, the cost of doing business for the services I've rendered to all you fools. Regardless, once you take a sip from your glass, you'll be in the express lane, for whatever comes next after this life, in less than an hour. When others pay you no account, it actually affords the power to do just as you please, and no one's none the wiser. Should have just let me crash at your pad, dude."

SWING
BY
KORTNEY Y. WATKINS

Author's note: the following is a tale that can be seen in a number of ways. It is a tale of hope and mercy, of trauma and vengeance, of refuge and reckoning; it is a tale of extremes and in-betweens. Though this tale is in part very loosely based in (alternate) history, and gives a nod to personal lineage, it was created with the understanding that humanity can choose to be at its best or worst.
Therefore, I propose to you, dear reader, that contemplation regarding your views of this humble story is worth the intellectual and emotional exercise.
So saying, may the ghosts and their horrors give you enlightenment—and if needed, peace.

I

February 1715 brought the end of the Tuscarora War and with it everything that Charles Justice Woodcreek knew. With his parents, aunts, uncles, brothers, and other older family now missing, dead, or fled, Charles inherited the role of patriarch at just twenty-six. It was a burden, but one that was necessary for the remaining family to survive. For him to survive. Pieces of him had died bit-by-bit with every rape, every kill, every atrocity that humankind was never meant to experience, but family members and friends did. He needed to survive.

The challenges of a man's survival were an accepted part of life, but trouble was not. It was not natural, and Charles felt that within his soul. The trouble was that trouble did not end when the war did. Years of mistrust between the ever-increasing number of European settlers (a direct result of the propaganda spread

by European powers always lusting for more and colonial enthu-
siasts running away from perceived and sometimes real oppres-
sion and injustices) and the Indigenous peoples—peoples that
had been in conflict with one another since the beginning of colonization—had come to yet another head, and the impending
shadow of still another war was brewing.

Charles could feel it weighing on him like a full urn of grain
waiting to be stored in the silos. *The Yamasee are just as discontent as the Tuscarora were,* he uncomfortably mused, twisting ab-
sentmindedly at his beard, the slight waves hinting at his mixed
blood. It was a nervous habit of his. A tell that his papá had
warned him about which attentive people could see, recognizing
moments of his vulnerability. "Justice," his papá had implored
many times, "close your curtains. People are peeping through
your windows." Oh, how he missed him, how he missed hearing
his father call him by that loving name: Justice.

But his papá was gone now and he figured that it was best to
do what he could. If his papá was still so concerned, his ghost
would let him know. *I pray his ghost will come. I pray he can
still be here to tell me the right thing to do.* Charles blinked back
his emotions, cognizant of the many people—his family, his
clan—huddled in the eight-room house who looked to him for
strength and comfort; they were the remnant, all that remained of
what he once knew. As he surveyed the crowded room of the
many young on the well-worn wooden floor, holding tight to each
other, covered in grime from which the shine of their hollowed
eyes glowed back at him as intensely as a blood moon at midnight, he shifted in his chair, sitting taller, willing himself to make
his presence dominant, commanding, authoritative.

His wife, Mercy, and their own children were morose, quiet in
the unnaturalness of the aftermath of the last siege. Mercy
hummed because she could no longer sing, and their eight-month-
old baby, Thaddeus, whimpered because he could no longer cry.
The last weeks had been the hardest yet and everyone was tired.

*There's nothing to be gained by the listlessness of a leaf in a
stream, being swept away by the current. It's the rock in the
stream, steady and strong, that the drowning can look to for survival. I am now their rock.* They had to survive.

Charles continued to look around, assessing the damage of the house from his current viewpoint. Most of the windows were shattered, and there was charring along the west wall where a fire had been set ablaze with home-grown grenades—pinecones coated in pitch made bright with the damned fires of hell and made to alight on curtains and clothing… and people. They had been thrown in after cowards shot the windows through in the deep of night where children should have been dreaming good things but instead awoken to a nightmare. It was nature made unnatural. *That's what hate does. We cannot live in hate. We must survive.* With a nod of his head, certain in uncertainty, Charles came to a decision: it was time to leave.

While many of his tribe fled northward to New York and Ontario to reclaim their ancient heritage as part of the Iroquois, Charles decided to go southward to a place where Europeans had not yet completely overtaken territory—even if it was close to another tribe's territory. He would pay the tribute if it meant that he could create his own community, a safe haven for his mixed-race family. Without the protection of the Tuscarora, they were all in danger now that enslavement was based upon racial preference, and racial disloyalty.

"Uncle," Charles approached David Stern the next morning, "we are leaving. Come with us. The hunt is on for survivors, and I will not see my family decimated. You know that I consider you a part of my family."

"When?" the war-hardened forty-six-year-old grunted out, having paused swinging his axe to split wood in front of the tilting shanty less than a thousand feet away from the Woodcreek house. Though still attractive with a slight muscular build, light brown hair, and green eyes the color of forest moss after a light rain, the war had aged him, especially in mannerism, not so unlike the disposition of elders who find no temperament to treat with trivial things or people.

"Dusk. We leave under cover of darkness. I have heard rumors of others giving chase to survivors, and especially to those families who are not solely of a certain lineage. That was two days ago. In truth, we have lingered far too long. We have little, so at least that will make traveling fast and light. If you are coming, bring with you no more than you can carry, since it is likely that the men will have to assist the women and children. If you are not coming, God be with—"

"I will be at your dwelling within the hour to assist. We will not make dusk without it." David turned and entered the shanty without another word. Charles exhaled a slow and halting breath, his shoulders painfully untensing at the release of weight he fully was not aware that he was carrying. Uncle David was a welcome addition for many reasons, and truth be told, Charles could not endure another loss, as they would likely never see each other again if Uncle David declined the invitation. He counted this as a sign of good fortune to come, that better days would unfold, that God gave his consent for the move, and Papá, his approval. The family would survive.

II

By October, the Woodcreek clan, as they were now known, had negotiated with the regional Cherokee and Creek regarding a modest tract of land and made a settlement. After months of a harrowing journey on foot, spring of 1716 brought the arrival of Joseph Smith, leader of The Traders Dozen, a group of organized traders that started with twelve members but had grown to more than two dozen. They, along with their families, had been looking for a safe place, fleeing the Yamasee War and knowing that the established English colonies offered far less to exploit, as it had been over a century since the original colony at Jamestown.

They were a homogenous group of Europeans, non-indentured, many of whom had lost loved ones in native raids. Several older ones remembered hearing of the indignity of their grandparents being indentured alongside the African and Indigenous peoples. It was an insult that after all their bloodlines had endured that land and resources still eluded them, despite the propaganda claims that had circulated far and wide in Europe. That is until the discovery of the Woodcreeks.

Joseph Smith was not so arrogant that pride would make him miss an opportunity to take the land that he and his clan so deserved. No, he would make nice with the Woodcreek clan. His clan was, after all, in hostile territory, but the Woodcreeks seemed to get on well with the Indians, and his clan would need to gather their strength and expand in order to stake their claim.

But after both the Creek and Cherokee met the Traders Dozen, now known as the Smith clan, the elders were not keen on them dwelling in the neutral territory between the tribes; they observed the auras of the Smith clan members and knew that they would be trouble. So, the tribal leaders entreated Charles to drive the Smiths away before they themselves had to intervene in order to ensure there would be no trouble. The agreement made for the Woodcreeks were only for the Woodcreeks, and as they found kinship and brotherhood in the spirit of their African-Native-European mixed brethren they did not mind their presence, so long as they respected their nations and were able to trade and pay tribute.

Charles had listened and agreed, but now that summer had passed its pique and autumn would be upon them ere long, he empathized with the Smiths impending plight. Winter's spell would freeze the woods, and the crops and animals would sleep or hide. Survival depended upon storing goods, and it was well-understood that the Smith clan had been hard-pressed to restock. To make matters more complicated, his dear-heart Mercy, having made friendly acquaintance with Joseph's wife, begged Charles that the Smiths could stay one more month before moving their own way. To the chagrin of the tribal elders and a foreboding warning of the shamans, Charles allowed the Smith clan to stay one more month.

By summer's end, the Smiths moved out of the Woodcreek settlement and resettled twenty miles southeast, further into the forested land—land that though abundant in trees had little to offer in the way of plentiful game and easy access to clean water.

The winter of 1716 came early and hard, leaving five to die between December and March. Three of the Smith bachelors left on a quest for trade with anyone, so desperate was their circumstance. They did not return. No one knows but speculated that either war or weather claimed them.

But the Woodcreeks are surviving and even thriving! Joseph thought to himself. Though the failure of leadership fell squarely on his shoulders, though his pride prevented him from forming a sincere alliance with Charles, though the situation that his clan now faced did not have to prove as dire as it was, Joseph needed someone to blame before he admitted defeat and his clan rightly found his faults.

"It is clear that the Woodcreek clan is thriving in spite of everything. I would gamble that the reason is due to their muddied blood—the great European peoples mottled in disgrace with African and Indian heritage," Joseph spat out his tobacco on the compacted dirt floor of the meeting house and sneered at the gathered group of male clan elders. A rumble of agreement hummed through the room. He had been scheming from the beginning, but now it was time to claim what was his, and he had a masterful plan.

When the weather allowed, Joseph and a few others travelled with the express intent to meet David in an attempt to meld the two groups. As David was the senior European in the Woodcreek clan, the choice for outreach was obvious. He would reveal his master plan, assured that it would not only make sense to David, but his alliance also be the assurance that the plan would work.

It was simple. The Smith clan would build a village in the following spring. The only caveat was that anyone with non-European pure blood would be made to be indentured, thereby ensuring a caste-system, one that provided skilled free labor. "Is your sanity lost?" David inquired of Joseph quietly, a calm and deadly censure haunting his seemingly simple reply.

"Surely, being who you are—what you are—is worth restoring a *right* order of matters. I do not mean to enslave anyone, but make no mistake, there is always a hierarchy and people like you," here Joseph gestured to David and his own clan members, "and me are at its pinnacle—where we belong." David turned his green eyes to meet Joseph's black ones, sneering in disdain.

"The head of my clan is Charles, my nephew. I do not make decisions on behalf of our clan, nor do any elders. We are thriving and are at peace. I doubt, in the fullest, that Charles will consent for any of our clan to be subjugated, including his own wife and children, let alone himself. However, I will make sure that Charles and the other elders are made aware of your offer."

Joseph snorted and his companions shifted uneasily, glancing at each other, though not shying away from David. "By last I counted, there are at least a dozen of you that could leave the Woodcreek clan, if you wanted to and join us. Leave the filth behind to find their own way. There are other opportunities to gain servants. We do not need the Woodcreeks. It is only for their sake—a repayment of their initial kindness—that we proposed indenturing instead of slavery for any other people. Now that it seems unlikely that they will take their rightful place in the natural order, perhaps we should just purchase ourselves some slaves. But make no mistake, whether indentured or slave, anyone not like us will serve us." Joseph completed his soliloquy with forceful determination and his clan members nodded their assent. He then turned, beckoning his people, and made to journey back toward their settlement.

Charles was not happy upon hearing the developments and the betrayal; despite the warnings from the Cherokee and the Creek, he was left reeling. A few days later, he sent an envoy to the Smith settlement, led by David, demanding that the Smith clan leave the neutral territory. But as the Smiths were not idle, because Joseph had a plan, they were now many, having replenished their numbers and then some. As it happened, in the days it took for the Woodcreeks to arrive at the Smith settlement, one of the missing bachelors returned with seven European families and four bachelors, comprising thirty-two additional people, most of which being skilled. Apparently, the returned bachelor had split from his companions after understanding early on in their quest to trade that reaching a port city in the East would be the only solution to the Smith clan plight.

Knowing that the Smiths are now in a stronger position, Joseph smirked, scoffed, and flat-out refused Charles' command. David, not knowing the reason, could feel the shift in Joseph's attitude, and left quickly to return home with his own brethren. *The Woodcreek clan is again in danger. Our land will soon be squatted and overrun,* thought David in dismay. He did not hesitate to ask Charles to call a meeting of the elders upon his return in the middle of the night. The Cherokee and Creek were notified by first light.

It was an uneasy silence for all involved. An entire month of uneasy silence.

April showers brought the storm of battle to the Woodcreek settlement. Before noon on a mild day full of the fragrance of honeysuckle upon the breeze, over one-hundred and fifty men, women, and children appeared on its outer edge, looking at their new home in anticipation. The atmosphere was thick with tension, as the Woodcreek young were ushered back into their homes and the elderly women and sick, the small meeting house. Charles, David, and the other young men as well as the male elders approached their foes, forming a formidable line to meet the would-be usurpers. Scythes used to reap food for life and hatchets meant for trees that would supply shelter, warmth, and fuel now were brandished as possible weapons for death, along with the firearms present.

Upon seeing this, a few visiting tribal members of the Cherokee and Creek, who had been sent to monitor the stalemate between the clans went their ways to immediately inform their respective peoples that the time had now come.

Joseph approached David, completely ignoring Charles. It was a sign of disrespect, but also an indication of Joseph's perceived new hierarchy.

"You have been given another chance, David," Joseph projected his voice over the eerie quiet, as if a leaf falling to the ground would not have made the loudest of echoes as it were. But David made no move except to look at his nephew in deference, a contrasting sign of Joseph's disrespect and a denial of his supposed hierarchy.

"Traitor of thine own race, David?" Joseph queried into the silence. He ranted on, "We have come to take what is natural and God-decreed. We, *our* people, *will* subdue this great Earth, David, and this is the corner that the Smiths are taking. We, *our* people, will rid the world of the weak and impure starting with the Woodcreeks. I declare that this land is now ours!" Joseph finished triumphantly in an animalistic roar. Shouts from the Smiths went up to meet their leader, their master.

"Is that so?" Charles retorted calmly, his arms crossing over his chest. He would fight and he would win. He did it before and would do it again. *The Woodcreeks must survive.* Charles chanted that mantra in his head as he was passed a rifle from a Woodcreek elder next to him. He took it, raised it, and with glorious precision, made the first shot—a fatal shot. Thinking of survival was what brought them into refuge before. It had to be the same now.

* * *

Outnumbered by firearms and a mercilessness too often seen before in humanity by the hosts of heaven, the Woodcreeks fell. The children. The women. The men. The young. The old. The defenseless. The defenders. All fell. It was a complete and total massacre.

Joseph, before giving the order to dispatch David and a few other of the surviving Woodcreek European males, were brought forward in his presence and asked a simple question. "Do you stay as one of us, or do you swing?" Pale, bloodied, and broken in heart, the remnant looked to each other for strength as they breathed out in unison, "Swing."

* * *

The bodies of the Woodcreek clan, hung and burnt beyond recognition, decorated six large white oaks near the base of the bald side of the mountain. From a distance, onlookers would have been able to see great lights, like beautiful low-hanging stars. But in close confines, one felt the putrid air remaining thick from desecrated human flesh, and the wicked flames held fast by the demonic candelabras that Joseph had lit for a feast to celebrate the Smith clan's lust did not move. The flames shot straight upward to the heavens, an offensive offering that had complimented their blaspheme of God. Time was tested himself, as the unnatural moment lingered far too long, forcing him to no longer walk his standard pace. So, he ran. For vengeance of the distorted order, he ran.

It was no surprise that because the Woodcreeks were beloved by both Cherokee and Creek nations, the Smith clan was soon chased away back northward within a week of the massacre, having lost half of their own number by the nations' brave warriors. The alacrity with which retribution was handed to the usurpers was astounding, and quite frankly unexpected by the fallen foes. The Smiths had quickly forgotten that it was the Woodcreek clan—and not they—who had established a treaty. It was a lesson that came at a great cost, for the deaths of the Smith clan members were unforgiving and gruesome.

The shamans buried the Woodcreeks, their bodies having been allowed to rot by the Smiths, save for Charles-Nathaniel, the eldest child of Charles Justice and Mercy, who ran and hid during the attack. Because the Smiths had torched the portion of the Woodcreek settlement during the raid where some of the children hid, it was assumed that he died in the fire. The lone survivor, Charles-Nathaniel had wandered the woods delirious for two days before being discovered by a Creek hunting party.

Shamans of both nations joined to summon forth justice for their fallen friends. Their restless spirits would be witnesses for the divine balance, true justice beyond the courts of men that would exact for every life taken throughout the generations of the Smith clan, however long that took. And it would take 300 years to the day.

* * *

Fifteen years after the murders, Oglethorpe, with the commission of the Crown, established the colony of Georgia in 1732. Thirty-five-year-old James, the younger brother of Joseph, a former bachelor while under his older brother's authority, had long-since married and is the father of five. He has made much money in the colony of Virginia after his narrow escape; his brother being taken by the Indian warriors before his very eyes. Yet, despite the pain, he could not deny that the skills he learned from the Smith clan, along with Joseph's ideology served him well, making him into the important slave trader that he was today.

On a peaceful afternoon, James reflected upon his life, smiling at the good, grimacing at the bad. However, the thought of returning to the place that defined him as a man overtook every sensibility he had. He remembered the mountain and its beauty and felt a sense of longing and belonging. No number of nightmarish memories could keep him from the desire to return to the mountain.

Alexandria, Colony of Virginia
Obituary
December 8, 1733

Local, Mr. James Smith of Alexandria, died by accident, having been flung from his horse near a cluster of white oak trees at the base of a small mountain in the new-found colony of Georgia. He was discovered by locals dead-upon-the-scene, a strangulating event whereby his mount's reins wrapped around his neck, promoting its break and subsequent suffocation. He is survived by his wife, Anna, and five children who mourn him immensely. His mother, father, and brother precede him in death. No auction is scheduled for his property, including his slaves.

III

I'm Black. That was the statement thought, but not said, which rang heavy in the air around Charles, dooming clangs of a deep bell like that of a clock tower in a historical square. He took a deep breath and slowly released it, the force of air through his nostrils making a high-pitched rasping sound, contrasting to the bells. He took another breath and then another and still another. His heart rate slowed. The bell tolls receded to background noise and his stunned stupor changed to deep contemplation. In a matter of a moment, his whole life—his children's whole life—had changed. *Speaking of,* he walked to the wall of his study and punched the house intercom button to summon the kids. Having gathered his three loves together in his study—really a library of sorts with a worktable, sofa, reading chair, and desk— along with his eldest son's fiancée, he geared himself to make the revelation aloud this time. He was a single father, widowed when the youngest was just three. He had found earlier that if the children trusted him, they could get through any challenge together. Trust meant truth. Even if it was uncomfortable.

The kids looked at him expectantly, and noticed the papers in his hands, an official printout of the DNA test that all of the Archer children had been dying to see. Zachary, Christian, Stephanie, and Kayla looked at each other with a bit of excitement. Oh what, oh *what* would the results they had been waiting on for three whole weeks reveal!? Zachary reached out to hold Kayla's hand, her modest, but beautiful engagement ring twinkling from the sunlight pouring through the study window.

"Kids—" began Charles.

"What did it say?" Stephanie leaned forward slightly, interrupting a bit breathlessly.

"Shut up and let Daddy speak!" Christian rolled his eyes at his sister, who typically annoyed him into oblivion, as little sisters tend to do.

"Don't tell me to shut up. YOU shut up," quipped Stephanie at the harsh rebuke.

"*Both* of you shut up!" Zachary had already mitigated a quarrel with his younger siblings not an hour before. He was the eldest and once again found himself at his wits end. Kayla squeezed his hand in sympathy.

"Kids! All of you be quiet! Please..." pleaded Charles. He pinched the bridge of his nose and rocked back in his desk chair, a soft squeak protesting his sudden shift in weight. Charles felt a migraine coming on, but he was determined to speak the truth to his children. He never lied to them before and wouldn't now, especially since fate had dealt its tricky hand; it was a high-stakes game for all of them now. Well, at least newly high stakes for all but his future daughter-in-law who had no illusions of being considered "Black" by herself and others, though when she traveled abroad sometimes people would look at her askance.

The way that Americans perceived race was quite different from the rest of the world. This fact wasn't lost on him, particularly since Kayla had become part of the family and traveled abroad with them often. Through dealing with instances of prejudice involving his future daughter and thinking about any children that would result of Zach and Kayla's union, Charles had become hyperaware concerning how people locally, domestically, and internationally perceived the concept of "Black". Though there were some instances of goodness, many other situations had left an acrid taste in his mouth.

But he was Black. They all were. The "One Drop Rule", a sometimes legal, but at all times American social law dictated that Black blood was a contaminate to White blood, no matter how small of an amount. In the day of DNA testing for ancestral answers, many people were finding out inconvenient and life-changing truths. Charles recalled having read a local news story where a fourth-generation Ku Klux Klan member wanting to prove royal European family lineage took a DNA test. While he did indeed descend from a royal house, he also apparently descended from a plantation house. His third great-grandfather being mulatto had "passed" as white; he was beyond furious when the Black branch of the family reached out to him on the DNA website, wanting to glean information about their long-lost family member and hopeful to establish a more meaningful connection. The moment someone outside of his immediate family found out, the moment he lost all connections with friends, White family, and business associates. He had to move his family to a completely different country for fear of what his former comrades could do, and also because none of his Black family, now understanding that he was a generational Klansman, would accept him and his family.

If Charles was honest, he could have easily been in the same position as that man. However, though his family didn't outright deny their heritage, they also didn't make it well known—especially when now and again some members would have deeper olive skin, a wider nose, fuller lips, and/or the tendency to keloid. At least with his own grandmother she had allowed their neighbors to justify their suspicions. Charles being around ten at the time recalled Mrs. Rebecca, his grandma's next-door neighbor, look at his little deep complected and broad-nosed cousin with an inquisitive look while they were playing in the backyard, the elder ladies sipping sweet sun tea. "Adelaide? Didn't y'all say you had some Mediterranean in ya bloodline?" Charles recalled his grandmother simply nodding. It wasn't a lie, as they did. But it wasn't also the full truth either.

The only time Charles knew for certain that things weren't as the public knew them to be was at the funerals the Archers would go to. It seemed like people were always dying in the family, but not his branch of the family. The Smith side always seemed to die young. Often, the Smiths would sneer at their cousins, making snide remarks about "mottled blood". There had been long, generational discord after the marriage of an Archer ancestor, Charles-Nathaniel Woodcreek to the daughter of James Smith. No one really spoke about what "mottled" meant when he was a child, so he grew up thinking that it meant that Charles-Nathaniel was of the lower class. It wasn't until Kayla and Christian had run across a secret compartment in a family heirloom, an old escritoire that contained documents, letters, and Charles-Nathaniel's journal that an alternative truth formulated in Charles' head. It was this that finally prompted DNA testing. And the dream—nightmares really started soon after.

It was always the same dream: two family clans fleeing for their lives, one Mixed people, one all-White; the Mixed clan resettles; the White clan joins for a while; Native elders looking concerned as the two clans interact; the White clan moving on and winter bringing death; the White clan leader making threats; a massacre; a retribution.

After talking to the kids for a few hours about their new status while trying to process their new identity in their new reality, Charles got a call. He had just been outbid by the last remaining Smith earlier in the week for family land south of the base of Stone Mountain. The cousin, being the last of his line, was rich beyond belief. That was saying something, as Charles' wealth was no trifle. But grandma Adelaide had always told Charles that the day would come when "fate would swing the Archer way" and that he should be kind to his cousins even if they were not kind to him. So, he let the family land go—land that was supposedly Smith, though by the records in the hidden cache it was most certainly Woodcreek.

"Charles Benedict Asher?" intoned a deep business-like male voice.

"This is he," responded Charles, equally all business.

"My name is Desmond Parker. I'm the family attorney for the Smiths. Or at least I used to be."

"Beg your pardon?" Charles was a bit confused and after the day he had wanted to take a nap before preparing dinner for his family.

"I apologize if you haven't yet heard the news. My condolences on the death of your cousin, Joseph Smith. As you know, he did outbid you on the parcel of land in Stone Mountain. Curious that it was even available, and relatively virgin at that. And the swath of land is quite large. He had plans to develop some of the land and then sell the rest to other investors."

"OK..." Charles was at the end of all patience, rolling his eyes heavenward.

"At any rate, I was calling to let you know that my secretary will be setting up an appointment with you to transfer the land deed. As you are the closest kin to the former Mr. Smith and the Smiths/Archer's have a long-standing agreement, you are to inherit the land." Charles blew out a shaking breath. Was it really over? The day that he regained his true identity was the day, if Charles-Nathaniel's journal was true, is the day divine justice was met.

"Thank you for letting me know," Charles said reservedly, his emotions all over the place. They hung up after a few more exchanges, Charles asking if Mr. Parker had builder referrals for a newly minted idea of creating Woodcreek Lodge, a place for people recovering from trauma.

* * *

The Woodcreek clan looked on as the groundbreaking ceremony for Woodcreek Lodge got underway. Suddenly, a door appeared in the mid-morning sky that seemed to lead to nowhere and everywhere. It sent outwards tendrils of hope and peace, and the ghosts grabbed at each string meant for them. It lifted them up and through the sky, then the firmament.

The last ones to pass the threshold were Charles Justice and Mercy, hand-in-hand. Charles Justice stopped. "Papá?"

"Justice," his papá smiled. "We've been waiting so long for you."

Mercy tugged on her husband's hand a bit impatiently, longing for the overdue reunions, and laughing in utter joy, Justice and Mercy moved along.

Papá swung closed the door until the next arrivals were to show—hopeful, now that the order was restored, time would walk again in harmonious steps, swinging his arms to the right rhythm of the world.

TALISMAN OF GAMBIT
BY
L. RENEE JAMES-GRIFFIN

Korah's eyes fluttered open to the gentle caress of sunlight filtering through her bedroom window, casting a golden hue across the worn wooden floorboards. She lingered in the warmth, savoring the tranquil moment before the demands of the day enveloped her. Each ray of light seemed to whisper secrets of ancient artifacts and mystical wonders, a silent invitation to embark on another journey into the realm of magic.

As she lay there, memories of countless hours spent pacing back and forth across the same floorboards flooded her mind. Each worn groove bore witness to her restless energy, fueled by a ceaseless curiosity and a relentless pursuit of knowledge. The floor beneath her feet was not just wood; it was a canvas etched with the imprints of her countless musings, a testament to her unwavering dedication to her craft.

With a resigned sigh, Korah finally stirred, reluctantly casting aside the comfort of her covers. The weight of responsibility settled upon her shoulders like a heavy cloak as she faced the reality of the day ahead. The artifacts in her possession awaited her meticulous attention; their mysteries waiting to be unraveled and their stories waiting to be told.

At least she didn't have far to go to get started. As a guardian of ancient artifacts and magical knowledge, Korah's modest dwelling served as both a sanctuary and workspace. Nestled within the weathered walls of a dilapidated building in Old Fourth Ward, a district steeped in history as the birthplace of the revered Dr. Martin Luther King Jr., Korah's home bore witness to the passage of time and the evolution of the world around her.

Though the years had transformed the neighborhood into the newly christened New Fourth Ward, the echoes of the past lingered in the air, a reminder of the struggles and triumphs that had shaped its identity. Despite the outward changes, Korah recognized the underlying truth that remained unchanged: the enduring presence of conflict and division, where ancient rivalries persisted and those deemed different or non-human faced discrimination and persecution.

Dressed and seeking her first cup of warm matcha, Korah noticed a sudden movement outside her window. Upon further inspection,

Korah found a sleek raven perched on the sill; its intelligent eyes fixed on her.

The raven hopped inside the moment Korah unlatched the window. It carried a small scroll in its mouth. The bird dropped the scroll at Korah's feet, cawing once before disappearing.

Korah picked up the scroll and immediately noticed the ancient runes etched into it. The runes glowed with magical energy. The runes meant one thing only — Professor Knox had sent her a message.

Though cryptic, the runes carried an ominous warning. The Peachshade Talisman is real and not a myth like many thought. Dark forces were seeking it, intending to use its power for destruction. Professor Knox ended his note with a date and time stamp. He wanted to meet. She already knew where.

Her need for matcha forgotten, Korah couldn't help the excitement that rose within her. For years, she apprenticed under Professor Knox who taught her how to properly find, preserve, and catalog magical artifacts of all kinds. Korah had handled powerful relics before, but legend had it that the talisman rivaled any in existence.

The Peachshade Talisman was well known in the magical underworld of Atlanta. Hell, children learned about the mythical gemstone in school. Carved from a rare peach-colored gemstone found only in the orchards of Georgia, the talisman supposedly possessed the ability to enhance the natural abilities of its bearer.

For a moment, Korah wondered what it would be like for a water mage like herself to gain heightened senses, increased strength, and enhanced magical prowess. The prospect of unlocking such potential stirred a longing within her, a yearning to transcend the limitations of her current abilities and delve into the depths of her elemental power.

But as quickly as the temptation arose, Korah quashed it with a mental shake. She couldn't afford to indulge in fantasies of newfound power, not when the stakes were so high. Professor Knox's warning echoed in her mind, a sobering reminder of the dangers that lurked in the shadows. As Professor's protege, the burden of retrieving the artifact fell squarely upon Korah's shoulders, a duty she accepted with a solemn determination.

Before she met with Professor Knox, Korah knew she needed vital information, and the bustling marketplace of Atlanta beckoned her. Its vibrant stalls and diverse vendors drew beings from all corners of the magical underworld, making it the perfect hub for gathering intelligence.

Korah made her way through the winding streets as vendors called out on either side, their carts and stalls overflowing with magical wares. Crystals, potion bottles, ancient tomes—Atlanta had everything an aspiring mage could desire. She kept her head down, avoiding eye contact. Her informant waited in the alley up ahead. As she slipped into its shadowy entrance, a figure detached itself from the darkness.

"I need information," Korah stated firmly to the shadowy figure before her. She was aware that Nyx might disapprove, but Korah's determination outweighed any concern for Nyx's reaction. With a reputation for secrecy and a network of connections that spanned both within and beyond Atlanta's underworld, Nyx was Korah's best chance at obtaining the crucial information she sought.

"You always do," Nyx stated, lowering his hood just enough for Korah to glimpse his pale and ethereal face.

"Tell me what you know," Korah said without preamble.

Nyx's golden eyes glinted. "Whispers in the dark suggest the Peachshade Talisman is real and close by."

Korah's pulse quickened. "Anything else?"

"Some believe the unusual storm last week unearthed something magical somewhere in the city. Rumors are flying about what it could be and whether it can be found."

Korah digested this silently. If it truly was the talisman, it could impact the fabric of Atlanta's magical community. Many mages, light and dark, would seek its power.

Korah threw a few coins Nyx's way, then hurried from the alley. She needed to find allies she could trust, those with abilities to complement her own. Water sprites came to mind, though they were rare in the city.

Lost in thought, Korah did not notice the figure barreling toward her until they collided. She stumbled back with a gasp as icy blue eyes flashed.

"Remi," she hissed, steadying herself. Remi Blue, her rival water mage. He was known for being ambitious, cunning, and ruthlessly desperate to outmatch her abilities.

Remi's mouth curled into a smirk as he gave an exaggerated bow. "Korah Thames. An honor, as always."

Korah tensed, ready to deflect his magic if necessary. "What do you want, Remi?"

Remi examined his fingernails. "Oh, I was simply passing through. Though, I did hear the most fascinating rumor." His smirk widened. "Tell me, have you had any luck locating the talisman?"

Rage boiled inside Korah. How did he know that it might be a talisman so quickly? She fought to keep her expression neutral. "I don't know what you speak of."

Remi laughed. "Come now, Korah. We both seek the Peachshade Talisman for its powers. But it is I who shall claim it."

Korah summoned her elemental powers, drawing upon the water present in her surroundings as her weapon. With a focused thought, she directed a powerful stream of water from her palm, forcefully knocking his hand back. Around them, puddles began to ripple and rise, responding to Korah's command as she tapped into her connection with the water element.

Being in Atlanta, Georgia, known for its abundant rivers such as the Chattahoochee, Korah's affinity for water magic was heightened by the presence of nearby bodies of water. In moments of need, she could harness the water's energy from anywhere, whether it be from the flowing currents of a nearby river or the gathered rainwater in puddles on the ground. Through her mastery of water manipulation, Korah wielded the liquid element as a formidable weapon, using it to defend herself and overcome her adversaries with fluid grace and precision.

Remi's eyes narrowed. "Impressive."

He sent a jet of water at Korah, who deflected it back. Snarling, Remi melted into the crowd before she could strike again.

Korah released the puddles, breathing hard. She had to reach the talisman before Remi. For if he gained its magic…the consequences did not bear thinking about.

She needed to speak with her mentor. After gathering a few supplies from home, Korah made her way to the Atlanta Underground, a network of tunnels and caverns housing the city's less reputable establishments. Music and raucous laughter echoed through the stone corridors as she descended into its depths.

Few would look for a scholar like Knox here. But through shadowy back channels, he kept his ear to the ground, monitoring the magical black market for artifacts. Korah slipped through a doorway into a crowded tavern, the air thick with smoke. Letting her senses guide her, she wove between tables toward the rear booth.

And there sat Knox, partially obscured behind a mountain of books and parchment. Korah slid into the booth without a sound, waiting for him to notice her. When several minutes passed without a glance up, she reached across and tapped the table. Knox jumped, one book thudding to the floor.

"Korah!" he gasped, adjusting his spectacles. "My dear, you startled me."

"Apologies," said Korah. She withdrew the scroll, brushing a smudge from its surface.

Knox's eyes widened. "All signs point to the Peachshade Talisman." His voice dropped to an urgent whisper. "If dark forces find it first, the consequences will be dire."

"Can it amplify a mage's power tenfold, as the legends say?" asked Korah.

Professor Knox nodded gravely. "In the wrong hands, the talisman's magic could bring Atlanta to its knees." He took a long sip of his drink before continuing. "I would love to retrieve it myself, but your skills have long since surpassed my own. I would be a fool to try."

Warmth rushed through Korah at his praise. "Tell me what I must do."

Professor Knox leaned forward, eyes gleaming. "First, you need a team… With the proper allies, you may succeed where others would fail."

Over the next hour, Professor Knox outlined her mission: Assemble a team of magical experts to help locate and secure the shard. He knew the perfect candidates, including some rather…unorthodox…choices.

"Adisa Ward, the shoplifter," Professor Knox suggested, ticking them off on his fingers. "Her powers of deception will prove useful. And Tariq DuPont. No artifact hunter is finer than Tariq, though his motives tend toward the selfish side. For magical intelligence, there is none better than Ramirez White. On the streets, they call him Spark. And finally, you will need a healer."

Professor Knox scribbled something on a scrap of parchment and passed it to Korah. "Seek out Emiel Reid. A reclusive but gifted healer. Tell him I sent you."

Korah tucked the parchment away and nodded. "I will gather them immediately."

"Make haste," Professor Knox urged. "Even now, dark forces congregate in search of the talisman's power. Trust in your allies but rely on your instincts above all. And Korah. . . be careful. It is said the talisman calls the most to those attuned to water since it was created by a water mage. What most don't know is that it was infused with dark magic."

Korah returned to the bustling market in search of her allies. Her first stop was a curiosities shop run by Adisa Ward. As the bell jingled above the door, Korah froze. Where the counter normally stood was instead a raging inferno.

A sound behind made Korah whirl, hands raised in defense. But it was only Adisa, extinguishing the false fire with a wave of her hand.

"Korah Thames." Adisa grinned, her form shimmering into its true visage—a tall, slender woman with olive skin and piercing amber eyes. "To what do I owe the pleasure?"

Once Adisa was caught up, she readily agreed to join the mission. "A merry chase for a mythical talisman? I'm not sure if it is real, but you can count me in."

Next was the artifact hunter, Tariq DuPont. Korah found him in one of Atlanta's ransacked antique shops, examining a shelf of crystals. Though perhaps "ransacked" was too kind—the once polished shelves were smashed to splinters.

"Your work, I take it?" Korah surveyed the damage.

Tariq glanced up, unperturbed. "The valuables here already disappeared. I was simply…searching for hidden compartments." He straightened, brushing dust from his jacket. "What can I do for you, Korah?"

She relayed the situation. At the mention of the talisman, Tariq's green eyes gleamed with interest.

"A powerful magical artifact, you say? I'd be delighted to assist."

Suppressing a sigh, Korah moved on. For what Tariq lacked in morals, he made up for in skill. His expertise would be invaluable.

The telepath, Spark, proved more difficult to locate. After hours of following dead ends, Korah finally spotted him engaged in a game of cards, his brown eyes flickering from his cards to his opponents. With Spark's mental abilities, his winnings piled high.

When he noticed Korah, he bid his disgruntled opponents farewell before slipping out to speak with her. Though wary at first, Spark's sense of duty won out in the end.

"I want that talisman as far from the city as possible," he muttered, shuffling the deck absently. "Too much potential for destruction here. I'm in."

Last was Emiel Reid, the healer. Korah consulted Knox's parchment before making her way deep into the forest outside the city. There she found a quaint cottage tucked against a hillside, smoke whispering from its brick chimney.

She approached the weathered door and gave three solid knocks. Moments later, it opened to reveal a powerfully built man with olive skin and striking gray eyes—Emiel. He wore simple robes, and his head was shaved smooth.

Though he listened politely as Korah described her quest, Emiel hesitated. "My place is here, tending to the land and people."

Korah persisted gently. "Professor Knox sent me. We need you. You won't have a place or others to care for if the wrong people find the talisman first."

At this, Emiel relented with a weary smile. "Very well, if my gifts can avert this evil, I will help."

With her team assembled, Korah gathered them at her place that evening.

"My friends," she began, meeting each of their eyes in turn, before explaining all Knox had revealed about the talisman.

They spoke long into the night, making plans. Tensions flared between brash Tariq and cynical Spark, cheerful Adisa, and contemplative Emiel. Several times, Korah had to remind them of the task at hand.

In the following days, they poured tirelessly over Knox's books and scrolls, searching for clues to the talisman's location. Emiel transcribed crumbling sections of text while Spark scoured them for hidden meanings.

They discovered the talisman was made long ago in a distant city, glittering even then with elemental magic. Over centuries, it passed between mighty kingdoms before vanishing. Legend said only a worthy mage could summon its powers. But if stained with corruption, the talisman would unleash chaos.

Tariq listened with thinly veiled boredom, eager to begin the hunt. "Legends and lore are all well and fine, but the talisman won't find itself."

Korah was forced to agree. Further research would have to wait— already, Remi sought the talisman, perhaps guided by sources beyond Knox.

After three exhausting days, Tariq proposed a new route for investigation: Atlanta's underground markets. Shady dealers trafficked in illegal magical artifacts—if the talisman had resurfaced, they might well know.

Korah hesitated to expose the mission by asking directly. But Tariq had contacts in those circles, and their leads had run dry.

Reluctantly, she agreed. That night, flanked by Adisa and Spark for protection, they met a skittish vendor in a deserted alleyway. While Tariq questioned him in hushed tones, Spark kept vigilant watch.

But their informant had little to offer—only unverified gossip about old magic resurfacing at the city's fringe. Few substantial facts.

Frustrated, they prepared to leave. But a whisper of sound in the alley's darkness gave Spark pause. He glanced about sharply, sensing ominous intent.

"We're being watched," he hissed. "We need to go. Now!"

But before they could flee, the shadows around them erupted. Dark figures rushed from all sides, including above, where they'd been lying in wait on the rooftops.

Korah's reflexes took over. She threw up curved shields of water, deflecting the blades of two attackers. Tariq pressed his back to hers, a short sword in one hand, an orb of light in the other to reveal their foes.

Spark was weaponless, but his mind lashed out, one assailant crumbling with a cry. Adisa had shifted into a great tawny cat, teeth, and claws shredding those who came too close.

Together, they might have prevailed. But their enemies seemed numberless, fresh replacing the fallen. They were being herded away from the alleys, out toward the open streets where they would be surrounded.

"We have to retreat!" Korah shouted, blocking another barrage of spells.

Spark nodded grimly, clasping Tariq's shoulder. With a flash, both vanished—Spark's teleportation ability could remove only himself and one other.

Heart pounding, Korah and Adisa fled for the alleys. Adisa took the lead in her cat form, Korah running behind, summoning walls of water to slow their pursuit.

Somehow, they managed to lose their attackers for a few precious moments. Adisa shifted back so they could squeeze through a broken window into another abandoned building.

Inside, they collapsed on the dusty floor, struggling to muffle their gasping breaths. Blows and shouts rang outside as their pursuers raced by. But the old building's crumbling walls sheltered them.

After an agonizing period, the sounds faded. The men had given up, for now. But they could return.

"We need to get back to the others and regroup," Korah panted, clutching a stitch in her side. She only hoped Spark and Tariq had made it safely away.

Adisa nodded wearily, struggling to rise. With their arms slung over each other's shoulders, they slipped from the building and into the night.

The trek back to Korah's building passed in a blur. Her side ached fiercely where a curse had slipped past her guard, and her water magic flickered weakly in her grasp.

But finally, they stumbled through the door. Spark and Tariq whirled from their places around Korah's table, relief breaking across their faces.

Emiel rushed to help Korah into a chair. His large hands passed over her, radiating soothing energies. The pain in Korah's side subsided.

Once she'd caught her breath, she turned urgently to Tariq and Spark. "Did you see who attacked us?"

Spark shook his head, brow furrowed. "They hid their faces and did not speak, but I noticed that several of them wielded water."

"Regardless of who they were, we were fools not to expect an ambush," Tariq stated.

Korah's shoulders slumped. She should have been more cautious. But it was too late for regrets.

"At least we are all safe," Emiel spoke gently, like a calming breeze after a storm. Korah managed a grateful smile. She could not have asked for a finer group with whom to weather this darkness.

"Korah, I can't see a clear path," Spark sighed. "I don't know what it means, but I see a cavern, strange runes, the gemstone . . . and darkness."

Cavern, Korah thought. There goes that word again. Glancing around the room, it came to her. Nyx and Tariq's informant mentioned something about rumors flying about magic being near the fringe of the city. Could the talisman be there? It couldn't be a coincidence. Korah didn't believe in coincidences.

"I know where we need to go," Korah told Spark, Tariq, Adisa, and Emiel.

Under the cover of darkness, Korah, Tariq, Adisa, Emiel, and Spark made their way to the outskirts of the city through a series of tunnels that started at the base of Atlanta's underground.

Their footsteps echoed against the cold stone walls. Adisa's keen senses guided them as they moved deeper into the tunnels. The group knew they were near the city limits when a faint etch of runes began to appear on the cavern walls. The air became heavy with the scent of damp earth and lingering magic. Up ahead stood a steel door that seemed out of place with its surroundings.

"Finally," Tariq stated as he moved past Adisa and the others to stand in front of the door. "We've been walking for hours."

Tariq pulled on the door and slipped inside before anyone could protest. A sense of unease crept over Korah as magic washed over them. The energy called to her, beckoning her to enter the room.

Glowing crystals of various hues dotted the walls, casting a soft, ethereal light illuminating the cavern in an otherworldly glow. In the center of the cavern, an alcove carved out of stone ran the length of the floor to the cavern ceiling. The peach gemstone rested atop a marbled pedestal. The Peachshade Talisman radiated warmth and light.

Tariq stood beside the pedestal. He reached for it when a faint humming sound echoed in the cavern.

"Watch out!" Spark said, diving to the left.

Just as Adisa began sniffing the air, a burst of energy coursed through the cavern, knocking everyone off their feet, except Spark. From the shadows, Remi and his men emerged, surrounding Korah and the others.

Remi stepped forward, his arrogant smirk sending a chill down Korah's spine as he drew closer. "Surprise! I knew you would lead me to the talisman, Korah."

With a flick of his wrist, Remi summoned a surge of dark energy and water, hurling it towards Korah and her team, but Korah sprang to her feet as she silently called forth water from the ground. A swirling barrier of water shot up deflecting Remi's attack.

Korah's actions gave Adisa and Spark the time they needed to square off with a few of Remi's men. Adisa shape-shifted into a bear and then into a cave bat to swipe and bite Remi's men. Spark used his telepathic abilities to briefly disorient Remi's men long enough to knock them down. No one noticed that Tariq had quietly backed away from the fighting.

"You're outmatched Korah." Remi laughed, as he threw another mixture of energy and water at her. "You've always been and just refused to see it."

In the heart of the chaos, as Korah and her team fought desperately to maintain their footing amidst the shifting illusions, Tariq attempted to retrieve the Peachshade Talisman. He lunged forward, reaching out for the artifact.

Before his fingers could grasp the talisman, a shadowy figure materialized from the darkness, seizing Tariq and the artifact with a swift, unseen motion. With a panicked cry, Tariq was whisked away into the depths of the caverns. Remi's triumphant laugh echoed through the caverns like a death knell.

Remi's men concentrated their attacks against Korah, Emiel, Adisa, and Spark, preventing them from going after Remi or Tariq.

Unable to push past or overthrow the men, Korah and her team retreated from the underground cavern, barely escaping from the men.

Outside, beneath the stark glare of the sun, Korah, Emiel, Adisa, and Spark huddled together, bruised and battered from the fight.

Korah's mind raced, grappling with the whirlwind of events that had just unfolded. Their failure hung heavy in the air, a bitter taste on her tongue. Remi's cunning had outmaneuvered them, leaving Korah to confront the harsh reality of defeat. The weight of responsibility pressed down on her shoulders like a burden too heavy to bear. They had faltered, and in doing so, they had unwittingly delivered the talisman into the clutches of their enemy. Tariq's absence gnawed at her, a stark reminder of the cost of their failure. They had not only lost the artifact but also one of their own.

Chest heaving, Korah stepped away from the group. She turned to face them. This failure wasn't on them; it was on her.

"Look at me!" She demanded of her team. "This isn't over."

THE DREAMER'S RING
BY
M. HAYNES

Georgia State University History professor Derrick Anderson turned away from his whiteboard to address his students. The sea of faces ranged from mildly interested to outright apathy, but he lectured on.

"Many believed that the decision of Brown v. Board of Education was a success, and ostensibly it was. It had been exceedingly clear that facilities for education were not 'separate but equal', so the access to any educational institution was an important victory. However, as the Little Rock Nine, Ruby Bridges, James Meredith…" Derrick turned to the board behind him to write the names down, "…and countless others proved, exactly how this access was to be given was still unclear. There was also a fairly vocal sector of Black people who were vehemently against this, or any, integration. Can anyone think of why?"

Derrick looked out into the classroom, and after a few seconds of awkward silence a basketball player in the second row of tables looked up from his drawing to answer. "They knew that it wasn't gonna go right. Some folks was cool with how things were and didn't wanna change."

"Thank you," Derrick paused for a second. "That's close, but I think there's a bit more to it. It can, however, be boiled down to an idea that you must be careful what you wish for." Derrick's eyes glanced over the classroom, taking in the still disinterested lot. He did notice, however, that a girl with a bushy afro towards the back of the classroom perked up a bit. Even if it's just for one student the show must go on, he thought, and continued his lecture.

After class ended, Derrick headed back to his office. Almost immediately after he settled into his office chair, he heard a frantic knock at the door. He looked towards the door with a hint of annoyance; it wasn't his office hours and he was already irritated from having so little participation in class. Judging by the knocks, though, this person really needed his help.

"Come in," he said, and immediately one of his students from Survey of United States History rushed into the room. He recognized her afro and the black shirt bearing some famous rap line from this morning. "Ms. Gibson? What's the issue?"

Shanice Gibson stood at the desk, staring at Derrick with pleading in her exhausted eyes. "Dr. Anderson, I got a problem," she said.

Derrick nodded and got up to close his office door. He frantically began searching his mind for his Title IX training from the beginning of the year. All it would take was one misstep for the department to have an excuse to get rid of the newest Black professor. He leaned forward on his desk and invited Shanice to sit down. "What seems to be the issue, Shanice?"

Shanice seemed to be trying to decide how to best explain the issue to Derrick. "Well...uhhh...there was this guy who gave me a ring and-wait that-um..." Shanice began. A crucial part of his training kicked in and Derrick stuck up his hand to stop her.

"I just want you to know that anything you tell me I am legally obligated to report. I want to help you, Shanice, so please—"

"What? Tell who?" Shanice asked in alarm. Understanding showed on her face when she realized what Derrick was getting at, but he continued before she could respond.

"Shanice, please, I have to. But it's okay, we can make sure that he doesn't hurt you again." Derrick kicked himself for assuming, but it was out there now.

Shanice laughed. "It's not like that, Dr. Anderson. I'm not being abused by no-I don't even..." she sighed and started over. "Do you think people wish for too much?" she asked.

Derrick relaxed a bit. "Yes. Kinda like I said this morning, you can think one thing is exactly what you need, but it ends up being not all it's cracked up to be."

Shanice nodded and reached into one of her pockets. "So basically, I wished for too much and I don't really want this anymore." She opened her palm and a silver ring with a gold trim sat inside of it. It looked like the class ring of someone who graduated from a fancy school in the early 1900s: it was big, ornate, and ancient looking. Derrick blinked as he inspected the ring. He could have sworn it had glowed.

"What is this, Shanice?" Derrick asked.

"Some guy gave it to me. He said it could help you get what you wish for, but it's ain't worth it," Shanice explained. "You research a lot, right? Maybe you've heard of something like this?"

Derrick bit his lip. He couldn't tell if that was a subtle clocking dealing with the piece of jewelry, or if she was poorly complimenting his intelligence. "You're right, but don't you think you should give the ring back to the young man who–"

Shanice interrupted him. "I've tried. I can't find him. Listen Dr. Anderson, I've gotta get rid of this thing." Shanice's voice was far more forceful than it was when she arrived in the office; she jerked her palm at Derrick as if to force him to get the ring.

Derrick thought for a second, but Shanice's face told him how adamant she was about not taking this ring with her.

"Fine, I'll take it," Derrick agreed. He reached out and plucked the ring from her hands. Surprisingly, it was warm to the touch.

"Thank you, thank you Dr. Anderson. I really appreciate this," she got up to leave and her face looked much fuller than it did when she stepped in. "Just don't sleep with it," she warned her professor.

"Okay…?" Derrick responded, still a bit confused by this exchange. Before he could inquire further, however, Shanice had dashed from his office.

"…and she was just gone?"

"And she was just gone," Derrick repeated. It was several hours later and he and his boyfriend, Michael, were sitting in the living room talking after eating together. A random episode of _P-Valley_ buzzed on the television in front of them both.

Michael rubbed the legs of his scrubs, a surefire sign that he was not pleased with what Derrick had just told him. He had gone from being confused about why his partner said that he "got a ring" today to worried about this poor girl in the span of minutes. "Did you tell someone?" he asked. Derrick nodded and went to put their plates in the kitchen.

"I went to the Title IX coordinator after she left, but random pieces of jewelry don't exactly fall under their jurisdiction," he yelled from the sink.

"Why didn't you leave it in like a lost and found or something then? It could be evidence or something!" Michael yelled at him.

"Evidence of what, babe? You think she's a jewelry thief?" Derrick replied with a laugh. When he returned, he could see the worry in

83

Michael's face and tried to lighten the mood. "It's too ugly to be stolen, anyway," he joked.

"That's not funny," Michael said, but he smiled, nonetheless. The gaudy ring on the folding table between them wasn't at either man's taste level. "Seriously Derrick, what if something is seriously wrong with this girl?"

A timely appearance from Uncle Clifford on the screen made Derrick smile. He turned to Michael and tried to keep joking.

"There is something wrong; she gave her gay professor a piece of jewelry and didn't give him the chance to thank her!" Derrick grinned even harder and leaned over the arm of the couch to kiss his lover. Michael moved his face and looked at him.

Derrick sighed. "I'll try to talk to her again tomorrow, but I really can't make her take the ring back."

"That's better," Michael said and allowed Derrick to kiss him. He reached over and brought the ring to his face to get a closer look himself. "What's this writing?" he asked, pointing at the inside of the ring.

Derrick shrugged. "I tried looking it up, but nothing comes up. It's not in any language I've come across or any mythology I've heard of."

Michael gave Derrick a look that screamed 'what have you gotten yourself into' before looking back at the ring. "Why do you think she said taking this would help?" he asked.

Derrick shrugged again. "I don't know, but she was sure glad to be rid of it."

Michael nodded and held the ring out for Derrick to take it. An idea jumped into Derrick's mind and he feigned shock and joy as he took it. "Oh my God Michael, I do! Oh, this is so sudden! How did you ever set up that type of proposal? I'm so happy!"

"Derrick shut up!" Michael said, but he couldn't keep himself from laughing at the exaggerated reactions Derrick was having to his 'proposal'. By now, Derrick had placed the ring on his finger and was taking pictures of it with his cell phone.

Derrick leaned over Michael, placing both hands on either side of him on the couch. "How can I ever say thank you? You've made me the happiest guy in the world!" The neck kisses he gave Michael after his statement suggested that he did have a way to express gratitude, however.

Michael breathed softly into his boyfriend's ear. "I can think of a few ways," he suggested.

Derrick smiled and scooped Michael up into his arms and the two of them headed to the bedroom.

###

After successfully putting Michael to sleep, Derrick walked back downstairs to review his next lecture before he went to bed as well. He turned the television on a music station to serve as the necessary white noise as he worked, but it had barely taken five minutes before he fell asleep on the couch.

"Hello Derrick," a voice called out to him. Derrick looked around his bright blue surroundings and saw the source of it: a positively gorgeous Black man standing shirtless in front of him. The man looked a bit like Michael, right down to the deep brown skin and infectious smile but was closer to Derrick's muscle tone and height.

Derrick was shocked for a moment, until he realized he was dreaming. "Well, hello. You're a new one. I've had these types of dreams before. Where's Michael? He usually likes to join—"

"I'm afraid this is not that type of dream, Derrick," the dream man said. "But I am here to please you, if I can."

Derrick smiled at the man. "I'm sure you could. But alright. If you're not here for…extracurricular activities…, what are you here for? What is this dream about?"

The dream man moved closer to Derrick, giving the professor a closer look at his perfectly shaped face. "I'm here to deliver a message.

Derrick scoffed. "Yeah right. Okay, I'll play. So what is this message? A prophecy? A vision of the past? Are you our future kid coming back to warn me not to blow up the Earth?" Derrick asked.

The dream man laughed. "None of the above. My message is that you have been chosen. You are one of the gifted few who have the opportunity to make your dreams come true. Whatever you wish, whatever you desire, I can bring it to you. Is that something you want, Derrick?"

Derrick raised an eyebrow at the man before him. His last therapy session told him that dreams are usually just the mind making sense of events around you, but he couldn't think of anything that would make him construct this otherworldly beauty in front of him.

"Sure. Do I get to choose what I want now or…?" Derrick asked, and the dream man laughed again.

"I told you I'm just the messenger and judging by your skepticism you need a stronger message. I'll see you again soon…"

###

Derrick awoke on the couch when his phone alarm went off. He cursed himself for not finishing anything substantial and ran upstairs to get ready for work. Derrick ignored Michael's complaints that he never came up to bed and dashed out of his house so quickly he didn't even realize he still had on the ring from the night before.

When he made it to work, he taught his first two classes and went back to his office. He was a bit off his game as if he didn't get much sleep the night before. He was so tired he forgot to email Shanice to talk with her like Michael wanted. Instead, decided to use his time between classes to catch a nap in his office.

"Hello again, Derrick." Derrick and the dream man had returned to the same bright blue empty expanse, but this time Derrick's analytical mind was piqued.

"I've never had a recurring dream two days in a row...Can I ask you what you're trying to tell me?"

"I've already told you the message. You have been chosen to get whatever you desire," the dream man answered.

"But why me?"

"Because you wear the ring."

"The ring...?" Derrick asked. He looked down and jumped backwards when he saw the gaudy ring glowing on his finger.

"The ring is a gift, a blessing brought to the lives of humans like you in return for the good that you do. You are a great professor, a great partner, and you try to be a great person. There are some perks to that," the dream man smiled an impossibly white smile and Derrick couldn't help but smile back.

"But wait!" Derrick said after a moment. "I wasn't chosen by anything. One of my students gave me this ring because she didn't want it anymore."

For the first time, the dream man's positive demeanor faltered. "Shanice Gibson is one of those few people who don't think that they deserve the great things that life has to offer. You teach people like her all the time, I'm sure you've seen how often they sabotage themselves."

Something about the dream man's words made Derrick uncomfortable. He instinctively backed away. "She seemed pretty convinced that having your wishes granted wasn't worth it," he pointed out.

"Only if you don't recognize that there is a cost. But you know that, Derrick. You know everything has a cost, didn't you teach about that yesterday?" The dream man smiled again.

"How did you...?" Derrick asked, but the dream man waved his hand and Derrick quieted as he saw what happened next.

With that simple movement a whirlwind of green bills began to swirl between Derrick and the dream man. Derrick's jaw dropped and he began to grab at the bills in spite of himself. Before he could start to stuff the bills into his pockets, however, they melted from his hands into a puddle beneath him. The puddles grew and formed upwards into the shapes of men: beautiful men in several different shades of Black skin. Derrick approached the man closest to him and they all began to melt back down, not into puddles, but into awards. He picked up a letter a few steps away from the dream man that announced him as a MacArthur Fellow.

"Or perhaps you desire something a little bit more immediate," the dream man said, and with another wave of his hand the awards all disappeared. "That HBCU job you always wanted?" Derrick turned to the side and gasped as he saw himself walking down what was unmistakably the promenade from his days at Clark Atlanta. "A great day with Michael?" A clutter of photographs bearing the couple at various venues floated around Michael. "All of this could be yours, Derrick. The ring can bring it to you for as long as you wear it."

"Is there any way I can get all of that? Maybe in smaller portions?" Derrick asked. "Or just a raise. I'd be cool with just a raise," he added.

The dream man laughed. "That's not what you desire," he said.

"Yes, it is. I promise you it is," Derrick countered.

The dream man looked at him earnestly. "You're one of the higher paid professors in your department. Not to mention you're dating a nurse."

"We could still use a few extra millions, though," Derrick muttered. The back of his mind did question how the dream man knew all of this, however.

The dream man moved so close to Derrick that he thought he was going to kiss him. "I can already tell that is not the type of man you are, Derrick. You want lasting things; the opportunity to make a change. That is what you truly desire. I can help you do that."

The dream man was right, but Derrick was still a little hesitant. "What's the catch?" Derrick asked.

The dream man smiled even wider than before. "There is no catch. This is yours so long as—"

"DERRICK!" a voice boomed into Derrick's office and woke him from his nap. He looked up to see his boss, the History Department chair Dr. Richards. The man's bushy gray mustache twitched almost comically as he stared at Derrick from the now open doorway. "Why are you sleeping?"

"Oh, I'm sorry Dr. Richards. I just had a long night and—"

"If you're having trouble maintaining we can cut back your course load. I've already had student complaints about your methods…"

Derrick's eyes narrowed. He prided himself on being a very effective teacher, but it was clear that some of his students didn't appreciate the fact that he even mentioned Black and gay people in his classes. The chair agreed with them, partly because he was one of the types that thought that "politicizing History" was a no go and partly because he was well aware that the Dean hired Derrick to eventually become chair.

"I can assure you that my exhaustion is not an indication of any type of ineffectiveness," Derrick said, barely restraining his anger. Dr. Richards turned beet red, but his tone was no less nasty than before.

"Just don't make us regret your hire," Dr. Richards said back. He turned and left Derrick to stew and fume in his anger. It was old white men like Dr. Richards that made their field as stagnant as it was. Sometimes he wished they would just get out of the way. Derrick got up and slammed the door to his office shut again. As if feeling so disrespected wasn't enough, he didn't even get to hear the entirety of what the dream man was telling him. Derrick was so upset with Dr. Richards that he didn't even notice that the ring on his finger had started to glow.

###

Dr. Richards turned a corner down the dark hallway, constantly looking over his shoulder as he ran. He could still hear the ragged breaths behind him, but he couldn't make out exactly who…or what…was chasing him. He passed by a few offices and a drink machine before turning back. He grabbed the handle of a few of the office doors, but none opened. Whatever his pursuer was, it was nearly upon him, and judging by the loud thumps he heard as it approached it wasn't anything nice. He ran more, listening to the footsteps getting louder and louder as he barely dodged sharp corners.

Then, almost as suddenly as they had begun, the footsteps stopped. He stood in place, looking down the hallway to see if they started up again. After a few seconds of silence, he breathed a sigh of relief and faced forward to see where he was. The scream barely had time to leave his throat before his throat and head were detached from his

*body by the giant creature in front of him. He was dead before his
body hit the floor.*

Derrick awoke with a start. His body poured sweat and his deep
breaths matched those of the beast in his dream. He looked around; he
was in his bedroom, Michael was still asleep, and all was well. At
least on the outside.

Why had he dreamt of Dr. Richards? Why did he die? First the
dream man and now this? Derrick wondered if his therapist would
take an early morning session, because these dreams were getting ridiculous. He swung his legs to the floor and put his head in his hands.
Something warm touched the side of his head and he pulled back a
hand to see the ring still on his finger. In the dark of the bedroom, he
was certain this time that it was glowing.

Derrick snatched the ring off his finger and threw it to the floor.
Thankfully, the carpet softened the blow so it didn't make a sound
loud enough to wake Michael up. If the glowing wasn't bad enough,
there was the question of how the ring got on his finger in the first
place. He didn't remember putting it on, in fact he distinctly remembered taking it off when he got home that evening. Somehow though,
he ended up putting it back on and it was as warm as if he had put it in
the microwave. He sighed loudly; he was losing it. Rings don't glow
and they don't magically appear on fingers. He looked at his phone on
the nightstand to see the time. 4:43 AM. There was enough time for
him to go back to sleep, but he needed a shower first. Maybe that
would calm him down.

As the warming water hit his skin, he tried to figure out why this
dream was affecting him so much. He had had nightmares before, everyone had, but this felt different. It felt so real. Then the dream itself
was weird. He dreamt about another person entirely, someone he
didn't particularly like, and they actually died. He had always heard
that if you died in a dream you die in real life, but what if it's someone
else? None of it really made sense and that worried him, but the thing
that worried him even more he could hardly bear to think of it.

Why had he liked watching Dr. Richards die?

Derrick didn't sleep much even after his long shower. He tried un-
successfully to lull himself to sleep, but all the TV watching and paper
grading failed to do anything but make Michael wake up to tell him to

quiet down. He gave up after about two hours and decided to just prepare for work.

His first class passed without much incident, but when Shanice Gibson walked into the second class, he realized he had to talk to her. He halfheartedly gave his lecture about the start of the Civil Rights Movement and called her over the moment he dismissed. As she approached, he couldn't help but notice how much happier she looked than she did two days ago.

"You wanted to talk to me, Dr. Anderson?" she asked. Her voice was even happier, but Derrick noticed a twinge of concern in it.

"Yes, I didn't get a chance to talk to you after you came by my office Monday. Are you alright?"

Shanice smiled. "Oh yes. Much better, thanks to you." She tried to turn to leave, but Derrick kept talking.

"I'm glad," Derrick said. He sat back in the chair at his podium and kept his eyes trained on Shanice. "But I do have to ask you something about what you left with me. The ring," he clarified. At the word "ring" Shanice visibly shuddered.

"I really don't wanna talk about that, professor. That thing is better off being left alone." Shanice said, looking at her feet.

"I'm starting to think you're right, but I have to ask you something. The man you said something about, was that the man from the—" Derrick began, but Shanice looked up and cut him off.

"Dr. Anderson you didn't! Don't tell me you slept with it?!" she cried.

Derrick's silence gave her the answer she dreaded.

"You have to get rid of it! Give it to someone else! Break it, hide it, something! Before something happens!"

"Something like what? What does the ring do?" Derrick asked.

Shanice sighed. "It's not so much what the ring does, but what that…thing…inside of it does. It's evil, Dr. Anderson. It starts off as this woman promising you good things, all your desires, but it changes." Derrick took note of the fact that for Shanice, the dream man was apparently a dream woman. "It tricks you into putting the ring on and it does what it wants to make things worse for you. You have these weird dreams and then terrible stuff happens that you never really wanted. You have to get rid of it!" The terror in Shanice's face couldn't be faked, and that made Derrick's expression match hers. The two looked at each other and Shanice gasped. She already knew that look.

"You've already had a nightmare, haven't you?"

"Hey Ms. Reynolds, is Dr. Richards in?"

"No, he stepped out for lunch. Would like me to have him contact you when he gets back?"

"No ma'am. I'll see can I catch up with him myself." Derrick left the chair's office before his internal scream became an external one. Shanice's story kept replaying in his mind as he paced the hallway. How one of her homegirl's boyfriends gave her the ring. How her dream person promised her good grades, a good job, and the 'baddest girls on campus'. How the ring only glowed when she was angry or upset, and how the people that caused that ended up hurt. Shanice had even told him about the nasty argument she had with her aunt last week, and how the next day her aunt was dead.

Derrick ran up to his office where Shanice herself was still waiting on him.

"Did you find him?" she asked immediately. When Derrick shook his head, she became more animated. "You gotta find him!"

"But what if you're wrong, Shanice? I mean, he was being chased down a dark hallway in my dream. He has to be safe at least until nighttime. I'll catch him before he goes home and tell him to be careful," Derrick surmised.

"No! Dr. Anderson logic don't work with that thing. For all you know he could already be dead!" Shanice took a deep breath to try to calm herself. "Remember the fight I told you I had with my aunt? That night I dreamed that a house fell on her. I called her to apologize, thinking that if I made up with her it would all be okay. Do you know what happened? She was driving when she answered the phone; her car got hit by one of those 18-wheelers carrying trailer houses. It don't care! Once you dream it it's going to find a way unless you keep him safe!"

Horror raced across Derrick's face. He paced his office again. "Why did I even put that thing on?!" he cursed himself.

"Don't blame yourself," Shanice comforted him. "It kind of calls to you, you put it on without realizing and it makes you think that what it's doing is okay until it takes all the important stuff."

"That doesn't help me now! What do I do? How do I help him?!" Derrick screeched.

"Chill!" Shanice snapped. Panic was all over her face as well, and it took that to make Derrick start to think rationally. There had to be something he could do to help Dr. Richards. Maybe if he brought Dr. Richards here, he and Shanice could convince him to let them keep him safe. At least until they destroyed the ring. He could only hope that Dr. Richards believed them, for his sake. He didn't like the man much, but he didn't think he deserved to die. No matter how he felt after that dream.

Derrick sat back behind his desk and looked out of the cracked open door. Shanice looked back at him anxiously. No sooner had he opened his mouth to try to formulate a plan did he see Dr. Richards walk past his office door with another professor. Derrick froze, and Shanice looked from him to the door.

"What? What is it?" she asked.

"I just saw him, stay here." Derrick said.

"Wait, Dr. Anderson!" Shanice called, but Derrick was already out of the door and walking down the hallway. He saw Dr. Richards and the other professor standing in front of the stairway and approached the department chair from behind. When he was close, Derrick called out to his boss.

"Dr. Richards!" he yelled. The middle-aged man jumped so ferociously at his name being called that he teetered onto the stairs. Before the other professor or Derrick could reach him, he toppled down them. He landed neck first on the first landing, leaving Derrick in complete and utter shock at the top of it.

Several hours later, Derrick was still shaking as he opened the door to his house. All the things the police said just kept replaying in his head. Phrases like "freak accident" and "he was dead before he stopped falling" haunted his mind, but what scared him the most was when one of them mentioned that things like this had been happening around the school all semester. How many people had accidentally sent this…thing after innocent victims?

Shanice herself had run off once the paramedics were called for Dr. Richards. Derrick didn't dare contact her; poor girl had already been through enough. No, he needed to destroy it himself and stop anyone else from accidentally hurting another person.

Derrick walked upstairs, thinking that the ring was probably still on the floor of his bedroom. He searched for the ring for what felt like hours, but it was nowhere to be found. Where could it have gone? Then, with a pang of sheer terror, it occurred to him. Michael.

###

"Michael, you look exhausted!" The female nurse sitting behind the desk exclaimed.

"Thanks, Tangie. I definitely needed that," Michael responded. When he yawned, he continued, "Dammit Derrick."

"Ooooo y'all kept each other up late last night?" she asked, leaning over the desk to look at Michael.

"More like he woke me up. And no, not like that," Michael clarified when Tangie's eyes lit up. "I'm tired and this lady in 333 just pissed me off. Talking bout I took too long to check on her and her mama. Lady, I have like ten patients on this floor, I'm sorry I couldn't race over to help you find the remote."

Tangie laughed and Michael yawned again. She motioned for Michael to come even closer so she could whisper in his ear. "If you need some time to get away, there's a closet that I use to sneak naps in down right before the ICU. Lock the door from the inside and catch you a cat nap."

Michael grinned. "Thanks girl! Cover for me, okay?"

"Got you," Tangie answered.

When Michael reached the closet, he saw a raggedy chair that Tangie had to have grabbed from a room before it was redecorated. He shrugged and sat down in the chair. Truth be told, he had thought he slept well after Derrick woke him up that morning. He had done some cleaning, which always calmed his nerves, so when he went back to sleep their bedroom was as spotless as he liked it. He had even dreamt of this gorgeous man that seemed so calming. Michael sat in the chair and tried to sleep with his head in his hands, but the ring on his finger was unusually warm on his face.

This ring was sure strange, Michael thought. It was sharp when he stepped on it heading back to bed that morning but so comfortable that he didn't realize that he had put it by the time he woke up. He shifted his position so that he could lean against the wall with his arms folded and almost instantly drifted off to sleep. He had one last fleeting thought of the patient and her parent who just worked his nerves as the ring started glowing on his finger.

"Hello again Michael," the dream man said, grinning at him. "That wasn't very nice of that woman, was it?"

UNCLAIMED
BY
W. ALEXANDER LAWSON

If there was one thing that RJ liked less than public transportation, it was the people who rode public transportation. They were rude, they were aggressive, and they smelled like they rode public transportation. The airport was no exception. In fact, the airport seemed like a beacon that summoned the worst travelers in the world to compete for the title of worst traveler of the year. Yet RJ had chosen to work at the busiest airport in the world, which made his near-daily ride on public transportation unavoidable. So, he held his breath as he was swallowed up by the group of people who rushed in around him to board the compact locomotive.

"Welcome aboard the plane train. Please hold on, this train is departing. The next stop is for Domestic Baggage Claim and Ground Transportation," the automated female voice announced.

RJ's right hand clung to his fast-food lunch as the vehicle pulled into the dimly lit tunnel. The not-so-subtle rocking of the train forced its inhabitants to become much closer than they'd ever intended. Passengers had the strength of their equilibrium tested as they moved swiftly down the track, but RJ stood unmoved as domestic and foreign bodies jostled against him. His extensive experience on the plane train had honed his sense of balance, and he was easily maintaining his footing until the large body of a man relaxed into him, sandwiching him between the man's husky frame and the wall, trapping him in place.

"Yo!" RJ exclaimed, tapping the man on the shoulder. "Excuse you!"

The burly man glanced back, but he barely acknowledged his faux pas, simply inching forward just enough to free RJ from his confinement.

"Bitch..." RJ grumbled, regaining his footing just as the plane train slowed to a stop.

"Please hold on, this train is stopping. Please collect your belongings and watch your step as you exit."

RJ watched as the burly man and his family pushed through the crowd of travelers to reach the escalator as though there was a race that only they were aware of. He waited as the train car cleared before stepping out to make his way back to his own dark corner of Harts-field-Jackson International: the lost and found office.

Before he even opened the door, RJ could hear the gravelly voice of his coworker Lawrence belting along to his favorite funk band.

"What up, Unc?" RJ called out, as he ambled into the back room. "You good? I thought somebody was back here whoopin' yo ass."

"Money man," Lawrence greeted RJ as he pulled his headphones around his neck. "You can't be a hater yo whole life. You know if you put me on the internet I'd go virus."

"I won't argue with you 'bout that," RJ chuckled, taking a seat in a corner and unwrapping his chicken sandwich. "I see they got you back here organizing this shit again."

"*They* don't got me doing nothing. This is part of the job."

"It's all going on the same truck," RJ answered through a mouthful of chicken. "It don't matter what it look like while it's back here."

"That's what wrong with you young cats now—wanna do every-thing halfway. You gotta take pride in what you do."

"You got it, Unc."

"Look at this," Lawrence gestured toward a box of wallets. "I got these organized by color and material to make 'em easier to go through. It makes stuff simpler for everybody."

"Well, here," RJ pulled a wallet from his pocket and removed the money, "add this to your pile," he mumbled around a bite of fries as he tossed the empty leather billfold to the older man.

"See, this is what I'm talkin' 'bout," Lawrence asserted. "Stealin' at your own job ain't smart."

"The way dude was pressing himself up against me on the train, he might as well had just handed it to me."

"Whatever you say, young buck. You don't gotta listen to me," Lawrence replied, placing the billfold in among the other wallets. "But you gon learn the hard way. You don't think them cameras see you goin through them bags?"

"Ain't nobody watchin' them cameras. Plus, I only go through the bags they shippin' out to be sold anyway. You think they ain't already checked 'em before they get back here? If anything, I'm just cleanin' up the leftovers," RJ reasoned through another bite of his sandwich.

"Knock, knock. Got a delivery for you, boys." A flatbed cart stacked with bags suddenly appeared in the doorway. "Another batch for the truck," the voice belonging to their shift manager explained, never stepping into the room.

"Looks like break time's over, Money Man. I'll start loadin' up the pallets. You can sort the new shit."

As Lawrence worked to organize the already-sorted outgoing bags, RJ began going through the pockets and compartments of the luggage he had been tasked with sorting. He scoured bag after bag in search of bounty, but he found nothing. No loose cash. No jewelry. No random trinkets. Nothing.

After searching nearly three dozen pieces, RJ was prepared to write off his search as fruitless, until an old, dusty suitcase at the bottom of the pile caught his attention. The pale, yellow handle and faded floral pattern embroidered stood out against the backdrop of nearly identical black valises.

Curious, he pulled it free and flipped open the latches holding it secure. He rummaged through the contents, but disheartenment spread across his face as he once again found nothing. Haphazardly, he shoved the loose clothes back into place in an attempt to reorganize the items he'd disturbed when a sharp sting caused him to snatch his hand from the bag.

"Fuck!" He exclaimed as he examined his finger, which had been sliced open and was starting to bleed.

Cautiously, he pushed the clothes aside in search of the source of his injury, and he noticed that a portion of the portmanteau's stiff lining had been lifted, and the area seemed to bulge. Curious, RJ slowly slipped his fingers beneath the gap made by the raised leather and pulled out a small, velvet bag.

The familiar sensation of metal greeted him as he softly squeezed the pouch, and a toothy grin crept across his face. He began to pull on the braided drawstrings to examine his treasure when a voice from the hallway startled him.

"RJ?"

"Yeah? What's up?" he responded, hastily slipping the bag into his pocket and reclosing the case before the face of his supervisor appeared in the doorway.

"Can you give me bag number 5004452233? It's yellow with pink flowers. I've got somebody here trying to claim it."

"Yeah. One sec," RJ responded, hesitantly passing her the mysterious floral suitcase he'd just raided before watching her turn and disappear into the corridor.

Absent-mindedly, he toyed with the ill-gotten gains hidden in his pocket. His paranoia was palpable as he eyed the clock and waited for someone to question him about the missing velvet bag, and his anxiety was rewarded when his manager called him to the front counter.

"RJ, do you copy?"

"Go for, RJ."

"Did you find a–," the manager began before static disrupted the communication.

"Can you repeat that? Over."

"Did you find a small, velvet pouch when you sent up that suitcase earlier? The guest from before is back, and she says it's missing. Over."

"Gimme a sec. Lemme check," RJ replied as he hurriedly pulled the velvet pouch from his pocket and thumbed through the contents, taking the items that looked the most valuable. "Yeah, I see it. I'll bring it up. Over."

RJ moved quickly, pocketing a few pairs of earrings and some rings before resecuring the bag and making his way to the front desk. As he rounded the corner, he spotted a little old woman standing at the counter. His nervous eyes darted over her visage, and at first glance, she appeared to be a typical senior: her silver-tinted curls coiled tightly to her head, her coffee-colored skin bore the finest of wrinkles, and her once pearlesque smile was slightly stained by decades of hearty meals. Everything about her appearance was innocuous, except for her nails—a set of long, sharp acrylics painted red.

"This what you was lookin' for?" RJ inquired, holding the bag before the woman's eyes.

"You found it! Thank you!" her gentle voice lilted as she took the pouch from his hand.

"No problem."

"Is everything here?" She asked, caressing the bag and watching him intently.

"I mean... I don't see why it wouldn't be," RJ answered before silence seemed to envelope the room.

"I see. Well, then I guess I'm all set," the woman said, turning toward the door to leave. "But just know," she added, looking back at RJ, "if something is missing, I'll be back to get it."

The remainder of the day moved along sluggishly but without incident. The end of RJ's shift arrived unceremoniously, and the inquisition he had feared never came.

"You outta here?" Lawrence asked, as RJ packed up his belongings.

"Yeah. I got some business to handle."

"Make sure you think about what I said... It ain't really worth it."

"Will do, Unc."

RJ wasted no time escaping the building with his prize. He moved with intense intentionality as he made his way to the parking garage. He could hear the subtle jingle of shifting metal that seemed to scream at passersby, begging to be saved from their captor. So, he didn't slow or stop until he was safely in the driver's seat of his sedan.

After breathing deeply and scanning the garage for other drivers, RJ pulled the jewelry from his pants and held it in his palm. A grin slid across his face as he eyed the several pieces before him. His fingers caressed the collection of gem-studded rings and earrings. Among the items there was one very ornate ring hanging from a thin chain. He lifted it and watched it oscillate as he held it in the air, examining it closely.

The exterior of the golden band was embossed with a delicate filigree pattern, and in the interior of the band, the words *divitiae ad sumptus animae tuae* were engraved. It seemed large, perhaps too large to be a woman's ring. Tepidly, he slipped the ring onto his finger and inspected it. It fit him perfectly, so he concluded that it must've belonged to a man. Satisfied, he removed the ring, placed the stolen pieces in a new bag, and headed out of the parking lot and into the city toward his favorite pawnshop.

#

"Man, you on some bullshit! I know you can go higher than that," RJ snapped at the man behind the shop counter.

"I can do 500 for these two rings 'cause the gold is real and 2000 for the earrings... And that's only 'cause those are real diamonds."

"What about this ring?" RJ asked, holding up the ornate loop.

"I hate to break it to you, but whatever's engraved on there must be Spanish for 'piece of shit' cause that ring is just a pretty hunk of metal," the owner said, sliding the ring across the counter to RJ. "Shit, the engraving probably cost more than the whole ring did."

"Bruh, that's cap!"

"You can call it what you want, but I know what I'm talking about. The most you're getting for this stuff is 2500."

"Do 3K like Andre and we locked in."

"Man, you needta be happy I'm doing 2500 and not asking you where you got this stuff from 'cause you can take this shit to somebody else."

"Whatever, man. Gimme the 25," RJ groaned.

The shop owner gathered his newly acquired pieces and disappeared into the back room. He reappeared a few moments later with a small stack of new bills in his hand.

"Pleasure doing business with you."

"Yeah," RJ grumbled, thumbing through the bills as he headed to the door.

"Yo. Don't forget this," the owner called out, tossing the ring to RJ.

"What I'm 'posed to do with this?"

"I don't know. Take it down to the junkyard and see if they still buy aluminum," the shop owner said through a laugh.

"Fuck you," RJ growled before he stormed out and tossed the ring across the strip mall's almost vacant parking lot.

He shoved the funds he'd received into his pocket and made his way to his downtown studio apartment. He entered the cookie-cutter space as though he was on autopilot and wasted no time changing into his street clothes before rolling up the remains of 'za he'd procured earlier in the week. He queued his playlist and took a seat on the kitchen counter, allowing the sound of synthesizers and 808s to fill the void where any meaningful thoughts might manifest.

In a matter of minutes, clouds of smoke hung in the air, creating a haze as thick as the fog enveloping RJ's conscious mind. His thoughts drifted to the ring he'd discarded at the pawnshop. He opened his web browser and navigated to a translation site, typing every possible spelling of the seemingly imaginary words carved into the metal he once possessed. But he failed to recall the wording of the engraving and the rapid chiming of a video call alert pushed the thought from his brain as he answered.

"What's good, bro?"

"Nigga, get dressed. Tonight we in the streets," the voice of RJ's friend Myles poured through the earpiece.

"Where you tryna go?"

"We at Blue Flame. You already know."

"Say less. I just hit a lick, so I'm wit it."

Within an hour, RJ went from looking like he lived under somebody's private jet to looking like he owned one himself. The tattoos that covered his arms glistened beneath a layer of cocoa butter that clung to his bronze skin. With his durag removed, his 360-degree waves were placed on full display. His cotton t-shirt wrapped itself snugly around his body, layered tennis necklaces glimmered around his neck, and the stones encircling his watch face danced under the strobing lights. The aroma of vanilla and sandalwood wafted around him, and the pockets of his low-riding jeans swelled with the spoils of his criminal exploits.

It didn't take long before RJ was offered his first table dance. After being served his first drink, he'd purchased five more rounds for the table, and he was showing no signs of slowing down. His low-hanging eyelids and pink-tinged sclera signaled that his body was in the throes of an elevated experience. The funds he'd obtained seemed to be fly-ing free from his fingertips, and the bare-bodied beauties that sur-rounded him seemed eager to take it from him.

One-by-one, the au natural entertainers who made their way to RJ's section increased in beauty, until he was approached by a dancer he'd never seen before. As if in slow motion, he watched as she crossed the crowded lounge, closing the distance between them. His heart pounded and his breathing became labored as she leaned into him and whispered in his ear.

"Private dance?"

"Y'all don't do no private dances," he slurred.

"We do if you can keep a secret," she responded slyly, a smirk spreading across her glossed lips.

"Well, don't mind if I muthafuckin do."

RJ excused himself from his friends and followed his seductress to a hidden room in the rear of the club. He trailed her expectantly as she pushed into the small, sparsely filled room where a single leather chair stood against a wall beneath a swinging blue light.

"Get comfortable," the woman commanded, forcing RJ into the va-cant seat before straddling his waist.

He could feel the pressure of her weight as she ground against his cloth-covered body. The blood rushing away from his brain had his head swimming, and the heat of her flesh radiated over him. His body trembled as the edges of her red acrylics grazed his neck, and he held his breath as her face inched toward his ear.

"*Divitiae ad sumptus animae tuae*," she whispered, her warm breath echoing in his ear as her fingers encircled his throat.

"What?" He asked, recoiling from her words.

"*Divitiae ad sumptus animae tuae!*" She repeated, her dark, sultry voice becoming distorted as she tightened her grip around his neck, her stiletto-shaped manicure slicing into his flesh.

RJ tried to force her away from him, but the wall behind his chair trapped him against her slowly contorting body. He opened his mouth to yell, but her grip blocked the air from reaching his lungs. His eyes widened as the beauty before him morphed into a grotesque, unrecog-nizable figure, and a single tear fell from his eye as he lost conscious-ness.

"RJ, you good? Get up, nigga!" Myles's voice cut through the darkness that had enveloped him.

RJ opened his eyes and leapt from his seat, panicked. He groggily surveyed the room, and slowly realized he was once again at his regu-lar table in the center of the club and security was towering over him.

"Where shawty went?" he asked, his rich baritone tinged with a hint of fear.

"Who?" A burly, bald bouncer asked.

"Shawty who just took me to the back room."

"Fuck is you talmbout? The Flame don't even got no back room," Myles interjected.

"I ain't think they did either, but shawty just took me back there. On God."

"Nigga, you trippin… You ain't move from that spot since we got here."

"Ima have to ask y'all to follow me to the exit," the hairless security guard interrupted.

"Come on, man, you ain't gotta do all that. My bro good now. See," Myles defended.

"He don't look good to me," the guard shot back, gesturing to RJ's bloodied neck. "So, y'all gotta go. Now!"

RJ and his friend made their way to their vehicles as he apologized and tried to recall what occurred to the best of his abilities.

"My bad. I don't even know what happened," he explained.

"Yo dumb ass took a couple shots and knocked out till you started yelling for somebody to help you."

"Ain't no way."

"Dead ass, bro!"

"Man, I don't know what's wrong with me. I'm trippin'," RJ reasoned.

"Yeah, you was wilin'. I shoulda told them niggas you was havin' a seizure. Now we gotta find another move."

"Actually, I think Ima call it a night. I gotta be to work early anyway," RJ replied, stroking the wounds lining his nape.

"You sure?"

"Yeah. Ima holla at you later."

"Word," Myles agreed, dapping up RJ and pulling him in for a hug. "Be safe, bro."

#

RJ drove down I-20 East in silence until he reached home. He entered his empty apartment and headed straight for the bathroom. With a gentle flick, he activated the light switch and illuminated the room. As he leaned into the mirror to examine the now-crusting lacerations that were sure to become scars, he noticed a subtle glinting from the corner of his eye.

On the gray marble countertop rested the ornate gold ring he had discarded outside the pawnshop. Hesitantly, he picked it up and examined it, carefully rereading the Latin words inscribed on the band. His attacker's voice reverberated in head as he pulled out his phone and searched up the words, hoping to decipher their meaning.

As the translation appeared, a shiver passed over his body. His rich, saturated skin became pale, and panic spread across his face. *Divitiae ad sumptus animae tuae*—wealth at the cost of your soul. Once more, he looked at the ring before dropping it into the ceramic basin and watching it slide down the drain before heading to the comfort and safety of his bed.

#

A few hours later, RJ was again traversing the airport, dragging himself back into work. Because it was early, the ever-bustling travel hub had not yet filled with people, which made it easy for him to get to his assigned area. However, when he arrived at the office that led to the work area, he noticed through the window that the little old woman who'd claimed her bag the day prior was waiting at the counter.

The jewelry bag he'd once pilfered of its contents rested in front of her. He took note of her crossed arms, tapping foot, and surly expression and immediately realized that dealing with her wouldn't be easy. He tried to ease past her as quickly as he could, but her frail, withered fingers grabbed hold of him.

"Excuse me," she said. "I need to talk to somebody about items that were missing from my bag."

"You'll have to come back when there's a manager here," RJ answered swiftly, hoping to end their interaction with as much haste as he could muster.

"Listen, I don't have time to come back," she said before sighing. "I know you know what happened to the things that were in this bag. I don't even care about most of the jewelry… but there was an engraved ring. It wasn't worth much, but it's very important." her soft, matronly voice chastised. "So, just tell me what you know because if I leave here without it, there will be ramifications that could've been avoided, and young man, I'd rather not see that happen."

"Sorry," RJ said, pulling away from her grasp. "I don't know nothin', so I can't help you."

"Son, I need you to understand that I will do anything I can to get that ring back."

"The best I can do is let you fill out one of the lost and found forms. Somebody will contact you if they find it," RJ acquiesced, moving to the file cabinet behind the counter.

Intently, he began to skim through the alphabetized files in search of the desired document, but when he found the folder he sought, he noticed that the words on the forms had been replaced. Each piece of paper he thumbed through read *divitiae ad sumptus animae tuae* over and over and over again. Then he noticed that the ornate gold ring, the same ring he'd sent down the drain hours earlier, was now resting on his left ring finger. Startled, he shoved his hand into the files.

"Is everything okay?" the woman queried.

"Yeah," he stammered, hastily stuffing his left hand into his pocket and turning back without the form. "I just need a second," he added before sprinting from the office.

He maneuvered through the steadily increasing crowd and slipped into the bathroom of a sparsely populated concourse area. In the bathroom, he snatched the unknown alloy from his finger and stared at it beneath the fluorescent lights, noting that the pattern and engraving matched the ring he'd now twice discarded.

As he read the words silently, the glowing bulbs overhead flickered gently and a faint whisper wafted through the air, barely audible.

"Who that is?" RJ called out to no response.

One-by-one, he pushed open the closed stall doors, revealing that he was alone in the space.

"Man, I'm still trippin," he muttered to himself as he walked into the final stall and dropped the ring into the commode before flushing.

He moved back to the sink and leaned down to splash cold water on his face, but as he returned to his upright stance, he saw that the clear reflection once cast by the freshly shined glass was now obscured. The words he'd been introduced to the day before, the words which had now begun to torment him, were scrawled across the mirror in red nail polish.

Frantic, RJ began to wipe at the script. His body quaked as the whisper from earlier called out to him again. This time it was clear that the disembodied voice was repeating the ring's inscription. He listened as its volume crescendoed until its shrill pitch pierced the air and shattered the glass panes lining the wall.

Now convinced that there was something amiss, RJ sprinted from the bathroom and raced through the terminal toward the parking area, fully prepared to abandon his station. By now, the hustle and bustle of the crowd made it more difficult to maneuver, but he pressed forward undeterred until he reached the parking garage.

Shakily, he pulled out his keys and repeatedly pressed the button to unlock his door until he saw his headlights flash. He ran to the blacked-out sedan and pulled open the door, but his face twisted into a mixed expression of shock and horror when he saw that the very ring he'd just condemned to the airport's sewer system was now resting in the driver's seat.

Panic showed on his face as clearly as his eyes, nose, and mouth. He slammed the door and made his escape from the parking deck. Determined to distance himself from the airport, he pulled out his phone to request a rideshare, and seeing that the driver was only minutes away, he ambled to the waiting area to watch for the silver sports utility vehicle that would soon arrive.

"RJ?" The driver asked cheerily as he opened the rear passenger door, the sounds of V-103 spilling out of the car.

"Yeah. That's me."

"Good to meet you. I'm Destiny. Hop on in," The driver introduced herself while RJ slid into the backseat.

As they pulled out of the pick-up area, RJ eyes darted from side-to-side, scanning the faces of the pedestrians they passed on their egress to the main road. His body was tense and his brow furrowed as the urban sounds of contemporary R&B scored the scene.

"Everything okay? You looking for somebody?" Destiny asked, glancing back at RJ.

"Nah. I'm straight," RJ curtly replied.

"Okay... If you say so," she answered before turning up the radio and humming along to the tunes.

In a matter of seconds, the rideshare merged into traffic and onto North Terminal Parkway. They navigated through the influx of vehicles piloted by locals and transients to make their way toward the interstate, putting increasing space between themselves and the airport.

RJ's body relaxed, sinking into the leather seat as he watched the massive building slowly grow smaller in the rearview. He closed his eyes and listened to Destiny hum as their lane of travel converged with the slow-moving traffic ahead of them. He had begun to drift off to her dulcet tones when the sudden blare of radio static filled the SUV's cabin and snatched him from his respite.

"The fuck?" he groaned, annoyed by the disturbance.

"Sorry," Destiny mumbled quickly, reaching for the knob to toggle the radio.

RJ's eyes focused on the red, acrylic-tipped fingers that grasped the dial and turned it. He shifted in his seat as Destiny toyed with the radio, unable to stop the static.

"Just turn it off!" RJ demanded.

However, Destiny's attempts to disconnect the radio were met with failure, and soon the radio began to go haywire, sliding across the range of FM frequencies available.

"I don't know what's going on," Destiny explained, as she continued to toy with the disruptive transmission. "It must be the *divitiae ad sumptus animae tuae,*" she added, her voice becoming garbled as the Latin spilled from her lips.

"Excuse me?" RJ questioned, fear in his voice.

"I said there must be something wrong the *divitiae ad sumptus animae tuae*," she repeated, her voice again becoming warped.

With a look of uncertainty, RJ asked the driver to repeat herself once more, and, as if on loop, the driver began to chant the inscription. He cringed as the timbre of her voice became rougher and rougher with each refrain and watched helplessly as she began coughing uncontrollably. His eyes widened as her neck contorted to bring them eye-to-eye, and the ring she regurgitated struck him in the face.

Using all the strength and speed he could muster, RJ pushed open the door and scrambled from the still-moving vehicle just as a pick-up collided with the open door, sending Destiny's SUV gliding down the pavement. He fled across the lanes of traffic in terror, narrowly avoiding contact with the metal machines that swerved around him. He froze as they blared their horns and slammed into each other.

Overwhelmed by the chaos, he watched helplessly as the trailer of an 18-wheeler that had veered to evade the wrecked automobiles barreled toward him. He tried to dodge the aluminum-composite container as it rolled in his direction, but there seemed to be nowhere for him to go. However, just before impact, he felt a pair of strong arms wrap around him and pull him out of the way.

"Thank you," RJ panted, unable to catch his breath.

"You're welcome," a garbled voice answered back, causing RJ to freeze.

That's when he noticed a crowd of drivers forming in the roadway, and he saw his body lying on the asphalt. Lifeless. He tried to walk toward the crowd, but he was unable to move. Confused, he looked down at the arms of his savior, still wrapped around him. He studied the inhuman appearance of the gnarled hands' leathery skin and how it contrasted with the sharp, red, acrylic nails, and his tear-filled eyes were met by the shimmer of an ornate gold ring as a monstrous voice whispered in his ear.

"Divitiae ad sumptus animae tuae."

FANGS AND CLAWS BRING DUE
BY
ASHLEIGH DAVENPORT

Kellece wove through the mingling people and the Fangs and Claws exhibits holding some of their attention. She had come in earlier to check for safe routes through the Fernbank's After Dark event with serving trays, but no one stuck to the designated walking areas. They were much too close to the staged predators and couldn't keep their fingers off the weapons of ancient tribes sprinkled throughout. The guards weren't there for the displays though. The big wig they were looking after was giving an uninspiring speech.

A muscle-bound man stepped in her path, holding a tray of crackers covered in chunks of meat paler than him and a dollop of red sauce. He snapped his fingers, and some cracker dust flung dangerously close to Kellece's face.

"Bring over a new tray," he demanded as he reached for her tray.

Kellece leaned back, then stopped to let him take the silver platter and walked around him before he could ask for anything else. Relieved of the food, she rubbed the old black coins fashioned into her beaded bracelet and slipped easily around the patrons to get to the café, doing her best to get a good look at many of them as she moved.

"Girl, I don't know how they eatin' this dry ass chicken and crackers," Nyla said as they joined Kellece in picking up new trays of an even drier brown meat skewered between cuts of unidentifiable vegetables.

Kellece grimaced at the tray and rolled her eyes, "Beats the hell outta me. I can barely see the pepper on these things." She grabbed one tray.

"There's pepper?" Nyla looked hard at the plate, "Oh, I see one." They pointed at the middle of the plate.

"Yeah, I got a dude who might take my tray and eat it like it's steak."

Nyla cackled. "It might actually be steak." They both giggled. "But don't give him your plate so you can cheat. The surprise makes it more believable."

"Whatever you say." Kellece smirked.

"I'll just tell you that Uncle Jack is gonna have a ball."

Kellece gasped, "You know he complicates everything."

"Yeah, yeah," Nyla waved their free hand towards the door. "Just look at the eye candy on the stage."

"You mean the boring dude that can't make property acquisition entertaining?"

Nyla sucked their teeth, "You know I'm talkin' 'bout your crush, Ms. Eva. You can add the sexy guard giving you the eyes too." They pursed their lips. "You know it's a good sign when a man's locs are well-kept."

"You mean the confused, angry lookin' dude?"

"Nah, those lovely browns have been zeroing in on you the whole night."

"If that's the case, he ain't doin' his job." Kellece shrugged.

"Not like you're makin' it easy wit' ya sexy librarian look."

Kellece grinned, "All of us are sexy librarians tonight." She waved a hand at the servers lining up at the door.

They wore form-fitting black pants, white button up shirts, and non-slip black shoes. Since they had the freedom to tie up their hair as they pleased, Kellece and Nyla rocked low buns. Although Kellece's braids made the bun so large, it touched the back of her neck. A comforting slide of softened kanekalon sprinkled with small golden beads and gold strings laced between.

Locking a professional smile into place, Nyla and Kellece stepped into the hall to some small praise for the new menu item. Swaying through the crowd, they separated to give more people access.

"We couldn't have done any of this without all of your hard work," the man on the stage, Joseph Tanner, droned on.

The slideshow of historical houses being replaced by gray blocky buildings with large parking lots didn't help to make his heartfelt thanks any more entertaining. Everyone was more interested in the cave bear that loomed over the crowd in the middle of the room or the saber tooth cat that stood in a frozen leap on the right side of the stage.

Kellece glanced at the curator standing on stage beside the personal guard of the boring speaker. The poor woman was struggling to keep the discontent off her honey brown face. When her hazel eyes caught Kellece's, a shy smile crossed her lips. Kellece couldn't resist smiling back at the curly haired cutie. But she caught the eye of the dark-skinned guard's piercing gaze and stopped. She raised her brows at him and he shifted his focus to the crowd.

The crash of glass hitting the hardwood floor shook gasps from the crowd. Kellece stopped returning the guard's stare and turned around to head towards the sound. Spotting the broken plate, she bent down to pick up the biggest pieces.

"You pushed my family out of their homes for this mess!"

Kellece paused to look up at the livid black woman in a green beaded dress yelling at the stage. Her large afro and wooden hoop earrings bobbed with her words.

Kellece tilted her head and smirked, "You did too good of a job, Nyla."

Joseph laughed, "Well ma'am, this isn't a court room. Do you know where you are right now?"

"Yes, you snake!" she yelled, "You took my land and I'm getting more back."

The woman moved forward, and Kellece stepped back as guards rushed to stop her from climbing onto the stage. The handsome one dropped down and put his arms up to stop two of the guards from helping the others.

"Don't manhandle her," he said.

"Damn, she strong," one of the buff men said as he struggled to pull her back.

Joseph laughed louder and directed his attention to the crowd, "Stuff like this is bound to happen when people don't take the situation seriously and read the fine print."

The crowd was focused on the scene. Now he had their attention.

The woman turned and slapped the handsome guard, "You should be ashamed of yourself, helping this predator."

The man put his hands up to placate her, "I'm just doing my job, ma'am." He sucked on his busted lip.

Another guard snatched the woman's hand behind her back and forced her to the ground. Kellece squeezed her hands and winced at the cut left by a large piece of plate.

"The dead will rise with claws and teeth, to take what you owe or your soul to keep." The woman chanted from the ground as a man twice her size put a knee into her back.

Kellece recited the words in a whisper then snapped her wide eyes to the woman. "Did she say claws and teeth?"

"What was that, a poem?" Joseph chuckled.

The audience rippled with nervous laughter. Kellece dropped the plate pieces and stepped forward. Then a gasp from someone beside her made her pause. She followed their gaze to the saber tooth cat. Its intense gaze was focused on the oversized guard. Was it turned that way before?

"What the f—" Screams cut off whoever posed that question. Everyone's attention went to the back of the room and the man who kept devouring the bland chicken bites was grabbed by the cave bear and dragged out of the room.

Kellece turned back to the saber tooth cat as it leapt and slammed into the man on top of the woman. She stepped to the side as the screaming man was dragged past her.

"Oh, shit!" Kellece shouted and dove out of the way of another bear barreling towards the stage.

When she turned over to her back, Joseph stood frozen in front of the growling bear. Eva stood just behind the man, fear rooting her in place. The angry woman was nowhere to be seen.

Kellece tried to get up and was knocked down by a screaming patron whose dress was in the jaws of a large gray wolf. Its paws slid across the floor as it struggled to shake the woman down. Kellece stammered up and moved around the bear to get to the other side of the stage. Nyla was across the Great Hall at the door of the café, yelling and waving people in.

Kellece reached out, "Eva, come on!" She screamed at the curator as the bear climbed onto the stage.

But the small woman kept her eyes on the creature, not noticing that it had eyes only for Joseph. He stepped back and Eva stayed still.

Kellece darted her eyes around the area and found a table that was unscathed and snatched up a steak knife from the table. Gunshots blasted through the air, and she turned to see the busted lip guard shooting at the bear as he used a free hand to get Joseph and Eva moving. Alarms blared, drowning out the screams. Mechanical whirs pierced the air and the screams towards the café were cut short by the thud of shutters falling in front of the door. The entryway to the hall was closed off along with two more doors.

"Fuck!" Kellece yelled.

They were trapped in the Special Exhibit Gallery. She climbed the stage as the bear advanced on the small group of people.

Eva was moving at the behest of the guard. He took one more shot into the bear's head, but the bullets might have well been pebbles.

Kellece looked at the small knife. "This wasn't the plan."

Looking up again, she focused on its fur and saw something sparkling on the back of the bear's neck. The guard's gun clicked several times before he fumbled to get it reloaded. The bear swiped a massive paw and sent him flying off the other side of the stage. Eva screamed as it focused on her.

"Not her!" Kellece yelled and ran straight at it. She jumped on its back and slammed the knife into the back of its neck. The knife pierced through a coin and the bear reared up, throwing her from the stage. She smashed onto a table and it broke under her. The bear turned towards her, raising its arms to attack and Kellece covered her face with her arms.

Nothing happened. She moved her arms, and the bear was still standing on the stage, but its eyes were unfocused and staring into the distance. Another set of thuds and then the screams died down. Kellece groaned as she got off the crippled table.

"Are you alright?" A low, breathy voice asked as a pair of tawny hands grabbed Kellece's arm to help her up.

She placed a hand over one of Eva's. "I'm not, but I'm alive." She gave her a pat and looked at the shutter covering the café doors. "You have any idea how we can get in there?"

"No, the security system is under lockdown because of the gunfire." Eva looked around at the disarray.

Most of the tables that sat close to the stage were toppled or broken. The exhibits were either running around other parts of the museum or scattered across the floor.

"Do we need to wait for help?"

"Yes, the alarm should have alerted the perimeter security team. They'll get the police before trying to come in."

"Great!" Joseph shouted from the stage. He straightened his suit jacket as his guard clicked a new clip into his gun. "We just have to wait for the real protectors of the peace to get here." He cut his eyes at the guard. As if he could do anything himself.

Kellece rolled her eyes and let Eva go to help another patron up. Eva starts helping others too, ignoring the man.

Six other people had escaped the clutches of the reanimated creatures.

Kellece picked up a chair and guided a wounded man to sit. She lifted his pants leg and found bruises forming. He had been trampled. She pulled another chair up and gently placed his foot on it.

"I don't know how to deal with this, but let's keep you off your feet," she said to the man, and he nodded as a young crying woman joined him at his side and held his hand.

The lights flickered and blacked out, shocking a yelp from everyone. The central air quieted and the heavy silence weighed down on everyone. The lights came back on with the air and a collective sigh filled the room. Then, one of the shutters that closed off the room from the special exhibit store and the Great Hall lifted.

Everyone stilled as a shadow passed over the entryway to the store. Kellece lifted the bent knife and took cautious steps towards it. Then, a dark puff of hair came into view before a girl's face peeked around the corner.

"I-is it okay to come out?" the girl stammered.

Kellece relaxed and said, "It might be best you stay in there, just in case another door opens."

The girl nodded and disappeared.

"If we can get to the security office, we might be able to open the door to the café," Eva said as she held out a set of keys. "I can get us in."

Kellece picked up a spear from one of the destroyed displays and headed towards the door, peering into the hall. The other end was closed off by another shutter. At least nothing was moving, but it was still a wide-open space. She looked at the stairs, to the next level, but couldn't see much.

"Shit, we can't get anywhere through here." Kellece swore and turned back.

Eva felt along the wall near the stage. "There's a storage connection that might not be blocked."

Kellece left the hall and joined her.

"Wait a minute," Joseph calls after them. "You need to stay here."

Kellece narrowed her eyes and pulled back a lip in disgust at his demand.

"I mean to say, I would like to pay you to keep me alive."

Kellece sucked her teeth, "I ain't got the time."

"I can pay you a million dollars."

Kellece raised an eyebrow then shook her head. "I gotta get to my family."

Joseph stepped to the edge of the stage and said, "Right, just make a little money while you're on the way."

"Just pay that dude extra to do the job." Kellece pointed at the guard.

The guard smirked. "Omari."

"Yeah, pay Omari to keep you alive."

"He is getting paid extra." Joseph spread his hands out in front of him. "You seem to know how to handle the animals here and the more protection the better."

Kellece looked him up and down and sucked her teeth. "Right, like you'll actually pay up."

"I keep my word."

Kellece stifled a laugh then looked at the guard Omari, who still had one side of his mouth quirked up. "Who handles the money, Omari?"

"I do," Joseph said. At the same time Omari answered with, "A team of accountants."

"Okay, big money grip, you're gonna call your little accountants to send over a deposit as soon as we get to the security office."

"We don't need to go anywhere, and what makes you think you can give me orders?"

"You want to stay alive, and I want to get paid." Kellece shrugged, "So, you're going to do what I say or no deal."

Joseph narrowed his eyes at Kellece, then sighed. "Deal." He held out his hand.

Kellece stayed in place and stared at him as he looked down from the stage.

"Oh." He scrambled down the edge with the help of Omari and held out his hand again.

Kellece looked at his dirty nails and grimaced. How can his tailored suit be so clean, yet he didn't bother with his nails? She gave him a quick shake and wiped her hand against her pants.

"Ah, found it." Eva gave a sigh of relief. She pushed on the wall and a door released with a soft click.

It opened towards her and the small smile she dared to have at the discovery disappeared. Kellece pushed her out of the way as a thick boar the size of a small pony rushed down the corridor. It slammed into the door as Kellece grunted and pushed against it.

"Help her!" Eva yelled from the floor.

Omari rushed to plant a shoulder on the wall beside Kellece. Eva turned and scooted back to press her back against the wall. After a few seconds of the boar squealing, the door clicked and they sagged against it.

"Why the hell was there a display there?" Omari asked no one in particular.

"They couldn't find a place to display it properly, so they put it back there for later." Eva answered.

Kellece bent over and planted her hands on her thighs. "A damn pig is a predator?"

"Did you see that thing? Absolutely," Eva asked and answered.

Kellece shook her head and asked Omari, "How many bullets you got?"

"One."

"We got any other options to get out of here?" She asked everyone.

A few minutes and a shoddy plan later, Omari stood in the middle of the room with his gun pointed at the door. He nodded and Eva pressed the door and lets it pop open. The boar snorted and took a few small steps forward before walking back. It bumped into a crate then ran towards Omari with a squeal.

Kellece stood at the edge of the door with her back to the wall and an ancient spear in her grasp. Her eyes closed, she listened to the beast's pounding steps. She raised her arm and slammed down the weapon. The metal smashed into the neck of the hog, and it crumpled to the floor. Everyone watched as it went stiff with three of its legs straight and another bent to take a step forward. The display rocked up to its feet as if pulled by a string. Kellece backed up, pointing the spear at it. The head of the boar slumped down, the shattered bones in its neck too damaged to hold it up. Kellece poked it and the heavy creature didn't move.

"That's so fascinating," Eva marveled and moved closer from the other side of the door. "It's like they have to get back into their display positions."

"Let's get out of here, then you can start studying the damn displays," Joseph said as he walked up to them and peered around to see the dimly lit hallway.

"Why do you think they have to do that?" Kellece asked, ignoring Joseph.

"Your guess is as good as mine," Eva shrugged, "I would have thought you'd know more since you figured out how to stop them so fast."

Kellece used the bladed end of the spear to poke through the stiff fur of the boar's neck. She revealed a cracked black coin embedded in a shaved patch of skin. "I just noticed something that shouldn't have been there."

Eva moved closer and touched the coin. She sucked in a quick breath and yanked her hand back.

Kellece rocked her head to the side, "You okay?" She assessed Eva.

"Yeah," Eva looked at her fingers. "It didn't hurt. Just buzzed, like a battery or something."

"Well, let's leave them alone for later." Kellece straightened and looked down the hall, "Can we get to the control room through here?"

Eva rubbed her hands together and walked to the door, "We can get close, but it will open into the Great Hall. Then, we'll need to go up two levels."

"Well," Joseph dropped a hand onto Kellece's shoulder, "It looks like we should just stay here."

Kellece shook off his hand with a sneer, "Stay here if you want to, but I suggest everyone who does should go into the store."

She looked at the other people in the room and they headed to the shop. Two of the guys helped the injured man and brought in extra chairs for him.

Kellece grimaced at Joseph and walked towards the corridor.

Joseph took out his phone and turned on the flashlight.

"Make sure you turn that off when we get to the other side. Don't need a target on our back if we run into something," Omari said as he followed Joseph in and closed the door behind them.

Crates obstructed the path halfway down the dimly lit hall. Kellece hoisted herself on top of one and held out a hand for Eva. But the curator backed up, took a few quick steps to kick off the wall and grab the edge of the box. Kellece smiled and backed up to let her pull herself up.

Omari started to climb up, but Joseph stopped him with a hand on his shoulder.

Kellece moved across the box but didn't get down. When Eva turned around, she told her to hold on. Guilt tinged her chest as Eva backed up to the box in fear. But she watched the top of the two men still on the other side.

"We need to clear something up." Joseph failed to whisper low enough for her not to hear.

Omari let go of the crate and moved back out of Joseph's grip. "Clear what up?"

Joseph crossed his arms and said, "You've been undermining me since all this started."

"You mean when you told me to take care of the old woman while your other guards manhandled her?" Omari cocked his head to the side, "Or do you mean when you lied to her son six months ago when he came to refinance their home?"

Joseph scoffed. "That's who that was?"

"Of course. He looked just like her. The family resemblance was obvious."

"That doesn't matter. You need to let me handle the Zulu warrior up there and stop undermining my answers."

"Right, because you'll keep your word."

"Yeah, just like you'll keep your job for the health insurance."

Omari narrowed his eyes on Joseph.

"Nothing to say to that?" Joseph smirked. "I'm sure Janie will be just fine either way."

Omari gritted his teeth and mumbled, "Yeah, boss."

Omari grunted as he pulled himself atop the crate. Kellece reassured Eva as she slid down the other side. They squeezed past another set of crates and made it to the opposite door. Kellece pressed her ear to it.

"You hear anything?" Omari asked as he stepped past the last of the clutter.

Kellece shook her head and listened again. Joseph tripped over a pile of smaller crates, sending them crashing down. The clatter echoed down the hall, and everyone turned to stare at him.

"What? It's not my fault this place is such a mess."

Omari and Kellece scrunched their brows and pursed their lips.

"I will reprimand the employees that did not know this back area would have guests." Eva chided with a whisper full of anger.

Joseph nodded. "Good."

Kellece rolled her eyes and put her ear to the wall again. Hearing nothing again, and she slowly pressed the handle down to release the door. Peering into the dark, still room, she took light steps with the spear at the ready. Eva opened the door completely, taking care to stop it from hitting the wall. When she pointed at the center of the opposite wall, Kellece nodded at the door partially covered in shadows.

They took slow steady steps as they weaved a single file through the toppled displays. They were halfway across the room when a crunch of glass stopped everyone.

"Shit," Joseph whispered.

Kellece curled a lip at Joseph, willing him to pay more attention but he just stared back. Kellece took another step when something in the opposite corner caught her eye. The lights flickered overhead to reveal part of the terror bird's head.

A collective sharp intake of breaths. Then everyone was screaming and scrambling to get out of the way of the rushing bird. Joseph tried to pull Omari towards the corridor they had just come out of, but the creature slid on a tray and slammed into the door.

"Go!" she yelled at Eva, pushing her towards the other door.

Omari yanked Joseph's arm and yelled, "Move!" Then he raised his gun.

Kellece stepped beside him and pushed his hand down to step in front of him and whisper, "You don't have enough bullets." Then she held her spear steady and down as she took a small step back. Omari took a bigger one, allowing Kellece to move faster. She kept her eyes on the bird as it straightened and turned to them.

"Hurry up!" Joseph yelled behind them.

The sound of keys hitting the tile was followed by Eva screaming, "You're not helping!"

"Calm the fuck down," Omari called after them at a lower octave.

A light behind them jiggled their shadows across the floor. The creature cocked its head to the side.

Omari grumbled. "I told him about that light."

"Ay!" Kellece shouted and it moved its head back to focus on her. "Yeah, keep your eyes here."

She and Omari started moving back again as the frantic jingling and yelling continued. Then the keys calmed and clinked slowly.

Kellece glanced back at Eva trying to focus while Joseph shook and bounced from one foot to the other, not able to hold the light steady.

"Dammit!" Eva took the light from him and looked through the keys. She picked out one and jammed it into the door. Turning it to finally release the lock.

Joseph pushed her out of the way and slammed into the door.

Kellece moved to block the bird's eyes and tapped the ground with the spear tip. "This asshole was going to get all of us mauled," she grumbled.

"Pull, you bitch!" Eva yelled as she shot back up.

He pulled it and they crammed into the door and tumbled into the hall.

Kellece and Omari sped up as the terror bird adjusted its body to line up with theirs. It lunged and they jumped in opposite directions. Omari raised his gun and aimed, but the bird zigged and knocked him toward the other two who were fighting to get up.

Kellece ran over and smacked the bird in its bill as Omari righted himself and ran to the door. He stuck his booted foot in just before Joseph could close it.

Eva jumped on the CEO's back and screamed, "You fuckin' bastard!" as she slapped him across the back of his head.

Omari pushed Joseph back and they crashed into the hall. He turned around with a hand on the inside door handle and told Kellece to keep coming as the oversized bird chopped its beak at her.

The wooden clack snapped through the air. Kellece braced and side-stepped another lunge to bring down the spear. The bird turned its head and caught the metal with its beak. It wrenched it from Kellece's grasp and threw it across the room. Kellece punched it in the neck, ripping a squawk from it and ran for Omari.

"Bitch! You bit me!" Eva screamed from behind him and rolled off Joseph.

Kellece reached for Omari. But Joseph yanked his arm back and ripped the gun from his hand.

"What the hell?" Omari yelled, not able to help Kellece.

The bird caught the back of her shirt and yanked her back. It slammed her on the floor.

When Omari turned and yelled, "Give me the gun!" Joseph had it pointed at him.

"Close the fucking door!"

Kellece swiveled to avoid the bird's massive beak as it slammed into the floor, aiming for her head. Another strike and she wrapped her arms around it and rolled over, craning its neck. "Come on, you playin' too much," she groaned.

She heard Omari yell, "There's two bullets," and a door slammed.

Then something crashed into the beast's side and Kellece couldn't hold on. The bird shook Omari off and stood. It kicked him over and stepped on his chest. Kellece spotted and grabbed the spear just in reach. Before the bird could finish rearing back to strike, she swept its weight baring leg with it.

It squawked and stumbled back, catching itself before falling. She grabbed it by the nape, making it look at her.

"Focus!" She yelled, "Wrong target." When it calmed, she let it go and turned to a shocked Omari who had moved to an elbow to try to get up.

"Sorry, the spell gets a little depending how old the medium is." She said as she squared the blunt end of the spear at him.

"Spell? What—"

"Thank you for trying to help." Kellece cut him off and knocked him in the head. He was out cold. The terror bird made a deep chittering click.

Kellece sighed and went back to the door. The keys were still in it. She shook her head and pulled it open. Joseph was pointing his gun at Eva as they entered an illuminated room at the other end of the short hall.

Joseph pushed her in to the room full of monitors and commanded, "Get us out of here."

Eva grabbed one of the chairs, but when it wouldn't turn, she let it go. It pushed back and turned to reveal the woman that had disrupted that dinner. She stood and smiled at Joseph as Eva backed against the wall.

"Been waitin' for you, boi."

Joseph trained his gun on the woman. "You mean, you've been waiting on this bullet." He pulled the trigger and the woman's head rocked before she crumpled back into the chair.

Eva screamed and dug her hands into her hair.

"She was trying to attack me!" Joseph yelled.

"What?" Eva panted, confusion blending into her fear.

"Just get us out of here!" Joseph turned the gun back to Eva.

She took some deep breaths and moved over to the console. Staying as far away from the body as she could, she reached to enter a code on one of the keyboards. Eva sighed as the sound of shutters moving up and locking into place echoed around them.

"Thanks," Joseph said.

Kellece slammed a fist into his face, throwing off his last shot into the monitor. Holding his bloody nose and busted lip, Joseph stumbled against the wall. Then, she used the spear to hold him in place.

"You were going to shoot me!" Eva yelled.

"Always willing to use and dispose of those around you."

The old woman stirred in the seat, to the shock of Joseph and Eva. Kellece just smiled.

"My grandbaby told me scaring you wouldn't be enough." She stood up and straightened her dress as Eva blacked out and slumped into the chair she had vacated.

The bullet in her skull popped out and bounced along the floor. The torn flesh stretched and sealed shut, leaving the smooth surface of her forehead untouched.

Joseph screamed and yelled, "Let me go!"

"No need for all of that yellin'."

Kellece let Joseph go and used her spear to make him trip into the hall. When he tried to scramble up, he saw the terror bird coming from the other end.

"Don't get up on my account," Kellece sneered.

"What's going on?" Joseph spoke through his cupped hand.

Kellece put a hand on the bird's nape. "Simple, I've come to collect what you owe."

"I don't owe you anything."

The bird snapped and squawked at Joseph. Kellece kept petting him and cooed, "Now, now, Uncle Jack, I think he's playing with us."

"That toy doesn't scare me."

The bird moved closer, and Kellece leaned forward to speak by its ear. "You see, he just doesn't understand the gravity of the situation."

Joseph groaned. "You're going to jail or in the ground!"

Kellece stopped smiling and petting the bird. "I think it's time you took this situation seriously and read the fine print." She lifted her hand from its neck. "The dead will rise with claws and teeth, to take what you owe or your soul to keep."

The terror bird lunged for the man. Snapping at his kicking feet as he screamed. It snagged one and jerked him down the hall.

Kellece turned back to the security office. "Is she okay, G'mamma?"

"She'll be okay," She said as she checked on Eva. "Did everyone get out?"

"Nyla got most of them outside, and the family took care of the rest," Kellece answered as she watched Joseph being slung around the hall.

"Some folks got hurt," G'mamma stated as she stepped beside Kellece.

"Yeah, old bones don't make for a smooth job with magic."

"Girl, I know that." G'mamma popped Kellece in the head. "You can thank Jack for talkin' Nyla into this one. Next time, we'll stick to your plan."

Kellece smiled, "He in the bird, ain't he?" They laughed and shared a quick hug.

"Well, it's almost time to go."

"Alright, see you soon," Kellece said as she took the necklace holding the black coin off G'mamma.

The woman smiled and moved her hands into a graceful pose above her head. Her skin glossed over, becoming wax, and the light faded from the dancer's eyes. Not as lifelike as before, but Kellece smiled at the sculpture her cousin had masterfully created.

"Please!" Joseph yelled, making her suck her teeth.

Kellece walked up to the flailing Joseph, until his head was even with her feet. She took her time pulling out her phone as the bird continued to ravage the man's legs. He grabbed onto her calf and tried to pull away, but it held him in a vice grip. Kellece swiped through some photos as he pleaded for her to help him until she found the photo of the new development and turned the phone around. When Joseph couldn't stop screaming, she let out a sharp whistle and the bird stopped shaking its head.

Kellece grabbed Joseph's face and held the phone close, "I think you owe a bit of interest."

*The world is full of obvious things which nobody by any chance
ever observes."*
— *Arthur Conan Doyle*

TETHERED GOAT
BY
GERALD L. COLEMAN

They called themselves gods, we called some of them demons—
they were neither. But some of them paid well. Medusa sometimes operated as a go-between, which is why, when Radamensis agreed to pay
her for help, she said yes. He was desperate and in need of an introduction only she could facilitate.

The restrained, though ornate, foyer opened into one of the biggest
houses she'd ever been in. It was a Victorian manor in the historic In-
man neighborhood and looked exactly as you'd expect. She chuckled
quietly, to herself, while gazing at exquisite crown molding, an enor-
mous, crystalline chandelier, and a carpet-covered floor, which flowed
like a winding river pouring into a brief set of wide stairs cresting onto
a landing, with a round, heavy wood table upon which sat a vase filled
with a bouquet of flowers the size of hedge. A matching chandelier
hung over the giant bundle of purple dahlias beaming with muted white
light.

Historic, she thought. Mortals were funny.

Zazu lumbered into the foyer and motioned for her to follow with
the largest hand she'd ever seen. He led her down the hall, up the short
flight of stairs, past the largely scentless dahlias, to the back wing of the
first floor. He obscured everything in her eye line with his bulk. The
behemoth stopped at a door twice his size and extended a thickly muscled armed, which seemed more like a tree trunk covered in fine, black
wool than a human limb. *Scratch that*, she thought. Human was an as-
sumption and Medusa knew better than to make assumptions. They
were the cause of horror and trauma, in her experience, and she knew
better. She affixed a smile to her face as she looked up at the giant and
gingerly stepped past him.

The expansive room dripped with more of the refined opulence she'd already witnessed. Thick bookcases, made of what she guessed was wood from the eastern African bubinga tree, lined the walls. It produced a violet-colored timber with muted, purple, growth rings that became faint lines in the processed lumber. A hardwood floor, made of what appeared to be red zebrawood, was covered in large, plush rugs woven in multiple shades of purple. A dark-stained, mahogany desk sat opposite the room's sitting area, with a semi-circle of floor-to-ceiling windows behind it, adorned with thick, purple drapes. The ceiling was so high you could build a second floor in the room if you were so inclined.

Elwood Periwell Chisholm was dwarfed by the size of the desk and the leather chair he lounged in. He was nose deep in a thick book with a heavy, leather binding. She mouthed the title—*Codex of the Invisible Night*. The crown of his brown, clean-shaven head barely peeked up over the top of it. A manicured hand reached out for a fine, white, bone china cup perched on a matching saucer.

"Would you like an espresso, Medusa?"

The voice had the erudite tone you'd expect from a thaumaturg of the First Order. Chisholm hated the term wizard. He thought it reductive.

"That would be lovely, El."

He closed the book with a soft *thump* and laid it on his desk.

"Zazu, an espresso for our guest."

"Yes, sir."

She nearly jumped at the deep, rumbling voice. She hadn't realized he was standing behind her. It was unnerving for a man that large to move that quietly. Chisholm motioned toward another large, leather chair positioned across from him, in front of his desk. Medusa got ahold of herself, smiled perfunctorily, and crossed the room, dropping into a chair so comfortable she had to refrain from stroking its arms.

The small man straightened the vest of his black, three-piece suit, pulled a gold watch from its pocket by the chain, and checked the time. He was handsome, if not pretty. His salt and pepper beard was cut close, save for a stylishly fluffed bit on his chin. It suited his chiseled face and brown skin.

Medusa was no stranger to style. She caught the extra-wide, peaked lapels on his jacket, the French cuffs and spread collar of his white shirt, the luxurious silk of the black tie, and how the sunlight, streaming through the windows behind him, glinted off the large, gold, signet ring on the ring finger of his right hand as he sipped his espresso.

Zazu appeared out of nowhere to place an identical cup and saucer in front of her on the desk. She cursed under her breath. She'd almost jumped out of her skin again. She glanced up at him and saw a warm smile beaming back at her. But she only managed a weak one in response. Someone should put a bell around his neck.

She couldn't stay angry though. He was pretty—very pretty, and draped in black from head to toe. The shirt was in a style she knew was a thousand years old, reminding her of another time and place, with a fold over breast that tied at the shoulder with two small strings. He wore loose, sweeping leggings like a skirt and black sandals. His head was clean-shaven too, but unlike Chisholm, so was his face. He had a strong chin and high cheekbones. His brown skin was a shade lighter than her's and his employer.

The espresso was delicious. Just the right mix of bitter, sweet, and sour—nice and hot, with a thick layer of crema on top.

She took another sip and said, "Thank you, Zazu. Perfection."

The man rumbled his thanks and disappeared into the hallway.

"We pride ourselves on great coffee in this house," Chisholm said over his own cup. "Life's too short for bad coffee, among other things. Now, to what do we owe the pleasure of your company, Medusa?"

She swallowed, nodded, and sat her cup on its saucer, before snuggling back into the most perfect leather chair. "I have a job for you, El. I know you've played detective, here and there, for the right client, at the right price. You have a singular mind, love a good mystery, and aren't opposed to a fat payday."

In point of fact, Elwood Periwell Chisholm was the greatest detective the world had never seen—the mortal world at least. He had a photographic memory, and an IQ that was off the charts. But what Medusa liked most about him was his kindness—he wasn't necessarily nice, but he was kind.

She reached into her pocket, produced a cashier's check for fifty thousand dollars, and placed it on the desk in front of him before returning to the comfortable chair. He glanced down at it, steepled his fingers together, and his pretty eyes narrowed to slits.

She opened her mouth but he forestalled her with a raised finger. He stood, straighten his vest again, and stared at the check for a moment before making his way around the desk.

"May I?"

She liked that he asked for her consent—kind *and* considerate. "Sure, El." She also liked that he let her call him, El.

He leaned in and took a deep whiff of her locks. Then he inspected her mole hair sweater and knelt down to grab hold of her boot. He looked it over and studied the sole closely. When he stood, he straightened his vest again and made his way back to his chair.

Once he was comfortable, he took another sip of his espresso, leaned back, and said, "What could Radamensis possibly want from me?"

She nearly choked on her espresso. "Get the fuck outta here, El." Her face plainly said, *explain*.

The barest hint of a grin crossed his face.

"There's a lingering hint of the scent produced by the starflower lily in your hair and a bit of pollen from its stamin on your sweater. It's the only flower Radamensis allows in his home—something to do with the flower's strong fragrance warding off the smells of the home he escaped. There are small bits of the thorny needle shed from *Cedrus atlantica* or 'Glauca' in the tread of your boot, which matches the massive tree in the manicured arboretum in his backyard—if you can call the twenty acres behind his house a yard. I suspect that's where you and he talked and where he asked you for help?"

Chisholm warmed to the moment with a broader smile. He was in his element. "There are foreign shades in your aura, not of this dimension, fading but still there around the edges, which says you've been in the company of someone—let's say *notable* in a very particular way. And were he to need my help he wouldn't come himself. He would need an intermediary. And you are one of the only people who would be allowed in my home. Taken separately, they are inauspicious bits of observation, and obviously inconclusive. But their sum, taken together, makes for an easy deduction. Not certain, mind you, but probable enough to assert with modest confidence."

She couldn't stop the low whistle that escaped her lips. "Damn, El."

The broad smile faded to a simple grin behind his steepled fingers.

"Yeah, you got me. I'm here on behalf of Radamensis. He has a problem only you can solve." Medusa crossed her legs and rubbed at her chin. "Let me rephrase that—It's a problem only you can solve fast and he needs it done fast."

Chisholm lowered his hands and said, "He's lost his ring?"

"What the actual fuck, El!?"

He chuckled and waved a hand dismissively. "Now, now, Medusa. It's simple deduction. He sent you—particularly you, because you're one of the few people I'd let into my home unannounced. He sent you because you sometimes work as an intermediary. And you just said it was something he needed done fast. Given all the givens, and knowing what I know about him, it seems logical this is about his ring."

She nodded. It made sense once he laid it out for her to see, but it was still unsettling.

She shook her head, took a deep breath, and said, "Yeah, El. His ring is missing. And given the state he was in when I left, it's clearly a big problem for him. I mean, he's got enough money to replace it, no matter how expensive, so I figured there was more to it. But he wouldn't tell me why."

Chisholm just nodded his head. Just then, the ancient grandfather clock on the other end of the room chimed six times. The small man's eyes lit up.

"Are you hungry, Medusa? It's time for dinner. While I don't generally talk business over a meal, we can continue this at the dinner table if you'll join me?"

He was up and moving before she could say yes or no. She was starving, so she followed him out of his office, down the hall, past several more rooms on the first floor, and into a spacious dining room. He made his way to the end of the broad, mahogany table and took a seat at its head.

She nearly jumped out of her skin when Zazu appeared out of nowhere to point her to the other end of the table. Colorful curses poured from her mouth. Though they were uttered under her breath, she still blushed and murmured an apology to her host as she took her seat. By the Fates, she was going to personally tie a bell around his neck even if he was an unassailable mountain.

Circe appeared from a door behind Chisholm, in a flowing soft-green dress with long sleeves. Her hair was fiery red and fell to the small of her back. She smiled down the length of the table at Medusa—it was as radiant as her golden skin.

"I see we have a guest for dinner?"

Medusa smiled warmly at the woman and gave her a knowing nod. She was happy that Circe was happy, comfortable, and most importantly—safe. Chisholm nodded and gave Circe the biggest smile Medusa had seen yet.

"Yes, Chef. I hope it's not an imposition?"

"Not at all, El. I'm glad to see her." She turned back to Medusa and continued, "I hope she likes fish."

"I'm sure I'll love whatever you bring to the table, Circe. Your skills are legend."

The woman blushed, inclined her head briefly, and said, "Then we'll start with an aperitif? Martinis?"

"Yes, perfect, Chef," Chisholm said with unvarnished delight.

The woman returned with a tray in hand and placed a glass in front of each of them. She shook a large tumbler with steady, but delicate hands. Her pour was practiced—starting at the rim of the glass and climbing into the air above it. She finished by dropping olives into the thick, clear liquid with a soft *plopping* sound, before disappearing back through the door. The drink was stiff, tasty, and perfectly balanced.

Chisholm sipped on the martini and munched on the olives, speared on the end of a toothpick. He looked like a happy kid eating candy. She knew he was, famously, a gourmand of unrestrained taste, so it had been no surprise when he'd enticed Circe to come work for him. Chisholm had enough money so that she could ply her trade with abandon. He made sure she had the best of everything, from ingredients to the tools of her trade. And because she lived under his roof, she could do so un-molested. No one in their right mind would dare come looking for her at Chisholm House—god, demon, or other. You did not mess with the Thaumaturge. Some had tried, to their lasting regret. Medusa loved see-ing how Circe moved with a lightness that spoke of being free and un-burdened.

Chisholm once shared an incredibly private story with Medusa. Af-ter a late night of food, drink, and engaging conversation on a book he'd once shared with her—the *Mysterium Thaumagistis*, he'd turned quiet and reflective. What he shared about his mother helped her understand him. Chisholm hated bullies in general, but the kind who hurt women—those he despised with a hot, burning heat. He'd only been four or five years old, but it was seared into his memory like a brand. It made him a different kind of man once he was grown—a dangerous man to men who hurt women.

Medusa would've liked him anyway. He was just a deeply, likable human being, if intensely private. That night made her love him. She'd never told a soul what he shared with her. She was good at keeping a confidence.

She knew one of the things he liked about her was her ability to enjoy a silence between friends—the not needing to speak just to fill the void. They enjoyed their drinks, quietly, while patiently waiting for the meal to arrive. When it did, she was glad he'd invited her to stay. Circe was a genius with food.

They started with a tray of what Circe called pulled brisket barbacoa, atop mini jalapeño corn muffins, garnished with chopped parsley. The finger food was followed by rocket soup. Circe delighted in explaining each course. It was a blend of spinach, arugula, cilantro, and potato warmed with nutmeg, allspice, and turmeric, drizzled with olive oil, and finished with a large dollop of yogurt. The third course was a mixed-greens salad with sliced, red onion, a crumbled, blue-veined cheese, tossed with champagne vinaigrette, which she mixed right there at the table. Finally, the main course was salmon grilled in a mango chutney sauce, with garlic green beans on the side.

Medusa leaned back in her chair, rubbed her stomach, and said, "Brava, Maestro. Brava!"

Chisholm joined in. "Yes, brava Circe. As always, most excellent."

The woman beamed as she whisked the empty plates back through the door.

"Thank you, El. That was the most delicious meal I've had in an age. Circe is incredibly talented. I'm so glad she has a place where she's appreciated."

"I'm delighted she agreed to come work for me. She's a culinary artist." He settled back into his chair and sipped the espresso Circe brought them when she reappeared for the last time. He looked like a satiated dragon sitting on a mound of gold.

Medusa heard a door slam followed by muffled cursing. She darted a glance at Chisholm, who continued quietly sipping his espresso like nothing whatsoever was the matter, so she stayed in her seat and waited. A familiar voice echoed down the hallway.

"Home skillet, go easy on the threads, my guy. FYI, this is vintage Prada, ya dig? Take a chill pill, bro. You are hella disrespectful. It's not that serious. I'm going, I'm going."

Medusa was already chuckling to herself before Zazu even entered the dining room. It was only then she realized the giant had been missing through the entire meal. He was *helping* a man into the room. By help she meant dragging him along by the scruff of his neck and dumping him into a chair halfway down the length of the table.

She pressed her lips together in a firm line, then pursed them out, working her mouth, this way and that, in a failing effort to keep from smiling—all the while choking down the laughter bubbling up inside her like an overpoured beer with too much of a head.

Chisholm lowered his cup onto its saucer with a soft *clink* and said, "Hello, Hopscotch. Thank you for joining us."

"Sup, Chisholm. Was this strictly necessary, my guy? Your acrimonious thug didn't need to bug out on me like that. I was minding my own, chatting up this long-legged, full-on, smoke show at the Red Phone Booth—you know the one in the Dailey's Building? Well, not the one for the mortals, the *other* one. And here comes your oversized Mr. Belvedere dragging me away from a sure thing."

Zazu's chest rumbled like the sound of a distant avalanche. It appeared to be as much for the reproach as the low-key misogyny, but she appreciated Zazu for it. Hopscotch's head sunk down between his shoulders and his hands turned up in supplication.

"Yo, bro—Take. A. Chill. Pill. My guy. Seriously, you're trippin.'"

Medusa failed at keeping a ripple of laughter from running through her voice. "Hopscotch McGavin. Still spewing thirty-year-old slang with a side of misogyny. What was it again? Oh, right, you think it makes you sound retro—avant garde, right?"

The rakishly thin man scratched at his beard, moved a bit of dirty-blond hair out of his eyes with a pass of his sun-booth-tanned hand, and flashed her a smile so greasy she almost checked her pockets to make sure everything was still there.

"You're feelin' me, huh?" He winked at her. She responded to it with a look so hard he cleared his throat and turned his attention back to Chisholm.

"So, uh, my guy. What gives? Why the rough house routine? If you needed to see ol' Hopscotch all you had to do was shoot me a text."

Chisholm emptied his cup and replaced it on its saucer with delicate precision and said, "I do not *text*, Hopscotch."

The wizard made the word sound like it was too dirty to touch without a handkerchief wrapped around his fingers. He probably just thought it was beneath him. Chisholm was a bit of a throwback, but Medusa liked that about him.

Hopscotch said, "Ok, so what's the big deal?"

Chisholm steepled his fingers, with his elbows balanced on the arms of his chair.

"What do you know about Radamensis?"

Hopscotch shifted, uncomfortably, back and forth in his chair, glanced around the room before landing his eyes on Medusa and Zazu, then turned his attention back to Chisholm. You'd have thought the room was suddenly warmer—or possibly bugged.

"Oh, that dude. Listen, my guy, I don't want any trouble. Everyone on my side of the fence knows you don't mess with the big, bad, wizard Elwood Chisholm, and I dig that about you, bro."

Chisholm bristled at the word *wizard* before smiling warmly at Hopscotch. "No need to worry, Hop. I'm just after some information. I like to keep an eye on possible threats to the mortal realm. Can you help me?"

Hopscotch glanced around the room again. This time he looked even more wary, like he was in an interrogation room at a police precinct, and he didn't like it. But he managed to purr in that slick tone of his. He was slippery as fish just out of water.

"Sure, my guy. No problem. Easy peasy." He wiped his hands together and turned them up, showing Chisholm, like a magician performing a card trick shows you he doesn't have anything up his sleeves.

He leaned in toward Chisholm like a man sharing a confidence and continued. "Look, folks from back home don't care much that I escaped. I was so low level that no one gave it a second thought when I disappeared. But that dude? What do you call us? Infernals? That dude was a top-tier Infernal. Like, the Big Guy knew his name. So, when that dude legged it, people noticed."

He pulled on the collar of his red, flower print shirt. It was, actually, quite lovely, even on him, and went well with his blue Prada suit. He licked his lips, looked from Chisholm to Zazu, and back again—raised his hands, and shrugged. "How 'bout a glass of water? Or, even better, something stronger?"

The wizard nodded at Zazu who disappeared through the door Circe had used to bring in dinner. He returned with a rocks glass, containing a clear drink with ice. Hopscotch took it, gulped from it, wiped his mouth with the back of his whole hand and wrist, and gave Zazu a shaky smile.

"My man! Grey Goose on the rocks. That's stellar, my guy—completely lit and legit."

Medusa blurted, "Don't say it."

The thin man grinned and said, "Too legit to quit," and preceded to relish in the groan it elicited.

He took another long gulp, sat the drink down, placed his hands flat on the table and said, "Now, you gotta realize if the Big Guy lets someone like Radamensis get away with lambing it, all hell would break loose—wait."

He chuckled at himself for the pun he'd inadvertently spun.

When he finished, he said, "Where was I? Oh, right. So, the Big Guy puts the word out that Radamensis was to be brough back in chains, my dude. Like, wow, right? Full on stand and deliver. Critical, man, critical."

He scooped up his glass and drained the rest of drink as he warmed to his subject. Chisholm didn't interrupt him. He just let Hopscotch spill his guts. He motioned to Zazu who grabbed the glass and refilled it with a shaker Medusa hadn't seen the giant retrieve. She was, absolutely, going to get that dude a bell for his neck. Hopscotch half-drained his fresh drink and carried on.

"Now, Radamensis knows if he gets caught the Big Guy is going to punch his ticket but good. So, on his way out he snags an artifact—a thing so old, dark, and powerful, only the Big Guy ever used it. Now, most people think it's a ring, but that's just how it manifests itself here. But the thing is powerful, powerful enough to keep him hidden from anyone who's looking, especially anyone from back home."

With that, Hopscotch nodded, wiped his hands together again like he'd done what he'd come to do—despite having been dragged to Chisholm's house involuntarily, and said, "Tah Dah, motherfuckers. The whole thing's a gas, right? Right?"

He waved his hands over the table like a magician revealing the end of a trick. But when he looked over at Chisholm, he immediately turned to Medusa and said, "What gives?"

She glanced across the table and saw the wizard still had his fingers steepled together, but now his eyes were closed.

She'd seen this before. "Just give him a minute, he's thinking."

Medusa didn't know what he'd score on an intelligence test, but she knew it would be off the charts. She hadn't met many authentic, dyed-in-the-wool geniuses in her time, but Elwood Periwell Chisholm was the genuine article. Right now, he was putting that prodigious bit of genius to work.

When he finally opened his eyes, he looked at Hopscotch with a raised eyebrow, while chewing his lower lip. "What would the ring be worth?"

He caught Hopscotch with his glass halfway to his mouth. The man didn't blink before assuming the sketchiest interpretation of the question.

"You sly dog, Chisholm." He swirled his glass around with a roll of his wrist and continued, "To the right party? You could name your price. There's always a mortal, or two, trying to dabble in the 'occult.'" He paused and made air quotes with his fingers as he chuckled. "They're fools with money and I'd have no problem being the cause of the two parting."

"Good," Chisholm said. "Arrange for a meeting tonight with any interested parties. Tell them to come with cash."

Hopscotch nearly spit out his drink. "Wait, are you saying you've got the ring? Ballsy, my guy. Straight gangster."

Medusa noticed that Chisholm didn't answer him, he just got up and motioned toward the front door.

Hopscotch downed the rest of his drink with a *clink* of ice against glass, stood, and said, "Oh, oh, got it big dawg. Right away. Tonight, you say? When and where?"

The wizard said, "Midnight, High Museum of Art. Top floor, your side, not the mortal side."

Hopscotch nodded curtly. "Got it. And my cut for facilitating this lucrative meetup?"

"Don't worry, Hopscotch. You'll be fairly compensated."

The slimy man saluted Chisholm, rubbed the gold-ringed fingers on his right hand together, and whispered, "Cha Ching," before turning on the heels of his brown, snakeskin, Saint Laurent boots and disappearing down the hallway.

Medusa said, "Interesting."

Chisholm's only reply was, "Dessert?"

* * *

Medusa could still taste the deliciously exquisite cheesecake Circe served them for dessert. The creamy body was thick, with a graham cracker crust. It was just on the other side of cool—not cold, but refreshingly chilled—with a heaping spoon of five berry compote on top. She joined them with her own plate and espresso. They ate, talked, and laughed until it was time to leave for their clandestine meeting.

Chisholm was mum about his plan. Medusa knew not to ask. She was ninety-nine percent sure he didn't have the ring. So, he was playing some deeper, more complex game, like a *Senet* master who sees not only their next move, but the next dozen.

Zazu appeared with one of Chisholm's Senet boards as the dessert dishes were being cleared—a game similar to chess, but much older, created in *the Two Lands* called Kemet by its inhabitants and Egypt in modern times. The board had three rows with ten squares each, accompanied by ornate pieces you moved across it after casting small, throwing sticks to work out your turn. As with most things when it came to the wizard, his Senet board was an ornate thing of wood, leather, and burnished brass. Even the tiny throwing sticks were made of brass—with inscriptions filled with diamond shards.

Medusa enjoyed their spirited matches but always resigned herself to losing. She spent each game simply trying to get as far as she could before an inevitable defeat. She felt a bit like a piece on that board as they entered the gallery on the top floor.

They were in the High Museum but in the *Otherworld,* on the side they called the *Hidden Places.* Beings like her, Hopscotch, and Radamensis went by many names in the mortal world. They were called Fae, or Fairie, others used Shadowwalker, Undying, or the Extramundane. Some even labeled them gods or demons. They were many different names, all describing the same thing—beings from another dimension. It was reductive. Some of them were actual natives of the mortal world, particularly the Fae. But human beings, especially these contemporary incarnations, were allergic to complexity and enamored with ease, even if it was wrong—sometimes, particularly if it was wrong.

Those of the Otherworld took to calling their places, which existed in the same physical space as the mortal structures, by the same names the mortals used. It was just easier. So, even though they were standing in the Otherworld reflection of the High Museum, they just called it by the same name. The Hidden Place's High Museum was currently hosting an exhibit on mortal religious practices. Otherworlders were fascinated by the rites, rituals, and artifacts the mortals used to fight off their existential dread—the fact that they would one day cease to be. They had created elaborate visions of an afterlife to combat that experiential crisis. Their beliefs made some of them better. Others, it made worse.

Medusa was staring at a painting of the black Madonna and child, which should have been hanging somewhere in the Vatican, but had somehow made its way here, when Hopscotch showed up. He kept looking around like he was expecting someone to jump out of the shadows cast by the soft, overhead lighting. Nervous wasn't even close to a good description. It made her skin crawl. The apprehension radiated off him like an unpleasant odor. It was infectious. She wanted to tell him to get it together, but she was just a spectator. This was Chisholm's show.

"Hey, peeps. It took some doing, Chisholm, particularly given the short timetable, but I managed to scrape up three bidders."

The bidders—the people with money and their small entourage of assistants—entered and stood on the other side of the gallery, making sure to keep their distance from each other. Medusa recognized Aristobulus. He had two men standing behind him trying to look like they weren't armed guards. Ari was tall, slim, and pale as the white walls of the gallery. He wore blue pants and a tweed jacket with a silk pocket square puffing out of his breast pocket like a flower in bloom, and a silk, polka-dot ascot. He had long, wavy, black hair and a matching beard. Medusa wasn't the least bit surprised by the cape and cane. That was Ari.

The woman, being fawned over by three much younger assistants—two women and a man—wore an all-white pants suit and red pumps that looked like they cost more than the building. She had silvery-gray hair hanging to her shoulders and fierce, red nails decorating pale, wrinkled fingers adorned with a large diamond ring on one and an even larger gold ring on the other. Her entire look screamed money so old it might have been made during the Roman Empire.

The other man was by himself. He wore a tailored suit with a brilliant white shirt and matching silk tie. His blond hair was coiffed in a five-hundred-dollar cut. Cool, blue eyes stood out against sun-tanned skin and stared right through you. Medusa thought she recognized him but couldn't quite put her finger on from where.

Her blood went cold when Chisholm said, "Hardgraves."

That's how she knew him.

Hardgraves was a nasty piece of work. He came from the same place that had produced Hopscotch. But where Hopscotch was hopelessly small and inconsequential—which allowed him to escape without having to look over his shoulder—Hardgraves was high up on the food chain. If he—maybe *he* was an *it*—had gone missing it would certainly ring some bells in dark places.

She hissed at him before she could stop herself. His voice was melodic, but it raised small goose bumps on her arms.

"Now, now, Medusa, isn't it? Put away your claws and try not to turn anyone to stone. There's no need for animosity. I'm not here for you. Though, I confess, tangling with you might be a pleasant experience. Maybe another time?"

His bright, white smile made her shiver. She hissed at him again. This time on purpose.

Chisholm took a step toward Hardgraves.

"Whoa, wizard. At ease, my good man. I'm not here for you either."

A rich, vibrant voice drifted from the shadows in the back of the Gallery.

"He's here for me."

Radamensis stepped into the dim light of the open room. Rotund was the best way to describe him. Like Chisholm and Hardgraves, he wore an expensive suit. It was a warm blue shade but covered in a floral brocade of salmon-pink, white, and sky blue. It was accented by a large, weepy, black, velvet bowtie, crisp white shirt, and red pocket square, which poured out on his chest like a small stream of silk. His pale face was engulfed by a glistening pompadour of brown hair on his head, held up by enough hairspray to supply a salon for a month, and a thick, bushy beard. Black, suede, Gucci loafers made a soft *click clack* as he crossed the wood floor.

"Well, Hardgraves, I see you've come up in the world. At least as much as a sniveling degenerate comfortable with kissing ass might."

Hardgraves sneered and pulled out a gold cigarette case. He retrieved a cigarette, clicked the case closed, tapped it on the case and laid it on his lip with a practiced ease. He retrieved a small, gold lighter, encrusted with red and green stones that glittered in the soft light. A flourish of his hand brought it up to the cigarette and he lit it without looking. Smoke engulfed his words as he spoke.

"You fat, pompous goat. I wondered if you were brave enough to come after the Inglorious Relic of the Dark Night yourself or if you'd settle for sending an emissary, like the coward you are. I'm glad I was wrong. It'll make dragging your corpulent carcass back much easier."

Chisholm had stepped to the center of the Gallery while the two traded insults. Something had caught his eye. He chuckled. Everyone turned and looked at him.

"It's as I suspect," he said.

Medusa gazed around the room trying to see what had caught Chisholm's eye.

Hardgraves took a long draw of his cigarette and said, "Making pointless deductions, wizard?" The words floated across to Chisholm on the smoke the man expelled.

"In point of fact, Infernal creature, you'll find this particular deduction interesting. You see, I knew the quickest way to get at the center of the question of who took Radamensis' ring was to intimate that I had it and to see who showed up for a sale of the thing. I had a suspicion about the nature of the theft, so I decided to test my hypothesis. And lo and behold, it turns out I was correct."

Chisholm paused, and Hardgraves looked around at the other bidders and then Radamensis before leaping into the silence with exasperation.

"Well, wizard? Share with the rest of the class."

Chisholm took three steps back and said, "I'll let Azriel Stone explain."

Hardgraves growled just as Azriel Stone stepped into the light. Medusa was startled. She wasn't sure how the man had managed to stay invisible, but there he was, the cursed immortal and sometime, erstwhile, Infernal hunter himself.

Everything happened almost at once. Hardgraves leaped at Stone, who slammed his hand onto the floor. The tattoos on his forearms glowed softly with a radiant, white light. Hardgraves ran smack into an invisible barrier, which flashed white when he slammed into it, stopping him dead in his tracks. The Infernal howled with rage, made a slashing movement with his right hand, and a churning portal of black light opened on the right side of the Gallery.

A dozen infernals poured out of it looking like a pack of demons the mortals might depict in a film or novel. They had warped faces, claws, fangs, and blistering skin. Oddly, they were dressed like they'd step out of a Victorian drama. There were long jackets, waistcoats, and top hats. There were also women, but in tight pants and double-breasted coats with flared sleeves. They were all in unrelieved black.

Aristobulus and the unnamed woman, along with their retinue, fled. Hopscotch also pulled a disappearing act, which didn't surprise her. Radamensis hid behind Azriel who pulled a black, 1911 handgun from its holster behind his hip. The thing glowed with blue scrollwork along the grip and slide. He produced a knife from somewhere on his body with his left hand. It glowed like the gun.

Chisholm's voice was hard. It was the first time today Medusa had seen him upset.

"You break the Code and Covenant? It is forbidden for your kind to hunt in Terminus. Your Lord and Master was present, witness, and party to the Accord. How dare you."

Hardgraves banged his fists on the invisible barrier Azriel Stone had trapped him in. Each time he hit it, large warding symbols flashed white on the walls and the floor around the gallery. They must have been cunningly made for her to have missed them. It seems Azriel Stone had only grown more powerful.

Hardgraves sneered at Chisholm.

"We are not afraid of your threats Wizard. Nor will we be denied our prey." He looked at the small, seething horde of Infernals and said, "Get Radamensis. Leave none alive."

The horde howled, hissed, and growled as they surged forward. Elwood Periwell Chisholm took one step toward them and raised his hands.

"I am the Keeper of the Light of Khepri, Holder of the Keys of Gbadu, First Adept of the Thaumaturgis and Guardian of the Mortal Realm. You are not welcome here!"

He slammed his hands together in a resounding clap, but there was no sound. Well, there was, but it was like a sound so overwhelming, so piercing, that your ears stopped working. Medusa had just enough time to throw her hands up to cover her eyes. Even so, the burst of white light penetrated both them and her eyelids.

Once the light was gone, it still took a few moments for her vision to clear. Her ears, however, started working as soon as the sound of Chisholm's clap dissipated. The screeching made the hair on her neck stand on end.

She blinked furiously and slowly her eyesight returned. What she saw was disturbing. There were black scorch marks on the floor where the Infernals once stood. The black portal was gone. Hardgraves was crouched on the floor with his hands up as if he was still trying to shield himself. The left side of his body was scorched. He growled like a feral dog.

Azriel was lowering his arm and a mystical shield made of blue light was fading into nothingness. Radamensis was folded up in a quivering mass behind the immortal, somehow still whole and untouched thanks to the cursed immortal. The wizard lowered his hands and looked on what he had wrought with firm lips and hard eyes.

He was kind, and considerate, she thought, *but not to be trifled with.*

He tugged at the bottom of his vest before making his way over to Azriel.

"Well played, Stone. You managed to snag your quarry with the help of an escaped Infernal who, I'm assuming, you *invited* to help you?"

Azriel put away his knife and holstered his gun with a broad, white smile. The tall man was fit, lithe, and handsome to boot. He was wearing a black t-shirt, jeans, and dress boots. The tattoos on his arms were no longer glowing. He looked back at Radamensis, reached into his pocket, and tossed the man his ring.

"Correct, El. I needed to draw Hardgraves out so I could put an end to his visits. I saved a descendant of the Consecrated a while back and discovered Hardgraves was hunting in Terminus, which is expressly forbidden, as you well know. He's also butted into my personal business once too often. Bringing Radamensis out into the open seemed the easiest way to get his attention."

The immortal jerked a thumb in the escaped Infernal's direction. "He wasn't happy about being a tethered goat, but I made him see reason. It was help me or I'd send him back to his own dimension myself. After that, he was very amenable to making himself useful. Thank you for playing along. I hope you don't mind?"

Chisholm looked around the Gallery, stopping for a moment on Hardgraves, who was still huddled on the floor, and then turned back to Azriel Stone.

"Not at all, my good man. It afforded me the wonderful company of Medusa at dinner and gave me a reason to get out of the house. You also saved me the trouble of taking care of this miscreant myself. The Infernals have been getting out of hand lately and a message needed sending."

The two men clasped hands and Chisholm turned to go. Azriel pulled out a pair of golden cuffs, covered in indecipherable script, and bound Hardgraves before dragging him off with Radamensis in tow.

Medusa raised her hand like a kid in class, lost in the day's lesson, and said, "Wait, so you're saying this was all a set up?" She let her hand drop with disgust, raised her voice, and barked at her client on his way out the door. "Goddammit, Radamensis, you're going to pay extra for wasting my time."

The Infernal froze mid-step, ducked his head, and waved his hands in submission before hastening to catch Azriel who had not waited for him. Zazu appeared out of nowhere next to her and Chisholm as she watched Radamensis go. She jumped a full step at his appearance.

"And, YOU." She poked a rigid finger in Zazu's direction. "I'm going to put a goddamn bell around your neck the next time you scare me like that."

Chisholm chuckled and said, "Zazu, get the car, please. I think there's more cheesecake at home."

The First Adept, and Guardian of the Mortal Realm, raised his eyebrows at her in an unspoken question.

Medusa growled softly and said, "Yeah. But I'm also going to need another drink. Maybe two."

She didn't stop fuming until she'd had a piece and two more martinis.

THE BODY FARM
BY
ALANA DAVIS

"Tanner."

"Yeah, Quint?"

"Before we get out this truck, let me tell you something."

"Yeah, Quint?"

"If I see any foolishness from you, any popping out and trying to scare me, I'm leaving your ass behind."

A nod.

"If I see anybody else out here, a worker, a cop, a homeless guy, whatever, I'm leaving your ass behind."

Another nod.

"And if any...*any*...of those goddamn corpses moves even an inch, I don't care if it's gas or whatever, I'm...I'm gonna what, Tanner?"

"You're gonna leave my ass behind."

Quint could see that Tanner was struggling not to laugh as he answered him, which didn't inspire a lot of confidence about how the rest of this night was going to go. The beleaguered Georgia Tech freshman gripped the steering wheel of his snickering roommate's truck and wondered for the eightieth time that night if he should just go back and tell the team that they went. He was sure he could make up some story about why they couldn't get any pictures as proof. Lost phone, dead phone, phone chucked at a zombie in self-defense. As he looked out the front window at the crawling mist obscuring the ground before them, he could almost believe that last excuse would work.

"Come on, man, don't be a punk," Tanner said, sliding out of the passenger's seat and landing on the gravel with a crunch. He bounced on the balls of his feet, a little unsteady from the alcohol in his system, but still bright enough to be way too excited for what they were about to do. "The sooner we get in there and take those pictures, the sooner we can get back to the dorm and you can play Fortnite or Minecraft or whatever."

"Fallout," Quint muttered under his breath before sighing and sliding himself out of the truck onto the driveway. He had imagined the entrance would be a huge wrought-iron gate like something out of an Edgar Allen Poe story, intricately crafted with choking vines and weeping angels. Instead, they found themselves standing before a much less intricate barrier gate, marking the entrance with all the sweeping romance of a parking garage. Before the gate sat a sign that read "Georgia Tech Forensic Anatomy Research Facility", a clunky mouthful of a name. Folks on campus just called it the Body Farm. And that night, Quint and Tanner were taking an unofficial tour.

~~~~

Quint Street was not a daredevil by nature, and he hadn't really planned on starting now. He had to lay his body and mind on the altar of late football practices, agonizing study sessions to keep his grades high enough to play, and hours on the bus to and from his crumbling town of Manchester to even think about getting to a place like Georgia Tech, and he wasn't keen to squander the opportunity. His interest in football had less to do with the beauty of the game, and more to do with the fact that he was a big boy from a poor family, and the places for boys like him were in the military or on the field. Quint did not fancy himself a hero, so he preferred the option that was less likely to get him shot at. In general, he had always been a kid that liked to keep his head low and his nose clean. But such conviction can be challenging in the face of peer pressure, especially when that peer was your roommate and the only friend you'd managed to make in the four months since starting school.

Tanner McGivens did not have Quint's same aversion to trouble. If anything, the running back sought it out like a homing missile. His growing up poor didn't give him the same sense of caution that Quint had. If anything, it made him more reckless. He had come to Atlanta from Floyd county with a rusted Chevy pickup and nothing to lose. The other guys on the team loved him for his proficiency at keg stands and his willingness to take every joke just a little too far. Once he figured out there wasn't going to be any tension, the other boy's antics went from obnoxious to entertaining. The guy knew how to have a good time, Quint had to admit, even if he was a little much.

The night they received their mission, their quarterback had invited the guys to his parent's backyard in the suburbs to celebrate their bowl game win. They had already started decorating for Christmas, and the back deck was alive with twinkling lights, gold and black satin bows and a stereo mixing holiday classics with top 40. It was the cherry on top of a great season, and even though they didn't win the championship, their record was undeniable, and the mood was high. Quint couldn't help but feel like he had made it, nursing a beer beside a heated pool in a gated community, admiring the new sneakers his grandparents had scrimped and saved to buy in honor of his first successful season. Tanner was acting a fool as usual, doing front flips dangerously close to the pool's edge. Quint was about to tell him to cut it out when Davis Reeves, the party's gracious and Heisman-bound host, stepped in to keep his teammate from busting his athletic hopes and dreams on the concrete. They chatted for a while, then Davis turned to where Quint was sitting and waved him over.

Quint walked over to them, more than a little nervous. He hadn't done much that season to make himself stand out. The more popular and accomplished players barely looked his way. Tanner's stats weren't that much better, but he had the charisma to get into the circles of the older boys. Maybe some of that magic was finally going to rub off on Quint. If it let him stay on the team and get through school, he was willing to play along to anything Tanner and Davis had cooking.

Davis gave him a smile and a head nod when he finally reached them. "Yo, Quint, not bad for your first season."

Quint tried not to let it show, but his face grew warm under the praise despite the winter chill. Even though Davis came from a legacy family, he put in work at practice and on the field, and he was an amazing player in his own right. He didn't dole out praise too often, especially to an average freshman, so it felt good to hear. He simply nodded in response and said, "You too, man."

Tanner slapped him on the back. "You and me, brother, we're getting drafted to the Dallas Cowboys, don't you worry. Or, shit, the Patriots! You might as well go ahead and give them your ring size." Tanner wiggled his fingers in front of his face, flashing his own class ring he'd said cost him 20 shifts at 'the meanest Waffle House in Rome'. Quint rolled his eyes at the hyperbole. The most he was hoping for was a free degree and a job. Davis's indulgent smile seemed to confirm Quint's analysis.

Davis looked around furtively, then waved the two boys closer and dropped his voice down to a whisper. "Now that the season's over, I think it's time for your rite of passage."

The warmth Quint had been feeling moments before faded instantly. His folks had warned him about all this hazing nonsense, white boys beating on each other just to play power games. The coach had said that hazing was strictly forbidden, and the most he'd had to do was run drinks and clean uniforms, but the season was over now. No need to protect their precious bodies now. Tanner seemed to have the opposite reaction. His eyes lit up with the possibility of a new challenge.

Davis dropped his voice even lower. "There's this field the university owns, right outside the city," he murmured. "They use it to study dead bodies, like, people who've been murdered and left to rot outside. It's about 45 minutes from here. If y'all two get some pictures and come back with proof, you'll be a real Yellow Jacket. And...," he reached in his pocket and flashed a wad of bills, "I'll make it worth your while in other ways, too."

That caught Quint's attention. Even with his scholarship, food, clothes, and books weren't cheap. The way Tanner looked like he was about to vibrate out of his skin, he would have done it for a nickel and a stick of gum, but Quint needed that cash to push him past his reservations. He nodded and looked Davis in the eye.

"Bet. When we heading out?"

"Y'all can head out whenever you want," Davis answered. "Hell, y'all could head out right now if you want."

Tanner whooped and his hand once again thudded against Quint's back. "Easy money. We'll be there and back before you even know what to do with yourself."

Quint did not relish using his first real night of relaxation to take pictures of a bunch of dead people, but when Tanner was revved up there was no stopping him. He sighed, gave Davis a nod and said, "We'll text you the pics, I guess. There better not be no Walking Dead shit going on out there."

Davis just laughed and shook his head. "Come on, you ain't scared of a few dead people? They can't hurt you, only living folks do that."

He did have a point. Tanner had his chest puffed out but was looking back and forth at Quint and Davis, his eyes darting a little too fast. That boy was scared shitless and didn't want to be scared shitless by himself. Quint pondered whether he wanted to be out in the winter chill surrounded by dead bodies with an idiot, but the flash of all that cash wouldn't leave his mind. Cemeteries didn't scare him, so he figured it wouldn't make a difference whether the corpses were above ground or not. Plus, the cold would make the bodies stink less, which was his main concern.

Quint shrugged and put his half-drunk beer down. "Alright, let's ride."

Tanner grinned at Quint so wide he could see his molars. His grin quickly disappeared when Quint snatched the keys to his truck from his pocket and started heading towards the gate.

"No way, man, that's my baby," the running back complained, running to snatch his keys back.

"If you drive like this your baby's gonna wind up in a ditch. Sober up on our way there." Quint replied as he held the keys out of Tanner's reach, dangling them tauntingly. Tanner punched him in his shoulder and laughed, and he laughed too, despite himself. Maybe they'd be in and out, take a couple pictures and have a story to tell. At the very least, it was an easy way to get a chunk of change. Something about the way that Davis looked when he turned back, though, made him nervous. It wasn't smug satisfaction or pride or anything that he expected. He couldn't place it then, but later on, he knew exactly what it was.

Guilt.

~~~~~

The smell snuck up on them when they first walked in. No amount of money was enough to prepare Quint for that odor. It almost didn't even register as "bad" at first. The rotted sweetness wasn't pleasant, but it wasn't outright disgusting. His brain took a minute to process what it could be, but it clicked when he saw two gray feet lying inches from his right sneaker, mere yards from the front entrance. They were so small and withered they nearly got lost among the roots and plants surrounding them. The toenails were purple with little white stars, and tiny insects wandered over the painted constellations. A brown cloth covered the rest of the body, but the feet were enough to shock him out of autopilot. He jumped back, holding in a potentially embarrassing yelp as Tanner stumbled into his back, thrown by the sudden movement.

"Yo, what—" His complaint was cut short by Quint's finger pointing at their first body of the night.

They could only see its swollen gray feet sticking out from underneath the covering, but that was enough for Quint's stomach to lurch with nausea. This was not like seeing his mother at the funeral home when she had passed during his eighth grade year. He'd felt unsettled then, but the smell in combination with the waxen, rotting flesh made him turn cold. Tanner didn't take the sight much better. He looked completely pale, and the light from their flashlight didn't help his complexion.

Quint nudged him. "You good?"

Tanner shook a bit and drew himself up to his full height. "Yeah, just…let's just keep going. That one wouldn't make a very good pic." He pushes ahead, trying to affect a bravado Quint was sure he did not feel, and whipped out his phone.

Oh, right. They weren't just walking through this place for the hell of it. They needed the pictures. Quint got his beat-up iPhone 6 out and started scanning the bushes and trees for photogenic bodies. Some were what Quint had expected to see: gray skin, sightless eyes open in swollen slits, the earth beneath them damp and rancid with fluids. Others were a little more disturbing. There was more than one lonely limb strewn about, and some of the bodies seemed to be a little young to be included in such a morbid study. Insects crawled in and out of orifices, and they came across one body that had clearly had chunks taken out, the jagged edges of the wounds implying that some animal had taken a meal where it could.

Quint took as many pictures as he could stand to, and just as he'd had enough and was at the risk of losing his chicken wings and Coors, he heard Tanner call out to him in a quavering voice.

"Quint?" He called from a few yards away. "I think.... I think you should see this."

Quint was pretty sure he should not see "this", whatever "this" was. But curiosity overruled his good sense, and he stepped around the copse of trees to find Tanner standing over a body that was not like any they had seen that night. One, it was much paler than the others had been. Two, it was writhing. Hard.

"Nah."

Quint barely registered that he'd taken off towards the truck until he felt Tanner's hand clamp onto his shoulder. Quint shook it off and whirled on the smaller boy, fuming.

"What did I tell you?" he snapped, gesturing behind them at the bizarre corpse. "If any of these things move, I'm out! That looked like movement to me!"

"Hold on, man! It wasn't moving, like, *moving* moving" Tanner said. "I was like...come on, would you just *look*?"

Quint glared at Tanner for what seemed like a full five minutes, but the other boy didn't back down. Finally, he sighed and started towards the body. When he made it back over, he saw that Tanner was right; the body wasn't moving. Instead, it was covered in something that looked like small, undulating cotton tufts, each latched on to a tiny area of blackened skin. The coursing movement made it look like the body itself was moving, though it was still under the sea of fuzzy white. A small tag was attached to the body, the faintly glowing words written in a language Quint had never seen before. Something about the looping, anti-geometric script made him nearly as queasy as looking at the state of the body before them.

"Are those bugs or something?" Tanner asked, lining up his phone for a shot.

"How the hell should I know? All I know is I don't like looking at that shit," Quint scoffed. The sight of the bugs or whatever the hell those things made his own skin crawl. Something about those bugs seemed unnatural, like no insect that he had ever seen before, but he wasn't about to get close to investigate.

Much to Quint's chagrin, Tanner was already walking past the infected body and shining his flashlight further into the dark. Quint stormed over to drag him back by the arm if he had to, but the body that was illuminated in the flashlight's beam stopped him cold. From the shoulders up, he could tell that the body had once been a woman. It was the least corpse-like thing they'd seen all night, her skin a warm brown with no grey cast, salt-and-pepper braids fanned about her head, eyes respectfully closed. When the flashlight travelled further down, things started to go wrong. Her body wasn't just broken. It was shattered. It was as if someone had frozen her from the waist down and taken a mallet to her remains. Shards of rock hard flesh and bone were spread across the grass, catching the light of the flashlight like gory crystals. The sight of her petrified intestines brought Quint to his knees, and he crawled to a bush to retch.

"Tanner," he rasped, spitting and wiping his mouth with the back of a shaking hand. "Tanner, this is fucked up. Man, we have to go."

As he stood, he saw his teammate standing stock still, looking beyond a copse of trees. Tanner turned to look at him, his face ashen.

"Man...I don't think we're supposed to be here. I don't think anyone is supposed to be here."

Quint stumbled to his feet and walked shakily to Tanner's side. He grabbed the other boy's shoulder and opened his mouth to tell him once again that they needed to get out of there, but he gagged on the fetid air before he could get the words out. God, that smell. He could practically taste it now, coating his tongue and threatening to send him back into the bushes for another round of gagging. He turned to look at the source of the stench in the clearing and immediately regretted it more than he'd regretted anything in his life.

More bodies than he could count were arrayed in the middle of the clearing, spiraling towards the center in a deliberate arrangement that looked less scientific and more cult-like. Some were covered in tarps, some were not, but all were tagged with the same strange language he'd seen before. When it came to the bodies themselves, Quint hoped to God that whatever the hell had happened to their bodies wasn't what killed them.

A man's head split in half, a long red stalk unfurling from his ruined face like a sapling. A body elongated, twisted in a corkscrew pattern as if wrung out like a towel, bones jutting from the tortured skin. Another had limbs sprouting from joints in fractal patterns, arms and legs and fingers and toes fanned out like a fleshy seraph. The minute Quint's eyes landed on the face, he broke.

"Oh, *fuck* this."

He was about to tell Tanner that they were getting the hell up out of there in search of their truck, the cops and a good therapist, but just as he was about to open his mouth, he heard it.

Footsteps. Not the heavy, blundering footsteps of someone walking at a normal pace and going about their business. These were soft, light, and slow. Only the occasional shuffling of leaves gave away the rhythm of the gait. Quint turned to Tanner and put a finger to his lips. His teammate looked at him quizzically, but after a beat, his eyes widened with panic. The footsteps were coming from the direction of their truck, blocking their means of escape. Quint told himself that whoever was sneaking beyond the trees was just hoping to catch them unaware so it would make an arrest easier. He couldn't afford to think of his body warped and corrupted with the rest of the corpses on the ground. He needed to act. He needed to move.

Quint locked eyes with Tanner and jerked his head. The other boy nodded and they began to walk in tandem in the opposite direction. More grotesque shapes spotted the ground in his peripheral vision, but he couldn't afford to look, nor could he bear it. The pace of the footsteps changed as theirs did, from a slow creep to a quick shuffle. Whoever or whatever it was, it was gaining on them, and fast. Tanner cut Quint a wide-eyed look, and Quint just nodded in return. The two boys broke into a run, and as the footsteps behind them burst into a flurry of rapid motion, Quint made the mistake of looking back.

It took Quint longer than it should have to register that the thing chasing them wasn't human. Its gangly body was covered in what looked like a tightly fitting hazmat suit that was a dark enough green to blend into the forest that surrounded them. Gray mesh covered the area where the face would be. The long, thin arms and legs would have been unsettling enough on their own, just stretched just beyond human proportions, but the giveaway was the neck. It was nearly as long as one of its arms, and it undulated as it ran, though the head remained fixed in place, intent on its prey. It held some kind of long, metal object in its hand, the end sparking with blue electricity. Quint didn't know what that thing was, and he had no intention of finding out.

Quint's legs pumped as hard as he could possibly make them. He was fast, but Tanner was leaving him in the dust, and that thing was drawing closer and closer with each stride. He barely registered that he was crying, the wind whipping away the moisture on his face. He just had to keep going. They would make it to the other side, they would make it to a building with people, human people, they would—

A burst of searing pain hit him in the center of his back. He went down hard, his body too limp to even throw up his arms to protect himself. His head slammed into the earth, his vision whiting out before fading into a hazy darkness. In his semi-conscious state, he could hear the footsteps of the pursuer rushing past him in hot pursuit of its other quarry.

Quint lay still on the forest floor, fighting nausea, agony and oblivion all at once. He dug deep, deep into the place that had finished punishing drills, that had toppled boys bigger than him, that had fought to have a life. The smell of moss, dirt and rot threatened to make him gag, but he shakily breathed in and out, focusing on his stuttering heartbeat.

Get up.

His eyes opened, and he found himself staring into the eyes of another boy, one that looked like he had been around his age.

His face was twisted in a grimace, teeth bared and cracked, the gums receded so much that many had fallen out and littered the ground before him. The body this head was attached to looked like it had been manually flattened and covered in a gray, chitinous crust. Judging by the expression, the boy had been alive when it happened.

Get UP.

Quint tried to move his limbs, but they wouldn't obey him. He let out a scream of frustration, but even that only managed to be a whimper. His silent companion looked on as he struggled, impassive as he barely managed to twitch his finger. And then, in the distance, a flash of light, a shock, and a scream.

Tanner.

GET UP. GET UP. GET UP.

He didn't have much time. He used everything he had at his disposal: prayers, curses, bargains, DMX lyrics, the voice of his coach, the voice of his grandmother. One finger twitch turned to two, which turned to the turn of his wrist, which turned to hope. His legs began to burn, which was an improvement over not feeling them at all. Then the sound of those footsteps again. Slow but not creeping. It was taking its time. And the footsteps weren't alone. There was a dragging sound now, too.

GET UP! GET UP! GET UP! GET UP! GET UP! GET UP! GET UP!

The empty eyes of the former boy looked mocking now. The only thing in Quint's body that seemed to be fully functioning were his tear ducts, which were overflowing as he twitched on the ground, helpless before the approaching monster. He could feel his movement returning little by little, but as he moved his body, he could hear the footsteps slow. The thing was hesitant now. Wary.

Oh. Wait.

Quint went still. He breathed lightly, making sure his chest didn't rise. He barely even rustled the grass right in front of his nose. He assumed the position: mouth slightly open, eyes cracked and unseeing, limbs limp. A huge lump of dead weight. The thing picked up its speed again, its confidence returning. Through his open eyes, Quint could see that damn prod

swinging by its side as its disgusting neck leaned over him to inspect the handiwork. In its triumph, it swung it a bit too close.
Now.

Quint moved like a flash. He curled his legs under him and shot across the ground towards the prod, grabbing it with both hands. The thing tightened its grip and tried to wrestle it from him, but even in his weakened state, Quint was still the powerhouse. He stumbled to his feet, ignoring the pain, the way the change in position threatened to make him black out again, the sight of Tanner limp and bleeding out of the corner of his eye.

The thing whipped its long neck and slammed its head on top of Quint's, temporarily making him see stars. His death grip on the prod only tightened, and the next time the head came around, Quint twisted it and jabbed hard at the incoming blow. The move knocked the mesh on the helmet askew, and Quint instantly realized why the thing had been so damn quiet the entire time.

The mesh, and by extension the whole suit, was soundproof. The minute the mesh slipped, a horrible screech like a pitched-up jet engine ripped through the quiet of the night. Quint buckled to his knees, the sound knocking him nearly as senseless as a successful hit would have. His grip on the prod loosened and the thing yanked it from his hands, still making that hellish sound. He could hear it charge as he crouched on the ground, barely able to move. Just as the rod began to swing down, he made a wild play. He reached for the flattened body next to him and held it up, blocking the shock that was meant for him.

Quint still felt the jolt, but whatever had coated the poor boy next to him had the benefit of not being a conductor. He staggered to his feet, angled his shoulder, and rammed into the prod-wielding freak with all his strength. He swore the thing *squeaked* as it hit the ground. Once it was down, Quint didn't even hesitate. He jumped up and landed on the thing's neck with both feet. He felt a crunch as the scream was cut off, the body twitching wildly for the brief moment before it stilled. Quint stood there, breathing hard, still holding his grim shield in his hands, not quite believing what he had just done.

Quint snapped back to reality when he remembered that the thing had been dragging Tanner with him. He tossed the body aside and crouched next to him. The boy was bloody, the side of his face scraped raw and gouged by the debris of the forest floor. Quint gently turned his head, and Tanner's neck lolled to reveal a dent in his skull above his right temple. He was still in a way that Quint had seen too many times that night.

"No, no, no, dammit, no!" Quint yelled, voice straining as he shook him. He checked his pulse and his breathing, but there was nothing. He didn't know how he had tears left, but there they were again, making tracks through the blood and grime on his face. A flash of light in the distance caught his eye. A spark, much like the one that had come from the end of the thing's prod, flashed somewhere deep in the farm. Another flashed a few yards to the left of it. Still another flashed, this one to the right, and closer. Much closer. There was nothing to be done. He had to run.

Quint looked down at the body of his first college friend and choked back a sob. He reached down and squeezed his rapidly cooling hand, sending out one last prayer to someone, anyone, to help him survive this. Then he got up, grabbed the prod, and ran like he never had during practice, like he never had in his life. By the time his body hit the side of Tanner's truck and he pulled his shaking body inside, there was no sign of the monsters. Only the light on the side of the gate flashed, the only witness to his narrow escape.

EIGHT MONTHS LATER

Quint pulled up to the decrepit brick building in his battered Nissan. He climbed out and opened the door emblazoned with the words "Georgia Tech Forensic Anatomy Research Office" to the sound of merry bells. A woman with red lipstick and an infinity scarf smiled wide as he came through the door.

"Morning, Quint!" she chirped. "You ready to get started?"

"Sure," he murmured, leaning over the low desk to sign in. He always found the sound of her voice to be a bit grating, especially this early. The sun had only just risen when he left his town to begin his first part-time job. A professor standing just beyond the desk noisily slurped on his coffee and nodded at Quint, spilling a bit of the liquid on the scarf around his own neck. Quint nodded back, fighting the feeling of unease he had to battle every Saturday when he interacted with the staff here. The man smirked a bit before returning to his cup, his eyes never lowering. Quint had peered over his shoulder once to find him writing something in a strange, looping language unlike anything he'd ever seen. Accompanying the writing were anatomical images of bodies, dissected for the purposes of scientific interest. The pictures of bulbous larvae and plants spreading wildly in dizzying fractals may have had something to do with them, but the notebook was snatched away before he could tell, and he was met with the same set of eyes that pierced into him now. For his own sanity, Quint decided not to follow up. He was no hero, after all.

After that night, the cops had been suspicious. Two boys leaving a party and only one coming back driving the truck of the missing half of the duo draws a little attention from the APD. He told them they had been attacked by some psycho with a cattle prod at the body farm, leaving out just enough detail to make himself seem sane. Every time he pointed his finger at the body farm, whatever cop he was talking to would just frown and nod, jotting something down his notepad, but not much. He only went through two rounds of questioning, and after that, the investigation stopped cold. No follow-up calls, no missing person posts on social media, no nothing. It was like everyone forgot Tanner even existed. Quint tried and tried in vain to reach out to Davis, but he kept his eyes down and mouth shut, until Quint finally gave up, disgusted. He went on to win that Heisman and was making headlines as an up-and-coming QB for the Dallas Cowboys. He had always been a good player, but Quint couldn't help but wonder if his success was paid in blood.

Then, at the end of the school year, the letters arrived. In it was some bad news about Quint's scholarship, some warnings about his "previous questionable night-time activities" and a fat wad of cash. The letter tucked right next to it extended an offer for a part-time university job, should he want to secure his position on the team and at the school. They made it very clear: this or return to Manchester. The decision was simple. That didn't make it any less hard.

Quint pulled on his white protective suit, grabbed his tape measure and cattle prod and walked out into the field. The morning dew sparkled in the soft September sun as it settled on grass, leaves and mottled skin alike. He walked past the now familiar gruesome sights with a notebook in his hand, jotting down the minute changes that had happened since he'd last been in the field. He worked through his route methodically, marking off the bodies in their respective locations, going through the motions, until he arrived at a place that felt a bit familiar to him. He looked to see the corpse that had saved him last year, eyes no longer wide and staring but jellied and collapsing, the graying, wispy hair barely clinging to tight brown skin. The carapace surrounding the rest of the body looked the same. If anything, it looked even shinier, though it could be because he was seeing it in the light of day.

Another body lay nearby. Other than the tarp covering most of his body, he was in the exact same position as he'd been in that night. Sneakers still on his feet, class ring still on his finger. The area under the tarp, however, suggested that other things had happened in the course of the past year. The surface was lumpy and warped, and Quint thought he saw slow, shifting movement beneath the cover. His fingers went numb as the clipboard in his hand shook. This was his last body of the day, matching the final number on his chart. Quint understood now that he hadn't just been given this job just to keep him quiet. He still remembered that feeling, the crunch underneath his shoes. It was clear that whoever, or whatever worked at the body farm offices remembered it, too. Maybe he would have gone down swinging if he knew that survival had a price to pay. Quint was no hero, but maybe he would have been, if he'd known that cowardice came with its own cost.

Slowly, carefully, Quint lifted the tarp.

VANTABLACK
BY
BALOGUN OJETADE

One

The campus was getting dark, lit only by the dim lights in the yard of the AUC. Dhoruba hit the walkway of Scholars Landing and headed toward the lab. By the time he'd walked a block, Atlanta was already falling into shadow, the city lights igniting to battle the darkness.

"Looks like it'll be a foggy night," Cynt said as she walked up from behind him to stare out at the growing darkness. "Not a good time to be a pilot."

"Crazy," Dhoruba said. "Even though we're landlocked." He smiled. "And we aren't near any mountains to cause cold air drainage."

"Aw shit, somebody's about to go full nerd on me," Cynt shook her head and ran a hand through her curly, black afro.

"Not full nerd," Dhoruba said. "Nerds don't rock locks like these." He shook his head like a supermodel in a diabetes medicine commercial. *May cause loss of hearing, erectile disfunction and constant body odor,* he thought.

"You need to trim 'em," Cynt said, pointing at the top of Dhoruba's chest, where the end of his locks rested. "How long do you want them to get? I know Mr. and Mrs. Akoli don't approve."

"Dad's cool," Dhoruba said. "Mom's the one that's trippin'; says I won't get a high paying job, like a good Uncle Tom, if I keep them."

"Well, you are a nerd," Cynt said. "Just a pretty one. But be careful. Atlanta can be dangerous for pretty boys from Missouri, especially at night."

"What, you worried about me, Cynt?" Dhoruba asked with a smile. "You've been giving me this speech since I was a little freshie!"

"Well, you're a little sophomore, and it's my role as an AT-Lien and your Big to ensure that you don't die." The young

155

woman put one hand to her chest and let out an exaggerated sigh. "Because then I'd have to do all of the dirty work in the lab myself."

Dhoruba chuckled. "You've got that right. Speaking of that, let's get to the lab before we end up late, and Professor Davis murders us both."

They walked briskly up the walkway toward the lab.

"He wouldn't do that," Cynt said. "Where would he get his free labor?"

"If we're late, we're not working, so maybe he'll find some students who aren't late?" Dhoruba said.

"Good point," Cynt said. "We wouldn't want to get fired from our unpaid job." Cynt rolled her eyes and opened the door to the laboratory. Dhoruba darted in. Cynt never let him open the door for her. Not because she was some kind of ultra-feminist... she had caught him checking out her booty once and never trusted him to hold the door for her again.

"I'm a sophomore. That means we're lucky to have anything." Dhoruba went over to the closet to grab his lab coat. "And remember, I am getting paid through work study. This lab job is why I don't have to share a room with four other people."

"Sharing a dorm room can be fun," Cynt said, checking her phone for any messages.

"Not if you're trying to get work done," Dhoruba told her. "One roommate is enough."

Cynt smirked. "Well, let's get to work."

The "work" was checking the various samples from the "city below the city" – Atlanta's Underground – with the records and ensuring that they had the right sample in the right case.

All because someone else decided to goof off on the job. Or at least that was the rumor. Since some sample cases hadn't been opened for decades, Dhoruba expected that the culprits had gotten away with it.

"Oh great," Cynt said. "Limestone in a case listed for some meteoric iron. Yeah, someone worked hard at their class for that." She started writing up the new tag—which would then have to go to Woodruff Library so they could scan it into the online catalog. Dhoruba had no idea why they couldn't do everything electronically, but nope, writing it was.

Dhoruba nodded, staring down at his open case. This one held what the label said, fragments of meteoric iron, some of them hammered into old arrowheads. "Hard to believe people have been digging up this stuff for a thousand years."

"Why not?" Cynt asked. "A gigantic asteroid hits the land even before it was called Terminus, but by some coincidence it doesn't hit hard enough to destroy the Earth and it's shallow enough that people could dig up chunks of pure iron before anyone could make iron from raw ore." She opened another case and held up a fist-sized piece of iron. "And even after they could, it was a long time before anyone could match this quality outside of West Africa."

Conversation lagged as the two worked in silence. Most of the samples were correctly filed, but enough weren't that the piles of replacement paperwork grew by Dhoruba's side. About halfway through their shift, Cynt yawned and got up.

"I'm going to get some coffee. The first-floor canteen should be open." Cynt glanced over at Dhoruba. "Want any?"

"Hot chocolate," Dhoruba said.

Cynt snorted. "Aight, I'll fetch the hard stuff for you."

Dhoruba laughed as Cynt left. She certainly wasn't a coffee snob, but she loved her cup o' Joe. But neither coffee nor hot chocolate would get his work done.

***

As Dhoruba kept going through the sample cases, he found one that was old. Ancient, by the looks of it. He carefully pulled the tag off and the paper started to crumble in his hands.

Limestone samples. Dhoruba fiddled with the case's lock. After several attempts to open it, he growled in frustration and grabbed a screwdriver to pry the case open.

"Lovely," Dhoruba muttered. "Somebody probably left you right under a leak in the roof." He bore down on the lock and pried it off the decrepit box. Then he stuck the screwdriver's head between the lid and the body, pressing down as hard as he could. There was resistance for a second, and then it just flew open.

Unfortunately, Dhoruba had been putting his weight into it. When the lid came loose, he lost his balance and pushed the case across the top of the wooden lab table... and over the other side.

"Shit!" Dhoruba flung himself over the table, trying to grab the case. *If I destroy a sample, I'll never hear the end of it*—his thoughts screeched to a halt as he saw what was inside the case as it tumbled to the ground. It was a sphere, so black that it seemed to pull the light from the very air. He hadn't seen anything like it before. And then it hit the floor...

And shattered.

Suddenly, Dhoruba was plunged into darkness. It was like the orb had devoured every bit of light in the room. He clawed at the darkness, some tiny part of his mind wondering how mere darkness could have mass, could resist his frantic attempts to free himself. Then he felt something going up his nose—Dhoruba tried to scream, but no sound emerged as he collapsed to the floor, the tile cool under his body as he sank into the darkness...

***

"Dhoruba? Dhoruba!" Dhoruba blinked. It was Cynt's voice. He opened his eyes and saw his Big's worried face looking down at him.

"Cynt..." Dhoruba stared up at Cynt. "What are you doing up there?"

"What are you doing down *there*?" Cynt asked. "Are you okay? I found you on the floor when I came in, along with an empty box."

"I..." Dhoruba frowned as he looked around. The room seemed uncomfortably bright. "Is it daytime?"

"What?" Cynt asked. "How hard did you hit your head, fool? Maybe we should go to the health office."

"I...No." Dhoruba shook his head. He held out his hand, and Cynt took it, helping him to his feet. The windows were still dark, but the lights were bright. Too bright.

How is that possible? The lights had two settings, on or off. He'd had no trouble at all with them when he'd walked in, but now... He blinked again and looked down to the ground to keep the painful glare out of his eyes.

"What happened?"

Dhoruba frowned. "The box. It was jammed shut, and when I opened it, I accidentally pushed it over the edge." He shook his head. "And there was nothing in it, so I almost fractured my skull for the sake of some lazy student who couldn't even be bothered to put the wrong thing in it. He probably figured nobody would ever check." Why am I lying? It wasn't like Cynt would care.

On the other hand, she might, especially if Dhoruba started talking about rocks that devoured the light and then vanished. Cynt might care enough to refer him to the Morehouse Medical psych ward, which might decide that a crazy man didn't need to be a college student. And he really didn't want to go back to Ferguson, Missouri. Not to a town who's claim to fame was the brutal murder of 18-year-old Michael Brown by police officer Darren Wilson. His memories of the riots that followed, the protests, and the National Guard now had a feeling of revulsion about them.

"Let's get you onto the stool," Cynt said and helped Dhoruba up. "You must have taken a hell of a fall." She shook her head. "Are you sure you don't want to get checked out?

"I'll... I'll just leave early and get some rest," Dhoruba said. "Can you cover for me?"

Cynt frowned. "I think I should walk you back to your room. I—"

"Ms. Johnson, Mr. Akoli, may I ask why you are not working?"

Shit. Dhoruba looked up to see his professor standing in the open door. Dr. Milton Davis was not popular with his students. Stooped over, his gray hair thinning with age, Dhoruba figured that the main reason Dr. Davis taught lab was that the college mandated that all science professors teach at least one lab class.

It wasn't because he liked the students.

159

"Sorry, Professor Davis," Cynt said. "I think Dhoruba passed out for a few minutes."

"Really?" Davis stared at the empty box. "And did this have anything to do with a missing sample?"

"There wasn't anything in it," Dhoruba said. "It had a label for some limestone samples, but I guess someone either stole it or just forgot to include the sample."

"I see." Professor Davis stared at Dhoruba for a moment. "A locked box... for limestone. Curious." He bent down and picked it up. "And this corrosion isn't what I'd expect..."

"I figure it was stored under a leak." Dhoruba winced as he touched his head. *Why am I lying? Oh, right. Professor Davis would never let me back in here if he found out I lost something unusual. For that matter, he might think that I really had stolen something...*

Well, he might also decide that Dhoruba was nuts.

Davis frowned at the box and shook his head. "I should expect such idiocy from students and interns, no matter when they attended this school. You are dismissed for the day, Mr. Akoli. Ms. Johnson, you can remain here, unless Mr. Akoli requires..."

"No," Dhoruba said. "No, I'm alright. I'll just go back to my room and rest for a while."

"Very good," Dr. Davis said, looking down his nose at him.

"You sure?" Cynt asked.

"Yeah—sorry to leave you alone here."

"It's fine," Cynt told him. "Maybe the air in the box was bad. You probably got a big whiff of it, and that was enough to knock you out."

"Yeah. Maybe." Dhoruba nodded as he pulled the lab coat off and hung it up. "I'm sorry, Professor."

"Yes. Be certain to notify the secretary if you cannot make classes tomorrow." Without waiting for his response, Professor Davis turned and left the room, still holding the box.

"What an asshole," Cynt said once Professor Davis's steps faded away. "You're certain you don't need some help?"

"I'm fine," Dhoruba said, running a hand through his hair. "It was probably just weakness brought on by your delay in returning with the life-giving brew I needed."

"Right." Cynt turned to where she'd put the drinks down and handed Dhoruba the warm paper cup. "Here you go. Use it to regain your health, like Popeye with his spinach!"

Dhoruba laughed, pulling the lid off of the cup and inhaling the lovely scent of hot chocolate. "I will. And man, you and those old cartoons." He shook his head.

"Seriously, if you don't feel better tomorrow, get your ass to the doctor."

"I will, Cynt." Dhoruba smiled. "For real for real."

Two

By the time Dhoruba got to his dorm room, the light was nearly intolerable. Every streetlight blazed like the noonday sun, forcing him to shade his eyes and stumble around like he was half-blind. Fortunately, the clouds were rolling in, dimming the lights, and blocking out the moon. He dashed through the door into the lobby just as the first fat droplets of rain started to fall onto his head.

Dhoruba ran his fingers through his damp locks, then winced and closed his eyes at the glare from the lobby's lights.

"You're back early," Anaiah, the residential adviser said, glancing up from her textbook. "You okay?"

"Yeah, just have a headache," Dhoruba said. "I'm going to go lay down for a while."

"You're in luck," Anaiah told her. "Derek's still out, so you can get some sleep."

"New girlfriend? Boyfriend?" Dhoruba asked, wincing at the way the light just seemed to drive into his skull.

"New girlfriend. Gon' off to bed," Anaiah told him. "You look like crap."

"Thanks." I feel like crap. Dhoruba walked down the hallway and up the stairs, looking away from the bright lights. He fumbled for his keys, thankful that most of his fellow students were studying for tomorrow, at late classes, or in the cafeteria. Dhoruba doubted he would have been able to get any sleep if this had happened on the weekend. He opened the door, staggered into his dorm, and closed the door behind him.

The lights were off. Normally, Dhoruba would be fumbling around, cursing whoever forgot to leave a night light on.

But now, he could see. Even better, it didn't hurt his eyes. Dhoruba walked to the window and looked down into the neighborhood that surrounded the AUC. A shroud of fog and rain concealed most of the city. Skyscrapers loomed out of the fog like they were flipping the bird to the rest of the Atlanta.

Pretty, Dhoruba thought. He'd always liked the view, but now there was something oddly comforting about how the city just seemed to sleep under its foggy blanket. Down there, even the streetlights would be barely visible, everyone walking along in their own little isolated world, protected from the light.

Safe.

He shook his head and walked back to the bed, toppling over onto the sheets, the fabric soft against his body. His headache was fading away, his eyes were fine, and now he could get some sleep.

***

Dhoruba slowly sat up in bed, looking around. He was still wearing his clothes, and it was still night. He could tell that from the clock. But he could see perfectly, even though…

"But the lights are out," Dhoruba murmured. Now that his headache was gone, he could think about that. Yesterday, the lights had been out, and he had stumbled around in the pitch-dark room. Now he could see like it was broad daylight, even if the colors seemed to be muted. Subtler. Dhoruba stood up and closed his eyes. He could also feel the shadows, the darkness in the room. Feel them, almost as if they were becoming… Dhoruba opened his eyes and then let out a tiny shriek as he saw the rising, twisting shadows. They didn't feel like a hallucination.

They felt real.

As Dhoruba scrambled back, the shadows dove for him, touching him and spreading across his clothes and body.

"Stop it!" he cried out.

And they stilled.

What the hell? He looked at the mirror. He was wearing the shadows. Dhoruba held his hand up to his face. He could feel the shadows in his mind, almost like they were part of him. He closed his hand and then focused on the shadows that covered his skin.

I want to see my hand. There was a bit of resistance to his command. It was like he wasn't doing something right. But then the liquid shadow rolled back down to his wrist, leaving his hand bare.

"Well, you're not eating me," he muttered. "What is this?"

No answer. Dhoruba held out his hand again and focused. "I want a drop." It took a while, but finally, a droplet of shadow appeared in his palm. Dhoruba held it up to his face and stared at it. It was darkness. Darkness but...

"But you have substance." Dhoruba said, focusing on the droplet. Moments later, it had become a pencil, or at least the shape of a pencil, the material still that triple-black shadow-stuff. He touched it with his free hand, and it was solid, like a pencil. Then he relaxed his will, and the shadowy material turned back into a wisp of darkness that was absorbed into the shadows covering his body.

Why am I not panicking? Dhoruba assumed that the natural result of being covered in some strange material would be to scream and run around the room. Possibly flailing his arms. But definitely screaming.

Except he wasn't. He wasn't unconcerned, but there was something about the shadow that just seemed normal. Like it was a part of him.

"Like it's a part of me."

"Hey, Dhoruba, I'm back!" the muffled shout from the hallway was accompanied by the sound of a key in the lock. Derek's key.

Shit. Dhoruba frantically looked around. The room was covered in shadow, he was covered in shadow, and—Dhoruba took a deep breath.

Go away! Dhoruba commanded.

But they didn't go away. At least, not like he had wanted them to. Suddenly the shadows seemed to just flow into

Dhoruba's body, sinking into his skin. Other shadows seemed to vanish into the corners of the room, leaving it looking dim, but at least it was a natural kind of dim. Even worse, he could still feel the shadows roiling just under his skin.

Dhoruba checked to see if there was anything incriminating in sight, then nodded as he heard the front door open.

"Dhoruba?" Derek called again.

"In here!" he called back as he walked to the bedroom door.

The moment Dhoruba pulled the door open, he winced at the blaze of light from the front room. Both the ceiling light and the table lamp were on. The light just spiked straight into his brain.

"What's with keeping the place dark?" Derek asked as he paused by the windows and stared out at the fog-covered city. "I know you like the whole foggy look, but isn't this going a little far?" He looked back at Dhoruba with a smile.

Dhoruba suppressed a moment of envy. Dhoruba might be handsome, but Derek De la Cruz was *foine*.

"I... I had a really bad headache," Dhoruba said. "I figured it would go away if I just got a little sleep, and the light was hurting my eyes."

"What? Shit!" Derek hit the switch, and the ceiling light died. "I wish you would have called me. I could have picked up some aspirin from the store."

"I don't think it's that kind of headache," Dhoruba told his friend. "It'll just go away by itself."

"If you say so, but if you have it tomorrow, go to the doctor."

"Why is everybody telling me to do that?"

"I don't know," Derek said. He brushed his hair, smoothing out a break in the waves. "Maybe, it's because of your famous 'I'm feeling okay, I'm just, cough, gag, wheeze, fart!' event."

Dhoruba blushed. "That was one time."

"What about the food poisoning incident?"

"Okay...twice."

Derek shook his finger in Dhoruba's direction. "So don't hesitate to go see a doctor."

"I can't lose this lab..."

"And you won't, because even an asshole like Dr. Davis won't hit you for this, especially given that you're acing every other class," Derek said.

"Derek," Dhoruba fought the temptation to giggle, "Professor Davis is—"

"An asshole. He barely tolerates his own students and makes it plain that he's the smartest person in the room, even if he isn't. Or were you lying to me during that rant?"

"No, I wasn't." Dhoruba shook his head. "I thought you were going to be out all night?"

"So did I, but my date had something come up," Derek said.

"What?"

"She double-booked, and her other most important man in her life ran into us. I decided to leave the lovebirds before hands started to get thrown."

Only Derek. "I—"

"Is it me, or is the light getting dimmer? Dammit, I thought they fixed the wiring." Derek muttered, turning away from Dhoruba, and pulling out his phone, likely to send a complaint to the maintenance people.

Dhoruba stared at Derek in horror. The light from the table lamp was dimming, but not because of the current...

Dhoruba glanced down at the floor and realized that his shadow was darker than it should be. Worse, it seemed to be moving of its own accord. He could feel the shadows under the bed, rising up, desiring to quench that annoying light, so they could be free.

They didn't like hiding, especially when there was light around, or at least light they could quench. No! He didn't know what he did, but the shadows seemed to fade back. His shadow only looked a little darker and the lamp once again blazed in all of its annoying glory.

Dhoruba glanced at Derek. If he sees... "Derek, I'm going to go lay back down and try to sleep it off."

"Fine." Derek nodded. "But if this lasts until tomorrow, I'm tying you up and taking you to the hospital."

Dhoruba nodded and retreated to his room. All the lights were still off, not that he had a hard time seeing. The moment he closed the door, the shadows came rushing back from the surrounding air, while some others just seemed to explode from his body. Some curled in the air around Dhoruba, their forms oddly solid, a liquid blackness where their skin should be.

"Shit," Dhoruba said. "What if he comes in?"

Forget Derek coming in, what if I lose my focus in class?

Dhoruba took a deep breath, then another. Closed his eyes. He could feel the surrounding shadows. He'd told them to go away, and they had, but here they seemed to be stronger. Dhoruba sat down and called the shadows to him. Or at least he felt like he was calling them. He felt them rolling onto his body, covering him in a second skin. Then he opened his eyes and stared at the reflected image of his body.

He was covered in the night-black material, coiling shadows swirling around his body. Dhoruba figured that anyone who opened the door probably wouldn't be able to see a thing.

So they'd open the door and see a room filled with living, hungry darkness. That was so much better.

Dhoruba tried to pull the shadows back into his body like he had when Derek had come in. He felt a strange sensation of resistance, and then the room cleared of the unnatural darkness, the shadows coiling around him then sinking into his skin.

Now stay there! Dhoruba thought as he lay down on the bed, pulling the covers over his body.

I should stay awake. Just in case.

Just in...

Before he could finish the sentence, Dhoruba was asleep.

***

"Dhoruba? Are you going to classes today, or do you need to go to the doctor?" Derek's voice caused Dhoruba to shoot upright in bed. He looked around, blinking at the bright light from the...

Overcast morning.

Normally, he'd be fumbling for the light on the table by the bed, but now the room was just barely short of uncomfortably bright.

"Dhoruba?" Now Derek sounded concerned.

"I'm—I'm okay! Just forgot to set my alarm."

"You sure?" The door opened, revealing a freshly showered Derek, already dressed in one of his fashionable outfits. "Wow, you didn't even put on your pajamas? You must have been really out of it!"

"Yeah," Dhoruba brushed his tangled locks back into some semblance of order. "I really was. I'll head out after I take a shower."

"Don't forget to eat!" Derek said, then paused. "Do you want me to stick around?"

"Nah," Dhoruba told Derek. "I'm fine."

Derek didn't look convinced but finally nodded. "Okay."

The moment the door closed, Dhoruba took a deep, shuddering breath, and then squeaked in shock when he saw a moving shadow slither from under the bed.

"You hid under the bed?" he asked the shadow. There was no answer, and it seemed to dissipate into the air.

Great. I'm talking to magic shadows! Dhoruba waited until he heard the door close behind Derek. Then he stomped out of the bedroom, pulling his clothes off as he went into the shower. On the way in, he turned off the lights, the soothing darkness making it easier to navigate around the room.

Fortunately, when Dhoruba turned up the shower, he found that his new issues didn't hurt his ability to enjoy a hot shower, so he leaned into the steaming spray and just sat there, trying to understand what had happened.

Okay, so a spherical rock vanishes, and suddenly I have shadows that do what I say, at least some of the time. And I can see in the dark. What the hell…

He inhaled, holding the air in for a moment before he exhaled. "I can worry about this tonight," Dhoruba finally said. "But I need to keep going to class." Classes were normal. Classes were ordinary.

He could do for some normal right now.

Dhoruba turned off the shower, dried off, and went to get dressed.

On the bright side, nobody is going to be bitching about me wasting electricity by leaving the lights on.

He dressed in a jeans and sweater combo, grabbing his leather jacket from the closet. The morning looked chilly, and the clothes should make it easier to hide any errant shadows. With that, Dhoruba grabbed his backpack and headed out into the uncomfortably bright hallway where he joined the throng of late-awakening students.

As he left the building, Dhoruba realized two things.

First, the hallway lights were dimming, not by much, but it was noticeable to him as he passed them.

Secondly, it was really bright outside. The sun was covered by a thick mass of clouds, the moisture in the air hinting at rain later in the day, but to Dhoruba, it was as bright as a cloudless summer day. Blinking the tears out of his eyes, Dhoruba made his way to the college store. Once inside, he winced at the bright LED lights blazing down from the ceiling.

"Got any sunglasses?" Dhoruba asked the bored clerk.

The guy looked up from his textbook and blinked in surprise. "Today?"

"Yeah," Dhoruba said. He glanced out the window at the dark clouds and shook his head. "I had an appointment with the optometrist. You know, the one where they put the drops in your eyes—"

"Oh damn, yeah. They're supposed to give you those little paper sunglasses, but they didn't, did they?"

Dhoruba shook his head. "Nope! So I've gotta buy a pair."

"Hang on," he said, vanishing into the storeroom. Dhoruba heard the clerk go rummaging through some boxes. "We never stock 'em except in the summer, so..." There was a pause. "Found a pair!"

He came back out, holding the pair of sunglasses. "I think these will be on the house. They don't have a price tag, and I don't want to have to go dig the stock number up." He stared at the big, lime green sunglasses with tiny leprechauns in the upper corners of the frame and shook his head. "Besides, you're paying enough just wearing them."

Dhoruba stared in disbelief at the glasses.

You've got to be kidding me. I—Dhoruba glanced outside and winced at how bright it was. "They're... unusual," he finally said, trying to sound like he really was thankful for the atrocity he'd just been handed.

The clerk shrugged, looking apologetic. "No problem. Good news, tonight when your eyes go back to normal, you can toss 'em into the trash."

"Yeah... Thanks." Dhoruba put the sunglasses on and sighed in relief as the dark lenses brought the light down to more tolerable levels.

Hopefully, he'd make it through the day without a headache.

Three

For the rest of the day, Dhoruba felt like he was a passenger on a slowly sinking ship. Everyone stared at his glasses, and Dhoruba had to use the eye doctor excuse several times. He could see just fine, the dark glasses keeping the glare down to a reasonable level. But even so, his eyes itched from the light. Thunder started grumbling, the sound muffled by the walls of the building, but at least Dhoruba wouldn't have to worry about the sun. When summer hit, he probably would have to walk around with welding goggles on his face.

I need to find out what's wrong with me. People just didn't gain... powers. Shadows didn't just start to move and change. He managed to sit through the last class before lunch, American History 300, and after an interminable time spent talking about the growing tensions before the Civil War, escaped from the brightly lit auditorium.

Outside, the wind blew, fat drops of rain spattering against the windows as Dhoruba pushed the door open. Other students were rushing to get inside, complaining, and struggling with their umbrellas. It didn't feel bad at all to Dhoruba. The heavy cloud cover was a blessing, finally letting him take the glasses off and stick them into his pocket, while the cool air and rain felt refreshing.

But then, he'd always liked the rain. Still, Dhoruba needed answers. And the best place to get them was...

Professor Davis. Joy. With that cheerful thought, Dhoruba turned and walked to the science lab, the rain cool upon his face. *What am I going to ask him?*

Dhoruba pulled the door open, the interior's warm air stifling after the outside chill. He sighed and stepped inside, the heavy glass door closing just as another flash of lightning illuminated the world, moments before the rumble of thunder shook the building.

The lightning isn't as bad as the interior lights. I wonder why? Maybe because it's just a flash of light? Dhoruba didn't know, but he hoped that he would find out. Putting his ridiculous sunglasses back on, he started for the office.

Like most senior faculty, Milton Davis had a secretary. The older woman stared up at Dhoruba, raising her eyebrows as she took in the lime green leprechaun sunglasses.

"My eyes," Dhoruba said. "They're sensitive to light, and this is all the store had."

"Better you than me," Dr. Davis's secretary replied. "By the way, he's in a mood."

"I—" Dhoruba fell silent as he heard voices from the inner office.

"It is not my job to manage your family affairs, Ms. Brown. If the dean wishes to excuse you, I will have to allow you to take the exam at a later date. However, I see no reason why you should expect him to provide that excuse merely because your brother is in the hospital."

Moments later, a crying freshman ran from the inner office, ignoring Dhoruba and the secretary as she escaped into the hallway.

Great.

"Professor, Dhoruba Akoli is here to see you," the secretary called through the open door.

"Of all the—yes, of course I have nothing better to do with my time. Send him in."

With a nervous smile, Dhoruba marched into the office.

Dhoruba had been to Davis's office once or twice before. It looked the same as always. One wall full of certifications and

academic awards, two walls loaded down with books and journals.

Dhoruba never failed to notice how impersonal the office
was. No family pictures, no awards unrelated to his profession.
Nothing.

He sometimes wondered if Davis even had a home, or if he
just turned himself off every night.

"Mr. Akoli, what are those ridiculous things?"

"Sorry, Professor, but my eyes are really light sensitive for
some reason, and I can't stand the inside lights."

"Are you requesting a leave from your lab work?"

"Ah, no! I should be fine by next week," Dhoruba said.

"Good. That remains 20 percent of your grade. Only a letter
from your physician can excuse a medical absence." He tilted
his head, his eyes gleaming behind his glasses. "As the previous
student discovered. I am not in the habit of pandering to those
who think that college is a lark or something to do between parties."

"Um, no," Dhoruba said. "But I had a question relating to the
meteor."

"Oh?"

"Has there ever been anything about black, almost lightless
meteor fragments?" He shook his head. "There's nothing like
that in the geology books, but someone was asking me…"

"The reason this subject is not covered in your geology books
is that it's not geology," Professor Davis said. "It is fantasy."
Davis looked even more annoyed than usual. "Legends of mystical fragments, orbs and spheres have been around for most of
recorded history. The meteor itself, as you no doubt recall, im-
pacted here just over 50,000 years ago. By the time the first humans had arrived in America, the crater from the impact of the
meteor had long been filled in by earth but every now and then
pieces of meteoric iron get discovered.

"The existence of meteoric iron led to a wide range of myths
arising about the crater." Professor Davis shrugged. "Black
spheres were one such claim. Various mystics found black
spheres that they claimed granted great powers." He snorted.
"And of course then there were the Shadow Wars of the 1900s

that added to the legends. I'm not surprised that you haven't heard about it—it's a bit of history that isn't widely known among non-residents."

"The Shadow Wars?" You would think I would have heard of something like that..."

"Mr. Akoli, I am a geologist, not a historian or philosophy professor. I suggest you avail yourself of the library, since we have arrived at the fact that the black spheres are simply a myth. As such, this is not an appropriate matter for actual scientists."

"I—" Suddenly, the desk lamp dimmed slightly. Oh, fuck! "I understand, sir. Well, I'll see you in class on Friday and at lab next Monday!"

Davis said nothing for a moment, staring at the lamp. Dhoruba tried to force the shadows back down like he had before, and moments later, the lamp flared back up to its normal brightness.

"Well," Davis finally said. "I expect you to be on time for class. If you'll pardon me, I believe I need to speak to the maintenance department."

"Oh-okay," Dhoruba quickly fled from the office. He didn't dare take the elevators, so he ran down the stairs, the sound of the storm muffled by the thick walls.

When he got out, Dhoruba felt the shadows just grow out of the air around him.

"Fuck, fuck, fuck!" he hissed. The rain was pouring down. Even so, if anyone noticed Dhoruba and his shadows, they'd probably panic and call the campus cops. Ignoring the rain, Dhoruba took off down the pathway, the walkway lights going dark as he passed them, flaring back to life behind him.

Where do I go? He needed to get someplace where nobody would bother him. He needed to be alone to figure out just what he could do. He couldn't walk around, never knowing if his shadows, or whatever the hell they were, would just decide to suddenly do something on their own.

Hell, he didn't even know if they were dangerous to him or to those around him. What if something had happened, if they'd become active while he was asleep and hurt Derek?

Shit. I hadn't even thought of that. The rain was starting to soak through his clothes. Dhoruba shivered and then gasped as he felt the shadows wrap around his clothes, forming a second skin over them. Now Dhoruba didn't even feel damp as the wind-driven droplets struck his now black clothes and just skidded off like he was wearing some kind of waterproof suit.

Great. The shadows double as a raincoat.

He needed to go somewhere nobody would bother him. Somewhere…

The Heritage Commons Dorm.

During the pandemic of 2020, which saw schools around the world – from elementary through post-grad – close for a year or more to physical enrollment, Clark Atlanta University, like many others, had suffered financially and Heritage Commons had to close its doors.

Nobody will be there right now. Dhoruba pulled out his phone and called Derek.

"Dhoruba? You made it to class?" Derek sounded concerned.

"Yeah," Dhoruba said. "I'm fine, but I still have a little headache. Need to chill, so I'll try to hit a movie later tonight. Don't worry if I'm late."

"You sure?" Derek asked.

"Yes, Dad…"

"Fine, fine. Well, I'll be late too."

"Oh, your date got rekindled."

"Nah, more like I ran into her ex-first boyfriend, and so we're planning to go out tonight to see if *we* hit it off."

Only Derek.

"Okay, Derek, but leave a note on the door. I don't want to surprise you again."

"When have I not left a note?"

"To warn me about a date? Every time."

"Fine," Derek said with a laugh. "You'll get your note. Have fun at the movie, Dhoruba."

"I will. Have fun on your date."

Moments later, Dhoruba put the phone back in his pocket with a sigh of relief. When Derek got concerned or curious, shaking him off was like trying to shake stink off shit. But now,

Dhoruba had time. Time to figure out what the hell had happened to him.

***

Technically, nobody was supposed to go down to Heritage Commons unless they had permission to be there from the school administration.

Nobody bothered with permission during the day. At night there were security guards. But right now, Dhoruba expected that not even the guards would be down there. Not in a storm like this. Even if they were down there, Dhoruba would see them long before they could see him.

Dhoruba put the sunglasses in his pocket as he walked down the winding walkway that led down to where Heritage Commons was. He could see perfectly, like it was a sunny day. *If only I didn't need sunglasses for anything brighter than an overcast morning.*

The place seemed odd, not just because of the rain and how deserted it was, but also because of the shadows that gathered around him. Dhoruba could feel them collecting, looking at him from corners and behind empty window frames.

It didn't take Dhoruba very long to get down to Heritage Commons' courtyard. He paused for a moment, looking up at the sky, still full of thick, roiling storm clouds, an occasional bolt of lightning flashing through the sky. Around him, the shadows coiled and moved in anticipation.

Dhoruba took a deep breath. "Okay, let's see what I can do."

He closed his eyes and tried to feel the shadows. He'd sensed them earlier, but now maybe he could get a better grip on making them do what he wanted, like not trying to smother any light sources in his immediate vicinity.

Because that would make his life very difficult.

Oh, and finding out if they were dangerous and if he could get rid of this ability would be nice.

Even if it felt normal to have the shadows surround his body.

He could feel them gathering at his call. When Dhoruba opened his eyes, he could see out, but he knew that anyone standing in the courtyard would see a great pillar of night that drank in every bit of light that touched it. He lifted his hand and felt some resistance. It wasn't just the absence of light, but a darkness that felt like some kind of syrupy liquid as he moved his fingers through it.

He tried to order the shadows to take a new form. The shadow obeyed him with even less resistance than he had felt from it in the bedroom. Not a pencil this time, but a heavy walking staff. He smacked it against the ground, the impact jarring his arm.

And it seemed... content. Content to do what he wanted. Not like it was intelligent. No, it felt more like a pet...

"My shadow cat," Dhoruba muttered. Then he nodded. Okay, go back to normal. No shadows.

And that time, there was resistance. It wanted to be out, to hover around Dhoruba, to bring the darkness to him.

"I can't function if every time I stop paying attention, I turn into Shadow-Man!" Dhoruba said, stamping his foot. There was a pause, and then the shadows started to turn incorporeal, swirling around Dhoruba and sinking into him. A few moments later, Dhoruba was standing alone in the courtyard.

But he could still see some twisting shadows in the corners. Not enough for people to realize it was him, but even so...

Worse, he could feel the power within him, a power that wanted to get out. Sure, he'd forced it back in now, but what would happen if he went to sleep, got knocked out, or hell, got surprised.

It was almost easier when it was... Wait a minute. Dhoruba opened his backpack. "Go in there," he ordered, blinking rapidly as the shadows rose from his body and then poured into the backpack. Then he closed it.

It felt...

Easier. Like they were happy to have a place to lurk, and they didn't care if it wasn't anywhere someone could see. Even the surrounding shadows were slightly less obvious.

Maybe they're trying to damp the lights around me because the light is dangerous or hurts them? If they can stay inside something, I don't have to pull the shadows inside of me.

And that felt better. Better that he wasn't forcing his shadows to act against their will.

That was perhaps the strangest thing. His new abilities felt natural. He shouldn't feel this comfortable talking about living shadows and light sucking powers and—

And it was then that a flashlight blazed from just outside the courtyard.

Dhoruba gasped and ducked behind a pillar. He could see the group out there, a bunch of men in raincoats. They were coming, flashlight beams stabbing out through the rainy night.

But they couldn't see him. Not like he could see them. Dhoruba kept backing up, to the gap that led to the front of the dorm.

I can get out front, and they can't see me. But who the hell were they? It wasn't exactly like the courtyard of an abandoned dorm was the kind of place you'd want to go in the middle of a rainstorm!

It was then that he saw a slim man or woman being brought forward, a hood over their head. They were tossed to the ground in the courtyard, their captors surrounding them. One captor, a big, beefy looking man, reached down and pulled the hood off, revealing a young woman with a short fade and huge hoop earrings with blood running down her bruised face.

"So!" the battered woman said cheerfully. "I take it I really wasn't invited to the party?"

Four

"Shut up," the largest man said, shining his light down on his captive.

From her refuge, Dhoruba stared at the bound figure.

She looked like an older teenager, maybe a freshman in college at most. The rain ran down her face, the water mixing with the blood from her split lip. Dhoruba could see the bruises on her face.

"But we were having so much—" The man cut her off by kicking the teenager in the face, knocking her back onto the pavement.

Dhoruba put his hand to his mouth. What are they doing?

Another man flashed his light into the teen's face. "Let her talk, Don. Isn't like she's going to be talking to anyone after to-night."

"Who knows," the teen said, wiggling herself back to a sitting position, blood pouring from her nose, "maybe you might find out something important. After all, what else are you going to do in the rain?"

"Shoot you, for one," Don said, drawing a large-framed pistol from the interior pocket of his jacket.

"Big Don, I thought we were connecting!" The teen spat out some blood. "I mean after you told me that you were getting ready to burn all those people out of their homes… It wasn't my fault that you didn't… or *couldn't*… read the guestlist for our little party!"

There was a snort from one of the surrounding men, quickly stifled as "Big Don" glared at them.

I need to call the cops. Dhoruba pulled out his phone and swiped his finger across the screen.

Nothing happened.

What? No!

"You know, you could have stayed alive if you'd managed to keep your nose out of other people's business!"

Dhoruba swiped the screen again. Nothing. He shook it, trying to get the water off of it, and then swiped one more time.

"Don't forget your calculus test! Study group tomorrow!" the phone cheerfully shouted. Dhoruba stared at his phone. His scheduling app. Maybe they hadn't heard it.

"Go find out who the fuck that was!" Big Don ordered.

Oh, of course he couldn't be lucky today. Dhoruba looked up as the men approached, their flashlights stabbing through the rain. They couldn't see him, not yet, but it would only be a matter of time.

"You know, if that's a college student, do you really want to off 'em, Big Don?"

"College students are a dime a dozen," Don told him. "And we wouldn't be doing this if it wasn't for—"

Only Dhoruba saw it. Even with the flashlights, the others missed the way their captive had wiggled herself into a squatting position and had her hands, bound though they were, in her pocket.

"Think fast!" she shouted, and then leaped up and ran, a small package falling from her hands and then there was light! Dhoruba fell backward, dazzled, a scream giving his position away, even as the thugs shouted, just as blinded as he was. The sound of shots rang out as they started firing at their captive, who was running right toward Dhoruba!

Dhoruba grunted, feeling the shadow cover her mouth and nose as the teenage girl managed to slam right into him.

She looked up at Dhoruba, spitting some blood to the side. "So you're the college student! Got a knife, or something?"

Dhoruba stared at her as she turned around and displayed her bound wrists. For a moment, he didn't know what to do, but then his shadows quivered around his hands, and in an instant he had razor-sharp talons, like those of a bird of prey. He dragged them down between her bound hands, the heavy cords parting like cobwebs.

"Great! Name's Ana!" She looked back to where the men were now coming forward, Don's obscenity fueled rant filling the air. "We'd better go."

"Yeah," Dhoruba said, and they turned to run back through the ruined storeroom.

"There they are!" someone shouted, and suddenly Dhoruba heard bullets whizzing over his head, sparking off of the exposed steel supports in the walls ahead of them. Their pursuers' flashlight beams bounced all over the place, but it was only a matter of time before they would be found. Then they'd be shot.

Put them out! Dhoruba thought as hard as he could, willing the shadows to serve him. Put out the flashlights!

And the darkness moved at his command, the bright LEDs fading to barely visible embers. The men started cursing, while some of them stopped shooting, shaking their flashlights in frustration.

"Guess there *is* a God, but how can we see?" Ana asked.

Right. She can't see in the dark. Dhoruba glared at the teenager and shook her head. "Come on." He grabbed her by the hand and dragged her with him, the girl stumbling in the

178

darkness. Then they were away from the dorm, running along the pathway. Behind them, the flashlights flared up again, evidently now beyond her shadows' reach. It didn't matter. She could see their pursuers long before they could see him.

"Okay," Dhoruba said as they got to the walkway that wound up to Clark-Atlanta. He turned and stared. The hunters were going in the wrong direction. "Who are you? Who were they? Why were they trying to kill you?"

"Well, I'm well, a…" She paused. "Can we wait until we get somewhere with better lighting? It's dark than a mug out here." She grinned, but her short laugh sounded really nervous.

Dhoruba sighed. "Fine. Once we're up in the school, we can talk. Then I'm calling the cops—"

"No!" Ana burst out. "No," she repeated. "Just… just let me explain, please? We need to do this quick."

"What needs an explanation?" Dhoruba asked. "I don't know you, and they were planning on shooting you." He shook his head and looked back down the curving path to Heritage Commons. "And what was that about burning people out of their homes?" Nobody was following them, and they were almost to where the lights of the college were. Nobody would be out, not in the rain, but they could head for Woodruff Library or any of the class buildings. One thing was certain, he wasn't about to bring this girl into his dorm.

"Look, okay, here's the thing," Ana began. "There's this dude, Pop Galloway."

"Pop Galloway…" Dhoruba stopped and turned to stare at Ana as they came to the first working light.

"Yeah, he's—" Ana looked up at him and paled as she took in the shadows that were wrapping around his body. "Shit!" she said, scrambling backward. "You're…"

"Covered in shadow," Dhoruba said. "Yeah, it's a problem I have. Now tell me about Pop Galloway and why we can't call the police!"

"Right." Ana took a deep breath. "Well, scary-ass shadow-dude, the thing is, Pop Galloway is the head of the Galloway Family, who's got their hands in everybody's pocket. He's also into real estate. Buy cheap, sell high. But sometimes people don't want to sell, like the tenants of an apartment building who voted to say no, and well, he burned it down and he's planning to do it again."

"And you didn't think to call the cops?" Dhoruba said, frowning.

Someone came by, shielding their head from the storm with a newspaper, ignoring the two while they ran for the library.

"You ever met a cop you can trust?" Ana asked. "Anyway, I didn't exactly have a choice because they caught me."

"Caught you doing what?" Dhoruba asked.

"Well… I do love my fellow man, but I also needed to supplement my income, so I figured I'd get my Robin Hood on, and I knew that Pop Galloway's house—"

Dhoruba stared at her. "You cannot be serious. You just got finished telling me that he's a crime lord who has murdered people, and you figured you'd just go break into his house?"

"Sneak."

"Doesn't matter." Dhoruba ran his hand through his locks, suddenly realizing that his shadows had kept them dry, no matter how much he'd been rained on. "So, why can't we call the police?"

"Because if we do, and if they are on the take, then the place will be burned down long before anyone can get there and we'll be toast too," Ana replied. "I say we go there, let the people know that they're in trouble, and then we can help them get away." She paused. "And I don't have any evidence other than hearing them talk while I was, you know, trying to steal from the house. They could always deny it, and then just burn the place down later."

"Right. You also want to stay out of…" Dhoruba patted his pockets, looked in his backpack, and then started cursing. A lot. For a while.

"What is it?" Ana asked.

"I lost my phone!" Dhoruba glared back down the path. "It's probably back down there somewhere. Do you know how much that phone cost?"

"Not really. So you'll come with me?"

"Yeah."

"Good..." Ana paused, then held up a cheap phone. "You should really keep a burner phone. Oh, did I mention that you're paying for the taxi?"

"Taxi?" Dhoruba said with a smirk. "Who uses taxis anymore?"

"We do," Ana replied. "All the Uber drivers in this area answer to Pop Galloway."

Dhoruba closed his eyes and counted to ten. He could hear Derek in his mind telling him that he needed to stand up for himself instead of letting everyone run right over him. But Derek wasn't there. "Fine. Let's go."

***

Ana called the cab while Dhoruba dug into his backpack for some cash. He wasn't about to show off his credit cards, not in front of his new "friend."

"So!" Ana said. "Here's the plan. We go there, warn the people, and then we can wait around to see if anything happens."

"That's..." Dhoruba dodged a spray of water as a campus maintenance cart zipped by them. "Do they even know who you are?"

"Um, no, but they'll trust me."

Dhoruba opened his mouth so say something, but then a car with "Yellow Checker" stenciled on the sides pulled up to the curb, flashing its lights at them. He gestured for Ana to get in, then slid in himself.

"Where to?" the driver asked, his voice muffled behind the thick, Plexiglas partition.

"Collier Heights Apartments," Ana said.

"You wanna go there? Not a good part of town. I'll need a deposit."

Ana looked at Dhoruba.

Why am I doing this? Dhoruba put several more bills into the slot at the base of the partition, leaving his open backpack on the seat. He should just ignore what Ana said, go to his dorm, pick up the phone and call the cops.

But the kid's right. We don't have any proof. Hell, the only reason I believe her is not many people just show up to murder a teen, but even ignoring what she said about the police, we just don't have anything to tell them.

While he was thinking, the cab left the college and headed toward the I-20 Highway. The driver passed one slow-moving truck, then merged onto the highway, the cab rattling as it drove over the patched pavement.

The driver peered over his shoulder, "I'll drop y'all off, but I ain't hangin' around. Y'all want me to come back, y'all walk to the end of the block, and I'll pick y'all up there. But not anywhere in that apartment complex."

"That's okay, we can just take MARTA," Dhoruba said.

The cabbie whistled. "Well, you're braver than I am, that's for certain. By the way, if you're trying to get a cab anywhere but the college, lose the mask. Nobody's wearin' masks no more... especially a mask like that."

Dhoruba nodded, putting his fingers to his mouth, still covered by the shadow. "Thank you," he mumbled.

They stepped out of the car. Dhoruba looked around. The apartment complex was of moderate size and each of its four two-story buildings was made of that orangish-red "projects-brick" – those bricks the project buildings in every big city were built from.

The insides of these apartments will burn, he thought, *but those bricks are probably asbestos... it'd take an exploding sun to burn those down.*

"What were you doing here?" Dhoruba asked.

"Hey, it's not that bad," Ana said.

"Right." *I wonder if she lives here.*

"So, we go in, warn the people, and then what?" Dhoruba asked.

"I... If they're warned they can call the police," Ana replied. "If enough people call, even crooked cops would have to respond." Ana's grin faded. "I hope."

Dhoruba didn't say anything to that.

The lights of the cab vanished into the fog, leaving Dhoruba and Ana alone on the deserted street. Dhoruba looked down at

the concrete, noticing the weeds rising up from the cracked surface.

How long has it been since anyone cared about this place?
Dhoruba thought.

"You'd... better take your mask off," Ana said.

"I... No." Dhoruba frowned at her. "You're involved with
criminals, and you said you're a thief. For now, I think I'll just
stay anonymous."

"Okay, but don't stand where anyone can fully see you." Ana
said. "I bet they're on edge."

Dhoruba sighed. *Right. Why did I come out here?* "I'll stand
behind you, let you do most of the talking." Between the fog and
drizzle, Dhoruba doubted anyone in the building would notice
him, even if they were looking out. With his face turned from
Ana and the door, he didn't even have to worry about her seeing
him so he could pull the shadows away from his face and enjoy
the fresh air. Dhoruba waited and looked around the neighborhood. The houses on the other side of the street looked like they
had seen better days.

"I'm telling the truth!" a voice behind him shouted.

"Bullshit!" another voice boomed.

Dhoruba shot a glance toward where Ana was, but she was
gone. He whipped around at the angry voices to see Ana being
marched out by two security guards.

Well, they were wearing jackets labeled "building security,"
even though one was holding a cane under one arm. They both
looked like they should be retired, not working as security. Ana
was squirming but not fighting too hard.

Dhoruba bet she didn't want to risk hurting her captors.

"Look, they're going to burn you out!" Ana cried.

"Uh-huh. And this is the story you're going with? Remember
the time you hit the fire alarm so you could snag some checks?"
The bald guard – the one without the walking cane – glared at
Ana, keeping a firm grip on her arm.

"That was a year ago!" Ana protested.

"Well, we still remember it!" The guards kept marching her
down the walkway until they stopped, looking at Dhoruba with
unfriendly eyes.

He quickly pulled the shadow back over his face, leaving only his eyes exposed.

"So you're working with this thief?" the bald man said as he flashed him with a flashlight.

Dhoruba winced. "No. But he was almost killed by some thugs, so I'm assuming she's… telling the truth? Sort of?"

"Sort of?" Ana glared at him from between the two men. "You were there!"

"I know. You also said you stole something from Pop Galloway?" She glanced at the guards.

The man with the cane snorted. "Everyone knows about Pop Galloway, so of course she'd talk to you about him. Probably stole something important and ran to the first person who'd help her."

"So why did I come here?!" Ana asked.

"To get in with a sob story. I mean, you already hit us with the lost kittens."

"They were—"

Dhoruba had enough and whistled. Everyone fell silent. "How old are you?"

"Fifteen," Ana said. "Almost sixteen."

"I went with a fifteen-year-old's plan," Dhoruba said, shaking his head. "A fifteen-year-old nearly got us both killed."

He turned his attention to the old "security guards."

"Look. All I know is that someone was trying to kill her, and they have a lot of thugs, and even if"—Dhoruba glared at Ana—"Ana was lying, something very serious is going on, and you need to call the police."

"Who's Ana? This here is Lashey," Baldy said.

"Told me she was Afrodil," his cane-carrying companion replied.

Of course she gave me a fake name. Dhoruba started to feel the onset of a headache that had nothing to do with the light. "Look, just call them!"

"Hah! The cops don't come around here, except when the mayor or somebody is walking around. They—" The bald guard fell silent as headlights turned onto the road and started approaching the building. Motorcycles. Lots of them. "Now, what the hell are the Unicorns doing down here?"

Unicorns... Derek had tripped about them. A biker gang... Fuck.

Dhoruba frowned at Ana, then turned to the guards. "I think that you'd better get inside and lock the doors. Now."

"Right." The guards started retreating into the nearest building.

"But we have to—"

Dhoruba whirled on Ana. "This was your plan?" he hissed. "Fine, you said the cops might not show up, but you didn't tell me that the people you were warning were retirees!"

"You went along with it!"

"When I thought you just looked young! I didn't know you were fifteen! Or that you had stolen from them!" He glared at Ana. "Call the cops."

"They won't get here in time—"

"Call the cops!" Dhoruba snapped. "And hide."

They ran inside the building behind the guards. Dhoruba stood just inside the doorway.

And maybe they'll just go away. Maybe they're just riding down through... And then the bikes started pulling off to the side of the road, directly across the street. The gang was hooting and hollering as they got off of their bikes. Worse, they were pulling bottles out from their packs. Bottles filled with liquid; rags stuffed in them. Molotov cocktails.

If I get out of this alive, I'm never leaving the AUC again. But right now... Dhoruba moved back to where the shadows were darkest. There were only a few working streetlights, and the yellow glow from the building behind him was dim against the foggy night.

Dhoruba called on the shadows, and they came to him, eager to respond, somehow sensing that he needed them. He let them crawl over his body, covering his clothes and skin. Other shadows gathered around him, orbiting his body like an honor guard. Dhoruba had no idea how he looked to anyone else, but...

"Jesus, Mary, and Joseph!" the guard shouted from his place at the top of the stairs and brandished his cane at him like it was a cross and Dhoruba was a vampire.

Guess I look pretty intimidating. But there was still too much light. Dhoruba looked up at the few streetlights and then just sent his shadows running up the poles, blocking out the light, leaving nothing but the interior lights of the building behind him and the headlights of the bikes to illuminate the street. And even those lights were dimming.

"What the fuck is going on?" a gang-member snarled, glaring at the streetlights. He didn't notice the dimming headlights of the bikes as he hefted a bottle in one hand and lit its cloth. "Can we do this without lights?"

Okay, what do I… Dhoruba smiled. If he could put out lights, he could put out fires… At his command, the surrounding shadows lashed out. Shouts of confusion and fear sounded as matches and lighters were put out. Even the flaming wicks in the bottles were doused by his shadows.

No fire, no threat. Dhoruba felt cocky as he walked to the front of the building. Several of the bikers pointed at his dark form.

"You're not going to burn this place down," Dhoruba said. "So why don't you—SHIT!" He ducked and backpedaled, desperately seeking cover as half a dozen biker gang members pulled out their guns and started firing wildly in his direction. The two guards yelled and ducked inside, closing the door behind them. The sound of bullets hitting wood and brick with the odd sound of shattering glass made Dhoruba want to piss his pants, but he was trying to impress Ana, or whatever her name was, and the guards, so he held it.

Suddenly, the shadows rose up in front of him, forming a shield against the storm of bullets. Dhoruba could hear the bullets hitting the shield, but it wasn't like they were hitting something hard—just something soft that seemed to rob them of all their force, so the spent slugs dropped to the ground.

"What the fuck is that?!" someone shouted, and then there were more gunshots.

Almost of their own accord, Dhoruba's shadows lengthened, forming tentacles that whipped out, pulling pistols from the hands of the Unicorns, and tossing them into the night. One of the Unicorns, a big, bald man with tattoos all over his arms, screamed shrilly as he crab-walked away from Dhoruba's shadows.

The cries of Unicorns permeated the night air.

"What the fuck—!"

"Shoot them, shoot them!"

"They're demons from Hell!"

"Mama!"

The whole gang stumbled onto their bikes and roared away, abandoning their Molotov cocktails, guns, and their booze.

Dhoruba pulled the shadows back to him.

He could feel a certain reluctance to return, but the shadows obeyed his command. Dhoruba's face was once again masked by his shadows, while the rest of his clothing had gone back to normal in the light drizzle.

The squeak of the front door opening interrupted the silence. Baldy stared out at the street and the abandoned gear, then looked at Dhoruba. "Who the hell are you? Some kind of Voodoo Doctor?"

"Um... No," Dhoruba said. "I'm just into special effects."

"Yeah. Whatever." The guard's gaze let him know what he thought of that story.

In the distance, Dhoruba heard the sound of sirens. "I guess Ana called the police."

"Young man, everybody called the police," the second guard said as he limped out onto the top of the stairs.

Dhoruba nodded. *Do I want to be here...* The answer to that was simple. Hell naw. There would be questions, they would demand ID and would probably call the college to confirm...

Nope. He didn't want to be here. But that meant...

"Where's Ana?"

"You mean Lashey?"

"I mean the brat!" Dhoruba hissed.

"Heh." Baldy laughed and shook his head. "She took off. You don't think she's gonna stick around where there's cops, do you? Even if they don't arrest her, she'd be sent right to DFACS."

"Still," the guard with the cane said. "She was telling the truth. So she did try to help us."

"Eh, maybe. I bet it was because she wanted something else to steal."

"From here?" Dhoruba said, looking around.

The guards snorted.

Dhoruba shook his head, then glanced up at the building. People were leaning out of their windows, staring down at him. Some of them had cell phones.

Aw naw, they're filming me.

It was pretty dim, even with the streetlights, but…

"Okay," Dhoruba said. "I'm going to get back home, so…" he checked his backpack, then blinked. He held the bag up, shook it a few times, then glared at where he'd last seen Ana.

Dhoruba's wallet was lying on the ground.

"Oh, you didn't…" Dhoruba snarled and stomped over to check the wallet. His bank card, his cash, everything but his ID was gone. He'd had it open in the taxi, and somehow… "That… That… Goddamn brat!"

"She got you, didn't she?" The cane-carrying guard asked.

"I—I saved her! She was going to be shot, and I saved her, and then I paid for the taxi, and she robbed me?" Dhoruba started stomping around in the tall grass in a fury, his shadows rising up in response.

"Uh, you gonna start getting scary again?" the bald guard asked as he and the other guard flinched and took a step back.

Dhoruba stopped and took a deep, calming breath. He held it in for a few moments and then blew the air back out.

"No," Dhoruba finally said. "I've lost my phone. The teenager whose life I saved took my money. Now I only have one thing to ask."

"Yeah?"

"I need to get out of here before the police show up, but I don't want to walk all the way home. Can one of y'all call me an Uber?"

Five

Later that night, Dhoruba was in bed, his blankets pulled up to his chin. He'd gone out to the Campus Store with Derek and had finally found some sunglasses that didn't make him look like a clown.

He'd actually bought a half-dozen, just in case he lost a few. Derek had been concerned, but Dhoruba had managed to get him to laugh it off.

But now that he was alone, Dhoruba played with his shadows, letting the darkness twine around his fingers. It felt nice. Comforting.

He shook his head and called some of the shadows back into his body.

The room was blanketed in darkness. Dhoruba took a deep breath, his heart thudding away in his chest. He closed his eyes.

"Go back," he commanded. He could feel the shadows resist the command. There was a sense of anger, a desire to protect Dhoruba. It was stronger than it had been when the Unicorns were shooting at him. But he kept ordering the darkness back, and slowly the shadows retreated into his body, under the bed, into his backpack. Dhoruba hopped out of the bed and walked to the window. He pulled the curtain aside.

The city was quiet... for now. It would need a protector soon enough. From Pop Galloway... from the Unicorns... from corrupt cops... and from fifteen year old pickpockets. He figured he needed to do something with his newfound powers and the darkness seemed eager to do something too, so that protector might as well be him.

I guess. He shrugged then hopped back into bed.

"So what is my superhero name going to be?" He pondered. "Blackout? Pitch? Tar Baby? Blackity-Black-Black? Shade?"

He thought for a long while, then he remembered reading about a class of super-black coating that absorbed nearly a hundred percent visible light. It was so black, it made crumpled aluminum foil look like a flat void, a hole that collapsed into nothingness... *Vantablack* they called it. And that's what they would call him...

Vantablack.

189

WHEN CARNAGE IS NO LONGER ENOUGH
BY
NADIRA JAMERSON

Every moment, there is a sacrifice. In pursuit of others, some options are yanked up from the root and tossed aside, so that only the shallow holes of unused possibility remain. Eventually, the wind comes, carrying away and rustling together the disturbed foundation, and even the holes are disappeared.

For her lunch at Jen Chan's, Zu easily decided on the familiar curry shrimp with fried rice, sacrificing the possibility of finally trying the General Tso's tofu. Instead of going up Boulevard and down Memorial on her walk back home, she quickly chose to cut through Oakland Cemetery. The heavy choices Zu was still pondering as she walked, however, were much more difficult to decide.

Maybe that's why she'd picked the cemetery route. During her two years of living in Atlanta's Grant Park, it had become one of her favored neighborhood fixtures. Named after its array of Oak trees, this cemetery was not dreary from the shadowy stories of frightful hauntings like most were. Established in 1850, the 48-acre stretch was home to greenhouses, detailed sculptures, and Victorian architecture. Gardens full of dark green lilyturf, white magnolias, and purple summer heliotrope hugged the burial plots during the warmer months. Atlanta's first Black mayor, Maynard Holbrook Jackson, Jr., was laid to rest there. It was a frequent wedding venue, art gallery, and classroom. For many who visited, Oakland Cemetery took death beyond tragedy and into a reminder to honor history and celebrate the present.

Yes, it was fitting that Zu's feet would carry her to this comforting marker of that which had been lost and remade when she was feeling crushed between the crossroads of "Should I stay or should I go?" Even the long stretch of black asphalt surrounded on all sides by the vibrant colors of plant life that led from the back of the cemetery to its tall, red-bricked front gate seemed reflective of her inner thoughts.

Zu's mind also walked, through all of the tears, separations, and blood that had pushed her to flee to a city she knew nothing of, except that it was different, those three years ago.

She slipped back in time to the days when her clothes and hands were stained with the insides of her little sister, So. Hiding her face in public in case they'd finally fingered her for the body she dismembered in retribution and left in her grandfather's bathroom. Fluttering so fast between one motel and the next with Ake, drinking and smoking, until she was disoriented enough to pretend the world around them no longer existed.

But if those times had been only pain, it would be easy to leave them behind for good. Instead, Zu also thought of the mornings laughing with So over breakfast before they went to school. The nights curled up in bed with Ake, warm and naive enough to believe that her first love would always be there to distract her.

For eighteen years, Zu had lived in fear before watching So die and finding her strength through violent rampage. One year spent on the road, drifting with Ake. And now? Could she really move on from all of that? Did she deserve to?

Since coming to Atlanta, Zu had tried to heal. She'd tried to become better. She no longer smoked all day, every day. She meditated when she felt anxious. Threw uncooked eggs at her walls when she was enraged. She watched videos that taught her phrases like "I am beautiful and deserving of love." She prayed to God at night for forgiveness and direction, and did her best to stay open to God's answers during the day. If Zu was honest, some days did feel lighter and more purposeful. There was even a stretch of a few months when she felt totally, "I have what I need!"

Recently, though, Zu found herself focusing on the still unanswered prayers. She had friends to go out with in the city, but none to confidently bare her secrets to. Blaming herself for her sister's death and contemplating suicide was less frequent, but on the days it emerged, she was again gutted by hope's absence. She could always call Ake, except after discovering so many of his lies, even his most sweet promises hardly filled her up anymore.

Had she really fought to survive just to be left alone in her wanderings through grief? Would she ever move past what she had done? Past what happened to her, and into who she could be?

Zu was so busy wondering "Is this all there is? Were the losses and the changes even worth it?" that she failed to notice the feet walking beside hers until their owner said "Hello."

"Oh. Hello," Zu responded, looking up. He was maybe six inches taller than her, wearing tan joggers and a sea-blue T-shirt. His hair was cut into short curls. Mellow, red-veined eyes and an eager smile painted his face. He appeared to be around her age.

"I was doing something back there when I looked up and saw you walk in. I had to say something," the man said.

"Oh? Doing what?" Zu asked at the same moment she noticed a jar filled with dirt grasped in his hand. Zu's recent spiritual and self-improvement journey had naturally led her further down the path of moon rituals and Tarot cards. "Magic?"

"What makes you say that?" the man laughed shyly, trying to tuck the jar behind his back.

"I don't know anything else cemetery soil would be used for," Zu replied with a knowingly wicked smile. "I like magic, too," she added, so he wouldn't feel caught. As they walked forward together, the man went on to tell her a lot about himself. He had recently been released from prison after doing a bid for breaking and entering. Next month would be his twenty-sixth birthday, but he did not know if he should celebrate.

"Birthdays are hard for me, too," Zu offered. "But I'm trying to learn that it's never wrong to celebrate your life, even if you have to do it alone." The man nodded.

"There's something about you," he said, staring deep at the side profile of Zu's face. "Your eyes. I don't know. There's something scary there." He chucked before adding, "Powerful."

Zu wasn't sure why she was so willing to talk with him. An existence plagued with guilt, much disappointment, and being on the run made her usually wary of connecting with new people. Yet, here she was.

The next words Zu spoke to him seemed to fly out of her mouth without her instruction.

"Ask me something you've been wanting to know," she said. They stopped walking and faced each other. It was undoubtedly a strange request of a person she'd met just minutes ago in a cemetery. The question he asked was even stranger.

He took a deep breath. "Is God proud of me?" And before Zu could question what authority she had to tell a fresh-out-of-jail stranger what the Divine thought of him, she answered.

"Of course," Zu said, and she believed it.

Those words and that belief rang between them, floated above them, and covered them until they were totally found in the irie moment.

"That's—That's all I wanted to know," the man finally said, breaking the vortex.

They continued to walk together in silence until they reached Oakland Cemetery's front gate. And then they parted ways.

BAT OUT OF HELL
BY
GLENN PARRIS

Andrew Christopher Estrada-Stryker opened the door to a strange man in a black suit wearing a brimmed hat tilted down over his forehead. The 18-year-old had seen that kind of hat before, but only in black and white movies on late-night television.

"Hello?" The boy said.

"Is this the residence of Marvin Stryker, son?" The man asked.

"Who's at the door, Andrew?" ACE's mother called from the kitchen.

"I'm not sure, Mom, but he's got a badge."

Naturally, the Dominican-born homemaker heard him out. After a quiet conversation in the living room, Mercedes Stryker walked the man to the door and closed it gently behind him. She trudged back to the sofa, sank into it, and began to sob.

"Mom?" ACE asked, caressing his mother's shoulder.

"That man is the devil!" Mercedes said.

"The G-man with the badge?" ACE asked.

"No. Your father!"

When his father finally came home, he was drunk. "I brought you here from the Dominican Republic. I saved you!" Marvin slurred his accusation.

"So why did you call the law on me?" Mercedes cried.

He leveled a bleary gaze at her. "Because you're shaking your tail feathers at Joe Bishop."

"He's our priest. Of course, I'm gonna show him hospitality. We're members of his congregation, part of his flock."

"Yeah, but I bet you're serving him more than coffee when I'm out working hard to keep this roof over your head."

"Marvin, you can't believe that I'm cheating on you."

"Look me in the eye, Mercedes, and tell me that you're not sleeping with him, and I'll call them off. I'll protect you again."

Mercedes crossed herself, looked beyond the ceiling above her, and hissed, "Dios Mia! There IS no one else, Marvin. You are my heart."

When the voices quieted, Mercedes Stryker slipped under a heavy arm and marched her husband to the master bedroom. The night was quiet in the Stryker residence.

Saturday morning, Marvin confessed what he had done. He told ACE the best way that he could. "Son, marriage is hard, and family is complicated. Your mother and I... had some issues that we had to work out. But it's all good now. I love your mom more than life itself. I told those men a lie and I'll have to pay for that. Earn your mother's forgiveness."

"Okay, Dad. Whatever you say."

"Let's play a little ball. Go get your ball and glove."

The old pitching net held court in the acute corner of a triangular backyard. Fifteen-year veteran of daily target practice, the Pitch-Back was kept in pristine order with tight springs and freshly strung industrial nylon mesh.

ACE planted his feet on his "spot." Precisely, ninety feet away in their double lot. He threw a few practice pitches at the strike zone defined by red ribbon threaded through the mesh forever judging his performance. He heard *Bang Bang*, his focus tune in his head and sang along, "Aw, beep, beep..." Four heaters, dead center. "Bang Bang!" The third one reached ninety-two mph. Marvin Stryker tracked it with the radar gun Officer Murphy across the street lent them from his patrol car when off duty.

Marvin nodded. "No matter how much pepper you put on your fastball, a good hitter will eventually catch you. Pitching is more about strategy then power. Takes most good pitchers a year or two to really understand that. You've got to have variety! Fastball, curveball, sinker, change up. Mess with the batter's head. Sometimes throw a ball outside, inside, low, or hang it high. Make him hesitate about committing to a swing. You gotta learn these things, ACE."

After an hour's demonstration of the various pitch techniques, Marvin and ACE retreated from the Atlanta summer heat to the living room for the afternoon Braves game. Two sandwiches, a cold beer for Marvin and a root beer for ACE were waiting on the coffee table. Marvin grabbed a sandwich in one hand and slid a notebook to his son with the other. Without looking down, ACE picked up the pencil, flipped halfway through to a blank page, dated it, and absently began making notes. So passed another afternoon with the Strykers.

The long days of summer followed high school graduation. The B average didn't get ACE more than the HOPE scholarship. Not enough to pay for Georgia Tech or UGA. ACE drove up into the driveway.

Marvin had wangled a summer job for his son with the Braves' Farm team as an assistant to the batting coach.

Marvin ratcheted the oil pan loose on the old Charger in the garage. He had a hard time getting out from under the car these days with his beer belly that began to swell above his belt. ACE might have to get a job at the local burger joint fulltime if he didn't get into college this year. He saw his mother pick up the mail from the box at the end of the walkway. She smiled as she sorted the envelopes strolling back to the front door. Mercedes walked with a dip in her step. Her smile brightened as she sifted through the envelopes.

ACE read her body language, "Good news?"

"Something special for you, Mijo." She handed the envelope to ACE as if passing the baton in a relay race. ACE scooped it up as he soared past her, beating her to the front door.

ACE plopped on the couch and hefted the letter, judging its weight as a jeweler might assess the karats of a gemstone. "Too thick for another rejection!" he beamed.

Mercedes leaned against the door frame; arms crossed in contented anticipation as her son poised to open what must be his first college acceptance letter. Marvin caught up puffing a little from the short walk from the garage.

ACE ripped the envelope open from one end and tweezed the sheets out. He unfolded and read from the top of the page: Morehouse School of Divinity is pleased to offer you a seat in the class of—"

"What, Wait! Did you say School of Divinity?" Marvin mopped beads of sweat from a corrugated brow.

Mercedes confessed with glee. "Yep. I sent it in."

"Hey Dad, there's a baseball scholarship! FULL RIDE." ACE slapped his thigh.

"My son ain't gonna be no priest." Marvin faced his wife, "No ma'am, no ham, no spam, no Kool-Aid."

"He doesn't have to go into the clergy, Marvin. The curriculum is extensive. There are always empty seats in the school of divinity." Mercedes fixed her fists akimbo. "Probably because everyone profiles the school like you do. He can get an undergraduate degree in philosophy or something.

"There's Georgia State and Gwinnett College. He don't have to study under no priests."

ACE sat up and scooted to the edge of the sofa and leaned forward. "Dad, it's Morehouse, Dr. King, remember. And it's all paid for. No debt. And I get to play baseball!"

"I got the pitching coach of the Gwinnett Braves to write him a recommendation," Mercedes said.

Marvin scowled. "And how did you do that?"

"I just asked." Her arms were now crossed in anger at her husband, "We're not going through this again!"

Marvin mirrored her posture. "Don't see it happening. Nope."

After more than a minute of silence, ACE spoke up. "I'm over eighteen."

That marinated in the living room until it was done.

"Your son's asking for your blessing, Marvin, but he doesn't NEED it." Mercedes pleaded. "College baseball. The two of you have shared this dream for fifteen years." She crossed the room to her husband and wrapped herself around his arm, "Mi amor, por favor."

"That romance stuff ain't gonna cut it, Mercy. I'm not wit it." He shook her off his arm and turned his back on them. "You do what you want. I'm done."

The dog days of summer were sweltering but the emotional temperature in the Stryker household was chilled. Mercedes had forgiven Marvin as any good Christian would but the light for him had gone out of her eyes. Ever a dutiful wife and an attentive mother, but no more.

Ace's freshman experience at Morehouse College didn't distinguish itself academically or athletically. He made the pitching squad, but he didn't make the cut as a starter. He put in hours in the bullpen. Chip Nobles played catcher. The two bonded, getting better as the year went on.

By the beginning of sophomore year, Coach tried ACE out as a reliever. Good. Not Great. One save, three losses after the starter led by one run by the seventh inning.

The coach sat back in the stands talking to a man ACE and Chip hadn't seen before.

Chip said, "I can't hear the conversation, but I'd bet my only nut the guys a scout."

In the stands, Coach Roberts ran down ACE's profile. "Andrew Christopher Estrada-Stryker, ACE. Kid loves the game of baseball. His Dominican mother wants him to be a priest, but his blue-collar father is a baseball addict. The boy comes by his love of the game honestly.

ACE Stryker: Got a legendary name for a pitcher. Just wish he had the talent to go with it."

The quiet man said, "Let me talk to him for a minute."

The coach called ACE over.

"Hello, son. My name's Drake Hooker. I'm an independent scout. I'm team agnostic." He chuckled, "Strange introduction to a kid at a divinity school, I guess. I place a lot of second-string positions for a variety of teams that need urgent, last-minute players."

ACE whipped off his cap and scrunched it in his hands, almost begging, "Sir, if you could get me something, anything, I'd be forever in your debt."

Hooker smiled a sympathetic closed-lip smile and laid a gentle hand on the boy's shoulder. "Every ball player dreams of being a major league pitcher. They learn the basic skills, maybe master a couple of pitches but when they come up against some of the best prospects out there, they find their hopes evaporating every time. I hate to raise false optimism for anyone not willing to do what it takes to succeed."

ACE beseeched him. "Please, sir. I'll do ANYTHING for a shot at a major league mound."

"I hear that all the time," Hooker's eyes dipped in sorrow, "but when the going gets tough, young men falter. They see a line that they can't cross."

"I've worked for this all my life. There is NO line I won't cross. Not for this, sir."

"Yeah, everyone says that until the pint of blood and pound of flesh comes due," Hooker said, his eyes rising towards ACE's.

"Give me a chance, sir. I won't let you down. I swear on my mother's soul." ACE stuck out his hand to shake. Hooker left him hanging.

"A handshake? Really. It's going to take much more than that to get my help. We're talking about a gift that will change your life. I need more commitment than that." Hooker stared deep into ACE's eyes.

"Just tell me what you need, and I'll give it, Mr. Hooker."

"My birthday's this Friday. I'm having a party at the Gold Digger's Gentleman's Club on Linden Place. Why don't you drop by?"

"This Friday? That's my birthday, too!" ACE exclaimed. "Who could have guessed we'd have the same birthday? This is destiny, Mr. Hooker."

Hooker grinned, "Yeah. Who?" He scribbled a mark on his clipboard then handed ACE a Gold Digger business card. "This will get you in free. My treat. There's someone I want you to meet."

"I usually spend my birthday with my folks... but this would be my honor. I'm sure they'll understand, just this once." Excited, ACE turned, cherishing the business card invitation then hesitated and half smiled. "You're not a priest or anything like that, are ya, Mr. Hooker?"

Hooker frowned, "Why do you ask?"

ACE chuckled. "My Dad doesn't trust the clergy."

Hooker's voice grew a tad deeper, "No... I'm nothing like that."

"Great. I finally met my guardian angel!" ACE jogged off to the locker room.

Hooker wiped a rivulet of drool from the corner of his mouth before the coach caught up with him.

"So, what do you think? Can you use him?"

"Oh, yeah. He's a once-in-a-lifetime prospect, Sam. Got all the right stuff. We can use him to the quick."

* * *

ACE came in and dropped like a cannonball onto the couch next to his father and slapped his dad's thigh. He called his mother in from the kitchen where she was making every kind of dinner noise. "Mom, I talked to a scout today. He said I had the stuff. He says he can get me a tryout with the big leagues."

Marvin sat up from a slump, sweating in the 70-degree living room. "Who does he work for? What team?"

"No team, Dad. He's independent."

Marvin raised his eyebrows and scowled. "Does he work for the church, ACE?"

"No Dad. I asked. He works for a secular talent agency."

Mercedes dried her hands on a dish towel and gave her husband the side eye.

"What?" Marvin shrugged, "Just to make sure this guy's legit and not some pervert."

She said nothing but fixed her eyes on Marvin as she left the room.

ACE elbowed his dad and whispered, "Dad, he invited me to a strip club for my birthday."

Looking at his son's naïve grin, he asked, "How'd he know Friday is your birthday?"

"You won't believe this but it's his birthday, too! He told me before I told him it was my birthday. You don't mind, do you, Dad? I mean it's the first birthday I'd celebrate away from you and Mom."

Marvin looked at his son and considered the ask. "You ever been to a strip club before, son?"

"No, sir."

Marvin swabbed his forehead with his sleeve. "You're going to be 20 years old. You're a man and you'll have to start making manly decisions. Don't come back to a drink you leave on the bar if you have to step away for a dance or go to the bathroom, no matter who you leave guarding it. You hear me?"

"Yes, Dad." ACE grinned. "I'm not an idiot, you know."

Marvin twisted his mouth into some distortion of a smile, "Yeah, you say that now. Let's see how much sense you got when you got all those boobs swinging in your face."

ACE effortlessly hopped up off the couch. "I got to pick out somethin' to wear Friday."

Before leaving the room, he noticed his father struggle a bit too much getting out of the low seat. He silently offered Marvin a hand up, as athletes did, without a word reflecting the implication of weakness.

* * *

The voice of his GPS came through ACE's cell phone and directed him to the doors of The Gold Digger Gentleman's Club. There were two of the biggest bouncers he'd ever seen, dressed in black suits.

"Excuse me. I have an invite." ACE hoped his hands weren't shaking when he presented the card.

"Business cards are a dime a dozen. This don't get you nothi—" The big man flipped the card over in his hand and saw the mark of Drake Hooker.

He waved to his partner, "He's good." Then to ACE, "Go right on in, sir."

When Ace disappeared through the heavy, double red doors, the guard touched an earpiece and whispered, "He's here, sir."

A scantily clad hostess greeted ACE by name. "Hello Mr. Stryker. Happy birthday!" She hugged him warmly, then showed him to a private event room. "Here you are. She patted him on the butt and said, "Have fun."

Drake Hooker lounged, arms wide across the back of a red velvet love seat. "Welcome my young apprentice, are you ready to become rookie of the year?"

"Yes, sir!" ACE said with a crisp salute.

Hooker returned the salute, "There's someone I want you to meet."

Like magic, a wave of Hooker's hand beckoned an exotic beauty that defied description. She owned the room like an apex predator on the prowl. Graceful sinews from shoulders to hips sang a rolling serenade to the senses. ACE felt, rather than heard, the music flow around her. Ruby-red bodice with milk-white gloves up to her elbows and stockings to mid-thigh. Her stilettoes clicked to the music until they stopped six inches from his toes. Her breasts were almost touching him.

She pushed a pinch of cake into ACE's gaping mouth. "Huh?"

Hooker said, "Birthday Cake, ACE. It's Devil's Food. Sorry. No ice cream."

"Happy birthday, ACE!" The copper-colored woman lightly kissed his cheek and grazed his lips as she withdrew.

Mesmerized, he stammered, "Th-thanks…"

"We all call her Dirty Penny." Hooker laughed at ACE's awkwardness, "Show him how you got your name, won't you Penny?"

As he became aware of the sounds, and the other people in the room, ACE resented the scant lingerie sheathing her beauty. He wanted to see more! He squirmed as if confined by a strait jacket restraining his arms to his side. His zipper was less successful.

Her widening coy smile revealed pearly teeth between full lips that curled at the corners. She took his hand so gently that he wasn't sure she actually touched him until he felt the tide tow him into a private room. He was as helpless as an antelope in the jaws of a lioness. She dominated him with no more than a gesture, guided him down onto a daybed, and straddled him. He moved like a prisoner just uncuffed from shackles. She laughed as he pawed at her bodice but she did not resist.

Who or what is this creature? His mother's voice echoed faintly through a fog of scattered thoughts. Then his father's voice rumbled, *Condom…*

Dirty Penny embodied his favorite features of every ethnicity he could imagine. Looking down at his lap, he couldn't remember how his zipper opened. When he looked up, Penny's bodice had vanished. The pulsing desire took him out to a warm sea of silken sheets like so much driftwood. The notion of *wood* pulsed in his mind all night.

The next thing ACE remembered was Hooker half-carrying him to a taxi. Someone opened the door and slid him into the back seat. ACE heard him say, "Get him home safe." When Hooker leaned in to give the driver directions, ACE glimpsed Dirty Penny over his shoulder turning away from the car with a sneer on her beautiful face. As he watched her disappear back into the club he glanced at a wet spot in his pants, then realized it was dark red.

Hooker tapped him on the chest and said, "Time of your life, eh ACE?"

* * *

Monday the call of a lifetime cured the remanence of ACE's hangover. "Hello?" Yes, this is ACE Stryker." Mercedes and Marvin stared intently. "What?" Seconds went by before ACE said to his waiting parents, "I'm on the Los Angeles Angels pitching staff." All three Strykers jumped up and down in a celebratory rhythm for three minutes. Marvin was the first to succumb to exhaustion.

"They want me on a plane tomorrow."

Marvin gasped and laughed at the same time. "Then git yo ass upstairs and pack, boy!"

The private jet waiting for him gleamed redder than copper but still, his mind wandered to Dirty Penny more often than his pitching strategy on the four-hour flight. Chip Nobles called him back to reality. "ACE come on, man. We ain't got no time to nap. Sleep when you're dead. You gotta get these signals down pat."

ACE rubbed his eyes, "Yeah, I know. No second chances." He opened the well-worn notebook and flipped through it to a page labeled change ups.

The plane arrived at LAX and bypassed customs. A black Lincoln limousine awaited them at the curb. ACE and Chip grinned in triumph and hopped in. No sooner did they arrive at the Hilton did ACE say, "Don't go anywhere, sir. We're just going to drop our bags and head straight to the ballpark."

After a rushed registration, the boys returned to the limousine, each with a backpack. Chip ordered, "To the Field of Angels my good man."

They entered the bullpen to see two veteran pitchers practicing. ACE grinned from ear to ear. "Mind if we share the pen, fellas?"

The pitcher stopped and looked at the pitching coach. "You must be ACE Stryker," he said. The two pitchers coughed and burst out laughing. "What the hell? 'ACE Stryker,' seriously? Dude you can't come in here with a corny moniker like that!"

Coach Greer bristled at them. "Believe it or not guys, that's his REAL name. He's a Drake Hooker prospect, and I hear he's *that* good."

The players shrugged and went back to throwing.

ACE and Chip said nothing more and humbly took the farthest pitching lane and warmed up. After a few fastballs, one of the veterans stopped and walked over to the radar gun. ACE raised an eyebrow and Chip hunkered down for some heat. The pitch clocked in at 96 miles an hour.

Coach Greer puckered his bottom lip and said, "Not bad kid." He nodded to the catchers. "Let's get you out in front of some guys who can hit. We'll see what you can do."

* * *

ACE made the reliever's roster. He had twelve saves before the All-Star games. The Angels sent Red Benson to the American League team. The other three pitchers were all Yankees.

Coach Greer clapped ACE on a sweaty shoulder after the game. "Well, you got some fans, son. The players have spoken. ACE, you're Red's backup in the All-Star game."

ACE stood up and almost lost the towel wrapped around his waist. "What?"

Greer held his hand out and mock turned his head shying away from ACE's junk. "Calm down, bud. It's just symbolic. We've got four pitchers who are real 'Aces.' It's more a nod to your impressive rookie season. You grab pine on national TV."

ACE cinched his towel and gave an appreciative bow. "Thanks, Coach."

Greer fist-bumped the rookie and waddled out of the locker room. ACE scurried a row over to find Chip Nobles. "Chip, did you hear? I'm on the pitching roster for the All-Star game!"

"I heard. This could be your big break. Just one inning, that's all you need to show your stuff."

"Nah. I'm just a placeholder." ACE clenched his right hand around his left fist as if it were a baseball. "But still…"

Game day, ACE proudly took his place at the far end of the bench, ignored or sneered at by the veterans who earned their places on the team by seasons of great ball playing. Top of the third and the Yankee's starter hadn't gotten to pitch. Red Benson was hot. Only one hit in two scoreless innings. Rick Ellison and Red had history, ugly public history. No one knew the background except that Drake Hooker recruited both of them in their early careers. Red climbed the stairs to take the mound. As he turned to acknowledge a kudo from a coach, Ellison spat on the step in front of him. Red's foot slipped and he went straight down on his right elbow. ACE thought he heard an audible crack when he fell. Red clutched his elbow. The pitching coach saw it all and called the penalty on Ellison.

"No spitting on the field or dugout. That's sacred!" He admonished Ellison.

The umpire ejected Ellison from the game.

The American League dropped from two Cy Young winners to one. Tony Postel didn't look happy when he took the mound. The National League took a walk and a double on the next two batters. Postel showed no remorse or effort in his pitches. Nothing topped eighty miles per hour. The next batter brought the two base runners home on a hard, off the wall double. Postel snickered when the catcher shrugged a wordless "WTF" expression.

The pitching coach trotted out to the mound to have a word with the Yankee's bad boy. Flush-faced, the pitching coach glanced back at the head coach for permission and got a vigorous nod. "You're out jack ass. Hit the showers."

Postel wobbled his head, "Yeah, who you gonna replace me with? You think Paulson's gonna throw real heat for the guy that threw out TWO of his fellow pitchers?"

The pitching coach's face went from tomato to beet red. He turned his back and stomped back to the dugout. "Kid, you're up!" He glared back at Postel who couldn't believe the decision to call his bluff.

ACE popped up like crispy bread from a toaster. He pounded his glove and charged the hill giving Postel a wide birth. The boos from the stands were deafening.

The announcers talked as ACE warmed up for his first pitch. "This rookie's had a good year but he's out of his league here. I don't know what Coach Robinson's thinking. The American League's in trouble out there. He thinks this kid's going to get him out of this jam?"

ACE took a deep breath and played his focus theme song in his head. *Bang, Bang.* The first pitch blazed past the Met's centerfielder at 99 miles an hour and backed him off the plate a foot. He adjusted his helmet, tipped approval to a worthy adversary, and dug his cleats in for a deep cut at the next pitch. The next came low and outside nipping the corner of the strike zone at 102 miles an hour for the second strike. The outfielder swung too soon at the sinker that came in dead-center of the strike zone at 80 miles an hour. The 500-batter struck out to a rookie on three pitches.

One announcer asked the other, "What's the kid's name again?"

"That is ACE Stryker. I think that's going to be a name to remember."

Robinson kept ACE in for six more innings. Nary another run scored for the National League team for the rest of the game. ACE made front page news and owned the news cycle on the cable channels. He moved up to top reliever for the Angel's late summer games. The Angels found themselves in the American League Pennant race with none other than the New York Yankees.

By game four, the Angels were up two games to one over the Bronx Bombers, but the Yankee bats were hot. The Angels starter got behind 6 to 2 by the seventh inning stretch. Red Benson remained on the injured list. ACE took the mound. He cooled the Yankees' bats like a one-man blizzard. The Angels clinched the American League Pennant with a 7 to 6 win over the struggling Yankees.

ACE burst through the front door with the news, "Mom, Dad, you're not gonna believe—"

Marvin lurched forward and coughed up a clump of blood into a merlot-colored puddle on the coffee table.

Mercedes ordered, "ACE, Call an ambulance."

* * *

ACE brooded in the molded waiting room chair, "How long has Dad been sick?"

Mercedes stared glassy eyed into the corridor that swallowed her husband. "The night sweats started six months ago, then the weight loss."

"But his belly. It's so big," ACE asked confused.

"The doctors call it ascites." Mercedes shook her head. "There's some kind of blockage. He has lymphoma. They tried chemotherapy. It worked on the cancer but wiped out his bone marrow."

ACE nearly didn't ask the obvious question. "Is he going to die?"

Mercedes stared at her hands as her fingers desperately wrestled one another. "He needs a bone marrow transplant. I can't give it. He has no brothers. No sisters. His parents are gone."

"What are you saying?"

Mercedes looked deeply into ACE's eyes, "Your father may not last to get an anonymous donor. You may be his only chance."

ACE backed away looking to the ceiling as if searching for heaven's mercy. "I-I can't."

"What?"

"Mom. I can't." Tears welled in his eyes, "I have been chosen. Chosen to be the starting pitcher in the World Series." ACE dropped to his knees. "He told me. He TOLD me!"

"Who told you?"

"Mr. Hooker. He told me I would face a challenge—a choice few men could make."

"What? ACE, this is your father. Your father's life. That's what's in your hands. Not some filthy baseball."

"Mom. I promised. I swore before God."

Her eyes opened wide. Tears spilled out of them as her head trembled rather than shook side to side.

"This was Dad's dream, too. We gotta have faith, Mom."

She had no words. She slapped him hard enough to spin his head. He couldn't meet her lingering gaze. ACE moped out of the hospital doors into the night.

* * *

The first week in October, ACE reported for pitching practice. Chip tapped him on the shoulder, all grins. "Let's load up that gun."

The opener against the Braves found Angel Stadium packed. The Braves drew first blood with a single homer on ACE's third pitch. ACE settled down and went to work.

The morning headlines were all about the pitching phenom called ACE Stryker and the amazing coincidence of the name. His performance ruled the news cycle; ACE Stryker was the talk of the nation. The Angels looked unstoppable. By game five, it all turned sour. The Angels led three games to two, as Marvin Stryker took a turn for the worse.

ACE dodged paparazzi and traditional reporters navigating through the hospital lobby. Breathless, he burst into his father's room demanding an update on his dad's status.

"They can't break his fever," Mercedes said through tears. She curled up on the floor at her husband's bedside clutching his hand. "—but his hands are so cold."

ACE gripped the bed rails as he surveyed Marvin's fragile frame. "What's the prognosis?"

"His white cells are almost nonexistent. He has nothing to fight with."

The doctor swept into the room right behind ACE. "Your father is in a fight for his life. He desperately needs a bone marrow transplant. Have you been tested, son?"

ACE nodded, "Yes, sir."

"So, I see. You were a match." The Doctor concluded.

"Doctor, I'm pitching in the World Series."

The physician's eyebrows arched upward. "For the Braves?"

ACE shook his head and glance away toward his father. "No. I'm playing for the Angels."

The doctor's gaze also drifted toward Marvin Stryker. "Well, can't someone sub for you?"

"I'm the starting pitcher and the series is tied at 3 to 3. This is the final game."

The doctor stared at him for a long minute. "Your dad is not stable. Definitive treatment is time sensitive. There's a good likelihood that we'll have to intubate him tonight. That's a stop-gap measure. He won't last long if we do that. Do you understand what I'm telling you, son?"

"Doctor, this is not only my dream, it's my father's, too. Ever since I was three. This is a once-in-a-lifetime chance. I gotta take my shot, for him and for me."

Mercedes began bawling frantically.

Both men turned to her for a heart-breaking moment then met each other's gaze. ACE said, "The game is at 6 tonight. It should be over by 9, 10 at the latest. Can I sign in for the... procedure then?"

"It's very irregular, but this is one for the textbooks. I'll arrange it. I just hope it's not too late."

After a forlorn look at his distraught mother, ACE disappeared into the shadows of the hall.

* * *

After a soulful rendition of the national anthem by the last Grammy-winner, two veteran Brave retiree announcers opened the game with the history and stats of the championship challengers.

"Well Brian, this is it. Who'd have guessed the Angels could beat the Yankees to face the invincible Braves?"

"That's right, Jon. This is going to be an interesting matchup: The home team's defense led by Damon Wynn has shut down every team in the National League. The red-hot Braves bats against the Angels rookie hurler. The Braves have racked up the highest scoring average I've seen during regular season baseball in years."

"That's right Brian, but the long balls have been evading the Braves' bats in the postseason. They actually entered this series as underdogs. If it weren't for the two injuries in the Angels' pitching staff, the series would be over by now. The pressure's really going to be on this young pitcher tonight. Question is, can he live up to his name? ACE Stryker. The gods of the game must have sent this guy from Baseball Valhalla. He's got an ERA of 0.7 in the postseason!" the retired Braves pitcher went on, "That beats the lowest ERA in baseball history previously set by Hubert 'Dutch' Leonard back in 1914."

"Yeah, but can he sustain that record against these hungry Braves batters? He's got a 'gun' and amazing stamina. This is shaping up to be a hell of a ball game tonight."

"One for the ages, Brian." He clapped, "Let's get this show going. Up first is..."

ACE took the mound, raised two fingers, kissed them, and silently raised them overhead, tossing tribute to heaven. The Atlanta crowd cheered him as one of their own.

"That's for his Dad, Brian. I just heard that his father is in critical condition at Hamilton Medical Center. Let's see if that burden is a distraction or a motivator for the kid tonight."

The applause died down as ACE wound up for the first pitch. He let loose with a scorcher down the middle of the zone clocked at 101 MPH. Chip Nobles had to step away and shake his left hand to work the feeling back. "Noble blew on it for show, but I can tell you, that's not all theater. After a 110 mph catch, that's some hot leather."

Ten minutes later, "Change of sides and ACE finishes the first inning with nine pitches, all with one baseball that never kissed wood."

The Braves ace rifled more than his share of strikes. The Angels didn't score their first run until the fifth inning. The two sixth-inning runs were hard-fought. Damon Wynn didn't let a ball drop in the outfield. The game was turning into a pitching duel.

Jon said, "The Braves starter is a crafty pitcher trying hard to hold a clinic on the field, but ACE Stryker is teaching a master class. NO ONE has hit a pitched ball by this kid all night. He's got that laser fastball workin' which he dishes with seasoning: Curveball 78 mph, sinker, slider, and that ridiculous knuckleball thing he's got going. It defies the laws of physics, Brian. Never saw anything like it."

The Angels were starving at the plate. If the Braves pitcher had a Barretta, ACE had a canon. By the middle of the seventh inning, ACE reigned with an honest-to-God, no-hitter. No foul balls, no walks, no fly balls, no bunts. On average, Braves fanned two of three pitches and got caught looking on the third. A Braves slugger got himself ejected when he threw the bat in frustration.

"Three zip, Jon. There's no stopping this guy. He ain't even broke a sweat!"

"Brian, I tell you, there's never been anything like this. This just in; the viewership has now topped three times the largest share any World Series game has ever drawn. All eyes are on ACE Stryker tonight."

Brian interrupted his colleague. "Wait. Pete Robinson's trotting out to the bump. What's up?"

"Don't know. I can't imagine any manager taking a pitcher running this hot out of a game."

Boos erupted from the crowd.

Jon pondered, "Something's really wrong out there. ACE looks like a statue. What's Robinson telling him?"

"Jon, I'm getting a feed in from the AP. Says Marvin Stryker's not doing well."

"Oh, man. His old man was in dire straits coming into tonight's game. This turn must be really bad."

Pete Robinson told him. "ACE, they say your dad arrested twice. They got him back but they're scared. The DOCTORS are scared." He patted ACE on the shoulder. "Go to your father, son. We got this."

ACE handed Robinson his glove with a grateful nod but no words. On his run through the dugout, Drake Hooker caught ACE's eye and slowly shook his head. Dirty Penny hung on the agent's arm and mirrored Hooker's expression.

ACE made his way to the locker room, peeled his shirt off, and grabbed his phone and wallet. He called for a private car service when Hooker appeared in the doorway.

"This is one of those times I told you about, ACE. A time when you'd have to make a hard choice. I'm sorry that choice is this hard."

Penny's shadow loomed in the dim hall light just outside the locker room.

"Mr. Hooker, it's my Dad. He's dying!"

"Are you a doctor, son?" Hooker asked. "What do you think YOU can do for him?"

ACE stared at the man in disbelief.

"You can comfort your sainted mother in her time of grief, but you're helpless to change your father's fate. You can, however, cement his and your legacy. Finish the game. I've spoken to the doctors for you. The soonest they can perform the bone marrow transplant is first thing in the morning."

Penny slithered into the doorway. "Don't throw away this magic night, ACE." She purred, "Listen to Mr. Hooker."

Hooker had a TV remote control in hand and turned on the monitor. The crowd was on their feet. The Angels relief pitcher had just walked his second batter. Hooker looked at ACE. "You can salvage this, ACE. Only you…"

Robotically, ACE found himself plodding back to the dugout. He watched the slow-moving trainwreck of the top of the eighth inning. Red Benson's arm was wilting. Chip stopped his second wild pitch.

A player somewhere behind ACE murmured, "He's behind in the count."

Another announced, "He's yippy as crap."

"Never came back from the nerve injury. We're at the bottom of the ninth. He shouldn't even be pitching…"

ACE punched the dugout railing and sidled up to the manager. *One lucky hit and we're in extra innings.* "Mr. Robinson, you gotta put me back in."

"What are you still doing here? You should be halfway to the hospital."

"The Angels need me more than my Dad. I can't help him, but I can save his dream, Mr. Robinson. Please. Put me back in."

Red Benson hurled another wild one. Ninety-two miles an hour. It got by Chip. He chased it down and checked the second base runner rounding third he turned back five feet from the bag. The Brave just did beat the ball back to third base. Chip Noble looked at Robinson and shook his head.

Robinson called the bullpen. Jay Walker staggered up to gasps from the crowd. Robinson intercepted him before he got to the mound. Eyes red and glazed, Robinson didn't know what the man was on, but it wouldn't end well for the Angels tonight. He hiked a thumb back to the locker room. He followed the dopy reliever back to the dugout.

"Walk this guy, Mr. Robinson, I'll take it from there."

At a gesture from Robinson, Chip flicked four fingers at Red. The Noodler hung his head before nodding and tossed a meatball two feet wide of the plate for walk number three.

ACE passed Red on his way to the mound. Red mouthed "thank you" as ACE patted him on the butt with his glove. No words needed.

The winning run at the plate, ACE sized him up. A lefty. A good one with no outs. ACE closed his eyes and began to sing softly, *Bang, bang.*

The batter ground his cleats into the chalked box.

ACE painted the lower outside corner and looked for the two-fingered gesture but didn't get it. The ump looked grimly at the scoreboard as a '1' appeared in the 'ball' column.

Squeezing the strike zone. I'm going to have to work for this one.

He curled a slider low mid-strike zone. The ump fingered a strike. ACE followed up with a 104-mph fastball. He ended the slugger's misery with a change-up. First out in the bottom of the ninth garnered a roaring cheer. ACE retired the next Brave from the batter's box with three pitches.

The Brave on Deck made Chip and Pete Robinson smile. Bane of the Angels batters in the outfield all season Damon Wynn held the worst batting average in baseball.

One of the announcers summed it up, "This has gotta give Pete Robinson a warm fuzzy feeling, Jon. I think the Braves just handed the Angels the championship. This Damon Wynn's like an air-conditioner: He fans every pitch within a mile of the plate. I don't understand why the Braves don't put in a designated hitter here."

"Yeah, I don't know. This guy needs to return his bat to Walmart, unused."

The announcers laughed as Damon Wynn knocked the dirt off his cleats with the bat stretched carried his bat through a swinging arc and braced for the first pitch.

"He ought to tell 'em, it's got a hole in it, Jon."

ACE threw a 92-mph sinker. As expected, Wynn swung through the smoke trail. Next, ACE's bread and butter caught Wynn looking.

"One pitch and we're done here, Brian."

"The crowds are already beginning to file out of the park, Jon. They know what we know. This kid's gonna punch this guy's lights out on the next pitch. Wynn holds the dubious record for the worst batting average in baseball history. There's never been a hitter below one hundred in a century of professional ball. This guy's not in a slump; he's in a grave."

The rest of this crowd wants to witness the first Perfect Series Game in decades.

"The count's 0 and 2. Bottom of the ninth, folks. ACE Stryker's is about to put a bow on this series for the Angels."

ACE checked the third-base runner. He threw a hanger just above the zone. Check swing. Nothing from the Ump.

ACE scowled, *Come on! That was a strike.*

"This umpire's got a postage stamp for a strike zone, Brian. ACE ain't gonna get away with any cheap stuff. He's got to deliver the goods."

ACE wound up and delivered a scorcher down the middle of the zone at 102 mph. Wynn just touched the ball in passing. Chip stopped the bullet but didn't catch it.

The umpire announced, "Foul!"

ACE squared his shoulders. He pierced the inside upper corner at 104. Wynn caught enough to send into the dirt right of the plate.

Foul.

Change up low and outside.

Foul!

Hanger at 106.

Damon Wynn found the heart of the ball and the crowd rose collectively to their feet. ACE sighed relief when the ball died west of the left field line.

"He tattooed that one, Jon. This is a Damon Wynn we've never seen. No one's hit Stryker's pitches like this."

ACE wound up and concentrated. He let loose with a fastball Wynn tipped it right of the right-field foul line.

"That one's a record for the fastest pitch in Series history. A 110-mile-per-hour scorcher. How did Demon Wynn even see that coming?"

The next five pitches rocked with the rhythm of a seesaw. Wynn moved to tap everything ACE spat at him. The batter and hurler danced for twenty more pitches.

"Wynn hits like he's possessed, Brian."

"ACE has never faced a beast like this guy. 'Demon Wynn' should be his new moniker, Jon."

For ten pitches the hearts of both Brave and Angel fans rose in their throats over and over again. A dozen armor-piercing pitches wound up deep in the stands on either side of the diamond.

"Wynn's bat found the ball in this marathon 9th but he can't seem to find the field."

"The threat can't be ignored, Jon. If the wind blows the wrong way, one of those Moonshots will win the game for the Braves."

"This is a case of pride going before the fall, Brian. The smart play here would be for Stryker to walk this SOB, sacrifice the shutout, keep the no-hitter, and mow down the next batter."

"He's doing this for his dad. He can't let it go." Brian said, "It may cost the Angels the series."

"What can Robinson do though? He's got no relief in the bullpen. The Angels have all their hopes pinned on this young ace. I just hope he has the maturity to recognize he has to take one for the team and do what he has to do here.

The pitching coach called time out and climbed the hill to approach ACE.

"ACE, walk this guy. He's got the devil in him tonight. Walk in the run and move on to the next one."

ACE cast his eyes down at the dirt and nodded.

Chip got the message. He stretched his arm wide of the plate away from Damon Wynn's swing. ACE tossed a 75-mph ball right at the mitt. Wynn caught the tip of it.

Foul.

Again, and again, Wynn went after the wide stuff.

"Man, ACE hasn't found leather in over thirty pitches!"

"Jon, we're in uncharted waters here. No mortal pitcher has ever gone this long without a strike, or a hit, and ACE is a thoroughbred, a God among pitchers."

Eight wide ones and Chip shrugged at Robinson. Pete buried his head in folded arm for a moment then raised it and gave the nod.

"Finally, Robinson just greenlit ACE to unleash a storm on Wynn, Brian. Let's finish this duel."

ACE went to work. No matter how great a job he did, he gained no traction.

"ACE has served up his full menu, folks; Low and inside, hung one at the top of the zone, Bender, nuclear fastball, followed by the filthiest changeups I've seen. This Wynn is like a Red Wall. Nothing goes past him, Brian."

"The pitch count is approaching fifty in this inning alone. Add that to the seventy pitches he threw in the first seven innings and ACE Stryker is now in record territory for the most pitches in one game."

"He's thrown fifteen balls this game, eleven in this inning alone. We've broken more records so far tonight than ever before, Brian. My worry is, what's this barrage of 100 mph bombs doing to this kid's pitching arm? His elbow, his shoulder, his back?"

"That last pitch clocked in at 100, Jon. Seems to me like he still has some gas left."

"We'll see."

Wynn laces a foul to the left. ACE removed his glove and massaged his right shoulder. Chip offered respite until the umpire signaled to get the ball back in play.

ACE tried some experimental pitches that he and Chip had practiced together. Wynn ate them up, sending souvenirs to the stands.

"That last meatball went foul. This has been a two-player game for the Angels. It's just a matter of time before Wynn finds the fences. The way he's spraying the park, the Angels can't even bring in the outfield. If one drops in the gap, a run will score with two outs."

Sweat poured into ACE's eyes. He wiped them clear and looked at the batter. Damon Wynn smiled. A demonic red façade greeted ACE and for just an instant, he could swear Damon's eyes flared fire.

What the what? ACE shook his head and found a mortal man at the plate.

ACE looked up in the stands to find Hooker for moral support. The scouting agent flashed a horned, red face for a second, fanging a sneer out to the mound. Penny wrapped snake-scaled arms around Hooker's neck as she blew ACE a kiss and flicked a forked tongue at the pitcher.

God, please help me.

"What's Stryker doing, Jon?"

"He's calling for another glove. Maybe he tore some laces or something, Brian. It's been a long game."

The bat boy trotted out with a right-handed pitcher's glove.

"Well, that takes the cake. He's switching pitching hands!"

"Did I miss something? Is ACE Stryker ambidextrous, Jon?"

"Not that I've heard." Jon said, "Let's see how he does here."

ACE crossed himself before the first left-handed pitch. Hooker frowned and whispered to Dirty Penny. "Yeah, that won't help him. The sinister hand is all mine. His father just pounded his last heartbeat. The kids ours."

* * *

As the code team called the final resuscitation attempt, a nurse pulled the sheet over Marvin Stryker's face. Father Bishop had already administered the last rites and now prayed with Mercedes. The game playing on the television in the room showed ACE switching to left-handed pitching.

Mercedes whispered, "No…"

* * *

ACE pumped 105-mile-an-hour fastballs and 98-mile-an-hour curves. Wynn nailed them all. Bounced each one foul at the right and left field posts in succession.

"This is a royal mess, Brian. ACE can't walk the guy, and he can't strike him out. Damon Wynn is just grinding him down. With the laser show he's performing out there, it's just a matter of time before he pounds one out over the fence."

"My count has ACE at 150 pitches this game. He can't keep this up and Wynn looks like he's only getting started."

"All ACE can do is hope for rain." Jon looked up at the starry Atlanta sky and scoffed.

A breeze rose as ACE wound up for his next pitch. The dust blew past the batter's box, momentarily blinding both batter and catcher. Damon Wynn swung and smoked one right at ACE. It caught him off-guard. ACE, accustomed to right-handed pitching, reached across his body with a bare left hand. Broken fingers deflected the blast to his right wrist. Lightning pulsed through his arm. ACE didn't realize the snow cone catch he made until he could hear the crowd cheering. He couldn't move his hands.

Damon Wynn smashed the bat against the plate in a fury of splinters.

In unison, the former Braves cheered from the announcers' booth, "Angels win, Angels WIN!"

The big screen displayed the split image of Mercedes Stryker on one side and Angels and Braves carrying her son from the field in triumph.

The announcers dubbed it, "The greatest game EVER played."

ACE looked for Drake Hooker. He found him gritting his teeth before flipping ACE the bird. He and Dirty Penny disappeared into the crowd, never to be seen by ACE again.

In an interview, a reporter asked Mercedes what she thought of her son and his decision to stay in the game while his father lay dying in the hospital.

"Some things are just meant to be. I don't know that anything could have saved my husband if it was his time to go." Tears welled in her eyes, "the Devil tried to take Andrew by the left hand. It was a sinister move in my boy's time of need, but I will always believe that before my husband's soul left this plane, he guided ACE out of that final inning. My boy came through it."

The closing remarks from the two sports announcers on the screen droned in the background.

"They say that spectacular defensive play cost him both hands. Rumor has it both bone and nerve injuries. ACE Stryker may never play again."

"My son fulfilled his destiny. His and my Marvin's. Come what may, they're both at peace now."

Father Bishop raised a hand and announced, "No more questions."

A tenacious reporter pressed, "What about ACE's career, Father?"

"I think the Angels have spoken, everyone." Bishop gestured to the television where they all gathered in the lobby. "There's nothing more to be said."

DAPHINE
BY
VIOLETTE L. MEIER

"You really have a type. You know that?" Zenobia asked as she tossed a fried shrimp into her highly glossed mouth and tossed the tail onto the edge of her dinner plate. She wiped her mouth; brown foundation and glittery lip gloss covered the napkin like sparkling mud thick with mica.

"My type is my business," Daphine retorted, leaning back in her chair, and allowing her eyes to take note of every older gentleman in the room.

"I'm not trying to get in your business but you're forty-nine years old, still piping hot, well-to-do, and cool as hell. Why do you date geriatric white men? By looks, your last date was at least eighty! Atlanta is full of fine men of every color. I'm not saying that you have to date a brother, but old Jim Crow looking men are not the move. A matter of fact, even when we were young you were picking up men twenty to thirty years our senior. Why them? Didn't yo' mama tell you that old men will give you worms?" Zenobia asked before taking a long sip of a turquoise blue cocktail with a rainbow umbrella leaning off the rim.

"Again, my business," Daphine snapped. She crossed her long yellow legs and let her high heel swing on the tip of her toes.

"I told you that my husband Van's business partner Christavius is crazy about you," Zenobia said. "He's your age, handsome, spiritual, financially stable, straight, and kind. His ex-girlfriend used to work with me. She told everyone that he's the reason why she's bow-legged," Zenobia laughed aloud. "He's a catch girl. If I were single, I would date him or at least take his stick shift for a test drive!"

"How can he be crazy about me? He doesn't even know me," Daphine chuckled, still scoping the bar for men.

"He met you last year at the Christmas party at my house. Ya'll danced together all night long. He even made your evil behind smile," Zenobia jested.

Daphine laughed too. She remembered him. She liked him, but he was not who she was looking for.

"I think you should give the man a chance. There's no reason to be alone for the rest of your life. The last time you were really happy was when you were seven," Zenobia said, the mirth sucked from her voice like a syringe. "That was forty-two years ago Daphine. Let the past go. We ain't getting any younger. The time for fun is now."

Daphine's eyes went dark. Forty-two years ago was the last time she had seen her twin brother, Davante' alive. A tightness in her chest made her gasp and exhale slowly trying to banish the emotional pain that throbbed within her.

"Bingo," Daphine whispered and sat up, quickly pushing away all thoughts of her twin brother. She pulled her shoe onto her heel and stood up.

"That's him," a voice whispered.

"I'll pay for your food. You can leave when you're done. I'll not be leaving alone tonight," Daphine said confidently, adjusting her dress. "Talk to you later Zenobia. Love you lots!" Daphine kissed her friend on the cheek and left the table taking slow sensual steps towards a liver spotted old man sitting at the bar.

Zenobia let out a sigh and rolled her eyes before she crunched on another shrimp.

"Anyone sitting here?" Daphine cooed, leaning so close to the older man that her lips brushed his ear.

He looked up at her, shocked to see a vibrant light-skinned black woman with thick curly red hair and a seductive smile.

"N...n... No one is sitting here. P.. p...please join me," he stuttered, pulling the barstool out for her to sit down.

"What's a sophisticated young man doing here alone?" Daphine asked as she looked into the old man's graying blue eyes. Cataracts bit at the edges of his irises. A hairy mole sat high on his cheek. Canyons of wrinkles were carved on every inch of his face.

The man smiled, the pink skin around his mouth curling.

"Would you like a drink?" he asked smiling with a mouth full of teeth all the exact same size and shape like yellowing ceramic rectangles glued together.

"No thank you," she sweetly declined. "Are you married?"

The old man hesitated. His eyes told her that he was.

"It doesn't matter," she said. "What's one night?" She smiled, running her tongue over her teeth.

The old man swallowed hard as she stood up from her stool and extended her hand to him. He accepted, stood up, and followed her out of the bar.

* * *

"Earlier tonight, the body of seventy-five-year-old real estate mogul, Richard Kramer, was found in the front seat of his car with his throat slashed and a mysterious marking carved into his chest. Witnesses say that he was last seen leaving a popular upscale Atlanta bar with a younger woman. He leaves behind his wife of thirty years and four adult children. Investigators say that this is the seventh victim of what authorities call the A-town Massacres in the last four years bearing the same marking," Aashvi Patel, a veteran news reporter reported through the flat-screen television hanging above the fireplace in Daphine's master bedroom. "The FBI has been called to aid in the investigation. Atlanta hasn't seen serial killings of this magnitude since the Atlanta Child Murders circa 1979-1981."

"He got what he deserved," a voice whispered.

Daphine turned the TV off and climbed into bed.

A heavy knock made her front door vibrate.

Daphine threw her legs over the side of the bed and slid her feet into a pair of satin slippers then grabbed the matching robe which hung on the back of the door. Dragging her feet, she made her way to the front door.

"Who is it?" Daphine asked through the thick wooden door, knowing exactly who it was.

"Kat."

Daphine opened the door and stepped aside to let a tiny, frail, blue-haired woman into the apartment. Her skin was pale and clinging to her bones. Thick white whiskers dotted both corners of her lips. Bulky dentures filled her small mouth. Hunched back and slow-walking, Katherine O'Hara, better known as Ms. Kat, took nearly two minutes to cross the threshold. At a hundred and nine years old, she remained a beautiful woman full of creativity and tenacity. Head of the apartment welcome committee, a choir member at church, and the sharpest shooter on this side of the Mason Dixon, Kat was a hardcore feminist, a vicious advocate for human rights, and a widow whose adoring husband died two-decades earlier. She lived alone in the apartment across the hall but made a welcomed appearance in Daphine's living room at least thrice weekly.

"What are you doing out so late Ms. Kat?" Daphine asked the elderly woman who was now sitting on the edge of a nearby chair.

"It's only eight o'clock my dear. The moon is barely out," Kat said in a voice rich with age. "I just came to tell you that my son Bobby is coming to stay with me for a couple of weeks so if you see a man going in and out of my apartment, you know who it is. I don't want you to worry my dear. You look out for me so well."

Daphine smiled and squeezed the old woman's hand.

"I'm glad you told me. You know I don't play about your safety Ms. Kat. You're like my nanna," Daphine said sincerely. Her blood-related grandparents meant everything to her when they were alive. Their wisdom and understanding brought her profound stability for the first half of her life. Now all of them were deceased and Ms. Kat helped fill a void in Daphine's heart.

"I know dear," replied Kat. "I want you to meet him. I warn you; he can be unpleasant at times because he idolized my politically incorrect brutish father, but like dad, in his heart, he's a good boy. Will you come over to lunch with us?"

"Of course, I will," Daphine agreed. "Set the date and time and I'll be there."

* * *

A short stocky doorman with olive skin and long blonde hair opened the door to Southern Elect, an elite country club for a diversity of Atlanta socialites and frequented by local celebrities and the bourgeoisie. Daphine, Zenobia, Van, and Christavius stepped inside.

Normally Daphine didn't have a stomach for such pretentious places, but her best friend begged her to go so there she was dressed to kill and apparently on a double date.

"I'm glad you agreed to come with us," Zenobia whispered into Daphine's ear as they walked into a grand ballroom decorated in lush fabrics, fragrant blossoms, ornate furniture, and angular chandeliers.

"How can I say no? You pestered me for weeks," Daphine replied. "Did I really have a choice after you threatened to come to my house and drag me out by my hair?"

Zenobia laughed, "You know I would have done it too!"

The couples found their table. Christavius pulled out Daphine's chair then sat down beside her.

"Thank you," she said avoiding his eyes. Kind, amber, and long lashed, his penetrating eyes made her stomach flip. Daphine had to keep her focus. He was not who she was looking for tonight.

"You're welcome," he replied.

A server came to the table almost immediately offering champagne, fresh fruit, and hors d' oeuvres.

Zenobia filled her plate with tasty bites.

Daphine declined everything but the champagne.

"It's been a long time since I've seen you," Christavius said, smiling big and wide. His handsome face was pleasant and his cologne intoxicating.

"Yes, it has been quite a while," Daphine agreed, unable to squelch the smile taking over her face. She had to admit to herself that Christavius was charming.

"Did y'all here about that man that got murdered last month?" Van asked while swallowing a whole strawberry.

Daphine was mentally preparing to do the Heimlich maneuver in case Van fell over the side of the table.

Christavius' smile vanished. He turned his attention from Daphine to Van.

"Yes," Christavius replied. "My firm is handling that case. The victim's family is suing the nightclub he was parked outside of for having inadequate security."

"The man that got killed kinda looked like the old coot that Daphine left the club with when we went out last month," Zenobia laughed. She bit into a strawberry then fed one to her husband.

Daphine rolled her eyes and took a sip of champagne.

"There's nothing funny about what happened to that man," Christavius scolded. "He was butchered. No one deserves to die like that. No one."

Zenobia's countenance fell. She looked away and stuffed another strawberry into her mouth. "Sorry," she whispered under her breath.

Daphine tuned out of the conversation. Her idea of a fun night did not consist of discussing murder over dinner.

"I'll be back," she said and disappeared before anyone could respond. She walked over to the window where the lights of the city twinkled like a concrete and glass universe. She leaned against the floor to ceiling windowpane until she spotted movement in her peripheral.

"I remember when this place wasn't so urban," an elderly man with graying blue eyes and a mole on his cheek said. He sat at a nearby table complaining to a woman who looked a decade or three younger than him.

The woman sipped her champagne and nodded. From the look in her eye, she heard nothing he said, nor did she care about what she missed. She was there for his bank account not his personality.

"In my day, everyone knew their place," he droned on. "Certain types were not allowed in exclusive country clubs. Now, anyone can get into anywhere!"

His companion nodded and sipped, trying her best to look interested. If her mortgage wasn't past due, she would cut her losses and go home.

"Excuse me sweet cake, I have to go to the little boy's room," he said getting up from the table and slowly making his way across the room; a shadow followed close behind him.

Daphine put down her glass and followed behind him into the men's room.

The old man unzipped his pants and began to relieve himself when Daphine locked the door behind her and stood beside the urinal.

"What are you doing in here?" he growled zipping his trousers so fast that he almost zipped his most prized possession in the zipper.

"I overheard your conversation about how urban the club has become and some people not knowing their place. Who are these people?" she asked, leaning against the wall with her hand in her purse.

"He's talking about us," a voice whispered into Daphine's ear.

The old man scoffed; his eyes burning with fury.

"You don't have a right to ask me anything. You people have no boundaries. A man can't even piss in peace! Did affirmative action give you access to the toilet too?" he hissed.

"It's him," the voice said.

"No, it just gave me access to you," Daphine huffed as she pounced on the old man like a feral cat on a maimed squirrel. Her hand was out of her purse, wielding a curved blade before he could move an inch.

The old man pushed her against the wall, but she was on his back before he could reach the door. Her blade dug deep into his pink flesh as his futile howl faded into a low gurgle. His body hit the floor. She tore open his button-down shirt and artfully engraved his left breast.

Daphine washed her hands and returned the blade to her purse. She rinsed off the bottom of her red-bottom heels and breathed a sigh of relief that she decided to wear all black. Bloodstains, if there were any, were not detectable on her dress. She took a paper towel and hand sanitizer and wiped her fingerprints from the door, then made her way back to the table to her friends.

"Where were you?" Zenobia asked loudly over the live band. "I took the liberty of ordering for you."

"Thanks. I appreciate that," Daphine said, her demeanor uneasy.

"You didn't tell me where you were," Zenobia prided, her voice slurring a bit.

Two empty champagne glasses and one shot glass sat empty on the table next to Zenobia's purse.

Daphine laughed, "You can never hold your liquor. Sit back and stop breathing in my face."

Zenobia leaned away from her best friend and sighed, her head bobbing like an apple.

"Where did you go?" Zenobia asked, trying to contain her buzz. "You got something on your dress," she slurred reaching for a tiny bloody ball of flesh.

Daphine knocked her friend's hand away and quickly disposed of the human meat within her handbag.

"I thought I left my mama at home," Daphine quipped, unease creeping into her voice causing it to crack, then turned her attention towards Christavius. "Are you from Atlanta?"

"I am," he smiled. "Born and raised in East Lake Meadows."

"You from the hood!" Van laughed.

"So am I," Daphine replied. "I grew up in the West End. Harris Homes until..." her voice trailed off. Her glossy eyes fixed across the room.

"You better not cry!" a voice whispered into Daphine's ear.

"Until what?" Christavius asked, puzzled by Daphine's sudden pause and demeanor shift.

"Until her twin brother, Devante' got killed during the Atlanta Child Murders," Zenobia answered. "After then, she moved to Stone Mountain where we met in elementary school and been friends ever since."

"Oh my God! I'm sorry that happened to your brother," Christavius offered his condolences. "That was a scary time for all of us. I remember my parents not allowing us to go outside to play and taking us to and from school instead of letting us walk like we used to. Rumors of children getting snatched on street corners and killers crawling through windows had us all shook. I can't imagine the trauma you suffered. Again, I'm so sorry for your loss."

Daphine diverted her eyes. Pools of mascara-tinged water accumulated and rolled down her cheeks.

"May I?" Christavius asked as he picked up a napkin.

Daphine nodded.

He gently wiped her face and folded the napkin into her hand then kissed it.

"I'm sorry," he whispered.

Daphine smiled at his kindness, took a deep breath, and pulled herself together.

"I like him," the voice whispered.

"Me too," she uttered a hushed reply.

"You too what?" Christavius asked, confused by her response. He placed his hand upon hers and waited.

"She too traumatized!" Zanobia belted, "Her brother getting killed was especially traumatic for Daphine. She said she saw the kidnapper. She said he was a white man with gray-blue eyes and a mole on his face," Zenobia yelped, her breath smelling of champagne and strawberries.

"How many of these did you let her have?" Daphine asked Van who was busy stuffing his mouth with steak.

"She grown. I can't let her do nothin'," he mumbled while chewing.

Daphine was amazed that such a bony man could eat so much food.

"Chris, can you believe she dates white men after she saw a white man kidnap her brother? He tried to kidnap her too, but she got away. Devante wasn't as lucky," Zenobia slurred, her hot breath blasting across the table. "They found his body days later behind the projects. Daphine ain't been right since."

"You doin' too much! I'm finna go!" Daphine barked angrily, picking up her purse and standing up. Her chair flew backwards and landed on its side with a booming thump. She couldn't believe Zenobia was so casually telling a stranger about her brother's death. Daphine wanted to strangle her, but before Daphine could storm away from the table, a team of police officers rushed into the ballroom.

"What's going on?" Van asked one of the servers who was trembling and crying hysterically. The woman pointed to the bathroom area.

"They found a dead man in the bathroom. Somebody killed him!"

* * *

Peaches' Pristine Porch, whose southern cuisine was praised throughout the south, was a black-owned landmark diner located on Auburn Ave next to the Royal Peacock "Club Beautiful" – a famous Atlanta nightclub that hosted greats like Ray Charles, Marvin Gaye, and Martin Luther King, Jr. Now dancehall reggae and freestyle hip hop battles keep its doors ajar. Peaches' Pristine Porch was one of the first restaurants that openly served an integrated clientele without danger in the south and its walls still boasts of its activism promoting civil rights.

Daphine and Ms. Kat were escorted to a small table with a checkerboard tablecloth and white cloth napkins. A lone daffodil bobbled in a skinny crystal vase in the middle of the table.

"What time will your son get here?" Daphine asked, picking up a menu and flipping through the laminated pages edged with gold.

"I'm not sure. I haven't seen him. I've been calling him for days and he hasn't picked up. He left my house a week ago all dressed up with a young bimbo on his arm. It seemed clear to everyone but him that the only thing she was interested in was his wallet," Ms. Kat grumbled. "I figured he has been shacked up at her house for the week. I texted him a lunch reminder. He didn't reply, but he never misses a date."

"Maybe he's just running late," Daphine said, patting the back of Ms. Kat's hand to comfort her. A worried frown bent her lips as she sipped water with trembling hands.

An old retro black and white TV sat on the dessert counter.

"Can you turn that up for me please?" an older man, with a voice so smooth he could narrate documentaries, asked the waiter nicely.

Ms. Kat smiled at the man whose mahogany skin matched his plaid shirt and trousers.

"That's my kind of man," Ms. Kat meowed.

Daphine laughed so hard that her whole body submitted to hysteria.

"I don't know why he wants to watch the news. It's nothing but chaos and disorder. The news is banned from my house! I have no room for fearmongering," Ms. Kat spat.

"The newest victim of the A-town Massacres has been identified by his partner as Robert O'Hara, son of 109-year-old Atlanta socialite Katherine O'Hara. He was discovered in the restroom of an elite social club in Midtown Atlanta. Robert O'Hara was an engineer in his mid-seventies. The victim's partner said he was visiting family in the Atlanta area," Aashvi Patel reported through the black and white television.

Ms. Kat grabbed her chest and slid from her chair to the floor. By the time the ambulance arrived, she was cold.

* * *

"I didn't think our first date would end with us being questioned by the police about a murder," Christavius texted. "Redo?"

"Sure," Daphine texted back.

"I know it's short notice but are you busy tonight?" he texted.

Daphine closed a file on her desk and put it in a drawer. Her administrative assistant waved goodbye in the doorway and exited into the elevator.

Daphine leaned back in her chair and tried hard to think of a good excuse why she couldn't meet him. She could think of nothing, so she texted, "I'm free. What do you have in mind?"

"Meet me at Grant Park in the small pavilion. I'll be there at eight. I hope you like sushi," he texted.

"I don't." she replied. "I hate it in fact."

"Sweet tea pizza?" he texted.

"Now you're talking. ☺ See you soon." She texted and dropped her phone in her purse.

* * *

Daphine walked beneath the trees of Grant Park. Warm air tousled leaves and tickled the skin of her arms and face. She leaned against one of the trunks and slipped her sandals off and allowed her feet to sink into the plush emerald grass. She walked until she saw Christavius's wide smile shining from underneath the pavilion.

"Hey beautiful," he greeted, trotting to her and throwing his arms around her like they had known each other for decades.

Daphine uncomfortably reciprocated and forced a smile.

He slipped his arm inside hers and escorted her to a picnic table set with fine china and silverware. A bottle of expensive wine sat in the middle of the table with wine glasses decorated with flakes of gold and a sweet tea pizza as big as a car tire. A pair of electric candles flickered on each side of the entrée.

"Wow, all this for me?" Daphine laughed. She admired and appreciated his creativity. She sat down and dropped her belongings next to her. "The pizza smells so good. How did you keep it hot for so long?"

"I can't tell you my trade secrets," he joked as he slid into the seat across from her.

The couple laughed and talked for hours. Conversation flowed easily.

"It's getting dark. Want to continue this at my place?" Christavius smirked and placed his hand upon hers.

Daphine blushed. It had been a long time since she had entertained romance. Her life had no room for it.

"Let me think about it," she whispered. "I'm going to run to the bathroom real quick. I'll be right back."

226

Chris stood up.

"I'll walk you," he said.

"No need. I'll be back before you know it," she replied.

"But it's dark and the park can be dangerous at night. I would be more comfortable walking you," he insisted.

"I can take care of myself," she huffed, her eyes and brows pinching. She stood up from the table so quickly that she almost lost her balance.

"I know you can, but I wouldn't be a man if I didn't look after your safety," he replied trying not to chuckle. He found her fierce independence foolish but kind of sexy.

"You're right," she softened and exhaled. "Thank you for being a gentleman. Please escort me."

The couple walked to the stone lavatory building located near a fountain. Christavius watched Daphine enter the ladies' room then went into the men's room.

Daphine exited the bathroom stall with her purse in hand. She placed the purse strap on her shoulder and exited the restroom. The strap hooked onto the doorknob and snapped, spilling the contents in her purse onto the concrete. A combination of obscenities exited her mouth as she stooped down to pick up her things. As she gathered her belongings, a pair of pale hands handed her a tube of lipstick and her wallet.

"Here you go ma'am," a man said as he dropped the items into her hands.

Daphine surveyed his ivory face and studied his gray-blue eyes. Kindness rested there but that didn't matter. Age seemed to subjugate the wickedness of youth. A humble smile often hid the stain of past sins. A small flat mole rested on his cheekbone. His off-white tank top and biking shorts blended into his rosacea blotched skin.

She cocked her head to the side and spied his bicycle leaning against a tree. He handed her a package of tissues and her keys.

"I think this is it," he said. He turned on his cell phone's flashlight to ensure that there was nothing left to pick up. He extended his hand to help her up. She stood without assistance.

"Thank you," she said. Sweat began to dampen her armpits.

"You're welcome pretty lady. It was my pleasure," he smiled. "Make sure you hurry out of the park. It's getting pretty dark. There can be some unsavory people out at night," he warned as he turned and walked towards his bike.

"He is the unsavory one," a voice whispered to Daphine.

Daphine slipped her hands into the inner pocket of her purse and retrieved a pocketknife, her eyes wild and stretched. Her teeth bared. Hot air pushing from her nostrils. She sprinted behind the friendly pedestrian and raised her knife above her head and drove it down between his shoulder blades with the strength of ten men. The blade slid through his back like a butterknife through a ripe strawberry. Blood splattered across her cheeks as she sliced life from the innocent. She turned the man onto his back and cut the front of his tank top open. She pressed her blade into his pectoral and began to inscribe her mark.

"Daphine!" Christavius screamed as he turned the corner.

Daphine looked up. Blood splattered across her face like raspberry jam.

"What are you doing!" Christavius yelped. His arms outreached. His eyes were affright. He took a step towards her.

"He…he…attacked me," she lied pulling her blade from the dead man leaking crimson at her feet. Daphine stood up and turned towards her date.

Christavius looked at the gnarled body then back at her. Except for the blood spattered across her face and clothes, she looked untouched. Not a hair was out of place. Not a wrinkle in her garments. Her makeup was flawless. Even her expression was serene.

He dialed 911 and put the phone on speaker.

"911. How can I help you?"

"A man has been stabbed in Grant Park. Please send help immediately. He's located near the public restrooms," Christavius said then hung up the phone, placed it into his pocket, then pulled out the gun resting in the small of his back.

"Tell me what happened," he whispered, his knuckles aching from his grip on the gun pressed against his thigh. "How did he attack you?"

Daphine's eyes alternated between his face and his gun.

"I was leaving the bathroom and he ran up on me," she whispered. "He rushed towards me, and I pulled a knife from my bag and stabbed him."

"What were you doing to his chest?" Christavius asked, anxiously tapping the barrel of the gun on his leg.

Daphine said nothing.

They locked eyes. Silence between them.

"Stab him," a voice whispered in her ear.

A small shadow darted in her peripheral.

Daphine's eyes followed the inky figure.

"If you stab him, you and I will finally be together," the shadow whispered as it stood behind Christavius.

Daphine leapt towards Christavius, knife overhead, face crazed. Christavius shot three bullets into her chest. She hit the ground in a twist of screams and cried. He rushed to her side. The shadow hovered over her dying face next to Christavius.

"Why?" Christavius asked as he kneeled and cradled her head in his arms. "Why?"

"He killed my brother," she gurgled, blood erupting from the sides of her mouth. "The man with the cold eyes and mole killed my brother. Every time I kill the man, he comes back, and I have to kill him again," she choked then looked past Christavius' tearing eyes into the face of the shadow. The inky black of the shadow faded into a technicolor being which shifted into the face of a light brown boy.

Sirens tore through the silence. Legions of footsteps rushed towards the bloody couple.

"Davante'," Daphine whispered; her eyes locked and staring in the distance. A smile bending her lips upward. Her chest stilled. Like her brother, she was gone.

MONSTERS ON THE MOUNT'
BY
ROBERT JEFFREY II

The sisters sat watching the news, the days tragic events flooding the small room. Footage of pitched gun battles over Stone Mountain Park rolled across the screen, while reporters and citizens rushed to cover. Taliyah held her tears in check; Lizzie let hers drop. Grandma sat next to them, her prayers rising to roof above her small Conyers home.

That's when a blinding blast erupted miles away at the park, forever changing the world.

* * *

Lizzie sat, her knees pulled up to her chest, looking out the room's window. She'd put in her earbuds, as the sounds of Anita Baker filtered through her ears. The young woman let the music take her away from the loud preparations taking place in the adjacent hangar.

Starlight sifted through the thick pained window, shining down on her. Outside sickly gray looking craters lined the Moon's surface. Many of the settlers found the terrain to be harsh, unforgiving, and "straight up ugly" as one of Lizzie's colony classmates had remarked when their contingent had arrived at the lunar base.

For the young woman there was something beautiful about looking at the craggy indentations that made up her home's surface. What she saw always reminded her of when her parents would take her hiking back home in Georgia. Sandy Creek Park. Sawnee Mountain Preserve. Ivy Creek Greenway.

Stone Mountain Park.

"Lizzie! You in there?"

She smiled, hearing the concerned hitch in her sister's voice over the music.

"Come in, sis."

The door whooshed open, allowing the tall frame of her sister to step through the doorway, carrying a tablet. Taliyah always joked she got the height from Daddy, and Lizzie got the short stack, frizzy fro' genetics from their Momma. Taliyah's sinewy frame was pushed into her jumpsuit, covered by the standard issue Seeker armor. The nano fiber combat bodysuit came replete with malleable insulation for protection from extreme environments, an adaptive camouflage layer, and enhanced plasma shielding against most types of weapon fire.

Taliyah had opted for bantu knots the last time they'd done each other's hair. Though Lizzie had done a good job following the lead of their mothers' lessons, she always admitted that Momma had always been better at doing hair. Lizzie remembered when she'd visit Taliyah for hair styling/ braiding sessions on base at Fort Stewart when she'd first enlisted. Lizzie would tag along, her attention alternating between her latest engineering class textbook, and Momma showing her the finer points of doing Taliyah's hair.

It wasn't just the height Taliyah had taken from her Daddy. She'd gotten the same dark skin, full lips, and hazel eyes as her father. She'd more than grown into the "imposing looking lady" their dad had always called her, pride rising in Taliyah whenever he said it.

Lizzie pulled out her earbuds. "What's the word?"

"The team's still prepping," Taliyah replied. She placed the tablet on a nearby table, typing in a set of figures. A holographic image of Earth appeared in front of them, glowing blue. Taliyah typed some more on the tablet, and the image zoomed in even further, showing the point of interest in greater detail.

Lizzie looked back outside, watching a lunar rover shuttle a group of settlers to an awaiting transport. The Jemison class vessel had become the standard ferry to their new home on planet Kamaal. The ship was cylindrical in shape, sleek in overall aesthetic, with FTL engines jutting from the end of the vessel. Convoys of the Kamaal bound travelers had slowed as of late, as ion storms on Earth had increased over the past few months preventing Seeker operations.

"I keep thinking, "When's our turn"? Lizzie asked.

"When the job's done," Taliyah replied. This conversation had been a constant and showed no signs of slowing down anytime soon.

"Taliyah, you say that every time they push our launch date back. There's always another mission," Lizzie said, frustration mounting.

Taliyah gave her a look, the "the serious stare".

"What'd I tell you when you joined up?" Taliyah said.

"Taliyah…"

"Nope. Like Grandma used to say, you want to have grown folks' conversations, let's do it. What did I tell you?"

Lizzie looked at the spectral image her sister's tablet was projecting, as if to escape from the escalating argument. Miniature holographic clouds rolled across the vast part of North America. The area was a wasteland, where ion storms appeared with extreme frequency and above ground living was fast becoming no longer possible. As a consequence of The Fall, the world had become almost uninhabitable, most of the planet now a scorched wasteland. Oceans had become charged glowing pools where sea life no longer existed. Cityscapes stood as burned and hallowed out testaments to the destruction wrought by the ion storms, constantly getting struck by the electrical tempests.

Back on the blighted Earth, Lizzie could hold her own with the other Seekers. She was one of the best Tech operatives the program had produced. Retrieval missions, search and rescue, and Scavyr strikes. She'd done it all on Earth. But confrontations with her sister: she hated them. She wasn't scared of Taliyah. In fact, she loved her sibling fiercely. Arguments with Taliyah though had become tedious over the years at the Tycho Alpha colony. And she did everything she could to avoid them. She'd often find ways to lose herself in the constant engineering work on base, avoiding Taliyah and showdowns any way she could.

And why? Taliyah was all the family she had left. Their entire world had gone to hell and swallowed everyone up in it. She couldn't afford to lose her.

Still looking at the hologram, she whispered, "The colony comes first. We come second."

"Exactly. So, if the Collective decides to push our settlement orders back again, we don't question it. I'm tired of having to repeat myself. Maybe it's a military thing. Momma and Daddy would've understood, us all being Army."

Lizzie's head jerked up. "No. You don't get to do that. I know Momma and Daddy would never back down from helping people who needed it. So don't throw that in my face like I don't give a damn about responsibility. That's some passive aggressive shit, and low coming from you."

Taliyah realized maybe she'd crossed a line. "Lizzie…"

"What's the mission?" Lizzie said, ending any further conversation.

The older sister took the hint and typed a few new commands on the tablet. Zooming further into the image, Taliyah brought up the Southeast region of the former United States of America. More zooming. Georgia. More zooming. The metro Atlanta area. More zooming.

Lizzie's breath caught in her throat.

"Taliyah, tell me this is a joke."

Taliyah looked up at her sister, the blue of the hologram illuminating the concern etched on her face.

"It's not," Taliyah replied.

Lizzie stood up, walking around the table, as if seeing the light construct from different angles might make it more real. In front of her, the bombed out husk of Stone Mountain stood in front of her. As if hollowed out by a frustrated deity, the top of the mountain had been ripped off, creating a hollow chasm which led to God knew where.

"Hell," was all Lizzie could muster.

* * *

The transport shuttle, the Ericsson, shook as it broke Earth's atmosphere. Though Mission Control back on Tycho Alpha had been able to gauge an opening in the blanket of ion storms, the skies above North America still rolled with fierce winds that buffeted the McNair class Seeker transport. As the piloting team breached the cloud cover, the world beneath was sheathed in a daytime darkness. Fuchsia colored lightning struck in the distance, its threat ever omnipresent.

A table stood at the top of the cargo hold of the transport's interior, projecting the same blighted remains of Stone Mountain Lizzie had seen earlier. Seeker Team Alpha-4 (STA4) were gathered, all not trying to lose their lunches as the ship shook. Lizzie and Taliyah sat next to each other, each assessing their mission briefs on tablets. To their left, sat Taliyah's second in command, and partner, Wren.

A superb tactician, and one of the best operatives the Seekers had produced, Wren was the ying to Taliyah's yang, smiling and optimistic, where Taliyah could muster a "meh" smile at best, ever the realist. Wren's hair was cut short to her scalp, and her ebony skin shone in the room's fluorescent lights as she leaned her 5'8" frame over to place a quick kiss on Taliyah's cheek.

She motioned to Lizzie, seeing the younger woman's furrowed brow, understanding her sour mood.

"Taliyah, you could've waited to tell her until the team was all together," Wren said, concern filling her voice.

"We don't have time for band aids."

Wren cocked an eyebrow in frustration, as if to say, "For real?" and walked over to Lizzie. She hugged the young woman she'd dubbed "Mouse", letting Lizzie lay her head on her shoulder.

"I know it's hard, but we've got you. Even your stubborn ass sister," Wren said, sticking her tongue out at her spouse.

The shuttle lurched to the side, the winds outside howling as the ship began its push along the Eastern coastline of the former United

States. Lizzie looked outside at the roiling waves smashing against the crystalized shoreline of Maryland

"So can all of us call the commander an ass, or just her wife?" Jacob said, smiling, his feet perched on the table.

Jacob was the team's long-range operator, and the resident irritant up everyone's butt. A scar ran the length of the right side of his face, ending at his perpetual smile. He'd always bragged the other guy got it worse. His long flowing hair was pulled back in a ponytail, a testament to his Polynesian heritage.

"Please try it. I'll definitely place bets on what happens after," Renata said.

Rounding out the rest of STA4 was Renata. An expert in hand to hand combat, infiltration, and heavy weaponry, the Brazilian had earned her moniker of "Bruiser" with glee. As their group's mission success count climbed amongst the other Seeker groups, a healthy bit of "off the books" competitions at Tycho Alpha was a constant. Some of these often involved cage fights, which Renata won consistently. The muscled warrior kept her fists wrapped in hand wraps, because as she often said during training sessions, "Fights are the only constants in life, and I don't like getting my butt whooped".

"Stow it and listen to the commander." Wren said nodding to Taliyah.

"Thanks Wren. Now, business. The tech heads on Tycho Alpha have found the Terminium motherload, and we've been tasked with retrieving it."

The room sat silent, Wren, Lizzie, and Taliyah's faces looking somber. Jacob and Renata watched them, confused.

"Commander, isn't this a good thing? The Collective's been praying for the ion storms to open up enough for us to make some more runs to the surface. I mean, y'all are looking like you've gotten the worse news in the world," Jacob said.

Lizzie pulled up the same hologram over the table from earlier. "It's at Stone Mountain."

Renata and Jacob sat a little straighter, now understanding the subdued mood.

"I've...heard stories about this place," Renata said, walking around the table. "Ground Zero. We called it "O Parque do Diabo" back in Rio. Never knew anything about the spot until The Fall."

"That's the location where them hicks, God's Patriots, they exploded the bomb? Some experimental shit that caused the storm? Created Terminium?" Jacob said.

234

Lizzie focused on the rotating exploded remains of the mountain, her emotions rolling. "That's the place…" Taliyah and Wren understood, but the others had no idea. "Our parents were there when it exploded." Her words were forced.

Taliyah looked over at Lizzie, as the younger woman closed her eyes, memories of the day flooding back. She focused on the projection, knowing time for sitting with her memories wasn't a luxury she could afford.

"Our Terminium stores are running low, and we've still got 25% of the populace left to shuttle to Kamaal," Taliyah said. "Though the ion storms have been hellish freak occurrences, they've also provided us with the main component of our FTL fuel: Terminium. Right now, all Seeker teams are spread across the planet, obtaining whatever remaining caches of the material they can. Whether it's stripping the resource from deposits or launching counteroffensives "liberating" illegal caches from Scavyr's worldwide, this is our last push to stock up on reserves. Yes, the Seekers are being stretched to our breaking point.

"But we need something that'll be long lasting, and that's where we come in. Our scientists believe if we can get a highly pure sample from Ground Zero, then they'll be able to synthesize the resource for years to come."

She felt Lizzie's eyes on her, and she returned the look.

"Then we go to our new home on Kamaal. No more fighting. No more living by the skin of our teeth. No more Seeker missions," Taliyah said.

The commander saw a hand raise and nodded her head. Jacob looked around the hold at the team, uncharacteristically hesitant to talk.

"Jacob, just say it," Taliyah said. She'd been prepared for this, after running through her "Eyes Only" brief about previous missions to the Mount'.

"Well, Commander, I know we've got the Scavyrs to worry about. I ain't worried about them. But…. I've heard things about the Mount'. Like weird shit. Recon groups, combat drones going missing. Whole mining teams, coming back, not the same. If they come back at all." The young man shifted in his seat. "Now, officially, I always thought the brass didn't want to spook the Seekers. Especially when some of us stopped coming back from Mount' missions."

"And then, there's…"

"The monsters."

Everyone turned to Lizzie, who'd spoken. She shot a glance at Taliyah, knowing she was treading on territory she wasn't probably supposed to be traveling on. Taliyah offered a brief nod, and the words came out in a rush.

"Eggheads talk. We're excitable like that," Lizzie said. "Biologists, engineers, computer technicians. We'd go over whatever data the Collective wouldn't classify as "redacted" or "classified". But we'd still talk."

"I heard about scientists and miners who'd gone missing during Terminium extraction trips. Strange, scanned data of the cavern system. Grainy drone footage of "things" hanging back in the shadows, deeper in the caverns. Whatever it was, it caused the Collective to halt mining operations in the area for years."

Wren noticed her partner was uncharacteristically quiet. "Anything to add? I find it sus that your lower ranking sister and our resident co-median might have more intel on something than our commander. I mean, you've got to know something."

Taliyah looked at the team, their faces carrying questions.

"All I'll say is this: keep your head on a swivel, and let's try and get the fuck out of here, ASAP," Taliyah replied.

Just then, the Ericsson was rocked by ground fire, lighting the skies around them in a fiery blaze.

* * *

"What do you mean "monsters", Momma?" Lizzie said, her 10 year old face scrunching up in confusion.

Vickie March looked away towards the part of the mountain which slopped down towards the iconic mural.

"Remember when Daddy and I talked to you about the Civil Rights movement?" Vickie said. "You learned about people like Coretta Scott King, Martin Luther King, and John Lewis?"

"Yeah, Ms. Avance had us do a report on it for Black History Month. We learned about Claudette Colvin, Medgar Evers, Rosa Parks, and a bunch of people," Lizzie replied.

"That's good," Vickie said with a small smile. "Well, there's more that you need to know about. About Stone Mountain. You know the mural on the front of the mountain? We see it especially close when we watch the laser show. Those men on the front of it, they fought for the Confederacy."

Lizzie's face fell, hearing her last word. Her parents had taught her about the Civil War, the South's fight to continue to force black people into bondage, and she remembered it giving her nightmares. She'd woken up some nights in a cold sweat, hyperventilating as images of the traumas her parents had spoken about played in the mindscape of her sleep.

"Why would they put people like that on the Mountain?" Lizzie said. Her young mind grappled with why something so disgusting might be celebrated on something as beautiful as the park she cherished.

"Because there was a time, and still is, where this state and country, was run by monsters," Ernest March said. "They want people to stay afraid of the bad things they used to do, but also, they want the Mount' to act sort of as a "celebration" of the terror they subjected black people to."

"The Klan even used to kick it here. Used to have cross burnings and rallies right where we're sitting," Taliyah said, the teenager drumming her fingers on the picnic table. Lizzie knew her sister only did that when she was angry.

"Taliyah's right Lizzie," Vickie said, concern etching her voice. "Your sisters older, so we've already had talks like this with her. She knows a little bit more about this place's history. But we want you to know also. Because even though this is a place we hike at, have picnic's at, and that's brought us a lot of good times, you always need to know the truth."

Ernest sat beside Lizzie, her brow still furrowed. "And if you decide you never wanted to come here again, because of what we're telling you, we get it," Ernest said hugging his youngest baby girl. "But Lizzie, because we know how much you love this place, we felt we needed to tell you everything about it."

Lizzie thought for a minute, her family watching. She looked in the direction her mom had pointed, remembering countless summer evenings spent at the Laser and Fireworks show the park would put on. She remembered looking up at those four men, riding on their horses, the lasers even bringing them to life and causing them to ride gallantly across the rock face.

But it was all a lie.

"Tell me more about the monsters," Lizzie said.

And they told her about the monsters of the Mount'.

* * *

The transport hit the ground hard, kicking up scarred Earth. The pilots were able to "land" the Ericsson on the Stone Mountain Memorial Lawn. For as far as the eye could see, the scorched ground spread around them, no plant life to be seen anywhere. Though the ion storms were now distant, gray clouds hung above the area, blanketing the expanse in a perpetual gloom. Dilapidated tourist structures including a museum, picnic areas, restaurants, and a children's park stood destroyed, burned, and falling into disrepair. The air stank of something forever burning, mixed with a metallic tinge.

Small arms and automatic fire peppered the transport, leaving indentations on the ship's side.

"I'm showing twelve holed' up at the museum! More heading in from the east!" the lead pilot, a seasoned veteran named Jamie, called over the system's intercom. "Wright's in a bad way!"

"Will he last?! Can we get airborne!?" Taliyah called through to the wall mounted speaker.

"Yeah, he's breathing, but there might be more going on inside!" Jamie replied. "Damn inbreds nicked us good with some old-timey surface to air projectiles, typical Scavyr scrapped shit," Jamie said. "But the longer we stay...."

Taliyah slammed a magazine in her modded MD Carbine. "Understood. Keep the engine running Jamie. We're going to run and gun this one. Computer, enact Kenneth Protocol, A84. Mark targets and lay down suppression fire."

Turrets jutted out from the Ericsson's side, marking heated signatures in and around the demolished remains of the museum. AI controlled massive rounds were let loose finding their targets, and the pained yells of the Scavyrs resounded across the lawn.

The suppression fire was just a stopgap, so they knew they needed to move quickly. The team checked their sidearms and secondary's, making sure they were locked and loaded.

"Lizzie, get 'em airborne," Taliyah said, as the group gathered on the lower level of the cargo hold near their ground vehicle dubbed the Odyssey. Her younger sister tapped a digital gauntlet on her arm, pulling up the schematics for a team she dubbed, "Gummi Bears". Six AI controlled drones lifted from their opened crates, flying a protective overwatch of the group in the cargo hold. The drones were modeled after the extinct eagles, replete with the latest recon and advanced weapons technology.

Arms fire continued to hit the side of the vessel, which the team ignored, finishing up with their gear check. A durable bullet proof material coated the outer lining of the Ericsson, so for now, they were safe.

"Okay, listen up. Wren, Lizzie, and I are going to get the goods," Taliyah said. "Renata, Jacob, as soon as the hatch opens, I need you both to lay down some cover fire. We've got to conserve ammo for the Ericsson's defensive systems. Only use the transport weapons systems if you see any of the Scavyr bringing in heavy hardware. Otherwise, just let them pop off with the small arms all they want."

"Once we get outside, Lizzie, get Tummi, Sunni, and Cubbi providing recon and cover fire for the transport. The rest of the drones go with us into the caves. Everyone got it?"

The team nodded, but Jacob raised his hand.

"So, we're just gonna ignore Lizzie basically said, "thar' be monsters in them caves"?"

"Well, like I said, they're in the caves doofus," Lizzie said.

"I ain't no doofus, doofus," Jacob replied grinning, loading his SB-40 sniper rifle. "Now, last question: what's separating us from winding up like everyone else who came to the Mount'?"

All eyes once again turned to Taliyah who simply replied, "I've got it handled."

Her response got a few arched eyebrows from Wren and Renata, while Lizzie sighed, used to the secretive nature of her sister when it came to Seeker work. The best thing to do she realized a long time ago was to "Trust in Taliyah". It'd worked so far.

"Zummi, Gruffi, Grammi, on me," Lizzie said. Three of the drones floated above Lizzie as she typed away at the digital readout on her gauntlet.

Stowing their weapons in the vehicle's cargo hold, Wren and Taliyah climbed into the front seats of the Odyssey, while Lizzie strapped herself in the backseat. The Odyssey was a Lunar Terrain Vehicle (LTV) designed to carry up to six passengers, an advanced version of the Artemis program era vehicles which had been used on the Moon. Upgraded to survive the storm stricken climate of Earth, gather and relay real-time scientific data to the Collective's Tycho Alpha colony, and provide offensive countermeasures in the event of an attack, the vehicle had come in handy on many Seeker missions.

"You good?" Lizzie said as Taliyah pulled up a projected navigation console, and the Odyssey's weapons network.

"I appreciate the check in, but remember, I'm the big sister," Taliyah said. "Don't switch up on me."

"Yeah, whatever. I'll do what I want old lady."

Smiling, Taliyah said over her shoulder, "I got your "old lady". Just concentrate on the tech stuff."

Wren flipped a pair of switches, powering up the vehicle. "Mouse, always clap back. Your sister ain't nobody."

Taliyah mouthed an "I hate you" to the driver, and Wren grinned as she gripped the wheel.

Taliyah activated the team's communication network. "Everyone, COMMS check,".

Each member raised a fist in confirmation. Renata and Jacob stood at the ready on either side of the transport, weapons raised to the closed hatchway.

"Let's ride," Wren said, remotely opening the transport hatch.

As soon as the doorway opened, gunfire erupted across the Odyssey. The bulletproof glass did its job and allowed Wren to push the mammoth vehicle out of the hatchway, the drones racing out to take on their respective tasks. A group of Scavyrs were concentrating their gunfire on the Odyssey as it raced out, not noticing the two remaining Seekers. Jacob lined up an attacker in his sight, took a deep breath in, and fired. The Scavyr dropped, and Jacob began his rinse and repeat routine, creating three corpses in all

As the remaining group of Scavyrs finally realized what was happening, it was too late. Renata let off her "shock and awe" part of the mission. She laid down cover fire with her upgraded Milkor MGL, dropping a pair of grenades on the terrified attackers.

The path cleared, the Odyssey weaved between the mammoth broken rocks littering the base of Stone Mountain, lurching forward towards the cave networks that extended beneath the destroyed Mount'.

* * *

The Odyssey barreled down the caverns underneath the dead mountain, as the minutes wound down. The path to the last recorded Seeker mining site was a twisting one, eating up time the team didn't have. Cave walls were illuminated by the headlights of the LTV as Wren expertly guided the vehicle through the network of grottos. Taliyah kept her eyes on the navigation display, the system of hollowed out tunnels stretching out for miles in front of them.

Wren's eyes stayed steadfast on the meandering passageways in front of them. "How we looking honey?"

"We're good...so far," Taliyah said adjusting the display in front of her to allow for a course correction. "Right."

Wren wrenched the wheel in the indicated direction, whipping Lizzie against the vehicle's side. "Ouch."

"Sorry," Wren said pressing her foot even more on the pedal.

"Left, then a sharp right," Taliyah said not looking up from the nav console.

They continued in silence, Gruffi following in their wake, floating like a silent sentinel against the dark.

Lizzie read an indicator which'd come through from Grammi and Zummi. "Taliyah, I'm sending something to Nav. New coordinates."

"Received. Wren, bank down and hug the wall," Taliyah said, watching water drip on the windshield from hanging stalactites above them. "We're circling around to the bottom. So, keep it slow."

The Odyssey soon reached the bottom of the chasm, headlights shining on the remnants of an abandoned Seeker mining colony. Ripped research tents, broken excavation machinery, and bloody torn uniforms were strewn across the muddy cave floor. The only sound to be heard was the dripping of water from the ceiling and the soft hum from the drones. Zummi and Gruffi patrolled the area above, and Wren climbed to the top of the Odyssey, scanning the cave walls with a pair of thermal goggles.

"There," Lizzie said, pointing at a crevice set deeply into a nearby rockface. Grammi raced forward, shooting a laser at the solid granite, sediment and rock shards flying off. Lizzie watched the progress, guiding Grammi with minor input from her gauntlet, ensuring they eventually hit the right vein of Terminium.

"Commander! Commander, do you copy?!" Renata's voice said through the COMMS system. Gunfire, and muffled explosions could be heard through the staticky connection.

"Renata, I copy," Taliyah said, watching her sister guide the hovering drone. "Give me a sit-rep."

"It's getting messy up here," Renata said, more gunfire punctuating her conversation. "Wait Commander-Jacob, tell Jamie to load more ammo into the turrets! What?! I don't care! We're not gonna make it another minute if we don't handle those gunners! Do it!"

"Boss, the Scavyrs have shown up with the heavies! Two mounted RPG launchers. The drones are doing their best, taking them out but it's not enough. Don't know how much time we have!" Another loud boom. More static. "Dam-! Comman-"

Renata's voice disappeared in a mass of static and then was gone. "Lizzie, where are we at?"

As she saw her sister, her spirits soared. Lizzie stood in front of her, hands gloved, holding a shining object. Terminium. Many often described the ore as heaven sent, whenever they had a chance to glimpse its lilac and aqua green brilliance shining firsthand. To see the material up close was close to a religious experience for some, and a symbol of the future the material spelled for humanity.

Lizzie placed several samples of mineral in an awaiting container, which was quickly carried to the cargo hold of the Odyssey by Grammi.

"Taliyah, Lizzie. We need to leave. Now," Wren said, her voice carrying a tone which Taliyah didn't hear often from her spouse. Fear.

Looking up at the earthen ramp which spelled their escape from the chasm, Lizzie gasped, while Taliyah's grip on her weapon tightened. The stench was the first thing they noticed. Musky, earthen, and sour. It hit their nostrils in a silent wave, reeking of decay. The sources of this scent stepped forth, the reflecting headlights of the Odyssey showing the creatures partially.

Their skin was blotchy in places, the illumination of the headlamps made it look almost waxen. They shuffled with mouths open as if trying to speak, but all that came forth were guttural growls and pained moans. Clothes hung to their bodies in tattered rags, the years spent underground showing visible wear. But the thing which made Taliyah's skin run cold, bringing back memories of the survivor's accounts that she'd read in those "Eyes Only" reports, were the creatures' eyes.

They glowed the same lilac/aqua green color as Terminium.

For a moment all was still. The creatures assessed their prey, while the members of STA4 stood ready for anything. Suddenly one of the creatures yelled a grating shout, and they rushed the crew.

Some of the things leaped down from the wrapping pathway which led to the gorge floor, their bodies hitting the ground in sickening thuds. Others charged the Odyssey, clawing up at Wren, who now fired in short yet effective bursts into the hordes of attackers. The other mountain dwellers turned their sights on Lizzie and Taliyah, who stood back and began firing as the howling monstrosities rushed them.

"Body mass, Lizzie" Taliyah said, feeling her Carbine "putting in that work" as Wren would often joke when they were at the shooting range.

Pull, fire, rinse repeat. Five more down. Lizzie used her Nova Edge, an engineering marvel utilizing a precision AI controlled targeting system, firing bursts of rounds with kinetic energy. She unloaded multiple rounds into the creatures' stomachs, ripping through their sickly flesh.

Tapping her sister's shoulder, Lizzie wrapped around to her sibling's back, reloading her weapon while Taliyah laid down cover fire for more of the violent hordes.

"Wren, we're coming to you!" Taliyah yelled over more shots ringing from her weapon. "Lizzie, get the Gummi's the to clear a path!"

The younger sister typed commands into her gauntlet, and soon the three Gummi's were cutting a bloody swath through the beasts. As they fell, Lizzie and Taliyah ran behind, rushing to the doors of the Odyssey. Wren hopped from the top of the vehicle, whipping to the left as one creature attacked. Up close she could see the tattered remnants of a Seeker uniform and armor, but the scarred face had now wasted away to no discernible features. Wren dropped the creature with a head shot. The right side of its face wasted away to pulp.

As the trio hopped into the vehicle, Wren powered the Odyssey to life. Monsters had landed on top of the LTV, beating from above, trying to wrench open the carriage ceiling. Others wrapped around the sides of the immobile vehicle, beating on the doors, and windows, moaning, yelling, and shrieking.

Wren tried her best to push the LTV through the ever growing hordes in front of them on the upward snaking route. "I can't drive through these things! There's too many!"

"Taliyah, now might be the time to show us how you got "this handled"!" Lizzie yelled from the backseat.

Pulling up the Navigation on her console Taliyah yelled, "Odyssey enact "Ogun's Shield"! NOW!"

A hum grew from inside the Odyssey and built to a shrill peak. The women covered their ears, gritting their teeth as Taliyah shouted, "Close your eyes!" A shimmering field erupted from the vehicle, hurling the creatures. An opaque sheath covered the Odyssey, flickering as monsters tried to burst through the shielding.

"Wait! The Collective has shields now?!" Lizzie said, her engineers mind racing.

"Prototype," Taliyah said. "So that means- "

Grinding the pedal to the ground, Wren pushed the Odyssey forward, hurtling up the steep path. "This shit might break down at any point. Got it."

More of the creatures hurled themselves on the front of the vehicle, flying back upon contact with the shield, or being flung off the edge of the pathway. The barrier flickered with every impact but still held true.

"Um, I'm getting a live feed from the drones. Passing it to Nav," Lizzie said, her tone worried.

A shaky live feed from all three drones came up on Taliyah's side of the dash console, and her stomach dropped. Following in the wake of the Odyssey were hundreds of the creatures, rushing forward with inhuman speed. If not for the flickering partition, the vehicle would've already been overrun. The Gummi's were doing their best to stem the tide with gunfire, small projectiles, and even the mining lasers.

But the mountain creatures just kept coming, appearing now from alcoves in the ceilings, and skittering along the walls.

"Drive, Wren," Lizzie said, as death pursued them.

* * *

The Odyssey broke above ground with mayhem in front and behind them. Tracer fire from Scavyr weapons tagged the Ericsson from all sides, and Taliyah could see the scorch marks from where the heavy weapons had hit the transport. Behind them the creatures howled, frustrated their prey had not been eviscerated. The monsters of the Mount' stumbled over each other, tearing at those too slow, as an almost bloodlust drove them all forward to destroy the interlopers. Their eyes began to blaze even more, as the ion storm now threatened its return.

"Renata, Jacob, cover us! We're coming in hot!", Taliyah yelled, as the Odyssey took another burst of gunfire from the Scavyrs.

"Aww hell naw! What is that behind you!?" Jacob replied over the COMMS channel.

"Just drop the hatch!" the three women in the Odyssey screamed as the vehicle whipped around massive rock debris.

The vehicle sped into the hatchway, the creatures close on their heels. Renata let loose with a pair of RPGs, thinning the ranks of the attackers with explosions which lifted broken bodies into the air. Jacob, now switched to an automatic Tempest 24, cut down the beasts with concussive impacts from his weapon. As the tail of the Odyssey climbed over the hatchway's threshold, skidding and crashing into the giant cargo restraint net, he slammed his hand on a wall switch, firing out the closing doorway at unseen ghouls that tried their best to climb aboard.

"Jamie, get us out of here now!" Taliyah yelled, and the group felt the thrusters of the ship rise.

Lizzie jumped out of the passenger's seat of the Odyssey, looking out at a nearby window at the mayhem erupting behind them. Below the swarm of beasts rushed the remaining Scavyrs. As they lifted higher, she could only make out arms fire and small dots fleeing the area. Tiny explosions sent yellowish orange plumes of fire up into the air blocking out what was left of the side of the Mount', and it was only then she turned away from the unfolding massacre.

244

* * *

"You good?"

Lizzie looked back at her sister who'd just left their debrief with the Collective. The tech wizards had already gone to work studying the Terminium sample they'd brought back, all other projects in the lab halted. She'd never seen the minerologists this excited, raising her hopes the mission had been a success.

She'd silently stepped out to the hangar, watching the remaining Seeker teams arriving back, and listened as the good news started to circulate. STA4 had done it again. They'd saved the day.

"Yeah, it's just, it just doesn't feel like it's real Taliyah," Lizzie said, leaning over the guardrail. A maintenance drone shuttled past, performing its nightly cleaning rounds. "I know it's real, but sis', we've been doing this for so long. I don't know anything else."

Taliyah leaned forward by Lizzie, staring off into the dark starry expanse outside the hangar holographic sheathed entrance. "And I hate that, Lizzie. Momma and Daddy didn't raise you for this life."

"Are we seriously going back to this again?" Lizzie said side eye-ing Taliyah in frustration.

"Lizzie, listen," Taliyah said. "I'm proud of everything you've accomplished in the years since The Fall. You've proven yourself, again, and again, and again. I'm glad to have you watching my back."

The younger sister leaned forward for a hug, but Taliyah pushed her back playfully.

"But girl, this ain't what any of us wanted for you," Taliyah said. "You're supposed to the next Mae Jemison. The next Aprille Ericsson. The next Shirley Ann Jackson."

"Well, technically I couldn't be the next "Shirley Ann Jackson", since she was a theoretical physicist, and that's not my field of study," Lizzie said. She saw her sister's deadpan reaction and smiled. "But I get the point."

"I've always seen Kamaal as being the place where you can truly put your brain to use in the way that it was meant," Taliyah said. "To help lead all of us towards something better. To help build our new world. That's why I've been pushing you. Girl, you are our future."

Lizzie ignored her sister's gruff demeanor, and leaned forward hugging her in a deep embrace, which was returned. They stood like that for a while, simply existing in the moment. At peace, the future ahead of them with no monsters to exorcise.

RIVER GHOST
BY
AZIZA SPHINX

On a quiet street off River Road, near two schools sharing the name Cedar Grove, be a house that was once red, white, and blue, with a haunting tale I might share with you. The house unobtrusively sits painted now with its colors demure and its non-sneering mouth. But I know all its secrets those hidden about behind shuttered windows and door facing south.

A shudder still consumes me whether walking or driving past, I know it still watches behind the masked window glass.

"Shh don't tell. I leave the ones here be."

"Then why are you still taunting and ever haunting me?"

"You should have returned when the sign first called."

Yet self-preservation overrode my downfall. "What is it that you feel I must always see."

"Ask yourself that. You're here visiting me."

The house was right as it tended to be.

Why am I here. Why do I care as I exit my car and turn to stare. The music still plays though the records are old. The jukebox cord now sits in a roll. No plug for power or electricity but from the beyond came energy.

"I know you hear it. You'll never forget."

Dang-it its right. That's what I get. Shut it out. Go on your way. It isn't my visitor on this sunny day.

"You cannot ignore me. I'll always be here. The music will continue; a worm in your ear."

I ignore the taunting and go on my way; I refuse to allow the past to ruin my day. My visit is pleasant my old neighbors are well. Not much has changed though my memory swells.

The night rushes back to the dark in the garage where the board speaks to others and ignites the bard. The crash of an object we're all now on guard and youngling take off running their breath coming hard.

A joke of the olders. Or dismissed as so. Except the creep of another power slithers across my toes. The game packed away their night coming to a close they retreat into the house as if no one knows.

I slip from my spot and creep to the door for the silence is broken with music once more. "Make it stop! Just go away!"

Not even my pleading will keep it at bay.

The radio. The song. Just change the tune. Hop in the car lest ye meet your doom. Speeding away eases the hell, the further the distance, the weaker the spell.

"You'll never escape. You can be sure of that. Till you know why I'm here and what I want back."

"I have nothing of yours."

"I will have what's mine. Or maybe a substitute I might be inclined."

The sun is now setting and thoughts of spirits hover as I settle in bed and hide in the covers. I banish the thoughts let sleep take its place and welcome the sandman's soothing embrace.

A river of blood. Now, this can't be real. An illusion designed to test my will.

Dealing with dark things is never the way. They poke and they prod and keep good things at bay. It weakens the resolve and then it dissolves any inkling of hope until it has it all.

You can't run forever. Sooner or later you'll need a conversation to be had between you and me.

"I've nothing to say. Just let me be!"

Silence then falls. I wait for a blow. And whisper. A clink. Another part of the show. Yet I feel the change as I return to the waking. Me piled on the floor in a bed of my making. My fingers are crooked and they hurt like the devil and I know in that moment I've just fought an evil.

"I'm not your enemy."

"Then leave me be!"

"Like you did that night after trapping me?"

"You are definitely mistaken."

"No. I know the truth. Think long and hard. I challenge: do you?"

"Why all the circles?"

'Why run away. This could have been settled on that faithful day."

"I was but a child."

"And now you are not. Yet you still fear the end. I saw what you got. Free to live open. Free to be free. While trapping another where they didn't want to be."

"I did no such thing!"

"You now know you did. I'll go my waiting. Live out my assigned bid."

The presence now gone. The room is light and bright. Still my shoulders weighed heavy at the truth of its plight. Did I do what it said. Did I make it believe it was stuck in a place that it could never leave.

Now that wasn't hard. Now I can be. An even trade. A gift for a key. I hit me then. I never chose. My gift was stolen, and it hurts now to know. I'd been wrong all along. It protected me. From the hurt and the curse and the bad things I'd see.

HOMECOMING
BY
MILTON J. DAVIS

The Night of Lights Celebration began at sundown in Summerhill and Synthia was almost ready. She checked her makeup one last time then ran her hand over her bald scalp. Stubble scratched her palms; she would need to shave soon. She summoned her holoscreen to confirm her sources were fully charged. Satisfied, she waved away the screen, exited her twenty-first-floor condo and strode to the lift. Her palm pressed the control and moments later she was greeted by the friendly faces of other celebrants from the floors above her, all dressed in the traditional black robe with high collars radiating bright colors bordering their exuberant faces. No words were shared; no one wanted to spoil the energy with words.

The lift door opened, and they spilled into the condo lobby then out into the lighted streets. The crisp air chilled her brown skin and she grinned. Fall was her favorite time of year. Bradford Pear trees and sugar maples blazed autumn orange, adding to the festive atmosphere. Synthia blinked and her eyes turned yellow, matching the hue emitted by the inside of her robe. The others around her did the same, surrounding her with reds, blues, greens, and almost all the colors of the spectrum. While the others paired off, Synthia strolled the leaf littered Summerhill streets alone. She was new to the neighborhood and had yet to make friends. It was just a matter of time. There were only so many of them in Atlanta, and there was safety in numbers.

"Synthia?"

She turned and her eyebrows rose. Bryan, her brother, forced a smile to his face as he approached.

"I thought that was you," he said. "You've changed . . ."

"Everything," she finished for him. "What are you doing here? I thought you hated synths."

"I do . . . I mean I don't, at least not you. You're not a synth."

"I am, Bryan."

"No, you're not!" Bryan blurted. "Not inside."

Synthia placed her hand on her younger brother's shoulder then smiled when he flinched.

"Who sent you?" she asked. "I know you didn't come on your own. And who told you how to find me? Mama?"

"Yeah. But nobody sent me. I came on my own."

"So why are you here?"

Bryan's eyes glistened. "It's daddy. He's dying. He asked for you. But . . ."

"But what?"

Synthia waited for Bryan to answer.

"I don't think he'll want to see you like this."

"Is that what daddy thinks, or you?"

"I'm just the messenger," Bryan said. "Do what you want."

"I'll think about it."

Bryan turned then marched away. "Don't think too long. He doesn't have much time. Not all of us choose to live forever."

Synthia watched him walk away. She should just let him go and be done with it, but she couldn't. He said he came on his own, but Synthia knew better. Mama didn't send him to Aytee-El for them to fight. She could have texted.

"Bryan, wait."

She trotted up to him then grabbed his arm.

"How did you get here?" she asked.

"I took the bullet from Valdosta," he replied without turning.

"You must be hungry. Tired, too."

Bryan turned his head just enough for her to see the side of his face.

"I am. Hungry, that is."

"Come with me," she said as she tugged his arm.

"Where are you taking me?"

"To my favorite restaurant."

He turned to face her.

"You still eat food? Real food?"

Synthia laughed at his ignorant question.

"Yes, I do. Now come on."

She tried to take Bryan's hand, but he pulled away. She started to say something sarcastic but decided not to. They were inseparable growing up, only two years apart. Time and circumstances changed everything, for some more than others.

They weaved through the growing crowd of lighted revelers. Bryan was making a huge effort not to bump into anyone. His noticeable avoidance drew laughs and scowls from passersby.

Synthia was relieved when they finally reached Shay's Ramen Shack.

"Let's eat outside,' she said. "It's such a pleasant night."

Bryan followed her to the nearest empty table. A server appeared seconds later, his voluminous afro strobing from red, to black, to green then back to red.

"Hey, Synthia!" he said. "Who's your friend?"

"Tay, meet Bryan, my baby brother. Bryan, Tay."

Bryan struggle to smile. "Nice meeting you, Tay."

"Same here," Tay replied. "So, what'll you and the virgin have?"

"The usual for me," Synthia replied. "Bryan?"

Bryan squinted as he read the menu. "I have no idea. I've never had ramen."

Tay stood beside Bryan, and Synthia dropped her head when Bryan leaned away.

"You like spicy?" Tay asked.

"A little," Bryan replied.

"Let's start you off with the Dan Dan Manzeman," he said. "I guess since you're a South Georgia boy you ain't afraid of pork."

Bryan grinned. "From the rooter to the tooter."

Tay laughed and his hair color sequence quickened. Bryan's mouth fell open.

"I know, right?" Tay said. "It gets everybody."

Tay took their menus.

"I'll be back with water and edamame."

Bryan stared at Tay until he entered the restaurant.

"This is crazy," he said.

"You get used to it," Synthia replied. "I had to adjust. It's nothing like home."

"You can say that again," Bryan agreed. "Why would he do that?"

Synthia shrugged. "Why not? If you're buying a new model, you might as well go all out."

"You didn't."

"I'm from South Georgia."

Tay returned with their waters and a bowl of edamame. Synthia took one of the salted soybeans then popped it into her mouth. Bryan took one from the bowl then studied it before he did the same.

"This is good," he said.

"Yep," Synthia replied.

"Is this real food," Bryan asked.

"No, it's synthetic."

Bryan grabbed his throat and Synthia laughed.

"It's real," she said. "You'll be shitting it out in a few hours."

"Your sense of humor hasn't changed," Bryan said.

"Why should it?"

Bryan ate more edamame. "I don't know."

Synthia reached out and took his hand. This time he didn't pull away.

"It's the same me, Bryan. Nothing's change."

Bryan folded his arms as he leaned back in his chair.

"Well, nothing important," she finished.

Bryan was opening mouth to reply when Tay appeared with their bowls. He placed Synthia 's down first, then gave Bryan his plate.

"Thank you," Bryan said.

"I love Southern folks," Tay said. "So polite. Now eat up."

Bryan scooped up a spoonful then ate.

"Wow. This is delicious!" he said with a full mouth.

"My job is done here," Tay said. He winked at Synthia. "Enjoy!"

Synthia began eating her ramen.

"Is he synth?" Bryan asked.

"We all are," Synthia replied.

"No, I mean is he one hundred percent synth?"

"Does it matter?"

Bryan fell silent. Synthia watched him eat, expecting him to continue.

"I guess it doesn't matter here," he finally said.

"It doesn't matter anywhere, except in South Georgia."

"There are other places," Bryan said.

"The list gets shorter every day," Synthia said. "Japan is 85% synth. China's not far behind. Europe's up to 40%, and Africa and South America are around 50%."

"What about Atlanta?" Bryan asked.

"Around 40%," Synthia answered. She picked up her bowl then slurped down the remaining broth.

"Hurry up and finish," she said. "I got a great pastry shop I want to show you."

Bryan finished his ramen. Tay came, took their bowls then scanned Synthia's wrist for payment.

The crowd was thick, synths and reals mingled together. Synthia could sense Bryan's mood easing and it made her smile. She was still big sister, looking out for baby brother. They got separated for a few minutes; when she found him a cute petite woman with glowing turquoise eyes that matched her robe lights had him pinned against the wall, talking so fast she didn't give him any time to reply.

"There you are honey!" she exclaimed. "I've been looking all over for you!" She grabbed his hand then dragged him away, the woman scowling at her as she waved.

"Thank you!" Bryan said.

"You're welcomed," Synthia replied. "Although she was kinda cute."

Bryan looked embarrassed. "Yes, she was. Except for her eyes. They were creepy."

"You mean like this?"

Synthia's eyes went from subtle to glaring yellow. Bryan shaded his face.

"Stop that, please!"

Synthia almost laughed until she detected the tone of his voice. He was terrified.

The sound of bongos, djembes, and bass rose over the crowd noise. Synthia grabbed Bryan's hand.

"Come on! It's starting!"

The entire crowd surged in the same direction, the music louder as they neared the outdoor stage. The band was deep into an amapiano vibe, their holoimages flanking their performance. Synthia and Bryan pushed their way close to the stage. Synthia warmed inside when she saw the genuine smile on her brother's face.

"Come on," she said. "Let's show them how the Dobsons get down!"

There were two things Bryan and Synthia loved more than anything else: music and dancing. They cleared a space with their flamboyant moves, drawing an audience that began cheering them on. Other dancers joined them and soon it was a true celebration. They danced until the band and DJ gave up the stage to a jazz trio.

"I haven't danced like that in a long time," Bryan said as they sauntered away from the outdoor stadium."

"I don't believe that," Synthia said. "Not Mr. Partyman himself."

"Hasn't been much partying in Moultrie," Bryan replied. "Everyone is preparing for Transition."

"I can imagine," Synthia said. She glanced up to the near invisible dome that covered Aytee-El. The United Cities passed the Human Separation Act thirty years ago and construction of the domes began immediately afterwards. Now that the cities and the domes were almost complete, the hard part was beginning. Synthia 's life wouldn't change much; she'd been living in the city for three years and her lifestyle fit the new normal. But it would be hard for people like Bryan and the other members of her family.

"Are you coming to Aytee-El?" she asked.

"No. Jayville," Bryan replied. "It's closer, plus it's near the ocean. You know how I love the beach."

"You won't be able to visit it."

"Yeah, but at least I can see it."

Synthia hooked her arm around Bryan's.

"You're staying with me tonight," she said.

"I don't think that's a good idea. I need to get back to mama and daddy."

"Call mama," she said. "Let me talk to her."

Bryan took out his phone.

"Mama . . . How's daddy . . . Yes, I found her. She wants to speak to you."

Bryan gave the phone to Synthia. She hesitated before taking it.

"Hey mama."

"Oh Lordy! Hey baby!"

The tears came before she could stop them.

"I'm sorry I haven't called."

"It's alright Cyndy. We're talking now."

"Bryan's going to spend the night with me. Is that okay?"

"Of course! Me and your daddy will be fine."

Synthia moved the phone closer to her mouth.

"Can I talk to daddy?"

"He's asleep. Why don't you give him a call tomorrow? I know he'd love to speak to you."

"Okay mama, I will. Bye. Love you."

"Love you, too, sweety."

Synthia gave the phone back the Bryan.

"You heard mama. You're spending the night with me."

"I'm a grown ass man," Bryan said.

"Who's spending the night with his big sister," Synthia replied.

Bryan looked like he was trying to keep a bee in his mouth when a smile finally burst on his face.

"Good! Now that that's settled, let's go get a Juicy Pop."

"Juicy Pop?"

"Only the best popsicle known to humankind."

Synthia grabbed his hand, and they ran toward the restaurant district.

* * *

Synthia 's apartment occupied a corner on the 14th floor of a complex overlooking Hank Aaron Boulevard. The eight lane divided highway that once divided the city had been ripped up and replaced with green space decades ago, so the view was now pleasant and soothing. She sat at her balcony table, sipping rum and seltzer water while gazing at the construction drones overhead working on the final phase of the dome. In a few more years humans would cut themselves off from Mother Earth in hopes that She would be able to heal without their presence. It was a biological first; the first time a virus quarantined itself from its host.

The glass door slid open, and Bryan stepped out. He grinned then sat at the table.

"What you looking at?"

Synthia pointed into the sky.

"It's really happening," he said.

"Yep."

"Doesn't seem right," he said.

"It doesn't matter," Synthia said. "It's happening."

"Why did you do it?" Bryan said.

"Do what?" Synthia asked, as if she didn't know.

"Change yourself?"

Synthia sighed. "Because I wanted to. And because I didn't have a choice."

"There's always a choice," Bryan replied. "At least that's what you always told me."

Synthia turned to face Bryan.

"If I tell you something, you have to promise not to tell mama and daddy."

"I promise."

Synthia swallowed then looked into the night sky.

"Five years ago, I was diagnosed with cancer," she said. Bryan sat up in his chair.

"Synthia! Why didn't you say anything?"

"I didn't want to worry anybody, especially daddy," Synthia said. "It was advanced. My doctor told me I had two options. I could fight it with radiation, but chances were slim that I would win. Or I could do this."

She swept her hand across her body. "Both were just as risky, but if I pulled through synth transition, I'd never have to worry about cancer again."

Bryan settled back into his chair. "That wasn't much of a choice."

"Tell me about it."

Bryan sipped his drink. "I wish you would have at least told me."

"Back then you were the last person I would have told," Synthia said. "I'm still surprised you came looking for me."

"I did that for daddy," Bryan said as he looked away.

"You you're still a member of Pastor Benning's flock?"

Bryan nodded.

"Flock," she said. "That's an appropriate description."

"Don't start," Bryan warned.

Synthia rolled her eyes then took a sip of her rum seltzer.

"You could have texted. My number hasn't changed."

Bryan looked up, his eyes intense.

"My plan was to talk you into reversal," he said. "I read somewhere that a person's body parts were kept in cryo for three months after transition just in case the central nervous system and the synth host didn't mesh. But I see that was no option for you."

"No, it wasn't," Synthia replied. "Not that it would have made a difference."

"You saying you would have done it anyway?"

"Yeah, one day down the road," she admitted. "You still hate me?"

"I never hated you," Bryan answered. "I never could. I just didn't understand why."

"What's there to understand?" Synthia said.

"You're going to outlive us all," he said. "We're going to die, and you're going to be alone. That's not what God intended. Earth ain't Heaven."

"Who knows what God intended? I'll bet you good crypts Paster Benning doesn't. Besides, you don't think I didn't think about that?" Synthia replied. "I did. I still do. Every day."

"But I still don't . . ."

"Bryan, do you love me?" Synthia asked.

"Of course, I do," he replied.

"Then let's just go with that," Synthia said. "Let's just sit here, drink, and look at the stars."

Synthia took out her phone and then turned on her playlist. Jazz wafted from her stereo on the patio and the two of them listened until they fell asleep. The sun sent scattered beams of light between the high rises hours later and woke them. Synthia stretched and yawned; Bryan blinked his eyes then stood.

"You hungry?" she asked.

"Yes," Bryan replied. "What you got inside?"

"Nothing. Let's go get something then we'll catch the bullet."

"We?"

256

"Yeah, I'm going with you."

Bryan's eyes widened and he smiled.

"Mama and daddy will be so happy!"

"Calm down," Synthia said. "I'm not coming for good."

Bryan's shoulders slumped.

"Oh."

"I can't. This is home now. But I'll make you a promise. I'll stay as long as daddy wants me to. Okay?"

Bryan's smile returned. "Okay."

Synthia stood. "I'm going to wash up then we'll get some grub."

"You don't need to eat, do you?" Bryan asked.

"No, but I'm going to," she said. "Can't let my baby brother pig out alone."

"You were right," Bryan said. "You are the same."

"Of course, I am," Synthia replied. "What I changed out here, didn't change who I am in here."

She placed her palm on her chest as she stood.

"Now let's freshen up and get going. Those cinnamon rolls at Big Tarts don't wait for anyone."

Bryan jumped from his chair then hurried inside. Synthia watched him go then followed, closing the sliding door behind her.

They washed up then walked the two blocks to Big Tarts. The woman waiting on them was a real.

"Welcome to Big Tarts," she said with a flat Midwestern accent. "What'll you have?"

"I'll have a chocolate croissant," Synthia said.

The woman turned to Bryan. "And you?"

"I'll take a cinnamon roll," he said.

A wide smile broke out on the woman's face.

"I love your accent! Where are you from?"

"South Georgia," Bryan said. "Moultrie."

"Never heard of it," she said. "Looks like they grow them big and handsome down there."

Bryan smirked. "If you say so."

"You eating here or to go?" she asked.

"To go," Synthia said.

The server picked up Synthia's croissant with the tongs then dropped it in a small brown back with the store logo stamped on it.

"Here you go," she said.

"Thank you," Synthia said.

"You're welcome!"

She repeated the process with Bryan's cinnamon roll, but when Bryan grasped the bag with his fingers, she didn't let it go.

"My name is Heaven," she said.

"I'm Bryan," he said. "Your parents gave you an ambitious name."

"You should get to know me," Heaven said. "I live up to it."

Synthia covered her mouth to hide her grin as Bryan tugged at his bag. Heaven held onto it a little longer before letting it go.

"Thank you," he said.

"You're more than welcome. See you again soon."

"I don't think so. I'm going back home today."

"That's too bad," Heaven said.

Synthia and Bryan left the store.

"Look at you!" she said. Coming to the A and getting everybody hot and bothered."

"Leave me alone," Bryan said. "Folks up here must be desperate."

"You sure you want to move to Jayville instead of here?"

"I have to be with mama and daddy," Bryan said. "Besides, Aytee-El is too fast for a country boy like me."

"We'll all be on the same speed soon," Synthia said.

As casual as she attempted to be, Synthia worried. It was such a drastic thing, closing humanity off from the Earth. But the truth was they really had no choice. Even such a radical decision didn't guarantee the world would heal its wounds. And even if it did, it wouldn't be in her lifetime.

They returned to her apartment, packed their items then caught a Rideout to the bullet station. The traffic was sparse; Synthia and Bryan found empty seats, with Synthia getting her favored window seat. Ten minutes after sitting the rapid rail streaked from the A and into the agricultural sector. Every inch of ground outside the city was cultivated to supply food for the soon to be crowded city. All 15 million of the state's inhabitants would soon call Aytee-El home, and the Ag sector would have to supply them with most of their food needs until the city reached full sustainable status. The same process was occurring in states, provinces, countries, and territories around the world. Aytee-El had been designated the population hub, expanding on the covert plans The Elites created before the Hacker War. Central Georgia was designated the agricultural sector. It was the richest soil in the state and would be used until sustainable farming was incorporated into the megacity core. The other regions were being abandoned and given back to nature. South Georgia, Synthia 's home, was the last Georgia region to transition.

The landscape changed as they entered the Coastal Plain region. They streaked by abandoned cities left to decay, pine trees emerging from sidewalk and road cracks. Buildings slowly succumbed to kudzu and muscadine vines while flocks of crows and pigeons maneuvered between them. Synthia glimpsed a herd of feral cows grazing on what was once Interstate I-75 and smiled. Humans weren't the only creatures in transition.

The bullet slowed then stopped at the Adele terminal, which in reality was a temporary shed large enough to protect a handful of people from the elements. No sooner did they step out of the rail did Synthia begin looking about.

"Where's the Rideout?" she asked.

Bryan let out a grim laugh. "Are you serious? The UC cut off public transportation for the outliers five years ago. Another step to force us in line."

The heaviness was back in Bryan's voice. He stared at her in the way he did when he saw her at the festival. To him, she was part of what was forcing them to give up their life.

"So, who's coming to pick us up?"

Bryan took out his phone then sent a text.

"Somebody will be here in a few minutes," he said.

The good vibe they shared in the Metro was sucked away by the dismal surroundings. Every minute Synthia stood at the station reminded her why she left . . . no, fled this place. The grumble of a diesel burning truck engine broke her musing. When the dingy white Dualie came into view, Synthia felt bile rise into her mouth.

"You called him?" she said.

"He's the only person that does this," Bryan said. "Sorry. I should have said something."

The truck pulled up close and Khalid stepped out of the driver's side, his grey eyes locked on Synthia.

"Well, I'll be damn," he said. "Never thought I'd see you back here again."

Synthia didn't reply. She was too angry. She stomped to the truck, opened the passenger door then climbed inside.

"Hello to you, too," Khalid said.

Khalid and Bryan got into the truck, and they traveled to the farm, the truck bouncing and rattling over the dilapidated roads. Synthia seethed. If there was any person that could make her feel more out of place, it was Khalid.

"So how you liking Aytee-El?" he asked.

"It's fine," she replied. She looked up to see him gazing at her from the rear-view mirror.

"I see you cut all your hair off. That's a shame."

"Can we just do this quietly?" Synthia said.

Khalid grinned. "I see some things haven't changed."

Synthia let out a sigh when her parents' family came into view. Bryan had done a good job maintaining it, the orderly fallow fields and freshly repaired fences resembling a landscape painting compared to the unkempt properties surrounding it. The truck rumbled up the gravel road leading to the house. Mama was on the porch, her hands clasped together with a gracious smile on her brown, weathered face. Synthia's bitterness melted away. Mama wore her favorite sweater and house dress, with a new pair of house shoes. The pickup had barely come to a stop when Synthia grabbed her bag, opened the door, and jumped out. She crunched her way to the porch, up the stairs then into mama's waiting arms.

"Hey, mama," she said.

"Hey, baby girl."

They held each other tight for a long minute before mama's arms opened to Synthia 's disappointment. Mama stepped back then inspected her.

"At least you been eating," she said.

"You know me," Synthia said.

Mama's eyes focused on her bald scalp.

"You never did like doing your hair," she said. "Guess that's not a problem anymore."

"Nope," Synthia said.

Mama looked over Synthia 's shoulder and her smile faded.

"How you doing, Mrs. Dobson?"

Khalid stood at the steps beside Bryan. Mama's eyes narrowed.

"Hey boy," she said. "Don't you have other things to do?"

"Not right now," Khalid said, his voice expectant.

"Well, we about to spend some family time. You best be on your way. I appreciate you bringing my children home."

Khalid's face drooped like a sad bloodhound. He nodded at Mama then trudged back to his truck, making a ruckus spinning his tires on the gravel before speeding away.

"Never liked that boy," Mama said. "I was so glad when y'all broke up."

"He broke my heart," Synthia said.

"Sometimes you need to go through a little pain for better things," mama said.

Bryan walked by them into house.

"Mama still Mama," he said.

"Come inside girl," Mama said. "Your daddy been up all night waiting to see you."

Synthia entered the house and the sights and smells of her past overwhelmed her. She passed the kitchen on the way to Mama and Daddy's room, spotting the old greens pot on the gas stove, a mess of greens simmering to perfection inside. Beside it, hot oil crackled from water escaping the greens pot. Mama was cooking fried pork chops, her favorite.

They entered her parents' room. Daddy lay in the bed, the mattress raised high enough for him to see her enter. He smiled and his eyes squinted.

"There's my baby girl," he said.

"Hey, Daddy!"

Synthia sat in the chair beside the bed then leaned over to hug daddy. He returned the hug with his left arm.

"I need to finish dinner," mama said.

Synthia stood. "I'll help."

"No, you won't," mama replied. "You'll stay right there with your daddy. You and I will talk later."

Synthia sat down then held daddy's hand.

"How are you feeling?"

"Terrible," Daddy replied. "But that's every day."

"I'm sorry, Daddy."

"What you got to be sorry about?" Daddy said.

"You know what I mean," she said.

Daddy laughed until he began coughing. He pointed to the glass of water on his nightstand and Synthia gave it to him. He sipped until his cough subsided.

"So, Bryan said you souped up."

Synthia chucked. "I'm not a car, Daddy."

"You know what I'm talking about."

"I guess he told y'all everything."

"You should have."

"I didn't want y'all to worry. I'm alright now."

"Let me see."

Synthia rolled up her sleeve exposing her arm. Daddy touched her skin with his finger then traced it up to her elbow.

"I'll be damn," he said.

"You should have done it," Synthia said. Daddy shook his head.

"Too old," he said. "Body couldn't take the strain."

Synthia eyes widened in surprise.

"You talked to Dr. Cane about it?"

"Of course, I did. Checked out all the options."

"I'm surprised."

"Why?"

"Bryan said . . ."

"Since when you start listening to Bryan? He's your baby brother. That boy ain't the sharpest knife in the drawer. He takes after your Mama's side."

"He looks just like you."

"The only good thing he got from me."

Daddy was teasing, which meant he was in a good mood.

"Dinner's ready!" Mama shouted. Daddy began shifting in the bed.

"Help me sit up," he said.

Synthia leaned over then wrapped her arms around Daddy's torso as he hugged her neck. She lifted him to a sitting position.

"Good. Now help me stand."

Synthia drew away. "Daddy you're not supposed to . . ."

"Come on help me stand, girl," he said. "I already know you stronger than you look, and I'll be damned if I'm gonna eat in that bed with my whole family here."

Synthia wrapped her right arm around daddy's waist, and he put his left arm around her shoulders.

"Okay then," he said. "Let's make a grand entrance."

They made their way to the kitchen, Daddy shuffling, Synthia carrying. Daddy was doing less than he thought, and Synthia was thankful for the bionics that helped her walk/carry her daddy to the kitchen table. Mama had back to them, giving the greens one more stir.

"I said, dinner's ready!"

Mama dropped the lid then reached back to untie her apron.

"I swear every last one of them is deaf," she whispered.

Mama turned around as Synthia eased Daddy into his chair. Her hands went to her cheeks.

"Samuel Dobson, what you done made this girl do?"

"Don't worry about it, Gurdy," Daddy said.

Bryan walked into the kitchen and his eyes went wide.

"Daddy! What you doing in here?"

"I'm about to eat my dinner if y'all don't mind," he said.

Mama and Bryan glared at Synthia.

"What? He told me to do it."

Mama rolled her eyes. "Well, it's too late now. But I promise to God if you die at my table and fall face first into my rice, I'm gonna leave you just like that until they come get you."

Daddy laughed himself into another coughing fit and Synthia ran to get him his water. Once he calmed down, she helped Mama make his plate then took it to him.

"Go on sit down, Mama" she said. "I'll make your plate. too."

"Thank you, sweetie," Mama said. She sat beside Daddy, and they shared a smile.

Synthia made Mama's plate then her own. Bryan made his plate and joined everyone at the table. They joined hands and Mama said grace. No sooner did she finish did everyone pounce the food prepared. There was never much talking when folks sat down to eat Mama's food; silence was the complement to an excellent meal.

Daddy was the first to finish. He leaned back into his chair then rubbed his stomach.

"I swear your mama is best cook in the world!" he said. He grabbed Mama's hand. "You know that's why I asked you marry me?"

He looked at Bryan and Synthia as a devilish grin formed on his face.

"She thought it was because she had a big booty. Used to wear the tightest jeans she could find whenever we went out."

"It was both," Mama said. "You used to look at my ass like it was fried chicken."

"Oh my God stop!" Synthia said. "I don't need to hear this."

"They do this all the time," Bryan said. "At least they don't do it in public."

"Shoot, y'all grown now," Daddy said. "How you think y'all got here?"

"Let's talk about something else please," Synthia said.

"Yeah, let's do that," Mama said. "Let's talk about why our baby girl was about to die and decided not to tell anybody."

Synthia cut her eyes at Bryan, and he shrugged.

"They needed to know," he said.

"You should have told us," Daddy said. "It would have made everything simpler."

"So, I had to be dying for y'all to handle my changes?"

"I didn't mean it like that," Daddy said.

"Pastor Buckman said that which was not made by God's hands cannot enter the kingdom of Heaven," Bryan said.

"We ain't gonna talk about Buckman," Mama said. "He was the first person to run off the Jayville after filling everybody up with his fool talk."

Bryan picked up his fork and picked at his black-eyed peas. "I'm just saying."

"We didn't send for you to talk about things past," Mama said. "We sent for you so we could talk about the future."

"You decided when you're relocating to Jayville?" Synthia asked.

"Not exactly," Mama said. "We applied for a Relocation exemption."

Synthia's breath caught in her throat.

"A what?" Bryan asked.

"Relocation exemption," Synthia said. "I heard of those, but I thought it was a joke."

"It's not," Mama said. "We applied and we were approved."

"What does that mean?" Bryan said.

"It means me and your mama ain't going anywhere," Daddy said. "We're staying right here."

"Yes!" Bryan said.

Synthia glared at Bryan. He still didn't understand.

"Don't go celebrating, boy," Mama said. "The exemption is for me and your daddy, not you."

"Wait . . . what?" Bryan said.

"You a grown man," daddy said. "You have to make those decisions on your own. Besides, you're too young for the exemption."

"Mama, Daddy. If you're here when city construction is complete, you'll be permanently cut off," Synthia said.

Mama and Daddy held hands.

"We know," mama said.

"That means you'll be cut off from us," Synthia finished. A chill swept through her as she uttered those last words. "You'll die out here."

"What do you mean us?" Bryan said. "I'm staying, too!"

Synthia rolled her eyes. "Aren't you listening? You can't. The exemption only applies to anyone 55 years and older."

"All this change is too much for us," Mama said. "The UC will provide us with all the support we'll need. Y'all will be notified once we move on."

Synthia 's sight blurred. She stood then stormed out of the kitchen, across the porch then into the yard. She didn't stop until she reached the persimmon tree near the fallow cornfield. She took her cell from her pocket and stabbed the touchpad with her fingers. Khalid responded moments later.

Pick up?
Yes.
You just got here.
You coming or not?
On my way.

Synthia jammed the phone into her pocket then paced. She heard the screen door slam then looked up. Mama eased down the stairs then walked toward her. Synthia looked around for somewhere else to go as Mama came closer.

"Nowhere else to run to, baby," Mama said.

"How could you make a decision like this without talking to me and Bryan?" Synthia asked.

"We haven't seen you in two years," Mama replied. "And Bryan is Bryan. He does what we tell him to do."

"That's not right, Mama. You know how everybody treated me the last time I was home."

"We didn't treat you like that," mama said. "We've always been here for you."

Synthia felt the tears on her cheek. "Just because I haven't been here doesn't mean I didn't want to be. I always knew that if I wanted to come home, I could. But this? It's too much!"

Mama opened her arms. Synthia fell into them and sobbed.

"We can't ask you to do something you don't want to," Mama said. "And you can't ask us to do something we don't want. The world is changing, and it's changing us."

"I'll stay as long as I can," Synthia whispered.

"That's good to hear, baby. Now text Khalid and cancel that ride. Dessert is getting cold. I made apple pie. Sweet potato pie, too."

Synthia looked into Mama's eyes.

"I love you."

"I love you, too. Always and forever."

Synthia took Mama's hand, and together they walked back to the house.

"Everybody's losing something," Mama said. "It's the times. We're sacrificing for what we hope will be."

"I know," Synthia said. "It still doesn't make it better."

"We ain't gonna worry about that right now," Mama said. "We got this moment, and right now you're home."

"Yes, I am," Synthia said.

Mama intertwined her arm with Synthia's.

"Let's go back inside. That sweet potato pie ain't gonna eat itself."

Together they walked back to the house, Synthia's eyes glowing bright yellow.

THINGS THAT GO BUMP IN THE NIGHT
BY
KYOKO M.

What kind of lunatic brings Count Dracula, aka Vlad Tepes, aka He Who Conquers aka Father of All Vampires…to a murder mystery dinner on Halloween?

Me. I'm the lunatic. My name is Cassandra Moody. Nice to meet you.

You see, the Count and I have a uniquely weird sort of friendship. It has to be, considering he's the world's oldest vampire and I'm the daughter of the original Wolfman. He met my parents a few centuries ago and they've been dear friends ever since, meaning I got an introduction. I didn't really get to know him until a few years ago when he came to visit us in Atlanta and I took him out for a night on the town that ended in a brawl with rival werewolves…and us making out. Just a little. I'm a classy girl, after all—I don't just make out with any old vampire, no, I had to go and choose the Father of All Vampires. Go big or go home.

Ever since, he and I have had little…visits. That's the nicest way to put it, really. He comes to the states every few months to hang out with our wolf pack, see my parents, and…well…the man's title is He Who Conquers. I'm sure you can put together what we get up to each time he visits. A lady doesn't kiss and tell.

This year, however, the Count had enough time to stop in for Halloween, which is actually a big deal in the supernatural community. Most of us get to cut loose on Halloween since the march of technology is now so advanced that many supernatural creatures can walk around as themselves and most normies write it off as elaborate costumes or special effects. Since this would be the first Halloween we'd be spending in each other's company, I decided to make it an occasion. I'd gotten invited to a murder mystery dinner thrown by a friend of a friend, so Vlad decided to tag along for a night of thrills.

And trust me, vampires and werewolves hanging out is *always* a night of thrills.

The limousine rolled to a stop once we reached the mansion. Yes, mansion, since living for hundreds of years at a time usually means vampires are filthy rich from learning the tricks of the trade to making money. The driver walked around and opened the door for me, offering his hand as I stepped out into the brisk fall air.

I picked up the hem of my dress and carefully stepped out onto the little circle around the massive fountain. We were in the land of the rich, which for Atlanta meant the West Paces Ferry area aka the same side of town where Bill Murray's mansion resided. I'd never be able to afford a house out this way for a hundred years, not unless I used my werewolf powers to rob a bank or knock over an armored car. I could also admit being the only black woman at a fancy murder party wasn't the smartest idea, but I was a werewolf and could take care of myself in any situation, not to mention Vlad would go to bat for me in a heartbeat, pun fully intended. My dress flowed around me, heavy and silken, as it was a replica of the iconic, fur-lined brown dress that Bette Davis wore in *All About Eve*. That was the party's theme for the night—the fifties, which happened to be an era that our hosts liked a lot, so every guest would be dressed as a character from a movie within that decade.

As such, my long dark-brown hair had been set in nice pin curls like Bette Davis's look in the film. It was no mean feat; my hair was naturally quite curly, so I'd gotten a silk press, then set it with bobby pins overnight. It had been a pain, but it actually looked quite nice.

My date then stepped out behind me, dressed in a replica of the suit that Gary Merrill's character, Bill Simpson, wore in the very same film. And boy, was Vlad something else to look at in a vintage suit. He was a whopping six-foot-four with sooty black hair enough to fall into his crystal blue eyes, contrasting his trademark pale skin. He was extremely well built, but that was because he was a predator and prey came to him easier when he was a handsome devil. He had a very slight Transylvanian accent and one of the driest wits I'd ever encountered. There was nothing more fun than trading banter with Dracula, in my book.

Well. Maybe *one* thing, but I digress.

"Ostentatious, but it's what I expected," he mused as he un-folded that giant frame from inside the limo, brushing lint from his right knee. "And it's a house on a hill, no less. Quite fitting."

"Quite indeed."

He tucked my hand into the crook of his elbow, his sky blue eyes filled with good humor and affection. "Might I say again how radiant you look, Miss Channing?"

I did a little curtsey that made him laugh, affecting Bette Davis's unique accent. "Why thank you, Bill, darling. I try."

We walked up the steps of the gigantic house. The heavy door opened and a butler appeared. He was grey-haired and wore traditional fifties butler tails along with white gloves, bowing politely. "Good evening, Miss Moody and Lord Tepes. Thank you so much for joining us this evening. Please follow me."

He stepped aside and we walked into the massive foyer. I could hear orchestral music flowing in from the main living room. The archway to our right led to a dining room with a long oak table. There was a staircase straight ahead that led to the bedrooms. The hallway beneath it likely led to the kitchen. The one to our left sounded like it was where the guests were starting to mingle, and it was where the butler directed us to follow him. My heels clicked on the marble floors as we walked into the main area where our murder mystery would be taking place.

When we reached the door, the butler bowed and left. There was a young, pretty girl waiting for us wearing a French maid costume and a big grin, her scarlet lipstick gleaming in the over-head light. She offered us the top hat in her hands that had little folded slips of paper. Each slip was a different color, no two the same one. "Welcome to our party! Please pick a piece of paper from the hat to find out your character assignment and what ac-tions you will perform in the role. Make sure not to show it to anyone, not even your partner. Over there are your sheets for logging evidence during your investigation."

We thanked her, then both selected a scrap of paper, a murder suspect sheet, and a fountain pen. I peeked at my assignment. I'd chosen the role of suspect. Tonight, there would be a fake murder and a fake victim, so the rest of the party would be trying to figure out who killed them and why. The winner would be granted a lovely prize: a check for five grand as well as a little fancy trophy and some bragging rights. I saw Vlad glance at his role as well before pocketing it, his expression unreadable as usual. We thanked the maid and headed into the room to mingle with the rest of the guests.

There was a total of eight guests including me and Vlad: four men and four women. The first woman in the bunch was the most noticeable—Elizabeth. She wore the black flapper girl dress from *Some Like It Hot* that Marilyn Monroe had worn, meaning she'd chosen to dress up as Sugar Cane. And considering how rich she was, it was entirely possible it was the real damn thing if that dress hadn't ever been lost or destroyed. Like the character she'd dressed up as, she was rather buxom and had blonde curly hair, an artificial beauty mark on her cheek, her lips red. It contrasted with her pale skin, as she was a vampire just like Vlad. And I noticed that her eyes locked onto my date immediately, which raised my hackles. There were a lot of women after Vlad, considering he was one of the wealthiest men alive and was handsome to boot.

The man beside her wore a grey suit that clued me in to his character: Roger Thornhill from Hitchcock's *North by Northwest*. Lex was a tall, strapping man with dark hair smoothed away from his face, his cheekbones elegant, his brown eyes already slightly glazed over from alcohol consumption. Supernatural beings did like to party, after all, and werewolves like him were no exception. He nodded to me politely and then sipped more wine.

The woman beside him, Jamie, wore the striped dress of Joan Crawford's character, Milly Wetherby, in *Autumn Leaves*. Her dark hair was pulled away from her face and pinned up with a few neat curls near her forehead. It made her piercing blue eyes stand out even more. Her eyes looked even brighter in her werewolf form; she had white and grey fur. I'd always found it to be lovely.

The man on her right, Robert, was dressed as Frederick Loren from *The House on Haunted Hill,* or as most people who know the actor, Vincent Price's character. He had his dark hair oiled and had a fake pencil thin mustache to complete the look in his vintage suit. He was chatting with Jamie and sipping from a glass of white wine. Like I said, werewolves love their booze.

His partner in crime—in life and in the party—was Maxine. She was short and curvy, wearing the iconic purple and gold outfit of Annabelle Loren from *House on Haunted Hill,* with her blonde hair in soft waves, but away from her face. She had a Steuben with what smelled like whiskey in it as she talked to Lex.

The last guest was Paul, a male vampire dressed as Brick Pollitt from *Cat on a Hot Tin Roof,* particularly Paul Newnan's powder blue set of pajamas as well as his leg cast. He had a crutch under one arm to sell the look, his brown hair neatly brushed. He took a deep sip from a chalice and his lips were un-naturally red as he did so; lots of vampires preferred their blood this way, but there was no denying they still liked it fresh right from the source. '

The room we'd entered looked to be the family room. It had a long burgundy couch and a matching loveseat across from it with a few more individual, but equally nice chairs around in the center of the room. The fireplace was directly across from the door and the walls were adorned with framed paintings of au-tumn landscapes and snowy mountains. It was all on gorgeous hardwood floors with rugs dotted around under the furniture and there was a black grand piano in the corner.

Robert and Maxine were our hosts and we were the last to ar-rive, so they quieted the group and then addressed everyone.

"Thank you so much for coming!" Maxine chirped. "We can't wait to get started. Raise your hand if this is your first murder mystery dinner."

I raised mine, as did Vlad and Jamie. "Well, don't worry. We'll walk you through everything. Everyone has been assigned a part to play and you are not to reveal to anyone else what yours happens to be. In just a few minutes, there will be a murder. Our victim will play dead for the rest of the party and the rest of us are going to look for clues and interrogate each other until everyone has decided on who they think is the culprit. Once everyone has chosen, we'll go around and let them explain their accusations. Once everyone has had a turn, then we'll reveal whodunit. The person who wins is the one who guesses the culprit and the murder weapon. In the event that two or more people are right, we're willing to give out equal prizes and you can share the trophy. If no one guesses right, then it's void and we can technically shift the roles and try again if everyone is patient enough to do so."

Robert spread his hands. "Any questions?"

"Are there any particular restrictions or rules?" I asked. "Like 'don't leave this room' or something to that effect?"

"Oh, no, you're welcome to our home," Robert said warmly. "Please explore as you like. The entire place is part of the mystery, so you're welcome to go anywhere you want since everything counts as a clue or a possible scenario to figure out whodunit. You won't need to go outside, though, as all the clues are indoors or can be viewed from indoors."

"Will we split up, pair up, or stay in a single group?" Jamie asked.

"It's completely optional. Whatever you think will help you solve the mystery."

"Lovely," Vlad said. "Are the wait staff assisting us or are they off limits?"

"You're welcome to ask them anything," Maxine replied. "They've all been handsomely paid for participating. We try to keep them happy since they keep us so happy."

"Are any of them part of the suspect pool?"

"No, we decided to keep it to just the guests. They won't be any of the assigned roles, but they can assist if you think of things to ask them."

Robert walked over to the doors and pulled them shut, locking them with a key he tucked into his pocket. "And just for the murder itself, we'll keep the doors shut and locked and the lights will go off briefly right at nine o'clock on the dot. In the meantime, please enjoy some libations and get ready for the main event."

I took a moment to offer everyone a Cheshire cat grin. "Fasten your seatbelts. It's going to be a bumpy night."

Most of the group laughed, having understood the reference. If there was one thing I was good for, it was references. I *was* a millennial, after all.

"How've you been, Vlad?" Elizabeth asked. "I haven't seen you since this turn of the century."

"Oh, you know me," he said casually. "I suffer from wanderlust. But I've been making trips to the states more often on account of a certain someone."

He paused enough to wink at me. "And I like this time of year in Atlanta. It's a rather festive city, after all. There is so much to do and the culture is very rich."

"It's really coming along nicely," Lex said. "I live over in Little Five Points and it's such a good area for the creative crowd. My sister's a professional dancer with a troop over there so it's nice to see so many people in the entertainment industry working in that area."

"I've been interested in the movie industry's interest here as well," Jamie said. "Like that studio out in Fayetteville. It's exciting that Atlanta's becoming so prominent in the filming world."

"Well, it is cheaper cost of living here due to so much poverty," Elizabeth said. "I'm not sure I could live here."

Lex shrugged a shoulder. "Just depends on where you go."

"Atlanta's not a pretty town, but it's got a little bit of everything," I said. "If you know where to look. I'm trying to convince the Count to get a summer home here; I really do think he'd like it."

"Oh, yes, yes," Jamie said excitedly. "It would be amazing to have you in town more often, you know. That last soiree that you threw at the beta's house was incredible."

Vlad grinned. Had his fangs been out, we'd have seen them. "Why, thank you. The only hesitation is that if I buy a home here, I'll never bloody leave."

"The state would vastly benefit from your presence," Elizabeth said, and the comment finally made me really take notice of her. I'd only met her twice. She lived in SoHo, but I also knew she had properties all over the states. We'd never held a full conversation since my instincts told me she had no regard for me, either from being a werewolf, being black, or being Southern. There was something…selfish in her eyes. She gave me the impression she spent a lot of time looking down her nose at other supernatural creatures and humans alike.

"Perhaps," Vlad said smoothly, sipping from the champagne flute that a waiter offered. "The Moody wolf pack has been very good to me. I wouldn't mind settling down in a city this vibrant with so many beautiful women around."

I rolled my eyes but couldn't help smiling. He wasn't fooling anyone. "Yes, these are the priorities of He Who Conquers."

Most of the group chuckled. "Excuse us for just a second."

I tugged my date aside. It wouldn't be great since both vampires and werewolves had supernatural hearing, but I still wanted a moment alone with him.

"Problem?" he asked as quietly as possible as we stood by the fireplace. The crackling hearth would throw the sound off a little, hopefully.

"How much do you know about Elizabeth?" I asked.

Vlad frowned. "Not much. She comes from the Norwegian clan of vampires. I don't see her very often, truth be told. She keeps to herself mostly. Why?"

"My Spidey sense is tingling."

Vlad arched an eyebrow. "My darling, the copyright infringement."

I poked him in the side, glaring. "I mean it. Something's up. I can feel it in my gut."

He nodded. "You have good instincts. Trust them. I'll keep my wits about me much as possible, then."

"As much as possible?" I echoed.

He grinned again. "Well, you are quite bewitching in that dress. It's very distracting."

I scoffed but wanted to smile again. "Oh, stop it, you dirty old man."

His eyes gleamed as he leaned down to my height and dropped a soft kiss to my lips. "Never."

And, of course, that was the exact moment someone turned out the lights.

It wasn't normal predator behavior, but I simply froze in place. Vlad slipped his arm around my back and pressed me into his side. It was normal for him to be protective; we could both see quite well in the dark. It was simply part of the show that they did it at all. Vampires and werewolves could move faster than most people could see, so even with our excellent night vision, it'd be hard to catch the culprit. I heard a bit of movement, but by the time I turned around, the lights flicked back on.

And we all saw Paul lying face-down on the floor, pretending to be dead.

The ones standing closest to him were Lex and Elizabeth. Jamie, Maxine, and Robert were over by the loveseat. Vlad and I walked over to start our little investigation. By the time we got there, Lex was kneeling over Paul to examine him for the (obviously fake) cause of death. "Not seeing any visible marks, which could be indicative of blunt force trauma."

Ah, so Lex likely had been given the role of detective. As far as I knew, with most dinner parties the roles were the victim, the killer, the suspects, the red herring, the detective, and the witnesses. We had one role other than mine out of the way, so that meant narrowing down the others. With eight people total, it probably meant there were two or three suspects total and we knew I'd been chosen as one, but not the actual killer. I knew Vlad wasn't the killer since he'd had his arm around me, meaning he couldn't have moved without me noticing. The others wouldn't know that, though, so it still worked for the party.

"What objects were nearest to him?" Jamie asked. We all glanced around the room for anything that might've been blood-stained.

"Could've been the champagne bottle," I pointed out as I gestured to it still sitting in the bucket of ice. "It's heavy enough to bludgeon a man."

"No one heard the ice shifting, though," Elizabeth said. "Not sure anyone's good enough to kill him without hearing that sound."

"Right, so what could've killed him that didn't make an obvious sound?"

"Well, we are supernaturally gifted," Vlad said. "It could've been traditional fisticuffs, as they say."

I nearly smiled. Sometimes he still used older slang for things, being hundreds of years old. "And the question is if he was hit from the front or from behind."

Lex grinned. "That's what she said."

Maxine groaned. "This is a murder, y'know. No time for jokes."

"Apologies, couldn't resist."

I gestured to the crutch that was lying beside Paul. "What about that? It's metal, after all. If you really put your mind to it, one could hit hard enough for a lethal blow."

The others nodded. "A fairly decent theory," Robert agreed. "There are a few objects in the room heavy enough, but ones that wouldn't make a distinct sound, like maybe the poker over by the fireplace. We also can't rule out if it was a blow by hand."

"Or," Vlad added. "More than one killer."

The party guests sent each other surprised looks. "Really?" Jamie asked. "You think maybe there were co-conspirators? How so? None of the conversations before the lights went out were about who had what role; it'd be cheating."

"True," I replied. "But it would be clever to have it be two killers since they could try to throw the suspicions onto the other killer."

"And how would you know that unless you were one of them?" Elizabeth said, narrowing her eyes at me. I just smiled at her sweetly.

"That's the point, dear. We're all supposed to make each other think someone else is the killer."

She rolled her eyes and polished off her champagne in a single swig. Again, the alarm bells in my head went off and I couldn't truly explain why. But I had been a werewolf long enough to know to trust my instincts, no matter how weird or illogical they seemed. It was more than her disliking me.

Something wasn't right about her and it clung to her like the smell of durian fruit. Something told me she'd seen horrible things.

And she hadn't done a thing to stop them, either.

I decided to let it ride for now and scribbled a couple of things into my murder sheet. Based on their reactions, my first thought was Elizabeth for the killer. If there were two, I'd have to listen carefully to their responses. After everyone filled in a few notes, we decided to split up to inspect the room for clues about either the murder weapon or the killer. After all, it wasn't against the rules to do things like hide or tamper with the evidence. It was kosher as long as you got away with it, but doing so also could cast doubt on you so you'd have to be strategic about it. Good thing I'd watched the movie *Clue* so many times.

"You seem on edge," Vlad said as he and I ascended the staircase. "Is it still the matter we discussed earlier?"

"Yes."

"Any prevailing theories, pet?"

I snorted softly. "I think she has designs on you."

Vlad blinked at me rapidly. "Wait, what?"

"Elizabeth. I think she resents me for having your attention."

He glanced back down at the first floor over his shoulder, frowning. "Truly?"

"Mm-hmm."

"Then she is barking up the wrong tree, to use the vernacular," he said, shaking his head. "She is not a thing like the women I am attracted to."

I arched an eyebrow. "Oh? And what women are those?"

Vlad smirked and slipped his arms around my waist. "Brazen. Intelligent. Witty. Strong."

He dropped a kiss just under my right ear, his voice a sultry purr. "And absolutely beautiful in every way."

I chuckled. "There are plenty of those women around, you know."

He met my eyes. "No, there are not."

I blushed, invisible to all, but his knowing smirk meant he knew he'd flattered me effectively. "Damn tease."

Vlad chuckled as he laced our fingers together and nodded towards the far end of the hall, politely ignoring how he'd just made me bashful. "Why don't we start there?"

"Works for me. Though I feel like the universe is laughing at me. I'm dressed as a character famous for being insecure about another woman trying to take her place."

He squeezed my hand. "I assure you that it is impossible. There is no one else like Cassandra Moody. The world isn't big enough for two of you. It's hardly big enough for only you."

"You bloody flatterer."

"Always, my little honey wolf." We explored the bedrooms of the house, which were just as spotless and beautiful as the rest. There were four total along with the same number of bathrooms. I was certain our hosts had probably left at least one thing around here or else they wouldn't have suggested the search of the house, so I made sure to pay attention to as much as possible.

The first possible clue came in the form of references to the characters we'd each selected for the party. We'd told our hosts ahead of time, so I spotted Blu-Ray copies of each movie that each guest had dressed up as in the bedrooms. Vlad and I took special notice of the placement in each room and that's when I noticed what could be guilt by association.

"I might be overthinking it," Vlad said as he peered at the bookshelf, cocking his head to one side. "But I think the placement of these movies is a clue. The film that Paul's character is in is the only Blu-Ray in this whole row of books."

"I had the same thought." I pointed to the *Cat on a Hot Tin Roof* Blu-Ray. "Look at the titles of the movies on the row directly below it."

Vlad squinted at them. "*V for Vendetta, I, Robot, Constantine, Tombstone, I, Tonya,* and *Mad Max: Fury Road.*"

He rocked back on his heels. "My dear, you're right. The first letter in each movie title spells out V-I-C-T-I-M. It's most certainly a clue."

I grinned and scribbled that in my notes. What a clever thing to do. I was fairly sure it was just an example since we of course knew Paul was the victim, but examining the next room's shelves revealed that one of the witnesses was Robert. The other two bedrooms didn't have bookshelves, so those two were probably the only two clues included upstairs. That gave us a new list of assigned roles: Paul as the victim, Lex as the detective, and Robert as a witness. Since the roles were randomly assigned, they'd probably had the wait staff wait until everyone chose a slip and had then gone through the house to add in the clues.

We went to the kitchen next. It was nice and spacious with an island counter in the center and granite counters around except for the wall that had a door leading to the backyard. The kitchen crew had ceased cooking during the mystery, so everything for our dinner—which we'd have after someone solved the murder—was already plated under a heat lamp or warming in a tray. I circled the island counter reading the little place cards that had each dish and its ingredients while Vlad perused the wall of wine next to the walk-in freezer.

"I might have something," Vlad said. I joined him at the wine wall. "There are four bottles of wine missing: Cantarina, Akutain, Naia, and Emiliana. All single word brands, so that must be intentional like the Blu-Rays."

"C-A-N-E," I finished for him. "Elizabeth's dressed as Sugar Cane from *Some Like It Hot.* We have the clue, but not the whole clue."

Vlad rubbed his chin. "Mm…the other half of the clue could be a few things. The wine bottles' placements in the wall, the room it's in, or something else entirely."

I thought it over, then snapped my fingers. "Wait. Are all four of those red wine?"

He checked the labels. "They are."

"Red wine and blood have a lot of parallels in fiction," I said. "It could be referring to blood not just because she's a vampire, but because she's the killer."

Vlad nodded. "And we found this clue in the kitchen. Sugar canes are edible, after all, so it's likely that may be the right clue if it's not misdirection."

I added a couple more notes to the sheet, then we headed into Robert's office. He liked antiquities and rare books, so one wall was nothing but a giant shelf packed to burst with books. His desk was also a nice antique one with one of those old-fashioned green lamps atop it for lighting. He had a comfortable rolling chair, a Mac, and the usual office supplies in a desk organizer. A few of the drawers were locked for privacy. The wall behind his desk had framed photos of friends and loved ones. There was even one of me and my parents, and a separate one with Vlad and the married couple, though his was from a prior century since his face and height were completely different. He was a shapeshifter, after all.

"Do you think the letters thing is for every clue or just a couple of them?" I asked as I perused the framed photographs.

"Perhaps, but they may have considered it too easy if every clue is related to letters. We still have Jamie and Maxine's roles to figure out."

"Right. Jamie's dressed as Milly from *Autumn Leaves.* Hmm…" I continued examining the room, but nothing jumped out at me initially. Vlad and I then stood in the center of the room, back to back, each observing half of the room. It could be something related to the character she was dressed up as, so I returned to the desk to examine its contents. When I looked it over the second time, I noticed that his letter opener was out, but the small pile of mail was untouched. I decided to go with a hunch that it may have been intentional. The letter opener was also lying horizontally on the desk instead of vertically. I followed where it was pointing.

The window.

"Might have something," I muttered to my companion as I walked over to the window and then pulled the drapes aside.

Outside the office window was a rather large tree with thick, gnarled branches.

And its leaves hadn't all fallen off just yet.

"Autumn leaves," Vlad mused. "Nice catch, pet. Now what's the other half of the clue?"

I pointed to the foot of the tree. Vlad leaned over more to see. There was an old axe leaning against the trunk in a thick pile of leaves. "Ah. That likely means she's a suspect."

He lifted an eyebrow, smirking. "And that leaves you and me, no pun intended."

Vlad faced me, adopting a faux-serious look. "Are you a killer, darling?"

"Why, Vlad, how could you possibly ask that of a lady?" I sniffed. "I would never dirty my hands with blood."

"Of course. How rude of me to even ask." He winked and offered me his arm. I could divine from process of elimination what role he'd likely been given: the red herring. A quick glance into the living room revealed elegant paintings on the walls of their family ancestry. There was probably a hint in there about him and/or me, I'd wager, for the others to find.

We reconvened in the room where we'd started. Jamie and Robert were already there chatting about the various clues they'd already found since that wasn't disallowed in the game. Lex returned next, looking excited about what he'd found, and then Maxine and Elizabeth returned respectively since they'd gone by themselves rather than in pairs. The butler returned with a handful of toothpicks so we could see who would go first with their accusation, using the "draw straws" method of shortest piece goes first, then so on and so forth for the slightly longer pieces. Vlad and I both chose the longest ones, so we'd be the last to go. Vlad went first.

"And last but not least," Robert said, gesturing to me. "Our lovely Miss Margo Channing. Let's have your guesses."

I did a little curtsey that made them laugh. "Why, thank you. I think Paul was bludgeoned to death with his own crutch and Elizabeth is his killer. I think Lex is the detective, Robert and Maxine are witnesses, Jamie is a fellow suspect like me, and Vlad is the red herring."

Maxine wrote down my choices on the score card. "That's everyone's answers. Time for the big reveal of our winner."

Lex and Robert drummed on the nearby lamp table, which made us chuckle. "Our winner is...Miss Moody! Congratulations! You guessed the right roles and the correct murder weapon."

The others applauded. Vlad had been rather close, then—he'd only gotten Jamie and Maxine's roles backwards. Maxine then addressed Paul. "Alright, let's give it up for our victim, Paul! You can come back to life now, dear."

We cheered.

And…Paul didn't get up.

"Oh, you can stop hamming it up now," Jamie said with a roll of her eyes. "Come on, it's time for dinner."

Paul didn't budge.

Robert frowned and nudged his foot. "Come on, joke's over, bud. Let's eat."

Nothing.

Robert knelt beside him and shook his shoulder. "Paul? Come on, did you fall asleep?"

He then paled. "Oh, my. I…think he's really out."

"What?" we demanded in unison.

Jamie knelt on Paul's other side and carefully sifted her fingers through his hair. Her eyes widened. "He has a knot on his head. Oh my goodness! Someone *really* did hit him when the lights went out. Come on, let's get him on the couch."

We helped carry him to it and gently lay him face-down on the couch. I got some ice out of the champagne bucket and put it inside a handkerchief, which Jamie held against the wound. We fanned him and tried to rouse him, but it took a few minutes before he came around. He blinked at us woozily and tried to smile, wincing in pain. "What'd I miss?"

"We have a rather serious problem here," Maxine said. "Someone hit you for real and that was *not* part of the plan. Do you remember anything?"

Paul slowly sat up and kept a hand on the ice to hold it against his skull. "It's…hard to say? It all happened within a second of the lights going out."

Robert turned to Elizabeth, his face set in a frown. "Well? You were the killer. That was your assigned role."

Elizabeth didn't bat an eyelash. "Now, why on Earth would I actually hit him? What possible motive could I have for that? What would I even gain from hurting Paul?"

I left my face neutral, but my hackles raised themselves again. I didn't like her casual response and her aloof demeanor at the accusation. "Nothing," I said quietly. "Unless you hit him so you could shift the blame to someone else here and get them thrown out of the party and disliked by all their friends."

She fixed her eyes on me. "Excuse me?"

I shrugged. "Not saying that's what you did. Just saying that is a possible motive."

She crossed her arms. "And how would you know that unless you were the culprit?"

I smiled at her, because that's what you do at fools, after all. "I barely know anyone here except for Vlad. I have no need to make anyone here look bad; I don't know them."

Elizabeth worked her jaw. She apparently hadn't expected such a simple but factual response. Maybe she'd thought I'd fly off the handle into anger so it would discredit the statement. She definitely needed to play a lot more chess. "Are you accusing me of hitting Paul?"

"No." I smiled wider. "But I sure am thinking it loudly."

Elizabeth stepped towards me, but Lex intercepted her. "None of that. We're civilized people, not animals."

"Speak for yourself," she sneered. "You brought a dirty mutt in here and it bit someone, yet you're surprised? Typical."

"Dirty mutt?" I snarled, my hands balling into fists, my shapeshifter magic breathing through my body as my anger boiled over. The wolf that lived in my head wanted to tear her throat out for that one. I didn't abide any insult to my heritage from a vampire. The relationships between vampires and were-wolves had always been cooperative, but every once in a while you'd come up against a vampire that believed we were lowly animals.

"You wanna take this shit outside?" I demanded even as Vlad rested his hands on my shoulders to keep me from advancing. "I'll show you a mutt, you stuck up slop-tart from hell."

"Stop it!" Robert snapped. "No one is going to do anything until we find proof first."

Elizabeth rolled her eyes. "That could take all night."

"Oh, not really," Vlad said, his voice and expression colder than a penguin's ass. "I implore our hosts to take a gander at the ring on Elizabeth's right hand."

Robert and Maxine frowned, then looked at her. She adopted a confused look. "What are you talking about, Lord Tepes?"

Vlad chuckled and stepped forward enough to catch her wrist, dragging her into the middle of the circle of guests. He held it up in the light while she struggled, and then I saw it.

A strand of hair from Paul's head had gotten caught on the side of her diamond ring.

She paled—which is no mean feat for a vampire—and snatched her arm away. "I didn't do it! Someone must've walked up behind me while everyone was distracted and—"

"Save it," Paul growled as he stood, though on shaky legs. "I may not remember much, but I know the attack came from the same direction as where you stood, Liz."

"What the hell is the matter with you?" Lex spat. "Why did you hurt Paul?"

"Simple," I said through my teeth. "She figured she could convince you all that I did it, which would cast me in an unfavorable light and leave her free to try her best to steal my date. She hasn't taken her eyes off Vlad once since we got here. She knew she didn't stand a chance with me in the picture, so she cooked up a scheme to sneakily get me out of her way. Didn't have the ovaries to just kill me or something like a real woman."

"A real woman?" She let out a mocking laugh. "What would you know about that? You're nothing more than his lap dog. His obedient little bitch."

"Better a bitch than a bottom feeder like you."

Elizabeth tried to lunge for me, but Robert restrained her. "Give it up, Elizabeth. You've been caught and there is nothing left to do—"

"Oh, no, let her go," I said with my meanest smile. "She wants to come at me? Fine. Let's do it like the old days. Let's have a duel."

Everyone froze. Beside me, I heard Vlad chuckle under his breath. Jamie glanced between me and Elizabeth. "To the death?"

"No," I said with a maniacal grin. "To the pain."

"What's that supposed to mean?" Elizabeth sneered.

"Of course this uncultured swine has never seen *The Princess Bride,*" I sniffed. "No, I'm not going to dirty my hands by killing you. We're going to duel in the old ways: vampire versus werewolf. No holds barred. We only stop when one of us is unconscious or taps out. If you win, I'll cease my associations with the Count."

I stepped closer, lowering my voice to a growl. "And if I win, you'd better not so much as *think* his name for the rest of your miserable eternal life. It's beneath me to get in a cat fight with another woman over a man, but I'll make an exception in your case since you decided to insult my honor and insult my species. So take your Sugar Cane ass outside and let's go."

"Cassie," Maxine said sternly. "You don't owe this weakling anything. We are certainly fine kicking her out of our house and never speaking to her again unless Paul wants to file assault charges."

"You're right. She's weak, but I do owe her something. I owe her an ass-whupping."

Maxine smiled fiercely. "Well, I certainly wouldn't mind seeing that. Robert?"

Robert matched her smile. "Neither would I, my love."

Elizabeth snatched her arm free, brushed off the front of her flapper dress, and then marched for the foyer. The others flanked her. I stayed back with Vlad for a moment. He met my eyes and settled his hands on my shoulders. I expected to see disappointment, but instead he just smiled and whispered, "Show her who you are."

I grinned. "It'll be my genuine pleasure."

* * *

"In accordance with the old ways," Vlad said over the roll of thunder in the distance. "Miss Cassandra Moody and Miss Elizabeth Hansen will engage in a duel one-on-one. The duel will not be over until either one party taps out and surrenders or one party is rendered unconscious. No killing blows are allowed, as this is not a duel to the death. If either party attempts a death blow, it will be stopped and that person automatically loses the duel. The stakes are as described: the ladies are dueling for rights to court one Lord Vlad Tepes. Everyone not participating in the duel will be witnesses to its events and they will not interfere unless one of the rules of the duel, as previously described, is violated. Are we in agreement, all?"

"Aye," said everyone present.

Vlad bowed formally to both of us. "Very well."

The butler handed him a restored old-fashioned pistol. Robert was a collector, after all. "You will begin at the sound of the gunshot. Is that clear?"

"Clear," I said, hands at my sides. I'd naturally taken off my dress, leaving me in a black bra and panties. Nudity was not a thing in the supernatural community; no one gave a damn since we were all comfortable in our skin, whatever color and however furry. Elizabeth had opted to take off her high heels but remained in her dress albeit by hiking it up around her upper thighs. We stood in the open field on the east side of the house. The treeline was about forty yards out and so there was nothing to get in the way of the fight and there'd be nowhere to run. But that was intentional—if she ran, it would automatically count as a loss, so that's why we'd chosen this spot specifically so no one had a great advantage.

Vlad glanced at me, winked, and then fired the pistol.

Time for that bumpy night I was talking about.

Elizabeth lunged at me. She was agile. I only caught a bare glimpse of blonde hair and fangs bearing down on me, her nails stretching out into deadly claws.

But by the time she reached an arms' length from me, I'd already begun to change.

Dark brown fur sprouted from my skin all over. My face pushed out and formed a muzzle. My fingernails stretched into hooked claws, razor-sharp, and my legs bent back at the knees as I adopted my bipedal wolf form. Werewolves could all transform into giant wolves at will, but with someone of her kind as my opponent, I'd need to be able to maneuver faster.

I locked hands with her and roared in her face, exerting enough strength to keep her from getting close enough to gut me. She hissed, her eyes glowing like hot coals in the surrounding darkness, and snapped at my throat. I jerked my head back and then slammed the top of my skull down on her nose, bloodying it. I then twisted my upper body and flung her further into the field of grass, steadying my big paws for the next assault.

Elizabeth twisted mid-air and landed daintily on her feet, but that was the only dainty thing about her. She came in low this time and went for my gut, slicing her claws across my stomach. It hurt like hell and blood spilled onto my fur, but I took the blow so I could get control while she was close. I grabbed her right wrist and twisted it behind her back, gripping one side of her head with my other hand and slamming her down into the grass facedown. She wheezed as the body slam stole her breath, struggling with her other arm to reach behind her. She gripped my forearm and tried to shred it apart with her claws, and more blood oozed out, the pain sharp and alarming, but I held her down with as much weight as possible.

Yield, I snarled, using my telepathy since werewolves couldn't talk aloud while in this particular form. It would be audible to the witnesses as well, since we all possessed similar kinds of magic. But I knew it would be in vain; someone this stubborn and possessive wouldn't have the sense to know when to lay down their sword.

I was proven right a moment later when she *broke her own neck to spin it around backwards* and sank her fangs into the meat of my hand.

It was a desperate, creepy thing to do, but it worked; I jerked back on instinct and she slithered out from under me. She got to her feet, her head literally facing the wrong way like Madeline Ashton from *Death Becomes Her* and then reached up and snapped it back around to the front. Gross.

Well, at least I knew it was going to be *that* kind of duel.

She jumped over my head and tried to slash my ankles from behind. I dodged it by rolling and came up on my knees, grabbing her ankle. I slammed her into the dirt once, twice, full on Incredible Hulk versus Loki style, vindictive pleasure filling me at the sound her body made when it smacked the ground. She grabbed my forearm and sliced into it to make me let go, then leapt onto me like a crazed marmoset. She crawled onto my back and then encircled my neck with her arm, using the other to put me in a chokehold. Dammit!

I threw myself to the ground as hard as possible, letting the extra weight crush her into the dirt. She grunted, but didn't let go, and I had about a minute of air before I'd pass out. That was not an option. Vlad had been the best thing in my life in a while. I savored every moment we stole together during our little trysts and flings when he visited Atlanta. I wouldn't let some uppity bitch from Norway have a chance at the man of my dreams. I dug my claws into her arm and shoulder as hard as I could, painting us both slick with blood, but she didn't relent. Thirty seconds left.

Then I thought of Vlad's words. *Show her who you are.*

And that was the key to winning.

I shifted out of my wolf form. My larger size had been the only advantage she had for the chokehold, so when I returned to my human form, her arm slipped just enough that I could free myself. I flipped over and straddled her there on the blood-stained grass, one hand around her throat, my claws out. "Yield!"

Elizabeth struggled and tried to get her feet under her, but I pinned her lower body in place with my thighs. "Yield, damn you!"

She gripped my arm and glared at me with all of hell in her eyes. I squeezed harder still and she let out a wheeze as it cut off her air.

Then, finally, she beat the grass with her fist twice, tapping out.

Vlad stepped forward and fired the pistol a second and final time. "The duel has officially concluded. Cassandra is the victor. All witnesses in attendance say 'aye' to confirm."

"Aye," the others said.

I let her go and stood up. My magic didn't dissipate; I didn't trust the bitch to honor the rules, so I took a few steps back as she got to her feet. Without another word, she stomped away towards the driveway where her limousine awaited. She slipped

288

inside it and then all we saw were the red taillights as it disappeared into the darkness.

"Do you want to press charges?" Maxine asked Paul as we watched the limo vanish.

"No." He winked at me. "That ass whupping was more than enough punishment."

I smiled. "Glad you're okay. If she'd have killed you...I don't know what I would've done to her."

"What *we* would have done to her," Lex said, scowling. "What in God's name made her think smearing your name would endear her to the Count?"

"Simple arrogance," Vlad said as he draped his outer coat around my shoulders. "In my younger years, I was far less discerning about the women I slept with. She must've thought I am the same man from centuries ago."

He slipped his arm around me and kissed my cheek. "And she was sorely mistaken. I am sorry to have brought this kind of violence into your home. It certainly wasn't my intentions."

"Oh, please, you are always welcome in our home, violence or not," Robert chided as he hugged his wife to his side. "We like a bit of mess here."

"Love it, in fact," Maxine said with a giggle. "Come along. Let's get you cleaned up and have a well-deserved dinner."

"Sounds like music to my ears."

We headed inside to finish our Halloween night together. Before you ask, dinner was excellent: duck confit, scalloped potatoes, sauteed spinach, crescent rolls, and plenty of wine.

"Well, that's something I can knock off the bucket list," Vlad said as we strolled, arm-in-arm, for the limousine after dinner and drinks. "Two women entered a duel for my hand in courtship. How romantic."

I snorted. "Uh-huh. Your ego is properly swollen right now, isn't it?"

"Among other things," he added cheekily, waggling his eyebrows as he opened the car door. "Not many creatures would fight for my honor. I'm flattered."

"Forget your honor," I scoffed, tugging him close by his tie. "I don't share."

"But sharing is caring," he said facetiously.

"Not in this dojo. Wolves mate for life. You're stuck with me for good, count."

He kissed me. "And I wouldn't have it any other way, my little honey wolf."

COLORS OF THE COSMOS
BY
ALVIN JORDAN RICHARDSON

Jacob Smith always felt like he was meant for more.

Growing up in Atlanta, the son of deeply traditional Virgin Islander parents, he was taught to keep his head down, work hard, and honor his roots. But his mind was never on Earth. His thoughts stretched beyond the clouds, past the reach of human hands, into the endless void of space. He wasn't just fascinated by the stars; he needed to understand them.

Were there other civilizations? Could disease be cured with alien medicine? Was time a place that could be walked through? And, most importantly, was love confined to this planet alone?

His parents didn't understand. To them, space was just a cold, empty abyss. But to Jacob, it was a canvas of infinite possibilities.

On the night of his seventeenth birthday, as he lay on the roof of their house, telescope trained on the moon, something streaked across the sky. Not like a meteor. Not like a plane. It moved with purpose. It slowed as it descended, spiraling lower until it vanished behind a patch of trees on the outskirts of town.

Jacob's heart pounded. He had spent his whole life dreaming about this moment. But now, faced with the impossible, he hesitated.

Then, curiosity overtook fear. He grabbed his bike and pedaled furiously toward the landing zone.

The air smelled different when he arrived. It was charged, electric. And then he saw it: a ship, sleek and iridescent, resting silently in a clearing.

And something was standing beside it.

The being was tall, its body shimmering with shifting hues, as if it were made of liquid light. Its face was unreadable, but it didn't move toward him in aggression. Instead, it lifted a hand and without words, painted into the air.

Swirls of color appeared between them, images that pulsed with life. A city of floating towers under twin suns. A great ocean where luminous creatures danced beneath the waves. And then… a boy who looked like Jacob, standing among them.

Jacob's breath caught in his throat.

The alien wasn't here to conquer, or to abduct. It was an artist. A cosmic painter, traveling across the universe in search of inspiration for its next great intergalactic showcase. And somehow, in all the vastness of space, it had found him.

Jacob hesitated. He had spent his whole life looking at the stars, wondering if he belonged among them. Now, the answer was staring him in the face.

The painter extended his hand. An invitation.

To leave Earth. To witness the universe as no human had before. To finally know, beyond a shadow of a doubt, that he was meant for more.

For the first time in his life, Jacob didn't feel like he was chasing a dream.

He was living it.

Jacob Smith took the alien's hand.

The moment their fingers met, a pulse of warmth traveled through him not electric, not jarring, but calming. He wasn't afraid. For the first time in his life, he felt like he was exactly where he was supposed to be.

The ship's interior was unlike anything he had ever imagined. It wasn't cold or metallic, like the sci-fi movies made him believe. Instead, it was alive. The walls shifted with slow, hypnotic waves of color, like a living painting. Shapes morphed and rearranged in real time, responding to movement, emotion, thought.

Jacob realized then that this wasn't just a spacecraft. It was a studio.

The alien, his host, his guide, finally spoke, though not in words. Instead, the colors of the walls shifted, forming fluid symbols that Jacob somehow understood.

"You are not afraid."

Jacob shook his head. "No."

The artist studied him, its body shimmering in deep purples and vibrant oranges. Then, with a gentle touch, it reached toward his hair.

Jacob froze.

The alien's fingers moved with careful fascination, running lightly through his afro. Its shifting hues turned a curious shade of gold, as if his hair was something it had never seen before. Jacob wasn't offended; he was seen.

The alien's colors danced again.

"Your crown holds the universe within it. It bends light, like the space between worlds."

Jacob chuckled, running a hand through his own hair. "Guess I never thought about it like that."

They were both fascinated by each other, an artist from another world, searching for inspiration, and a boy from Earth, longing for something beyond the stars. And now, together, they were heading to a place beyond imagination.

The Gallery:

The ship moved in ways Jacob couldn't comprehend. There was no engine noise, no turbulence. One moment they were on Earth. The next, they weren't.

When they arrived, Jacob could hardly breathe. The creature gave him a breather and a control panel that resembled a palette. His excitement almost made him pass out.

The Gallery wasn't just a building. It wasn't even a city. It was an entire realm, floating in the void, glowing with a light that had no single source.

It stretched endlessly in every direction, an exhibition of art from across the universe. Towers of translucent glass held sculptures that defied physics, shifting and changing like dreams in motion. Gigantic canvases displayed landscapes from distant worlds, rolling crimson clouds over golden plains, waterfalls that cascaded upward, creatures that shimmered with bioluminescent patterns, floating mountains & diamond storms.

And the colors!?

Jacob saw shades that didn't exist on Earth, hues that had no name, pigments that moved as if breathing.

The art tools were just as mind-bending. Brushes that painted sound. Pens that bled raw emotion onto a page. Floating instruments that read thoughts and turned them into moving images.

Jacob felt his soul ignite. This was beyond anything he had dreamed.

The alien turned to him, its colors shifting to something warm and welcoming.

"Create."

Jacob hesitated, his hands trembling. "But I... I don't know if I can..."

The alien reached out, pressing something into his palm. A simple tool, like a pen, but weightless, humming with potential.

"Inspiration brought you here. Now show the cosmos what Earth dreams of."

For the first time in his life, Jacob didn't just feel like he belonged. He felt infinite.

Jacob took the palette. It was impossibly light, yet when his fingers traced its surface, it pulsed with energy. It was warm, alive, waiting.

Without thinking, he lifted his hand and swiped his finger through the air three feet in front of him.

Color exploded.

Not like paint. Not like light. Something more. The air itself became his canvas, bending and shifting beneath his touch. He traced a line, and it shimmered like a nebula. He swirled his hands, and the colors responded, blooming into a radiant vortex of hues unknown to Earth.

His heart pounded in his chest.

He painted a moon he had never seen, its surface rippling like water. He painted trees with glowing roots that extended into infinity. He painted the face of a woman, a face he had never met but somehow knew her soft eyes, a gentle smile, a presence that felt like home.

And then, for the first time in his life, Jacob felt something he never expected.

He had spent years searching the stars for companionship, believing that love was waiting for him somewhere, on some distant planet. But now, as he watched his creations come to life, he realized something profound, something that had been inside him all along.

Love wasn't just about another person.

It was this. This moment. This feeling.

The sheer joy of creating, of expressing himself without fear, without limits. The way the universe had called him here, placing him in front of the one thing he had always needed, not a soulmate, not a destination, but purpose.

Love was in the way his heart raced as the colors danced at his fingertips.

Love was in the way the alien artist watched him, its body shifting into warm, golden hues, a silent acknowledgment of the truth Jacob had just uncovered.

Love wasn't just something to find.

It was something to make.

And tonight, among the colors of the cosmos, Jacob had created his own.

Jacob had never felt more alive.

He moved his fingers through the air, and the universe responded. The colors, the textures, the energy, all of it bent to his will. He wasn't just painting. He was remembering.

With careful strokes, he painted his parents. Their strong, loving faces emerged in the air with his mother's warmth, his father's quiet strength. He painted their laughter, their sacrifice, the traditions they carried from the Virgin Islands. He painted the islands themselves, the emerald waters rolling beneath golden sunsets, the ocean stretching endlessly like liquid sapphire, the rhythm of steel drums woven into the very essence of the place.

He wanted the cosmos to know them.

To know the love that raised him. To know the land that shaped him.

The alien painter stood beside him, its colors shifting, absorbing every detail. Jacob could feel its admiration, its curiosity. It had traveled across galaxies, seen things beyond human comprehension, but this...the beauty of Earth, the depth of its culture, was something entirely new.

Jacob wasn't done.

He took a deep breath and painted something even more personal.

A vision of himself and the alien painter, standing together in the city of Atlanta.

The towering skyline glowed behind them, neon lights reflecting off the streets wet with summer rain. The air smelled of peach trees and barbecue, a warm night buzzing with life. Jacob's afro caught the city lights, and beside him, the alien shimmered, its body blending into the hues of Atlanta's evening glow.

They were home.

Not just on Earth. Not just in space. But in the art, in the connection between two creators who saw the universe the same way.

Jacob turned to the painter. It had no mouth, no human features, but in that moment, he felt the smile.

They understood each other. No words were needed.

Then.

A light.

Blinding. Consuming.

For a moment, Jacob felt weightless, as if the universe itself had inhaled.

Then...

He was back.

Standing in Atlanta, on the very same patch of earth where he had first touched the alien's hand. The ship was gone. The gallery, the colors, the paintings, all of it had vanished.

But something was different.

Someone stood in front of him.

A familiar face.

Jacob's breath caught. It was the painter.

Not in alien form. Not shimmering with cosmic hues. But human. The face he had painted. A presence he had known before knowing.

They smiled at each other, a silent acknowledgment of something far greater than words.

She was beautiful. A beautiful brown complexion. Her afro tied up, a simple dress, eyes that showed the future...

Jacob didn't need to ask if it was real. He already knew.

Some journeys don't take you away.

Some bring you home.

FAIRIES AT MAYOR'S PARK
BY
JESSICA CAGE

When life gets complicated, walk the hell away and choose a new place to call home. That was the motto I came up with when everything came crashing down around me. I was the girl on top of the world. Meka, the party girl with more friends than she could count in one day, and a total hermit the next.

When I loaded my car to make the move across the country, I thought nothing of it. Okay, maybe that's a lie. I thought about it a lot. My life had become boredom island, party of one. The goal was to go somewhere I could reinvigorate my life. Now why I chose Lovejoy, Georgia, as the destination to start over, I couldn't tell you.

The little area was cute enough. It had great walking paths nearby and enough stores and businesses where I didn't feel like I was in the middle of nowhere. It was also close enough to Atlanta where I could drive in for a night out on the town and then run away from the mayhem for the rest of the week.

Looking back on that decision making, I realize now how much that makes me sound like a little old lady and I'm okay with that. I think.

Two months into my new life and I realized nothing had changed. I never went into the city. Because I worked from home, I barely left my house at all. I'd made one friend who was more of a homebody than I was. Each day I worked online, did work around the house fixing things up and decorating before inevitably making dinner for one and sitting on my couch with an old episode of Living Single playing in the background while I doom scrolled on my phone.

"This is pathetic," I muttered as I read the text from Tiffany asking if I wanted to come to her house to watch the new *Real Housewives* episode. Reality TV wasn't something that I found interesting. I never paid attention to the mess, but she liked it. "How is this my life?"

"Not tonight. I'll catch the next one." I responded to her quickly before returning my attention to my doom scrolling.

Boom!

The noise outside my front door caught my attention just before the security system sounded the motion detection alarm. Someone or something was on my porch again. I opened the camera app on my phone but saw nothing.

"Is it that damn cat again?" I huffed as I got up from the couch. One of the neighborhood cats had made a habit of coming onto my porch to knock over the planters. Luckily, I hadn't chosen a plant to put in them. The damn thing had me worried I'd be a fool to subject a plant to that fate. Smashed and trampled by a dirty-pawed menace.

I entered the code on the security pad by the door and waited for it to disarm before I stepped outside. Part of me hoped I could finally catch the cat. Then it would be off to the shelter. Maybe they could find it a suitable home where it wouldn't bother me.

Just like the camera's view, there was nothing on the porch. No cat, and the planters were right where I left them. I searched the area, trying to find the source of the loud noise I heard, but everything was fine.

"Well, that's weird." I shrugged. Maybe I was losing it. Maybe I was so bored with life that my brain was making things up to entertain me.

I turned to go back inside the house and froze when I heard a strange trilling noise. If I were someone who believed in the supernatural, I might have claimed it was extraterrestrial. The high-pitched sound gradually transformed into a gentle melody and eventually diminished until it was no longer audible. I didn't bother to investigate it any further. I wasn't that desperate to break my boredom. Two seconds later, I was back inside with the door locked and the alarm engaged. If something was out there, it wasn't about to snatch my black ass up!

The next day, Tiffany refused to take no for an answer. Since I didn't want to jeopardize the only friendship I had, I reluctantly agreed to meet up for lunch. I really didn't need that much convincing after she suggested we meet at Rutabaga's. The café nearby had a unique and funky vibe. Tiffany was no fool. She knew I couldn't pass up their Asiago Chicken Panini! I bit down into my sandwich and moaned as the flavors danced on my tongue.

"You look like you needed that." Tiffany stared at me over her coffee.

"Yes!" I laughed and wiped the crumbs from my mouth with my napkin. "I didn't sleep that well last night."

"Why not? Everything okay?" She adjusted the headband securing her afro perfectly atop her head before she bit into her own sandwich.

"I heard some strange noises outside last night. It was right after you texted me. When I checked it out, I saw nothing, but it put me on edge." I sipped my drink. "Did you hear anything?"

"Outside of the drama on my TV? No," she shrugged. "Those women are crazy! I can't believe they put all that out for the world to see. But damn it if I don't gobble it right on up."

"I still don't understand it." I took another bite and moaned. "Watching it makes my brain itch, but I do it for you."

"You will. I'll convert you to my side!" Tiffany rubbed her palms together and her long black nails clacked against each other.

"At this rate, yeah, you will." I sighed. The last couple of times I watched with her, I actually found myself paying attention to the drama on the screen.

"What does that mean? Are you okay?" She dropped the evil grin she had plastered across her face.

"Overall, yes. I'm healthy, financially secure, and emotionally stable." My shoulders dropped after I listed the things that should have made me happy with my life. "I'm just bored."

"Bored?" She sucked her teeth. "That's the issue?"

"I moved away from home because I wanted to start something new." I watched a woman with long blue hair and nose piercings walk in the door. "The goal was supposed to be to reinvigorate my life but look at me. I'm just doing the same things I was before, only now I'm in a different location. Work, eat, sleep. It's pathetic."

"You can always go out more." Tiffany stated the obvious.

"Easier said than done. Don't mind me. I'll wallow for a few days, then find a new project to occupy my thoughts." I picked a fallen piece of chicken from my plate and popped it into my mouth.

"Or you could be more active in your life." Tiffany flicked my hand with her fingertips. "The Meka you told me about, the version of yourself before you moved here, didn't seem like the kind of girl who would sit back and let life just pass her by. It's time for you to put yourself out there."

"You are one to talk." I pointed out the hypocrisy in her comment. "You do the same things I do, actually maybe less, since that garden of yours is still crying out for help."

"Hey, I'm not the one bored. I love my quiet little life. That's why I moved here." Tiffany poked at me. "The stories I can tell about my past will keep me full until I die. And if I decide I want more, I'll get out there and grab it. Don't project this onto me. If you were looking for action, why the hell would you choose Lovejoy of all places? There's nothing but old people and gas stations out here."

"The name was cute." I laughed. "I hadn't really looked too much into it. It had a low crime rate and pretty pictures online."

"You made a major life choice based on the name of the location being cute?" She rolled her eyes. "Maybe I overestimated you. Yes, stay your ass in the house because clearly you have some poor decision-making skills. You might go out there and end up tied up in someone's basement."

"That's not a problem. Few houses around here have basements. I checked." I winked as I thought back to my home search. A basement would have been nice to store my recently accumulated craft supplies.

"I don't think I can help you. You need something stronger. Like therapy and possibly medication. Now you're hearing strange things go bump in the night because your brain is bored. Probably just creating drama for the thrill." She took out her phone and tapped on the screen before turning it to me to show a listing for a local therapist.

"That's funny." I pushed her phone away from my face. "Oddly enough, I had the same thought last night. Like my mind just made it all up because I was bored with life. I wonder if that kind of thing is possible."

"It damn sure is, and if you don't be careful, you'll be one of those people in the padded room." She put her phone back in her pocket. "No, but on a serious note, Meka, if you want to change your life, you have to be the one to do it. No one is going to come in and inject excitement into your veins."

"You're right. I know you are." I sipped my latte. "Maybe you should be a therapist or counselor. You're great at it."

"It's all the reality television I watch! Girl, I sit up researching what the hell is wrong with these people and end up reading psychology essays!" She tapped the thin frame of her glasses. "Call me Doc Tiff. That's cute."

That night, my budding therapist friend left me to myself. I expected another invitation to binge watch reality trash, but it didn't come. And because she gave me nothing to distract myself, I couldn't stop thinking about her words. That was no doubt her plan all along.

I needed to be more active in making my life something I enjoyed again. That was never a problem for me before. I was an extrovert who made the party jump when I stepped into the room. People flocked to me, and I loved it. But thinking about becoming that girl again, the girl who felt empowered by the energy of others, the girl who ultimately hurt so many people with her selfishness, it scared me.

I stood in my kitchen, clutching a dish rag and struggling to breathe. How could I even think about going back? How could I risk it? Even if I was worried about it, why did it scare me so much to think about putting myself out there? Was I doomed to spend my life alone? Is that what life would be for me? Just standing on the outskirts and wishing for more?

BOOM!

The noise broke through my panic and again, a moment later, my phone chimed. The security app announced motion detected. I expected to see nothing when I opened the app, but there was something. Or better yet, someone. A fuzzy figure stood just beyond my porch.

Common sense said stay in the house. Common sense on the edge of a panic attack said to run outside and investigate because that was better than standing in my kitchen hyperventilating. I disengaged the alarm and ran outside, but I was too late. They were gone.

"What the hell is going on?" I muttered to myself as I turned to walk back inside. "I'm losing it."

It would have been nice if that were the end of it. I would go to therapy, work through my issues, and move on with my life. But no, it continued happening for days. Each night, a loud noise, a fuzzy figure, and then when I made it outside, they were gone.

On the fourth night, I ate my dinner early and set up shop on my porch. Whatever it was, I wouldn't miss it. I sat on the small swinging chair I picked up at a yard sale and watched the cat menace jump across my neighbor's porch. I should have snatched him up, but I was on a mission. The warm summer breeze was lulling me to sleep, but as I was losing my fight and drifting off to sleep, I heard it again. That trilling sound.

When I woke up, I saw two women in the middle of the road. They moved like water flowing and a mysterious internal light illuminated their bodies as they danced along the street. My jaw dropped in awe at their incredible performance. At first my body froze because perhaps what I was looking at was, in fact, alien. Then I heard Tiffany's words echoing in the back of my mind. It was time to take action.

I jumped from the swing to follow them and nearly tripped down the steps. My instincts told me to keep a distance just in case they tried to cut my head off. But they didn't. They were lost in their own world of dancing and music I couldn't yet hear.

The strange women led me to Mayor's Park, where there were other people, all women, dancing and glowing from within. They laughed, sang, and bounced around in circles while holding on to each other. As if that weren't unbelievable enough, I turned to see more of them, taking off from the ground. They moved in a controlled line across the surface of the water, then floated effortlessly, gracefully gliding around the fountain at the center of the pond.

Anxious steps moved my body back away from the scene. How was it possible that this otherworldly party was happening and no one else seemed to notice? It was then that I realized I wasn't the only person out there. Cars drove by, people walked down the street, and everyone was doing everything but gawking at the scene in front of me.

"I have to get out of here." I meant for the thought to stay in my head, but it slipped out of my mouth and caught the ear of the woman near me.

She turned toward me and narrowed her eyes. I shouldn't have reacted. I should have just pretended like I was just as oblivious as everyone else. But I couldn't help it. I swallowed the lump in my throat after making direct eye contact, then turned to run. I didn't make it far before the illuminated lady appeared in front of me, blocking my path home.

"You can see us?" Her voice was an airy sound. One full of excitement and not the threatening tone I was expecting.

"Yes," I said nervously, then took a step back. It wasn't like I had anywhere to run.

"Oh joy! You must come and join us. We haven't seen a borderling in a long time." She clapped her hands, then skipped closer to me. Large green eyes leaned in close to me as she examined my features. "Hmm, you're not very close, but it's still in there."

"A borderling?" I questioned nervously. "What is that?"

"Oh? You don't know?" She tapped her chin. "Yes, I supposed few of you ever do. How rude of your ancestors not to pass that information down. A borderling is someone who stands on the edge of the supernatural. You're not one of us, but you can see us! It has something to do with your bloodline. It means at least one of your ancestors was like us!"

"I'm sorry, but what are you?" I lowered my voice to not insult anyone else. If they considered the question to be a rude one, I didn't want to broadcast it to the rest of them.

"We are fairies, silly! My name is Kilae, what's yours?" She laughed, but when I didn't give her my name her expression dropped. "Oh, you don't know? That's interesting."

"Know what?" The woman was already confusing me. Twice she said I didn't know something. That much was obvious. I had no idea there was a group of self-illuminating women who floated around the pond near my home.

"It doesn't matter. Come join us. Please?" She pulled my hand into hers and frowned when I flinched. "It will be fun, I promise. We won't hurt you. The others will be so happy to know you're here. We protect those who are like you. But it's been so long since we've found one."

I looked back toward my house and heard Tiffany in my mind again. '*Take action!*'

"You're not going to eat me or sacrifice me to your God or something. Right?"

"I'm strictly vegetarian, so no," she laughed, and it sounded like a melody from my childhood.

I shrugged. "Why not. How much more insane can this get?"

"Oh joy!" She smiled before pulling me back toward the party. "Fairies! We have a special guest! A borderling!"

As I approached, the other fairies, all women, turned their attention towards me. A deafening silence suddenly blanketed the party that lasted for what felt like an eternity. Then a wave of exuberant cheers erupted. They applauded the term that still confused me, and the next thing I knew, I was being swallowed up in a sea of laughter and aggressive embraces. That night, as insane as it sounds, I partied with the fairies.

Before I could reject the offer, the women were feeding me unimaginably delicious treats and drinks that made my tongue feel like a cloud. Every worry I had about hanging with those indescribable creatures melted away as their food filled my belly and their laughter and songs washed over me.

"So, are there fairies everywhere?" I asked Kilae as she handed me my second glass of what I quickly dubbed fairy juice. It was alcoholic and made me feel like I was floating on air.

"No, not everywhere. We stick to specific territories. There are other supernatural groups that are not favorable to us, so we have to maintain a distance. But there are plenty of safe spaces where we can gather."

"There are others?" The entire time I danced and sang with the odd group, I hadn't considered they might not be the only ones out there. Suddenly, I had to consider what my world had just opened up to.

"Yes! There are werewolves, vampires, witches, all types. Most of them you've probably heard about in one fairy tale or another. But I'll let you know something now. The elves are the absolute worst. If you see one, run away. They will try to sell you bad potions and they are terrible backstabbers."

"Sounds like you have a personal issue with an elf?"

"Yes, Jarciu can kiss my glowing ass!" She hopped up and slapped her butt.

I couldn't help but laugh at that. "My mind is spinning."

"I can imagine it would be." She chewed on a thought. "That's probably what drew you here. The desire to be near your own. Georgia, especially Atlanta, is full of supernatural beings."

"Can you tell what I am?" I asked. Part of me wanted to be fairy, and part of me wanted to wake up and realize this was nothing more than an elaborate dream.

"Not without drawing blood." She winked. "If you really want to know, I can do it."

"No, thank you. It can remain a mystery." I pulled my hand closer to my body. I wasn't that interested.

The party continued into the late hours of the night. Long past when the flow of traffic stopped and the dog owners made their final lap around the neighborhood. Instead of going home, I took action and continued to party with the fairies. Despite my willingness to take part in their festivities, I didn't trust them all. Throughout the night, I stayed close to Kilae because she felt safest to me. Something inside me told me she would protect me. Not that the others seemed threatening, but I was new to their world, and I didn't want to cause problems.

"Are you okay?" Kilae pulled me away from the group.

"Yes, I'm fine, why?" I swallowed the sudden lump in my throat.

"You've been clinging to me for the entire night." She nodded at the others partying around us. "It's okay for you to get out there and mingle."

"Not to be rude, but I'd rather not. This is your party. I don't really belong here."

"If you weren't accepted, you wouldn't be here. Trust me." She pulled my hand into hers. "We are here to celebrate our womanhood. You're a part of that."

"Your womanhood?" I frowned. "What does that mean? Is this about to turn into some kind of orgy?"

"No, silly! Nothing like that at all." Kilae cackled so hard her face turned red. I stood waiting for her to catch her breath before she continued. "Unfortunately, this is one of the last times we will all be together like this. Most of the women here, including myself, are due to be mated soon."

"Mated? What does that mean?"

She frowned at me. "I'm sure you're over thinking the term. We'll be married off to a suitor and set off to create the new generation."

"That sounds tragic. Do you not have a choice?" I imagined there were some rules that stripped them of their right to be single and free.

"Of course we do! Those who choose not to will continue the party for another century. Some of us want to settle down. I know I've wanted my own little ones for a while now."

"And this is what? Your farewell to your single days?"

"Exactly! I won't be traveling the world partying into the late hours once I have babies. I'll leave this chapter of my life behind." She sighed, but it wasn't a sad sound. It was a hopeful one. Like she was finally getting to do the thing she wanted to do.

"Odd, you're trying to leave it behind and I'm trying to find it again," I admitted.

"You say that as if you've lost a part of yourself." She pulled me over to a bench where we sat together. "How is that possible?"

"In a way, I feel like I have." I looked around at the women who danced, laughed, and held each other. "You all have such close relationships here. It's something I miss so much now. I have one friend here and even with her, I limit myself. I don't let her get too close to me."

"There is so much more about you, isn't there?" She stepped in front of me. "Tell me what's going on in your mind right now."

"Honestly, all I can think about is how I should be terrified right now, but I'm just happy not to be on my couch for another night." I looked around at the women. "I miss having friends to gather with. Sharing stories and plans for the future."

"What's keeping you on your couch?" Miniol, another fairy who had introduced herself to me before, sat cross-legged near my feet. "I couldn't help but overhear you."

"Nothing, I mean, I don't know. Maybe fear." I shrugged, thinking about the near panic attack I had at even considering stepping outside my comfort zone.

"What are you afraid of?" Miniol asked and played with the frill on the bottom of my skirt.

"Putting myself out there. Getting hurt or hurting someone else in the process." I paused. Why was I being so open? I looked down at the cup in my hands. "What's in that drink?"

"Oh, I forgot about that! For us, it's like tequila, but for borderlings, it can work like a truth serum… if you're not used to it. You build a tolerance over time," Miniol admitted, then narrowed her heavily painted eyes at me. "Funny enough, I have an observation. You're new here, correct? We scouted the area before selecting it for our festivities. We had to make sure it was safe. There's no way we would have missed a borderling."

"Oh, well yes. I am new to the area. But I've been here for a few months now." I admitted. "Moving here was supposed to give me a fresh start."

"Why did you need a fresh start?" Miniol stood and placed her hands on her hip.

"Miniol, stop it." Kilae sucked her teeth. "She isn't on trial here."

"No, it's okay." I pat Kilae's shoulder. "It's a fair question. My old life, well, it didn't go the way I wanted it to. One day I looked up, and I didn't recognize myself. The plan was to come here, start over, and make my life fun again."

"You wanted more fun, and you came here?" Miniol laughed before she echoed Tiffany's earlier statement. "You're really bad at making choices for yourself, aren't you?"

"I didn't used to be." I shrugged.

"Theres something more there." Kilae leaned in again. The little fairy really didn't understand personal space.

"Maybe." I stood from the bench to put space between us.

"Tell me. Your secret will be safe with me, I promise." She looked at Miniol and without another word, the colorful eyed fairy flew away.

"Have you ever done something that made you question yourself?" I asked Kilae after I was sure Miniol couldn't hear me. "Something that made you fear your own actions."

"I've made mistakes, everyone has. But I think you're talking about something different." Kilae grabbed my hand. "Tell me, please."

"I don't know how to." My heart raced. I wanted to tell her everything, but I didn't want her to look at me like everyone else had. "I hurt someone I loved. And I had no explanation for it. After that, no one trusted me again. I couldn't even trust myself, I'm still not sure I do."

"So you moved yourself to boring little Lovejoy to make sure that doesn't happen again?" She lifted her finger and tapped the end of my nose. "Your decision to make this your home wasn't as clueless as you make it out to sound. You knew the risk wouldn't be as great as other places."

"There's not much here." I nodded. "Most of the people who live here are older. There isn't anyone to hurt."

"What did you do that was so bad?" Kilae tilted her head, and her eyes widened as the pieces clicked together in her mind. "Did someone die?"

I dropped my eyes to look at my hands. The answer was yes, someone died because of me, but I couldn't bring myself to say it aloud.

"Okay, too heavy!" Kilae grabbed my hand in hers. "Let's have some real fun!"

"What?" I asked as she pulled me further away from the others. I looked over my shoulder to see them still partying as if nothing was happening. "Where are we going?"

"You need to get away." Kilae called out and as she spoke, my skin tingled. "You said you wanted more fun, right? It's time to start!"

The tingles spread further across my body like a thousand little sparks. The feeling changed into a muted sensation, like the fuzzy feeling inside my brain after a long nap. Large colorful wings sprouted from her back, and she looked back at me.

"Don't let go." She lifted our clutched hands in my face and I nodded.

Kilae's wings moved in powerful strokes against the air and lifted us from the ground. I couldn't believe it. We were actually flying. Within moments, the pond surrounded by her friends, still lost in their celebration, disappeared beneath us. I watched as the landscape changed from the thick treetops of the rural area, to bustling city streets and back.

"This is insane!" My voice broke through the rush of air that brought tears to my eyes. "I can't believe you get to do this whenever you want." I looked over at the fairy who used her magic to carry me across the night sky.

"We can go anywhere you want. Just say the word." Kilae tightened her hold on my hand as she called out over the rushing air.

"I want to sit on top of the world." It was the first thing that came to mind. For months since the accident, it was what I wanted. To get as far away from the rest of the world as possible.

"Perfect!" Kilae's wings stopped moving. She pulled me into a hug and her wings wrapped around us. It felt like we were spinning, tossed inside a cyclone. A moment later, everything came to a chilling stop. We were there. Atop a mountain, looking down at a vast valley of trees and splitting rivers.

"Oh my god." I gasped to catch my breath and clear the spinning in my own head. "How did you do this?"

"Is this what you had in mind?" Kilae said as she stepped back and stretched her arms out proudly. "This is the closest thing I could think of to being on top of the world."

"Where are we?" All I could see was a vast mountain range that stretched on for miles. The cool air that cut through the mountain tops brought a chill to my body. Kilae noticed my shivers and tapped my shoulder with her hand. A moment later, a rush of heat moved over my body and wrapped around me like a blanket I would never be able to take off. "Thank you."

"Of course." She smiled. "We're no longer in Georgia, if that's what you mean. But it's far away from everything."

"This is breathtaking." I sighed. "You get to do this whenever you want. Shift to unimaginable places at the drop of a dime, I would give anything to be able to do that."

"There are some limitations, but yes." Kilae twirled around me. "This is one of my favorite places in the world. Very few supernatural beings come here. They don't like the temperatures. For those who do, there isn't enough food here. But I love it."

I stood there, speechless, as I took in the scene unfolding before my eyes. Then, I finally reached my limit and couldn't keep it bottled up any longer. If I was ever going to admit the truth, this was the place to do it. "Yes."

"What?" Kilae turned to me. She'd been waving to a passing bird when I spoke.

"Someone died. Because of me." I looked into her gigantic eyes and waited for her expression to turn against me, but it didn't.

"What happened?" Her question was gentle, one looking for under-standing and not judgement.

"I don't know." I took a deep breath and went back to the night when I lost my best friend. "You don't know how many times I've tried to figure that out. But it's a fuzzy mess in my mind."

"Take your time." She stepped closer to me. "There is no pressure here."

"I was with my best friend, Mel." The birds whistled as I tried to grab hold of the fragmented memory. "We were hanging out, getting ready for another night out. She didn't want to go, but I insisted. I re-member feeling off for days. I couldn't shake it, and I thought a party would be the best solution. You know, it would give me something to take my mind off things. Just before we were supposed to leave, the feeling got worse. My head started pounding. Mel came into the room to check on me. I turned around to see her and then there's nothing. I can't remember what happened next. When I came to, I was holding her lifeless body in my hands."

"You don't know what happened to her?" Kilae's expression turned. It wasn't anger or judgement. It was pity. Like she already understood something I didn't.

"No. And because I could never explain it, everyone blamed me." I thought about the countless conversations I had with people I once called my friends. Every one of them eventually tried to convince me to admit to something I didn't do. Even though there was no proof of what happened, and I called for help as soon as I realized she was hurt, it wasn't good enough. When someone gets hurt, when someone dies, people want answers. I couldn't give them the answers they needed."

"I can find the answers, if you would like." Kilae's offer was the first time she hesitated when speaking to me.

"What?" I wiped the tears from my eyes. "You can? How?"

Kilae cupped my face in her hand. "You've locked away the truth because you feel guilty about what happened to your friend. If you want, I can unlock the mystery for you. It's there, in your mind. I can find it for you. But I can't promise it will make you feel better. The truth might be more difficult to face."

"Are you sure you can do that?" My stomach twisted. Did I really want to know the truth? If I could know what happened, how could I deny the opportunity?

"Yes, absolutely." She said confidently. "Only if you want to."

"Okay." I nodded and straightened my shoulders. "Do it. I don't want to carry this anymore. I need to know the truth."

"Okay, close your eyes and focus on the last thing you can clearly remember." Kilae instructed.

She placed her hands on either side of my head, and her palms warmed against me. Within moments, it felt like that warmth was reaching beneath my flesh. It penetrated deep into my mind and the deeper it went, the clearer the memory became. In moments, I was no longer standing on the mountains with a fairy. I was back in my old apartment with my best friend.

Music bumped in the background as I shook my hips to the beat and styled my hair in the mirror. My head hurt, but it wasn't as bad as I remembered it. Then, as I danced and adjusted the braided bun, my reflection changed. A soft glow radiated from beneath my skin. I stopped and stared at myself, backing away from the mirror.

"Meka?" Mel called out from behind me. I remembered then that she'd gone to get more drinks.

I turned to see my friend standing there, holding a bottle of vodka and staring at me. One second, she was a concerned friend and the next; she wasn't. It happened so quickly. Her features changed and the docile girl turned feral as her lips pulled back to reveal sharp fangs. Mel charged me and knocked me against the wall. She growled and picked up the wooden chair and tossed it across the room, nearly hitting me in the head.

"Mel, stop!" I called out. But instead of listening to me, she pounced again. This time, when she charged, that soft light beneath my flesh spread and my entire body grew hot like fire. That heat dispersed from my core and reached out to Mel. I watched as the glow of light wrapped around her like a cocoon.

The wrap pulsated around her body, frozen in midair. Mel slowly faded. Her skin paled, her eyes dulled, and then she stopped. Everything stopped. I took a step toward her and, as if commanded by my own actions, the cocoon dissolved into strings of lights that rushed back to my body. I ran to catch her before she hit the floor.

When I held Mel's body, something happened. That energy that the light stripped from her, I felt rushing through my own veins. I could tell instantly what it was. Stolen energy that didn't belong to me. And it hurt so badly that I screamed out in pain. I held my friend, sobbing as the light disappeared beneath my flesh and then I passed out.

The memory ended, and my consciousness returned to my body. I fell forward into Kilae's arms.

"Looks like you're not just borderling after all." Kilae held me tightly.

"I did that to her? I stole her life away from her, didn't I?" I looked up at Kilae. "What am I? How did I do that?"

"You're something more, something new." Kilae supported me as I lifted my head and straightened my body. "We call your kind neutralizers."

"What is that?"

"You're a borderling, who, when threatened, can protect yourself. You can take the magic away from others. Your body absorbs it. It strengthens you, but you can't use it. At least I don't think you can. Neutralizers are even rarer to find, so we know little about your kind. I'm not sure when your kind appeared, but I think it was a natural evolution to protect you from those who sought to harm you," Kilae said. "It's best we keep this a secret between us."

"So, Mel wasn't human?" I remembered the way she looked. The change in her features just before she pounced. She no longer resembled the friend I had. She was something different, a monster.

"No, from your memory, I'd say she was some sort of shifter. It's hard to tell because she didn't finish the shift. Maybe werewolf?" Kilae scratched her chin. "They were notorious for not liking your kind."

"So, my best friend was a werewolf or something like that, and my inherent magical abilities protected me from her?" My head felt like it was spinning even more than before. "How is that possible? Why would she have been friends with me?"

"She may not have known it herself. Or she did, and she chose not to hold it against you. Not every supernatural is the same." Kilae tried to offer an explanation. "Her instincts may have taken over when she saw you in your heightened state."

"I killed her. It really was my fault." My chest burned. "All that time, people blamed me. I kept telling myself there was no way I could do that to her. But I did!"

"You were protecting yourself." Kilae placed her hand on my shoulder. "It's not your fault the magic took over."

"That changes nothing, Kilae. Mel is gone. She was my best friend, and her life ended because of me."

"Listen, something I've learned is that the time allotted to us isn't infinite. Is it tragic that a life was lost? Yes. But it may have been her time to go. If it wasn't, your magic would have failed and hers would have prevailed." Kilae turned me to look at the scene in front of us. "I'm not saying that it will be easy to move on, because how can it be? But you must live your life. You have a role here, every living being does. I promise you; your purpose is not to hide away forever simply because you made a mistake. You didn't even know this was a part of yourself. Now you do. Now you can move on with understanding of the risks."

Kilae turned back to me and wrapped her arms around me. For the first time since the accident happened, I relaxed. I let out all the tears, and I accepted her embrace fully. For the first time, I wasn't afraid of someone being close to me. I remembered very little after that, just her embrace and the soothing sound of a song from my childhood. I woke up the next day, in my home, in my bed, with the weight on my heart a little lighter.

There were no fairies that night. For two more nights I waited, hoping they would return, but they didn't. There were no loud noises to set off the detection, no strange sounds or illuminated figures dancing down the street. Instead of waiting for them to return on the fourth night, I walked over to the pond where they had partied before.

They weren't there. I sat on the bench and watched the still water. Had I imagined it all?

"I figured you would be here." The soft voice spoke from behind me.

"Kilae!" I hopped up from my seat. "I was beginning to think I was crazy!"

"Of course you aren't," she laughed. "How are you?"

"I'm okay. Still really confused about everything. I thought I would never see you again." I moved to sit back on the bench, and she joined me.

"I really shouldn't be here, but I couldn't stop thinking about you." Kilae admitted. "It felt wrong to leave you after what I revealed to you.

If I did, I would be no better than your ancestors who kept the truth from you to begin with."

"Thank you for coming back." I hugged her.

"I came to offer you a chance to leave this life. To start over and leave the weight of your past behind," Kilae said. "It would give you a chance to learn about yourself and your history."

"What do you mean?" I asked. "Leave this life?"

"We won't be back here again, at least not for a very long time." She looked out at the water. "And I'm not sure when I will ever be able to get out again. I told you; it's time for me to be mated."

"Why not? Are you in trouble?" I felt a chill run down my spine. "Did someone find out what you were doing with me?"

I couldn't imagine her being in trouble because of me. Yes, I was grateful to know the truth about myself, but it wouldn't have been worth it if it caused problems for her.

"No. It's nothing like that. We choose random locations for our celebrations. And we never hit the same spot twice. Like I told you, there are beings out there who don't like us. They hunt us down. It won't be long before their scouts track the scent of our gathering here."

"Oh." I looked around as if the enemies she spoke of would pop out and chase us down. "What about me? Will they be able to find me?"

"Not unless you reveal yourself to them." She wagged her finger in my face. "Don't reveal yourself to them."

"I won't," I hurried and answered.

"Meka, I can't come back here, but you can come with me," Kilae repeated her offer. "I know you're not happy with the way your life is here. Maybe this can be the fresh start you were really looking for. Like Miniol said, something brought you to Lovejoy. Maybe this was it."

"If I go with you, that means I have to leave my human life completely? Wouldn't that also mean living on the run, hiding in your world?"

"Well, yes." She nodded.

"Thank you, but I'm not sure that's a better solution for me." My gaze shifted towards the clouded sky above us. "What you said was right. I need to live my life. I have to stop hiding."

"So, I helped you?" Her face brightened and her wide smile stretched across her face.

"Yes, you did. And I want to thank you for that. I'm so grateful to have met you."

"And you won't come with me?" she asked again.

"No." I turned my gaze back to her. "I want to live my life the right way. Running away again, that isn't right."

"In that case, I have a gift for you." She handed me a box. Inside was a small necklace with a spiraling stone charm.

"What's this?" Holding the charm in my hand, I could tell it was something more than a simple piece of jewelry.

"If you ever need me, use that to call me." Kilae took the necklace and placed it around my neck. She tapped it three times with her fingers, then lifted it to my lips. When it touched my lips, it lit up and a moment later, I could see the charm around her neck respond. "You're my borderling now. That means it's my job to keep you safe. I'll always be here for you."

"That's comforting. Thank you, Kilae."

She stood from the bench. Before she turned to walk away, she looked down at me.

"Meka, you are so much bigger than the mistakes you've made. Take whatever lessons you can from them, but don't let them cripple you. It's time for you to get out there and live your life."

I watched as her wings appeared and lifted her from the ground. I watched the fairy fly away and smiled. My hands warmed and when I dropped my eyes to inspect them, I could see the soft glow beneath my flesh. I knew then my life was only just beginning.

PENNY CANDY LADY
BY
DEDREN SNEAD

The summer of '95 tasted like Banana Now and Laters and sounded like *Southernplayalisticadillacmuzik.*

Marcus Williams hopped off his Black Label Cardiel slick skateboard and pressed his face against Ms. Evelyn's side window, his breath fogging the glass as he counted nickels and dimes for the third time. Still only seventy-five cents—not enough for the frozen cherry cup, two honey buns AND the Starburst Jelly Beans he would need to work up the courage to talk to Leoshi.

Late afternoon heat shimmered off Simpson Road—what the old folks still called it, though they'd renamed it Joseph E. Boone Boulevard after Dr. King's friend. Construction cranes loomed in the distance like a murder of crows with their long shadows falling across neighborhoods that used to have the old names, used to have the old families who remembered when sassafras trees lined these streets.

"Boy, you gonna wear a hole in my window," Ms. Evelyn called from inside, her voice holding that weight that made even the hardest brothas from the Bluff straighten up and say, "Yes Ma'am." "Come on here before The Deep Dark notice you a-lingering."

Marcus straightened up, tucked the small cloth bag around his neck into his faded Braves jersey, and wiped his feet on the welcome mat before turning the old crystal doorknob.

As he walked through the door, the brass bell above chiming a note that seemed to hang in the humid air too long, Reebok pumps creaking along the worn floorboards up to a series of coffee tables, longboards and chairs that were a showcase of sweets curated in several glass jars and bins. Ms. Evelyn's house sat right on the corner of Magnolia and Vine—the real Vine Street, not the White Folks version they were planning uptown, where corporate sponsors could Regan-ize the neighborhood for prospective out-of-towners.

The old folks said this corner had been sacred ground since before Atlanta was even a dream— first for the Muscogee and Cherokee Nations who first understood the crossroads as places of power, followed by the regional runaway slaves who followed the North Star to be anywhere else but there. Old trading paths had crossed with old freedom paths, and now were the streets of a community trying not to get washed away by a wave of Olympic money and real estate developer promises.

The inside of Ms. Evelyn's house smelled first like strong peppermint and then something older, earthier, like the red clay underneath all of Atlanta. Then the wave of goodness would hit you. All the candy you could eat in two lifetimes, sprawled out in the receiving room of the Victorian house as a makeshift haven for generations of Atlanta youth.

She had it all. Wax teeth he'd tried to eat once as a younger man. A handful of Tootsie Rolls that was always a go-to. His little sister's favorite were Bonkers, but he wasn't buying any for her.

Gummy Bears, Nerds, Bazooka Joe. Warheads, Reese's Peanut Butter Cups, Cowtails.

Classics like pillow peppermints, Milk Duds, Sweetarts, Dubble Bubble and Laffy Taffy.

Marcus collected himself from the blissful daydream, having forgotten to respond to grown folk.

"The Deep Dark don't come out in daylight, Ms. Evelyn." Marcus said in correction, trying to sound braver than he felt about it.

Every kid in West Atlanta knew the rules—you could play in the day, but the night hours belonged to the shadows and The Deep Dark. When the streetlights flickered on, your tail better be home.

At best it was a warning, random patterns flickering like Southern fireflies, parents leaning out screen doors calling you by your government name to come inside before something worse than bullets could find you. Marcus watched his older cousin Malik get caught up dealing down in the Bluff, seen him change from the boy who taught Marcus to dribble a basketball to something hollow-eyed and distant, another casualty of the war for souls that raged in every American city. The magic Hoodoo stuff Grandmama was teaching Marcus about didn't seem to save him. What if her lessons were no different from the dope dealers who worked the corners where English Avenue bled into Vine City, selling dreams that turned into nightmares in your veins? Grandmama Mertie always said he and the kids of Vine City were special, but he'd seen special kids in the neighborhood ending up dead or locked up in Fulton County jail. The Good Die Mostly Over Bullstuff. He knew The Deep Dark had plenty of competition trying to snatch up the souls of Black Folk on the Westside.

Ms. Evelyn's returned a laugh that was dry as an August drought, carrying decades of knowing in its hollow sound. "Chile, The Deep Dark got servants that walk in sunshine just fine. Whisperers, they called. Look like regular folk till you see their shadows moving wrong, reaching for things they got no right to touch." She arranged a handful of Sugar Daddies and Ring Pops in new glass jars, the latter catching a ray of light, sparkling like big red diamonds. Marcus noticed how she kept glancing toward the side window, toward the empty lot where the Johnson first family house used to stand, where the Pryors' behind it used to run their corner store before the developers came calling with briefcases full of promises and checks that never covered the true cost of doing business. Mrs. Washington's old house still had her garden growing wild in the front yard, sunflowers and collard greens reaching toward a sun that would never shine on her kitchen again, their roots drinking from soil that held the memory of every meal shared, every story told, every child raised in love despite a world that seemed determined to destroy black joy.

"Your Grandmama Mertie knew that. She used to get my special stock back when Washington Park still had those Sunday Jazz days, when folks could walk from here to Paschal's Restaurant after service and walk in the front door, not the back."

Marcus's hand went automatically to the small cloth bag tied with old Nike shoestrings. His grandmother had made it before she passed, filled with things that didn't make sense to thirteen-year-old logic—red brick dust from the old Western Heights

School where she'd taught for forty years, a Mercury dime she'd earned sweeping floors, root tips that smelled like his nightmares and dreams both, protection and purpose twisted together like a strand of DNA.

"She never told me about no special stock," Marcus pondered aloud.

"Course not. You weren't ready then." Ms. Evelyn studied on him with eyes that seemed to hold decades more wisdom than her elderly face suggested, eyes that had watched Vine City rise and fall and rise again through many a tribulation. "But now you getting ready to *cross over*, be a Watcher, ain't you? Got your eye on that new California girl, thinking some candy gonna win her heart."

A hot heat rushed to Marcus's face.

"Ms. Evelyn, how you know about—"

"I know everything a'going on in Vine City. Back then, now and on up the road."

Ms. Evelyn allowed herself a rare smile in personal memory and focused just that much more on Marcus.

"You ain't the first boy I seen with courting in his eyes."

In the glass jars around the shop, other candies seemed to glow faintly, responding to something Marcus couldn't name but felt in his spirit. "Been watching from this corner since before your Grandmama was born. Seen the Cherokee who camped at a creek that used to run through here, clear water singing over washing stones. Saw the freedom conductors pass signals with oil lanterns, with dogs barking hard in the blackest night you ever did see. Watched Alonzo Herndon count his first million in coins that clinked like old slave chains."

Sometimes Ms. Evelyn didn't make sense. She could confuse dates and people. Talk about times and things way past her living years like she was just there. She sounded old-timey at one point, then like a learned Spelmanite the next. But she was so serious along the way, you just had to ride along with the story until she came back to you in the present again.

An old stirring hand reached out to Marcus and buried a couple pieces of wrapped candy into his own.

"What do these do, Ms. Evelyn?" he asked, turning the root beer barrels over in his palm, feeling them pulse in rhythm with his heartbeat.

"Same thing root beer always done—burns going down, leaves you feeling a little stronger."

Her smile showed teeth that seemed sharper in the afternoon light filtering through windows that had watched decades of change, decades of resistance. "Your Grandmama knew. She helped me charge the first batch back in '88, when the city started making its Olympic plans and we could feel The Deep Dark stirring underneath all that development money, uptown folks deciding your neighborhood would look better without you in it."

Marcus wanted a bag of candy to give to Leoshi, but as Ms. Evelyn spoke, he realized his crush would have to wait. He was connecting to something larger than Teenage Love. Ms. Evelyn pulled out more special jars—Oshun's Honey Drops that shifted color like oil on water, like the rainbow sheen on puddles after summer storms; Anansi's Licorice Webs twisted into patterns that made his eyes water when he tried to follow them, geometry that existed in folktales and quantum physics both.

She didn't explain the candies—she just handed Marcus another root beer barrel that felt warm against his palm, heavier than it should be, pulsing with energy that made his grandmother's protection bag respond like a tuning fork struck by destiny.

"Girl from California, folks coming here looking for a home."

"Y'all little love story to be? It ain't gonna like that. That's the opposite of what feeds it.", Ms. Evelyn said, watching Marcus's face with the intensity of a chess master planning three moves ahead. "Just like all these families around here about to be pushed out. You can smell it in the air like rain —a particular desperation that comes when folks realize their home ain't their home no more, when the ground under their feet becomes somebody else's investment. The Deep Dark feeds on despair and lack of hope. Not-belonging."

Every crane was another family displaced, another piece of community carved away and sold to the highest bidder. He thought about the friends at school who'd stopped coming to Ms. Evelyn's house with him after Christmas, whose parents couldn't find anywhere affordable close enough for the bus routes, scattered to the wind like dandelion seeds with no guarantee they'd find good soil to grow in. Outside, he could hear the distant rumble of MARTA trains carrying folks to jobs they couldn't afford to lose, past neighborhoods they couldn't afford to keep, the Red Line that connected Vine City to the wider world but also brought strangers who looked at the community and saw only obstacles to their vision of The American Dream.

"How long you been fighting it?" Marcus asked.

"Long as I been living." She gestured toward a wall covered in photographs—daguerreotypes of folks, families in big famed black and white portraits, others in the faded Polaroid colors of the seventies and eighties when hope had different faces but the same determination. In every single one, Ms. Evelyn looked exactly the same age, as if time moved differently for Candy Ladies.

"Every generation, something tries to break up what we've built. Jim Crow. Integration. Crack. Now here comes the Olympics. We remember what was, protect what is, nurture what could be."

Marcus was putting the pieces together—how his grandmother's protection, Leoshi's arrival, the coming Olympics, even his mixtape project were all part of the same battle for the soul of the community.

They were patches in the same quilt, and something ancient and hungry was trying to unravel them all.

Outside, a shadow passed the window—wrong somehow, moving against the angle of the sun, too long and too hungry, reaching toward something just out of sight.

The bell chimed again, and Leoshi from LA walked in with her cousin from Oakland, bringing a collective West Coast cool into the humid Atlanta air. Marcus's heart jumped sideways, the way it did when he heard OutKast on the radio. She wore baggy jeans and a Magic Lakers jersey, her hair curled into fresh box braids with gold clasps that caught the same light as the Ring Pops. When she smiled at him, his mouth went desert-dry.

"Hey, Mar-Kiss," she said, her Compton accent holding a part of his name, teasing him with the "Kiss" he was longing for since she first got on Bus 8 before school let out.

"You coming to Washington Park later? We supposed to meet some folks by the tennis courts, maybe walk over to the basketball courts behind Herndon Stadium."

Before Marcus could answer, her cousin Tre'—the lanky Senior who claimed he could dunk, the one who'd been bragging about Lakers and Golden State basketball every time you saw him, the one he didn't like—stepped past him without acknowledgement to the makeshift counter. When he slid by, his shadow fell across Marcus's feet, and the protection bag around his neck burned like ice, like every warning his grandmother had ever whispered in his ear was shouting at him all at once.

Marcus looked up at the cousin's face and saw his eyes—flat, empty, like someone had scooped out everything human and left something else wearing his skin like an ill-fitting suit stolen from the closet of the living.

The shadow was wrong. It moved independent of the cousin's body, reaching toward the special jars with fingers too long to be human, stretching like it wanted to devour everything sweet and sacred in the world.

"Actually," Marcus heard himself say, voice steadier than his heart, that was hammerin' like Hank Aaron with bases loaded, "I got to help Ms. Evelyn with something first. But maybe later? Washington Park's always got something happening on Saturdays." The lie came easy, but it wasn't really a lie—he did need to help, just not in any way the cute girl and the possessed boy could understand.

Leoshi looked a bit disappointed, but she nodded. "Aight. Don't take too long. I'm trying to see how you Atlanta boys play." She grinned, and Marcus felt that familiar flutter return in his chest,

As they left, the thing wearing Leoshi's cousin's face turned back, and for just a moment, Marcus saw something ancient and hungry looking out through those borrowed eyes.

Then the bell chimed, and they were gone, their voices fading into the street sounds of Vine City—cars with bass-heavy systems rattling windows, kids playing in the distance, the eternal hum of air conditioners working overtime against the Georgia heat.

"Good boy," Ms. Evelyn said quietly, shuffling over and locking the door, flipping the sign in the side window to 'CLOSED', transforming the shop into a sanctuary where different rules applied.

"You seen it, didn't you?"

"What's it doing with Leoshi?" as panic crept into Marcus's voice. "We gotta—"

"Calm yourself." Ms. Evelyn leaned into the window curtain, peeped outside like that Malcolm X *By Any Means Necessary* poster, or that of Boogie Down Productions' *By All Means Necessary* album cover, and moved back behind the counter with surprising speed.

"Whisperers can't hurt folks directly in daylight. They searching for the cracks in the wall, where The Deep Dark later can seep on in."

She waves Marcus to come behind the counter, where no kid he knew had gone before, and into the house part, past shelves lined with mysterious jars and bundles of herbs hanging from the ceiling—sage, sweetgrass, things that smelled like memory, like prayers said in languages he didn't understand, but appreciated someone was saying.

The house walls were fully covered in photographs spanning as far as the technology had been: families at church picnics in Washington Park, kids playing in the creek that used to run behind the elementary school, the grand opening of the first Black owned drugstore on Simpson Road. The Herndon mansion in its glory days, surrounded by other beautiful homes that had housed teachers and insurance agents and entrepreneurs, proving that Black excellence had deep roots in this soil. Martin Luther King Jr. with his children in their front yard on Sunset Avenue, back when Vine City was an address people aspired to instead of escaped from.

"Mertie was one of my best friends, and one of my best students," she said, pulling down a leather-bound book that smelled like graveyards and gospels, like the old Friendship Baptist Church before they tore it down for a parking lot that nobody used, another piece of community sacrificed to the altar of "progress". "She could spot a Whisperer from across Five Points, could mix a healing batch of ham hocks and collards that would see you through any ailment. But she knew you'd need more than protection. You'd need to fight now and again."

"I'm thirteen, Ms. Evelyn. I don't know how to fight no supernatural stuff." The old doubt crept back in—what if he was just a regular kid pretending to be special, the way kids in the neighborhood sometimes pretended to be older, harder, more prepared than they really were?

"You think David was any older when he faced Goliath? You think your ancestors were ready when they had to fight for freedom?" She opened the book, revealing pages covered in symbols that seemed to move like living things, like the shadows that danced on walls during the house parties his older cousins threw when their parents worked late shifts, geometric patterns that appeared in African textiles and rap album covers from X Clan.

"Besides, you got advantages they didn't know they had. You got the Sight, on your Grandmama's side that goes back to women who read futures in bones and tea leaves. You got this whole community's history running through your veins—Cherokee stories, Freedmen escape routes, civil rights organizing, and Jazzmatazz. You can't be taken from that."

She assured him with a hand on the shoulder.

"Let me get you in this kitchen and show you a thing or two, young man."

She was patient yet firm in the lesson. Hands steady as she showed him how to mix honey and red clay into paint for protection symbols, how to charge the soft candies with intent until they glowed with accumulated prayers. But she didn't explain everything—let discover through experience how the root beer barrels burned spiritual energy along with shadow-stuff, how he could sense he had maybe three charges in him before he'd be running on empty, how the power flowed differently depending on where he stood, stronger near the old intersections where ley lines met, weaker near the new construction that ignored the sacred geometry of place.

"Every piece of candy costs something," Ms. Evelyn explained as Marcus reached for a second root beer barrel. "These burn shadow-stuff, but they burn your spiritual energy too. Take too many too fast, and you'll hollow yourself out worse than any Whisperer could, become the very thing you're trying to fight."

"How do I get more power?" Marcus asked.

"Family." Ms. Evelyn said simply, and in that single word Marcus heard the entire history of Black survival, the secret that had carried his people through centuries of attempts at annihilation. "Every person who believes in you, every ancestor who approves, every connection you make—that's spiritual currency. Why the developers want to break up neighborhoods, scatter families, make folks too busy surviving to build relationships. Scattered folks are easier to feed on, easier to control, easier to disappear without noticing.

Why music matters. Why love matters. Why places like Paschal's Restaurant and the West Hunter Street Baptist Church matter—they're community batteries, storing up all that connection for when we need it most."

She reached in her apron and handed him canvas for his mixtape—a blank ninety-minute Hi-Fi Maxell cassette that had probably cost more than his weekly allowance, but she waved off his offer of the seventy-five cents with the generosity that was itself a form of magic. "Music carries power, especially when it's made with love and intention. Every song you choose, every transition you craft—that's a spell, baby. A way of weaving community together across space and time, connecting past and future in the eternal now of rhythm and rhyme."

Marcus spent the next few hours crafting the perfect mixtape, using the dual-cassette deck Ms. Evelyn kept in the back room, its analog warmth giving weight to every decision as he tuned into WHTA-FM, Hot 97.5 to catch the new flavor coming through the speakers. The order had to be perfect—each transition a spell, each song a step in the story he was trying to tell not just to Leoshi but to the universe itself. And the rap gods were generous that day. Side A opened with OutKast's "Player's Ball," because you had to start with the hometown heroes, the ones who'd put Atlanta on the map and proved that the South had something to say worth hearing. He followed it with TLC's "Waterfalls" and Ms. Evelyn was right about that song having power, something in the way Left Eye's rap cut through the melody like truth cutting through lies, like wisdom slicing through ignorance. The hometown hits kept coming.

Between tracks, he added harmonies from another tape he'd brought from home. He then carefully dubbed sections of his Grandmama's singing one evening on the front porch, ancient words weaving her soulful spirit into the modern beats. The song was in a language he didn't recognize but felt he knew—something that predated English, that had come from the Motherland on ships of sorrow and survived in tears and hums, in the call-and-response of church services and the rhythm of work songs, in the hidden cadences that turned survival into resistance and into art.

By late afternoon, Marcus skateboarded toward Washington Park, carving through streets that were becoming more unfamiliar as development pressure mounted. Past construction sites where families used to live, where memories were being bulldozed to make room for Olympic dreams. The construction workers were all white, he noticed—contractors brought in from the suburbs to build housing that none of the displaced families would ever afford to live in. They worked in air-conditioned trailers while the summer heat shimmered off concrete and rebar, the temperature reaching that particular Atlanta intensity that made the air itself feel thick enough to swim through, oppressive as history itself.

But Washington Park still stood, the first park in Atlanta open to African Americans, its trees older than the segregation it witnessed, older than a lot of the pain that had shaped the city. The tennis courts where Arthur Ashe had once played, proving excellence could bloom anywhere it was allowed to root. The pavilion where families still gathered for reunions and fish fries and birthday parties that spilled over with enough food to feed anyone who walked by hungry. The court had been sacred long before basketball hoops went up. Washington Park was one of the few places Black folks could gather freely in Atlanta, their music carrying messages of resilience and resistance. During the civil rights movement, organizers had met here to plan marches and boycotts, understanding that revolution often began in spaces where community gathered to play and celebrate, where joy itself became an act of defiance.

And there, shooting free throws with mechanical precision under the basketball hoops installed back in the eighties, was Leoshi. She wore a different Lakers jersey today—Eddie Jones instead of Magic—and when she saw Marcus rolling up on his board, her whole face lit up like the marquee at the Fox Theatre.

His heart did that sideways jump again, the way it did when he heard a perfect beat or watched the sun set over the downtown skyline, painting everything in shades of possibility.

"Finally!" She bounced the ball to him, a perfect chest pass with the kind of precision that came from growing up in gyms, from understanding basketball as a language of squeaking sneakers and swishing nets. "You ready to run? Got next on the good court."

But before Marcus could answer, her cousin appeared—the Snoop Doggy Dogg looking one with the wrong shadow. In daylight, it was still harder to see the wrongness, but Marcus had the Sight a bit more focused now, trained by Ms. Evelyn's teaching and sharpened by the charged candy dissolving on his tongue. The darkness writhing behind those stolen eyes was unmistakable, like storm clouds gathering behind someone else's face, promising violence disguised as weather.

"Actually," Marcus said, "I got something for you first." He pulled out the mixtape, hands only shaking a little, the J-card decorated with images cut from Word Up! and The Source magazines.

On the cover, he'd drawn the Atlanta skyline with the words "Vine City 4 Life" in bubble letters, a promise, and a prophecy both. "Made this for you. Some Atlanta flavor."

Leoshi's smile could have powered a thousand ceiling fans at once. "For real?!? Nobody ever made me a tape before." She looked at the track listing, reading each song title carefully, her finger tracing over the careful handwriting like she was reading scripture. "Oh, you put Monica on here! That's my girl! And what's this—OutKast? I heard them on the radio driving through Alabama, but I ain't know they were from here."

"Yeah, and some other stuff. Local joints you probably haven't heard." Marcus tried to play it cool as he kept his eyes on her, not looking directly at the monster wearing her cousin's face.

"Maybe we could listen to it together sometime? I could show you around the real Atlanta, not just the tourist stuff they gonna put on TV for the Olympics."

"Sounds dope." She tucked the tape into her gym bag like it was precious, which it was—ninety minutes of musical magic.

Then she asked, "You think it can cure what is wrong with my cousin?"

Marcus's eyes snapped into hers, seeing the intelligence there, the awareness that went deeper than basketball skills and West Coast swagger.

She pulled out a small bag from her pocket—not unlike his Grandmama's protection charm, but something her own grandmother had made back in Cali, filled with different herbs and artifacts but carrying the same intention, proof that magic crossed regional boundaries, connected communities of resistance across space and culture.

"Abuela Rosa taught me about *spirit-seeking* before we moved. Said Atlanta was powerful but dangerous. I don't know how, but Tre's spirit got jacked soon after we got here. He's talking, but it's not HIM talking."

She looked at the park around them, at the way shadows lingered in corners despite the afternoon sun, at the subtle wrongness that seemed to follow her cousin like a second shadow, darker and more twisted than any shadow had a right to be.

"Been having dreams since we got here. Dreams about big buildings with teeth eating families, about music that could heal. Thought maybe that's why your mixtape felt so... important when I held it, like it was humming in my hands. Crazy, right?"

Marcus felt something shift inside him—now he wasn't alone in this fight. The community of Spirit Folk was bigger than he'd thought, proving hope that love was indeed stronger than the forces trying to tear them all apart.

"We need to get him back," he said, nodding toward her cousin, who was dribbling a basketball with hands that moved too smoothly, too perfectly, like a machine programmed to imitate human motion without understanding the soul that should animate it.

"Let's run a game, little man." The thing wearing Tre's face spoke out, its voice carried a tenor that made birds fall silent in the trees around the park, made the dogs in the neighborhood start barking blocks away, a sound that bypassed the ears and went straight to the primitive brain where fear lived, and echoed to Marcus:

"Yeah, Marcus. Let me show everyone how weak you humans are against US."

Every bounce of the ball echoed with history, with all the games played and dreams shared and connections made on this particular patch of asphalt that had absorbed decades of sweat, laughter and tears.

"This ain't just pickup ball…" Marcus realized as he watched the crowd gather. Not just living people—translucent figures from different eras stood at the edges of the court, waiting and watching. His Grandmama Mertie nodded at him from beside a man in a striped zoot suit who must have been from the forties, next to a woman in a church dress from the sixties whose face looked familiar from civil rights photographs he'd seen at school, all of them connected by the common thread of choosing resistance over surrender.

"Winner takes all," the Whisperer said, its stolen voice a call to engage in this spiritual battle for Vine City.

The game started—three on three, Marcus teaming up with Leoshi and Dante from down the block against the Whisperer and two other local dudes whose eyes were starting to show that telltale flatness, that particular emptiness that came when something else was looking out through acquired faces. The shadows were spreading to more folks.

Marcus noticed things shifting around them. The court lines seemed to glow faintly, forming patterns his Grandmama would have recognized as calling symbols— sacred geometry that appeared in African textiles and Native American pottery, the same mathematical relationships that showed up in rap beats and jazz improvisation, beauty and protection of universal languages. The basketball itself felt heavier, more significant, like it carried the weight of the moment, every dream deferred and dream achieved, every moment when young people chose to compete instead of destroying each other.

The Whisperer was good—unnaturally good. It moved with inhuman adroitness, making shots that defied physics, calling plays in a voice that sounded like static and broken promises, like the war-charge to gentrification itself. And every time Team Whisperer scored, the shadows grew longer despite the afternoon sun, the air got colder despite the Georgia heat, and more kids around the park started showing that flat-eyed stare as The Deep Dark's influence spread like a virus through the gathered crowd, turning spectators into potential hosts.

Marcus found himself playing better than he ever had before. He'd always wished he was a little bit taller. But the charged root beer barrels he'd been eating throughout lent him speed and clarity of purpose, the protection symbols glowing faintly in the court concrete guided his movements like an invisible coach, and Leoshi's presence beside him made him feel invincible, like he could fly if the game demanded it. He realized that for this one game, he had indeed become a *baller*. And when he and Leoshi slapped hands after each of them made their shots and their fingers touched, a light sparked between them—not a metaphorical light but actual brilliant illumination, the kind of pure energy that Ms. Evelyn had talked about, a sweetness that could anchor souls to place and purpose.

The score climbed: 10-8, 15-12, 18-17. Each basket felt like a battle in a larger war, each defensive stop a small victory against the forces trying to hollow out the heart of the community. The ancestors gathered closer, their translucent forms becoming more solid as the game intensified, as if the spiritual contest was calling them back from wherever souls went to rest, summoning them to witness this moment when past and future collided on a basketball court in Washington Park.

The score was 20 to 19 Whispers, but game point for either team if Vine City could make a two. The Whisperer Tre' had the ball, dribbling with that wrong rhythm that hurt to hear, like a heartbeat skipping or a song played backward. It drove toward the basket, shadow-form rippling with anticipation of victory, of the right to claim this crossroads for The Deep Dark, to turn another sacred space into a feeding ground for forces that grew fat on broken communities.

That's when Marcus heard it—his mixtape playing from someone's boom box at the edge of the court. Leoshi had ran over and put it in one of the ghetto blasters' setting at the court's edge during the last stare down between Whisperer Tre' and Marcus.

Suddenly every ghostly ancestor in the gathered crowd was singing along in voices that carried across centuries, their combined power creating a barrier the Whisperer couldn't cross, a wall of sound and memory and stubborn love that said: *This place is ours. These children are ours. This community is ours.*

The thing stumbled, just for a moment, its inhuman prowess faltering as the music hit it like a physical force, like a sharp truth spoken in the face of lies. Marcus stripped the ball from the dazed Tre' and passed the ball to Leoshi. She pulled up for a jumper from the top of the key, the ball arcing like a prayer against the sky, like hope made visible.

"Jordan." She called, a yellow candied tongue ejecting from her mouth.

As it swished through the net, the Whisperer let out an earthly scream. Its human disguise peeled away like old paint, revealing the writhing darkness beneath—all hunger and void and the emptiness that fed on broken homes, the spiritual parasite that grew strong on disconnection and despair. The other possessed kids collapsed as shadows fled their bodies like smoke, leaving them gasping and human, confused but alive, their souls their own again, but Tre' still stood in place, solemnly as a black visage twisted in agony faintly above his head, then retreated back into his body.

"What the hell—" Leoshi started, then stopped as she really saw what had been wearing her cousin's face, as the full reality of the supernatural struggle settled over Washington Park like summer humidity.

"Come on," Marcus said, grabbing her hand and pulling her towards Tre.' "Ms. Evelyn can help him."

Leoshi and Marcus returned back again to Ms. Evelyn's shop as the sun set over Vine City, painting the sky in shades of peach and gold. The real cousin Tre' had been laid out on a fainting couch while the shadow-thing that had been wearing his face had retreated within. As Leoshi played the mixtape once more from Ms. Evelyn's radio, it finally and fully emerged, jumping up out of his mouth, lunging at Marcus with fingers like broken glass.

It screamed, sounding like every demolished house in the neighborhood crying at once, and as its claws scrapped against his jersey, the icy burn of Grandmama Mert's mojo bag returned. The fiend scowled and then dissolved into a shadow-dust that Ms. Evelyn swept up with an ordinary broom and dumped into a jar labeled with symbols Marcus was finally beginning to understand.

"Not today, Satan," Ms. Evelyn said, arranging the shadow-dust among other captured spirits on a high shelf like a librarian filing away a folio of dangerous books. "Deep Dark's getting desperate, sending so many in daylight. Bet it gets worse before it gets better."

Leoshi helped her Tre' to his feet. The boy looked around the house in delirium, blinking like someone waking from a long dream, seeing the candy shop and the magical jars and his cousin with a boy he didn't remember meeting.

"Where... Like...Yo, what happened? Last thing I remember, we were was getting off the plane at Hartsfield, seeing people and feeling like I was drowning in the crowd, like I couldn't breathe...like I been asleep since."

"You're safe now," Leoshi said, hugging him tight, her voice carrying all the love that had brought her family across the country in search of something better. She looked up at Marcus over her cousin's shoulder, her eyes bright with tears and appreciation both. "We're all safe, *primo*."

Marcus felt the truth of it all settle into his bones. The immediate threat was over, but more than that—he'd found a place in the larger story, in the continuing struggle.

Not just the boy with a crush, not just his grandmother's spiritual heir, but someone who could stand at the crossroads between past and future and master the patterns to see the people within them.

"Them Olympics still coming," Ms. Evelyn said, addressing them all while she looked through here special stock jars that caught the last light of day. "Deep Dark won't give up easy. We got to be ready for what's coming, got to build families again that can bend without breaking."

Ms. Evelyn handed Tre' a sour pickle sprinkled with green herbs, looking to him to take a bite.

"We will be, Ms. Eveyln." Marcus said, and he meant it with every fiber of his being. He touched the last root beer barrel in his pocket, feeling its warmth pulse in response to his certainty. Not a thirteen-year-old pretending to be special anymore, but a defender who'd could anchor souls to place even when everything else was changing. Marcus stepped outside to give a moment to Tre' who was still trying to grasp all that he'd missed between bites.

Outside, Vine City pulsed with life continuing despite every attempt to break it, to scatter it, to turn it into something profitable rather than precious.

The bell rang as Leoshi came out as well and stepped beside Marcus, slipping her right hand delicately into his, interlocking her fingers with his, her skin warm against his sweaty palm.

"Thank you for what you did back there. That mixtape really is magic, huh?"

"Everythang's magic round' here in the A." Marcus said proudly and awkwardly, then grinned at how much he sounded like Ms. Evelyn.

Leoshi squeezed his hand stronger, like the invisible forces that held the universe together.

"Then we better make more. Sounds like we're gonna need a whole new soundtrack for what's coming, Mar-Kiss."

Marcus felt a sudden warmth within him, a burning going down, leaving him a bit stronger.

But this wasn't from Ms. Evelyn's candy.

Under the shadow of a sassafras tree, a tender, pursed connection between Leoshi's face and Marcus's face had been initiated.

Neither could tell who was the culprit, but the deed was well underway.

For that Now and Later flavored first kiss with Leoshi, Marcus would have squared up with a thousand Whisperers barehanded.

It was just the beginning of a new summer song, and every good mixtape needed a strong finishing groove.

Just like every good story needed to leave room for the sequel, and every act of resistance needed to plant seeds for future.

Outside Ms. Evelyn's window, the streetlights flickered one by one, met with an ancestral hymn being hummed by the Penny Candy Lady as she straightened up her wares for tomorrow.

Dedicated to all the neighborhood candy ladies who made childhood sweeter, one penny at a time.
Mine were Ms. Williams and the Lady In The Alley.

CASALANTA
BY
MARCELLUS S. JACKSON

"To assess a threat, you must know more than just its position—you must know its potential."
– Chess Master's Rulebook, Vol. XII

Coffee doesn't taste the same when victory feels hollow. I sat at the Peachtree Pub across from the A.C.E. station, watching morning light dance through the translucent solar panels that lined downtown's elevated walkways. My reflection in the vintage windowpanes caught my eye – tall frame hunched over the counter, dark skin warm in the amber pub lighting, goatee needed a trim. The cinnamon toast wasn't my usual glazed donut, but the kitchen drone was on the fritz again. Just like my instincts about this case.

The curved walls of Atlanta City Police Enforcement headquarters loomed across the street, its self-cleaning panoramic windows reflecting the first sunrise of 2097. Another New Year's Peach Drop come and gone, leaving behind biodegradable confetti and the lingering scent of cheap liquor and burned-out glow panels. Inside the pub, the air was warm with a mix of nostalgia and something just shy of peace. Maurice, the owner, still used real wood for his bar top – said some things were better left unchanged. I agreed, adjusting the metal-trimmed fedora that earned me subtle eyerolls from younger officers.

Thirty-six hours after the biggest bust of my career, and something still didn't sit right. We'd caught Mateo Krishman—the Fire-Snake himself—in his Buckhead mansion. Three years of chasing him through back-alley chop shops and tech-drug dens, and finally, he was behind bars. The evidence was solid. The case was closed. Every chess piece was exactly where it needed to be.

So why did it feel like I was walking into a trap?

I nursed my coffee, watching a band of youngsters glide by on their new mag-lev boards. The city had changed so much since my days in Southwest Atlanta. The Frescoian revolution had transformed our skyline into something out of an old sci-fi film—self-sustaining towers that generated their own power, vertical farms that fed thousands, and A.C.E. precincts that operated more like community centers than the old-style police stations. Auto-drones patrolled alongside human officers, and crime scene holograms could recreate events down to the millisecond. The resource-based economy had lifted most boats, as they used to say. But human nature? That stayed the same.

An old chess master—Alexandra Kosteniuk—once said the most dangerous position is *thinking* you're winning. I couldn't shake the feeling that we'd missed something, that there was still another move on the board we hadn't accounted for. You don't just catch a snake like Krishman without rattling the nest.

Tech-drugs—Vapyr, in particular—had been tearing through the city like wildfire. What started as legitimate medical nanobots for healing injuries had become the newest poison on the streets. Now, every back-alley nano-chemist with an atomizing 3D printer was pumping out dangerous, unregulated tech enhancements. It wasn't just junkies anymore, it was everyday folks, caught in the crossfire between progress and survival. The things I'd seen . . . people turning into monsters, chasing a high that rewired their biology. The kind of people I'd sworn to protect when I first pinned on the badge fourteen years ago.

Sure, the tech revolution had saved lives. Medical advancements were light years ahead of where we were just a decade ago. But there's always a cost. For every miracle, there's a nightmare. And for every Krishman we take down, another pops up like a pawn, ready to be sacrificed.

In three years of hunting the Fire-Snake, I'd learned he never made mistakes. He was too careful, too calculating to get caught unless . . . My mind raced through case files, interviews, evidence, looking for the unturned stone. That nagging doubt crept in—the kind that had kept me sleeping on my office couch more nights than I cared to count.

The scent hit me first—jasmine and autumn spice, with something else I couldn't place. Then a voice that stopped my thoughts cold, warm as Georgia sunshine after summer rain.

"Still taking your coffee black as midnight, Marquis?"

I didn't have to look up to know who it was. Tavia Adesina. Just what I needed.

"The Queen combines the power of the Rook and Bishop in one piece. Yet her greatest strength lies not in force, but in the element of surprise."
- *Garry Kasparov*

"Heeeeeeyyyy, is that sludge you call coffee the only thing keeping you warm these days, Detective?"

The voice hit me like summer lightning – unexpected, electric, familiar. Eleven years dissolved in an instant as Octavia Adesina slid onto the barstool beside me, trailing expensive perfume and memories. The misty winter morning outside suddenly felt warmer.

Gone were the facial piercings and baggy clothes of the teenage hacktivist I'd supervised on probation. The woman beside me wore cream fingerless lace gloves and a matching body dress that made my mouth go dry. Tiny tech-fibers glittered with heat off the rose-red shawl folding around her, exposing parts of her skin. Deep golden brown like honey in sunlight, seemed to glow even in the pub's dim lighting. Still had a whole bunch of hair, but the rebellious sixteen-year-old who'd turned a stuffy political conference upside down had evolved into something else entirely.

That incident was legendary around the precinct – how this chess champion's daughter had hacked the conference's video stream, exposing a congressman's indiscretions to twenty thousand people. When I'd picked her up, she was all attitude and brilliant defiance. During her probation check-ins, that defiance slowly transformed into something else. She'd help me study for my law exams, teaching me chess principles between coding lessons with other kids. Her father even trusted me enough to work security at his company events. Then the family moved to Kenya for his business, and that chapter closed. She found me over the GlobalLink years ago, messaged me a congrats for making Detective. Not a peep since.

"You still calling me Marquis just to be different, Tavia?"

"Someone has to." Her smile hadn't changed – still that perfect blend of mischief and grace. "Though you've changed plenty, Detective. More seasoned than I remember."

"Seasoned?" I laughed. "That's a polite way of calling me old."

"Please. You wear it well." Her eyes dropped to my left hand. "Though I notice you're not wearing anything else. No ring?"

"Married to the job." The old excuse tasted stale on my tongue.

"Still? Some things never change." She stirred her drink, studying me. "Though your taste in hats has improved."

The next couple hours or so flowed like honey, sweet and slow. We caught up on lives lived apart – her global charity work, my cases, shared memories of those weekly check-ins. But something else crackled beneath the surface, a current of possibility I hadn't felt in years. I found myself noticing things I shouldn't: the way her neck curved when she laughed, how her fingers traced the rim of her glass, the subtle perfume that made my head swim.

"Beautiful piece," I said, nodding to the sparrow charm on her platinum necklace. The red stones caught the light like tiny flames.

"Not a cardinal," she corrected, touching it gently. "A crimson sparrow. My late husband gave it to me. Said it reminded him of how I transformed from that *hot-headed teenager* into someone who could lift others up, and I've grown to love it. Now it reminds me that even the smallest birds can soar highest when they're free."

Her eyes met mine, and the room seemed to shrink. Those same burnt sienna-brown eyes held secrets I suddenly wanted to learn.

"Speaking of transformations, what's clouding that detective's mind of yours? You've been somewhere else half this conversation."

"Just work. This case I closed—"

"Save the shop talk." She leaned closer, her voice dropping to a whisper. "I didn't come over here to discuss case files."

The heat in her eyes could've melted steel. My pulse raced as she traced a finger down my tie, each touch a whispered reminder of everything I'd been missing. Everything else – the case, the nagging doubts, even the sound of the pub around us – faded into background noise against the symphony of her presence.

"Careful, Ms. Adesina. I could still cite you for attempting to distract an officer."

"Officer?" She arched an eyebrow. "I believe you've been promoted since then, Detective. And I've learned a few new tricks myself."

"New ones, you say?" I smirked. Her modesty was cute.

The music changed, and I recognized the opening notes of *"Tell Me If You Still Care"* by S.O.S. Band. Atlanta soul from another era, all smooth bass line and velvet vocals.

"Dance with me, Marc." Not a question, but a dare.

The small dance floor was empty now, the New Year's stragglers long gone. The view of her from behind as she led me was a gut punch. Lord. Already makin' *easy work* outta me. We find a spot and she melted against me like she belonged there, each curve finding its home against my body, her hips moving with mine in that intimate slow-drag rhythm that spoke of midnight promises. Her head rested just below the hairs on my chin as we swayed, her perfume clouding my senses with thoughts I hadn't allowed myself in years. We moved, *grooved* together, between silences and whispers.

"Ironic," she murmured. "I've been in town all week, but this – right now – is the first time it's felt like home."

"Funny how that works." I pulled her closer, feeling her heart beat against my chest. "I haven't felt much like celebrating until now."

"When I first spotted you, you had such a mean face on." She traced my jaw with one finger. "I almost didn't—"

Mean face.

The words hit me like ice water. A photograph flashed in my mind – surveillance footage from the Krishman raid. A figure in the background. That distinctive scowl, those dead eyes . . . a face from the surveillance footage I'd dismissed. Someone who shouldn't have been there, hiding in plain sight. How had I missed him? The reality of the case came crashing back, bringing with it the weight of everything left undone.

I felt Tavia's body tense against mine as my steps faltered. She pulled back slightly, searching my face with concern. The warmth in her eyes turned to confusion as she watched the shield of duty slide back into place.

"I gotta go." The words hurt coming out.

"What?" Tavia stepped back, disappointment and understanding warring in her expression.

We walked back to the bar in silence, the moment shattered. Her heels clicked against the hardwood like a countdown. She gathered her things and mentioned she was heading back to New York today. I grabbed my coat, paid my tab, wished her safe travels, hating every word that moved us closer to goodbye.

"Stay out of trouble," I said, already turning toward the door.

The winter air slapped me awake the moment I stepped outside. Three steps down, I stopped cold.

What the hell was I doing?

I burst back through the heavy oak doors. Snatched my forgotten fedora from the bar, swiftly placing it on my head while crossing over to where she stood. One hand finding the small of her back, the other cradling her neck, her skin warm-mahogany silk beneath my fingers. I pulled her close and kissed her like a drowning man finding air.

She tasted like promises and possibilities, and I memorized every second of it – the softness of her lips, the warmth of her breath, the way her hands gripped my coat as if she might float away without an anchor.

"Happy New Year," I whispered against her lips.

Her eyes opened slowly, a smile playing at the corners of her mouth. "Finish it, then find me, Detective. I'm on the AeroRail back to New York at seven."

I didn't trust myself to speak again. Sometimes a good exit line is better left alone.

"In chess, as in war, the watchful player knows: a pawn left unchecked may rise to crown a hidden king."
- Master Antonin Kolvic, 1962

They say it's suicide, sacrificing your queen to win the game. But duty's a demanding mistress. I know Tavia understands. My second wind arrives with an ardent stride toward the A.C.E. cruiser, that nagging face still burning in my memory - something about those dead eyes, that pouty scowl. Like that old-school rapper. Marshall something, I think.

My wrist display reads 11:11 AM as I swipe one finger across the device. "Open says me." The door glides up with a soft hiss as I adjust my coat and slide into the seat. The squad unit's holoscreen flickers alive, bathing my cabin in electric blue.

"A.C.E. intranet. Scan streaming footage, Krishman bust." Body-camera viewpoints shift swiftly across my screen, each change bringing mounting frustration. "Shit, he's not here. Come on!"

Precious minutes tick by as my hunch guides the search . . . then, I see it.

"Wait, there he is." I lean forward, the seat creaking beneath me. "Zoom in, 50 percent . . . corner figure, crop the face." Damn, I need to call this in.

"Hail Sgt. Grasso." The network starts beeping while I replay the case in my head. I notice the indicators showing that he's not at headquarters, but a mile down at his *other* office, Precinct 4. He likes their cafeteria more. The beeps continue, then comes Grasso's voice booming through the unit's liquid crystal speakers.

"Danno! Speak of the devil. Hey, Johnson, tell Danno what the drunk party babe left in the holding tram for ya!"

"Well, as much as this breaks up the giggles . . . Sarge, this guy in the body-recording from the Krishman bust needs verification. The image comes from Officer Russert's cam."

The silly expression melts away from Grasso's rugged stubble-ridden face as his eyes focus on the screen. "Wait, what now? Image from last night? Well, hell, I don't know *who* the fuck that is. But there's the lieutenant's shiny bald head standing next to the prick. Hey, Drexel, isn't Russert one a' your guys?"

I shift in my seat as a turned-over white coffee mug attached to a bearded face enters the frame. "Good morning, Detective," Drexel grumbles, carefully backing away from the steaming mug. "Yeah,

Russert's one of mine. What's the deal?"

Since me chasing this mystery won out over a smoke-show level *sista* today, I choose my next question carefully. "Morning, Lieutenant. That officer standing next to you yesterday - you know him?"

Going for another sip, Drexel hums as his eyes draw back and to the side, then return to the screen. "Yeah, one of the city patrollers brought over from Peachtree 5. Something Warner . . . Warner . . . Warren! Yeah, Warren. Seemed a decent lad. Not much fuss. What's the matter Detective? Think I brought too many guys to the mansion the other night?"

If only . . . "Well, maybe just one guy too many, Sir."

Sarge leans back with a lazy sigh. "A.C.E. intranet, authorization Sgt. Marvin Grasso, badge two-one-eight-four. Locate Officer Warren precinct five."

I watch the on-screen windows shift as the fifth Peachtree precinct's insignia spins, leaving Warren's photo and info displayed. The digital voice announces: "Officer Daniel Warren cannot be located at this time. Last login for service . . . Monday December 31st... 8:27 AM."

Further commands reveal edited height measurements, changed photos. The lieutenant places his mug on the lunch table next to Sarge. "Alright, now there's cause for concern. What exactly are we looking for, Detective?"

I lean closer to the screen. "Wait, open up G-12. Blonde guy there! There's ol' Marshall," I mumble.

Sarge perks up, giving the screen the evil eye. "Who the fuck is Marshall? Says this scumbag is Alvin Shanks."

I take a deep breath before the revelation. "Intranet, place suspect Alvin Shanks' photo alongside officer Daniel Warren. Provide face scan and phenotype comparison analysis."

Blue horizontal lines multiply across both photos, scanning, processing with lightning speed. The intranet's chipper voice announces: "Analysis concludes a phenotypical attribute match of eighty-one percent."

Drexel stands straight, tilting his head. "Yeah, Shanks . . . real low key. Remember reading through this last spring. Might've been him, not Krishman, vaping those canines they turned loose on the informants. Trail pointed that way, but nothing solid enough for charges."

"What kinda sicko fuck gives that stuff to a dog anyways?" Grasso snaps.

"Not an animal lover, that's for sure," Drexel explains, retrieving his mug. "Forensics said that vape shit cuts any pooch's already short life in half after one use."

I take a yet another deep breath before laying it out. "Those pouty features, those empty eyes . . . Shanks used facial prosthetics, maybe even one of those off-market voice cloning strips, to infiltrate the lieutenant's squad during the bust. Watching us, planning something."

Drexel chokes mid-sip. "Wait, What?!"

"Oh, for fuck's sake!" Grasso's eyebrows rack downward, tone shifting from curiosity to concern. "Planning?! This case is practically done, and now you're making my fat ass fall out of this comfortable chair, Danno."

"If you're thinking about seeing Krishman, it won't be easy," Drexel interjects. "He was scheduled for transport at 11:15. Shit, we're already past that - they're probably halfway through moving him from holding to the new max city lockdown near Rice Street for state handoff."

The lieutenant straightens his tie, tucking in his shirt. "Look, Dannon... Grasso and I will beat you there. Half the streets around Rice are blocked off for the damn parade cleanup. Take Whitehall to Peters. It's the only clear shot. We'll handle the jurisdiction dance with the state boys until you arrive. Without this catch now, Friday would've been too late. Good work, Detective. Now move."

The connection cuts, leaving me alone with that face haunting the screen inside my cruiser's cabin. Eminem. That's it. Marshall Mathers himself. Funny how the old tracks help crack new cases.

"Ignition"

The command fires past my lips, and the Ion engine hums to life as a new chess game begins - one with pawns in police uniforms and a king in chains. Sporting a fresh set of carbon fiber wrist cuffs. Time to make my next move count.

"The master knows: a game lost is not a match surrendered. Yet wisdom lies in seeing how each piece, even in retreat, may spring the trap that claims the king."
- Grandmaster Viktor Petrov, 1987

Late. The realization burns like acid in my gut. Signs flashing like warning beacons – Shank's infiltration, the holiday timing, the perfect deception. He knew our move. Three years hunting Krishman taught me one thing: he doesn't just countermove, he sets the board.

In my cruiser, tearing through empty streets, emergency lights painting everything in cobalt blue pulses through another misty-grey sunup in Atlanta. Almost noon. Each second feels like drowning.

Tavia's scent lingers, jasmine and autumn spice threatening to pull on my focus. Her presence floods back; not just the sway of her hips or the warmth of her smile, but her voice cutting through my doubts. The desire swells, dangerous and deep, before iron discipline snaps my attention back. Three bodies found washed up in the Chattahoochee last spring flash through my mind. What Krishman does to those who lose focus.

Never learned chess. Not really. But her words echo like prophecy: *"When you see a good move, look for a better one."* My cruiser screams around another corner, the graphene tires fighting for grip. Life's funny that way–taking lessons from games never played, while hunting monsters who treat death like sport.

The square materializes through morning haze, GBI officials already locked in heated debate with Grasso and Drexel. The massive A.C.E. transport unit squats between marble columns like a steel fortress. Armed guards stand at attention, but something feels wrong. The air itself seems to pulse with tension.

"This way Danno!" Grasso's voice cuts through the chaos, he waves me over.

Mid-stride toward my superiors, movement catches my eye–a guard stepping away from his post. Wrong rhythm. Wrong stance. The guard's swift break from position, bee-lining away from the transport. A tattooed hand reaches up, hitting the helmet sensor. Time stretches like taffy as the visor lifts, revealing those dead eyes. The same eyes I've seen in surveillance photos, standing over broken bodies in warehouse doorways.

"It's him, Slim fuckin' Shady," comes out as barely a whisper, my hand finding the holster. Every instinct scream *ambush*.

"Quiet!" Grasso's voice booms. "Hey, Danno! What's the deal?!"

I drop into a crouch, blaster's laser indicators lighting up in sequence. "It's him, Sarge! It's Shanks! The face we saw in the . . ."

SHA-BOOM!!!

The holding unit doors explode outward like cannon fire, throwing bodies across the pavement. My ears ring as I roll from back to stomach, the taste of concrete dust coating my tongue. Through squinted eyes, I watch smoke canisters arc through the air, landing with metallic clicks that echo off the square's stone façades.

"Shit! Move Sarge! They're going for it! They're here for Krishman!" Ugh. Ears still ringing. Barely heard myself shouting.

A deadly light show erupts—lasers cutting cyan blue lines through smoke while bullets chip away at century-old marble. Each impact re-minds me of the LaVista Crossing shootout, when Krishman's crew shot their way out of a supply deal that went bad. Three dead inno-cents that day.

"Fuckin' scumbags!" Grasso growls from behind a parade parti-tion, his pistol already tracking targets through the chaos.

"Everyone down now! Take cover!" Drexel's orders carry the weight of experience. He's seen what comes next.

On my feet now, keeping low and swift, back toward my cruiser as rounds pepper the ground in my wake. My wrist com comes up. "Open defensive protocol!" The cruiser transforms, door lifting and reconfiguring into a reinforced barrier. Steel plates lock into position as I dive behind cover, the smell of scorched metal filling my nostrils.

"A.C.E. Network! This is Dannon! Explosion at the square, taking heavy fire! Access all streaming cameras, current position. Need eyes on that holding tank, building B front."

The cruiser's dash fragments into six angles, each showing the transport. Through the clearing smoke, my blood runs cold. A figure emerges; cuffed arms extended like a mockery of surrender. Three men surround him, one scanning the cuffs with a key-clip. My heart hammers against my ribs.

"Damn! It's Krishman . . . they've already cut him loose. Network, I've lost contact with sergeant and lieutenant on site. Need to warn the . . ." Movement in the bottom screen catches my eye. "Wait! What are they doing? Why all the hanging around? What's the . . ."

One guard passes Krishman a glowing yellow tech-vial. Even through the grainy feed, I recognize it; same design we found at the dog fighting rings, where he tested his "products." The bodies we found after . . . My face burns as I grip my firearm tighter. He cracks open the vial, inhaling the luminescent yellow mist. It starts. The spasms, convulsing. This just turned bad.

"No! No, no, no. He's *vapin'* out! Network, all ground units at the square, stay clear of the prisoner. Krishman's dosing Class C Vapyr! Be advised . . ."

[NETWORK]: "Calibrating . . . Personal devices offline due to in-cendiary discharge containing electromagnetic pulses. Three minutes twelve seconds until full network restoration for this area."

The firefight's percussion mingles with screams as I swallow rising bile. Through the din, a memory surfaces–Tavia's voice again, but dif-ferent this time. *"In chess, like life, sometimes you sacrifice position to gain advantage."* I peel myself out of the trench coat and roll up both sleeves, as eyes scan the cruiser's interior, seeking anything useful.

That snake had this choreographed from the start. New Year's skeleton crew, Shanks in place, timed charges. Okay. Alright. Think you can knock me off the board on a holiday? Think that tech-dope's gonna save you? The last time you *vaped* out, you left four officers in intensive care. Not today. Not in my city.

Something catches my eye—metallic glint from the passenger pocket. Krishman's weapon from the bust. The "toy" he used to carve up two of our informants before they could testify. Heard he took off three of his own guys' fingers with it for *buckin'* at him once. I reach for it, jaw clenched. I'm officially tired of snakes today. This bastard is going down.

After reloading my blaster, I ghost between shadows, working my way toward center yard. The marble columns of the square loom overhead—old Atlanta architecture about to witness new violence. Through thinning smoke, I spot two officers behind a courier truck, both looking shell-shocked.

Movement above—an armor-clad thug appears on a pedestrian walkway. I dive behind a weathered statue just as rounds spark off its base. Pulling a silver disc from my belt, I press, waiting for the light. The hunter becomes prey—I swing it wide around my cover. It lands perfectly, blue current dropping him mid-stride.

Reaching the officers by the truck, I find Oglesby, face streaked with sweat and soot.

"Detective, holy shit! What's the play here?

Before I can answer, a scream pierces the air. Through the smoke, a body flies past, spinning like a broken doll before crashing into the parade barriers. My stomach turns—I recognize the uniform. Rodriguez. Good cop, two kids. He'd complained about working the holiday.

"That's what Vapyr does," I explain, checking my blaster charge. "Turns users into living weapons. Last time Krishman dosed in public, he put a car through a storefront. The driver . . . didn't make it."

"You got a plan?" he asks between coughs. "Net says six hostiles left, not counting the beast himself."

Meeting his gaze, I nod. "Yeah, I took one down. Listen, Oglesby, you *alright*? Good. We flank these boys, push them toward the holding truck. Keep trying for Sarge. We need—"

Sha-WHIP! White-hot pain scores across my shoulder, spinning me down. Officers return fire as I scramble behind a concrete median. Checking the wound, time seems to stretch.

Visions flood in—case files, crime scenes, faces of those we couldn't save. But through the chaos, another scent catches me. Tavia.

The ghost of jasmine cuts through gun smoke. Her words from the dance floor echo: *"Sometimes the queen must be sacrificed to trap the king."*

The memory shifts—her thin fingers touching my face, those knowing eyes. "You're not just a knight on this board anymore, Marc. You've learned to see the whole game."

Time speeds up as a growl rumbles from my gut, climbing through my ribs. My chest expands and words fire out: "You heard the lady! Let's end this and get these animals in cages, keep Krishman away from the public!"

A tiny eternity of silence breaks with Oglesby's bark. "What lady, Danno?!"

"Shit, never mind! Take Schupp and get behind those pillars on Pryor Street's side! Keep Krishman's plants from using them as a hole to get away through. I'mma head through the parade banners on the other side to see if I can get to the big guy."

"Krishman?! You thinkin' that's smart while he's hopped up on that demon smoke?!"

"Well, no." The truth forces its way out. "But raging bulls hate red, right?! So I'll give him a target and try to distract him 'til GBI gets their people in closer."

Oglesby nods, taking a breath. "Watch yourself, D—Hey, Schupp! You're with me. You two, go east side, watch each other's six, try getting eyes on Sarge."

Taking the *tech-gangster's* weapon in hand, I run my thumb across the sensor, bracing for rejection. Orange lights whirl as my com device engages. A hologram blooms, accompanied by an eerily serene voice:

[DEVICE]: "Welcome, Detective Marquis Alonzo Dannon to Project Phoenix. Experimental plasma slicer. Model 714. Apple Corporation design patent D739,312 . . ."

"Apple?! Of course." Even psychopaths trust the brand. "Show me how to use this thing without bisecting myself."

[DEVICE]: "Tutorial Menu options: Taser, Bolt Cutter, Tourniquet Crafter, Plasma-Whip..."

"Plasma-Whip." My pulse quickens. "Like Christmas morning in a gunfight."

[DEVICE]: "Select lethality level: Control-Subdue, Injure-Maim, Full power-Kill."

"Control-Subdue." Keep him breathing for trial. If possible.

A groan draws my attention. An agent in a blazer struggles to rise nearby, cradling his wrist.

"Stay down," I warn. "Could have fractures."

"Norm Briggs," he manages. "That monster . . . threw me like a paper cup."

Moving toward the chaos, I hear him rasp, "Where you going?!"

"To the circus." Walking into hell with a borrowed whip.

Through clearing smoke, I witness Krishman's handiwork. Bodies scattered like fallen chessmen. The "Fire Snake" holds Grasso aloft, my sergeant's feet kicking air, face purpling.

"Put him down, Krishman!" Drexel commands from cover, surrounded by drawn weapons. "Half your crew's caught. Game's over!"

Krishman's laugh comes guttural, inhuman. Vapyr's effects visible now—skin glowing with volcanic patterns, eyes blazing amber. "Not over . . . until this piglet squeals!"

"Hey, snake boy!" My voice cuts through the tension. "Put the sergeant down. Got something that belongs to you."

He turns, Grasso still dangling. Even through the drug haze, recognition flares.

"Detective! Missing your hat!"

"Your boys shot it off, Mateo. Now, about the sergeant . . ."

His grin stretches unnaturally wide, showing elongated canines. Vapyr restructuring his facial bones. "Using my Christian name . . . touching my stuff . . . such disrespect deserves punishment!"

Grasso drops, gasping. Krishman's focus locks onto me, muscles rippling beneath prison garb. Three years hunting him, never seen him this transformed. This dangerous.

"Phoenix," I whisper to the weapon, "Help a brotha' out—make this count."

Krishman launches himself, covering twenty feet in a single bound. I quick-draw the blaster, firing a disc, catching him mid-leap. Blue lightning cascades over his frame, but he lands in a crouch, smoke curling from his shoulders. Where it would have dropped anyone else, he just snarls.

"That tickled. My turn."

He tears a marble bench from its foundation, hurling it like a toy. I dive, feeling the wind as it shatters against a column behind me. The square's historical architecture won't survive much more of this.

"Phoenix, display attack pattern!" The hologram grid appears, showing strike zones. Time to test *his* toy now.

The plasma whip cracks down, its red energy splitting the air. Krishman dodges, but the strike leaves a molten groove in the pavement.

"Whoa! Now that's hot!" *I love this thing already*. His eyes widen—recognition, then rage.

"You dare!" His voice deepens, Vapyr warping his vocal cords. "That's mine!"

"Should've used better security, Matt." Another crack of the whip keeps him back. "Tech genius like you, using default settings? That's sloppy."

He circles, looking for openings. The drug makes his movements fluid, predatory. "I'll peel your skin, slice by slice . . ."

A shot rings out—Shanks, trying to flank. Agent Briggs answers with return fire, pinning him down. "Focus on the big one, Detective!"

Krishman uses the distraction, closing distance. His fist grazes my jaw as I spin away. Even that slight contact feels like being hit with brass knuckles. The Vapyr has turned his body into living armor.

"Phoenix, increase charge to Injure-Maim!"

[DEVICE]: "Adjusting output. Warning: thermal feedback increased."

The whip's glow intensifies to orange as I strike again. This time it catches him across the chest, drawing first blood. He howls—part pain, part fury.

But instead of retreating, he grabs the energy stream with bare hands. His enhanced strength let him pull me forward, into his reach. His other fist cocks back for a killing blow.

Chess wisdom strikes like lightning—Tavia's voice cutting through adrenaline: *"The obvious attack is often a trap. Look deeper."*

Instead of resisting his pull, I drop and roll, using his own momentum. The sudden shift throws him off balance. As he stumbles forward, I spring up behind him, plasma whip singing through the air.

"Phoenix, full stun pattern, now!"

The energy stream wraps his throat like a noose of fire. He claws at it, enhanced strength meeting cutting-edge tech. Steam rises where plasma meets Vapyr-infused flesh.

"You . . . insignificant . . . piece of . . ." His words choke off as I pull tighter.

"Not so fun when the prey bites back, is it?" Memories of his victims fuel my grip. "This is for Rodriguez's kids. Those informants. Folks you've hurt. Those dogs you tortured. You're a real glorified fuck boy, Matt."

His eyes blaze brighter, muscles bulging as he fights the restraint. "I own this city! You can't . . ."

"Phoenix, maximum stun charge!"

[DEVICE]: "Warning: Approaching critical thermal threshold."

The whip's glow shifts from orange to white-hot blue. Krishman's knees finally buckle as the electricity volts through him. Even with Vapyr coursing through his system, there's only so much the human body can take.

A movement catches my eye—Shanks, rising with another weapon. "Cut'em loose, pig or . . ."

Laser fire from Briggs drops him instantly. "Not today, sunshine!"

Krishman falls forward, his enhanced strength finally failing. The drug's glow fades from his skin, leaving him looking almost human again. Almost.

"Check . . . mate," I manage through gritted teeth, letting the whip power down.

Grasso limps over, rubbing his throat. "Jesus Christ, Danno. Next time just invite him for coffee."

"Technically, this was his invite." Looking down at the unconscious crime lord. "He just didn't expect to be the one getting served."

Sarge, finally exhaling, big sigh. "Cute one, Hotshot. Now, let's get this shit show cleaned up."

Medical units swarm in as Drexel oversees Krishman's recontainment. This time with heavy-duty restraints and anti-Vapyr protocols. The lieutenant catches my eye, nodding slowly.

The noon sun breaks through dark grey haze, glinting off broken marble and scattered brass. Just after another New Year's dawn in Atlanta. My shoulder throbs big time where the bullet grazed it, but something else aches deeper. A good ache. The kind that comes from finishing what you started.

Holstering Krishman's weapon—evidence now—I can't believe that worked. Somewhere across town, I left a chess master at the bar. Then prospered, with a fraction of what flirting with her over coffee taught me. Maybe it's time to finally learn the game properly.

"Good game, Mateo. Happy New Year."

"The wisest player knows even as checkmate falls, unseen hands may have moved pieces on a larger board."
- Chess Master Isabella Chen, 2089

The elevator glides upward, my reflection ghosting against Atlanta's skyline through the glass. Twelve floors never felt so far. My feet feel like concrete blocks, the rest of me swaying like Spanish moss in a Georgia breeze. The couch in my office calls like a siren, but Sarge needs his debrief.

Images crash in waves: Krishman's enhanced face twisted in rage, his skin glowing with Vapyr's volcanic patterns. The plasma whip's heat against my palm as it caught his throat. The thunder of that marble bench shattering. My shoulder, still throbbing beneath fresh bandage foam, a souvenir from the late morning's dance with the Fire Snake.

Leaning one-handed against the glass, I watch the lobby shrink below. My reflection stares back, stubble darkening into what was once a decent line-up on a goatee. Then it hits me again—that ghost of sweetness rising through the day's sweat and gun smoke. Jasmine. Autumn Spice. Tavia.

My wrist snaps up: 6:06 PM. Something twists in my gut, a different kind of combat adrenaline. Hours ago, duty and stubbornness made me walk away. Kept me away. Now . . .

The elevator doors whisper open to applause. Screens around the office replay edited footage of the square showdown—the whip's glowing arc, Krishman's fall, that final takedown. I force a smile, shaking hands as they appear.

"Danno!" someone hollers from the back. Nikka, one of our routers, tries clapping while juggling her glowing schedule pad. "Nice work detective!"

Banks muscles through the growing crowd. "Hey, Dannon, Oglesby asked me to keep this til I saw you." He hands over my wide-brim hat, somehow intact after the firefight, save a few smudges. A smile tugs at my mouth as I wipe it down, memories of dodging Krishman's throws still fresh.

"Thanks, man. I just came up to—"

"Put it on, Danno! Let's see it!" The crowd picks up the chant: "Put-it-on! Put-it-on!"

Rolling my eyes, I place it carefully on my head, playing to the audience with a movie star pose. Reese, and old dispatcher yells, "We got *Indiana Dannon* up here today everybody!" The floor erupts in laughter.

Grateful for the levity after this morning's hell, I head for Sarge's office, finding him in mid-sip of coffee. He sets his cup down next to a half-eaten burger, screens rising behind him.

"I knew that was you out there with all the noise. Sit down, got something tracking on the important side since we locked up Krishman and his wolf pack."

"You and the captain looked good on the news, Sarge."

"Yeah, I looked real good getting strangled by that maniac." He adjusts in his chair, reaching for the burger.

"Well, at least the whole city didn't see that part, sir."

He whips around, still chewing. "Thank God! (cough) Good thing that kid in forensics edited that footage of you whippin' that punk knew to leave my ugly mug out of it."

My hands rotate the hat's brim as thoughts of Tavia push forward. "Sarge, I forgot about meeting someone at the Aero-Rail station soon. Everything's wrapped at the square, med-evac checked all the injured. Rodriguez will pull through, few months rehab. You know we found Warren. Shanks doped him up pretty good, but you'll see him back around Precinct 5 in a week or two. So . . ."

"This won't take long," Sarge turns to the monitors as they flip from news to financial graphs. "That scumbag Shanks isn't going any-where. Those stun rods hit him good—he'll wake up eventually, just won't enjoy it. What got me thinking was something that "psycho" Krishman was yammering about just before he grabbed me. About the cash and credits we seized, and something about 'disappearing digi-coins.'"

I sit back, hat resting in my lap. "Okay, so uh . . ."

"Well, I got all nostalgic about my ol' gumshoe days—turns out Krishman really did have over 17 million in cash and credits, plus an-other 4 million in digicoins. Right up until approximately 90 minutes before we seized only 8 million. No digicoins." He fumbles through desk items, searching. "Someone cyber-heisted his whole operation, right before our show. Wouldn't have caught it if he hadn't tried bust-ing out."

My mind flashes to Krishman's face twisted in fury, not just from Vapyr, but genuine rage. Maybe, about being robbed? The pieces start shifting.

"Remember that anonymous tip from October? About the Vapyr lab and stash? Boris, the kid who edited your takedown footage, found an encrypted call sign in it. Matched parts of the code to traces left when we tried tracking the missing money. Damn!" He lifts papers, growing frustrated. "Where'd I put . . . whoever did this was next level. Most hackers barely handle quad 3 AI protections. Same source that tipped us might've set up the money hit. Since Krishman was big on Britain's hacker logs before the vape business."

Standing, I check the time again. 6:27 PM. "Wild stuff, Sarge. Thank Boris for me."

"Ha! Here it is, under this fuckin' neck brace. 'Crimson Spar-row'—that was the call sign. Ring any bells, Danno?"

Time stops. Tavia's smile flickers through my mind. Her necklace charm swaying gently. Her voice, playful and knowing: *"It's not a* cardinal, it's a sparrow."

Heat crawls up my neck as her words echo: *"I've been here all week . . ."*

"Anything, Detective?"

Taking a deep breath, I meet Sarge's eyes. "Nah, nothing. Must be thinking of a movie or something. Head's still scrambled."

He sucks his teeth. "Ah well, it'll keep. Turn that whip thing over to evidence on five. Can get it back in sixty days if ya want."

Making it to the door, fixin' my Fedora, I hear: "Oh, and Danno!" His coffee cup raises in salute. "Happy New Year."

Walking out, my mind spins like a tactical display, rewriting everything I thought I knew. While I was playing cops and robbers in the streets, she was playing four-dimensional chess. The queen had been moving across the board all along, while the knight played his part in her game. And somehow, I can't stop a smile from creeping up. Of all the cities, and all the coffee joints in the world—yada, yada.

TERMINUS 3 AUTHORS
(ALPHABETICAL ORDER BY LAST NAME)

JESSICA CAGE: FARIES AT MAYOR'S PARK

Jessica Cage is an international award winning, and USA Today Best Selling Author. Born and raised in Chicago, IL, writing has always been a passion for her. She dabbles in artistic creations of all sorts but at the end of the day, it's the pen that her hand itches to hold. Jessica had never considered following her dream to be a writer because she was told far too often "There is no money in writing." So she chose the path most often traveled. During pregnancy, she asked herself an important question. How would she be able to inspire her unborn son to follow his dreams and reach for the stars, if she never had the guts to do it herself? Jessica decided to take a risk and unleash the plethora of characters and their crazy adventurous worlds that had previously existed only in her mind, into the realm of readers. She did this with hopes to inspire not only her son but herself. Inviting the world to tag along on her journey to become the writer she has always wanted to be. She hopes to continue writing and bringing her signature Caged Fantasies to readers everywhere.

GERALD L. COLEMAN: TETHERED GOAT

Gerald L. Coleman is a philosopher, theologian, poet, and Science Fiction & Fantasy author. He did his undergraduate work in Philosophy, English, and Religious Studies, followed by a master's degree in theology. He is the author of the Epic Fantasy novel series The Three Gifts, which currently includes, When Night Falls (Book One), A Plague of Shadows (Book Two), and the upcoming When Chaos Reigns (Book Three). His speculative fiction has appeared numerous anthologies including: The Cyberfunk Anthology: The City, the Roaring Lion Anthology: Rococoa, the Urban Fantasy Anthologies:

Terminus 1, 2, and 3, the 2019 JordanCon Anthology: You Want Stories?, Dark Universe: Bright Empire, Cyberfunk!, Spacefunk!, the JordanCon 2022 Anthology: Neither Endings Nor Beginnings, and Whether Change: The Revolution Will Be Weird. His essays appear in the Polish language Con-Magazine: KONwersacje, Apex Magazine 127, and the Hugo nominated Fanzine: Journey Planet. His poetry has appeared in journals, magazines, and anthologies including Pluck! The Journal of Affrilachian Arts & Culture, Drawn To Marvel: Poems From The Comic Books, Pine Mountain Sand & Gravel Vol. 18, Black Bone Anthology, the 10th Anniversary Issue of Diode Poetry Journal, About Place Journal, Star*line Vol. 43, Issue 4, the Locust Award nominated Year's Best African Speculative Fiction (2022), and This is the Honey: An Anthology of Contemporary Black Poets.

ASHLEIGH DAVENPORT: FANGS AND CLAWS BRING DUE
Ashleigh Davenport loves writing urban fantasies about monsters that bump in the night in more ways than one and the women who love them. She's always working on one writing project or another and fuels her late-night writing sessions with chocolate and bacon. You can find all things Ashleigh, through https://linktr.ee/AshWritesLots.

ALANA DAVIS: THE BODY FARM
Alana Davis is an author with a passion for all things horror and fantasy, with a dash of sci-fi for good measure. She has been writing as a hobby since she was a teenager, posting her stories everywhere from r/NoSleep to AO3. She can often be found hiking in the forest, or at home with her feline roommate Valkyrie.

MILTON J. DAVIS: HOMECOMING
Milton J. Davis is an acclaimed Black speculative fiction author and the founder of MVmedia, LLC, a publishing company dedicated to producing science fiction, fantasy, and sword-and-

soul narratives that highlight African and African Diaspora cultures. Based in Metro Atlanta, Davis has been a prominent figure in the Afrofuturist and Black speculative fiction communities for over two decades. In 2022, Davis was honored with the East Coast Black Age of Comics Convention Pioneer Lifetime Achievement Award, recognizing his significant contributions to Black speculative fiction. In 2024, he received the ConCarolinas Polaris Award, and the DeepSouth Con Phoenix Award for his contributions to Southern fandom.

L. RENEE JAMES-GRIFFIN: TALISMAN OF GAMBIT
L. Renee James-Griffin is an educator, editor, and writer with over two decades of experience helping others find their voice through the written word. She has an MFA in Writing from Naslund-Mann Graduate School of Writing at Spalding University. She is the co-founder of TLM Language Services and is passionate about nurturing creativity and promoting the art of storytelling. When not editing or teaching, James-Griffin is busy penning new stories, essays, and poems she hopes will soon find their literary homes.

M. HAYNES: THE DREAMER'S RING
M. Haynes' childhood was so filled with fantasy worlds that he just had to create one of his own. He began writing his own stories at the age of nine, creating characters who reflected his life experiences. As an adult M. Haynes recognized the lack of inclusion in speculative fiction and set out to correct that with his Elemental series and other writings. Now, M. Haynes uses what he has learned to show that protagonists can be more than just straight, blonde-haired, blue-eyed men or boys. Learn more about M. Haynes and his writing at his website, www.mhaynes.org

MARCELLUS SHANE JACKSON: CASALANTA

Marcellus Shane Jackson is an Atlanta-based graphic designer, illustrator, and storyteller with over 25 years of experience crafting bold, cinematic visuals. Known as "Mr. Shane" to many, he's created designs for a wide range of clients across the Southeast—including universities, HBCUs, and every organization within the Divine 9. His work, seen on countless homecoming and convention tees, carries a legacy of cultural pride and visual impact. Known since 2013 as the "movie poster style" cover artist of the Steamfunk anthology in the world of Black speculative fiction, he makes his literary debut as both cover artist and contributing author in Terminus Vol. 3.

NADIRA JAMESON: WHEN CARNAGE IS NO LONGER ENOUGH

As a Black queer woman, storytelling in all of its forms is one of Nadira Jamerson's greatest tools in building community. Through journalism and creative writing, her work explores themes including health, living beyond generational trauma, and the fight for Black and queer liberation. Her work has been shared in numerous publications worldwide, including DC Comics, Word In Black, and No Glum (UK).

TIARA JANTE': AN ECHO OF DREAMS

Tiara Janté is a Locus Award-winning, Hugo-nominated writer whose speculative fiction and non-fiction center Black spiritual traditions, ancestral memory, and liberated futures. She writes stories that challenge systems, hold space for healing, and honor the sacred in everyday life.

Tiara coined 'Hoodoofuturism', a genre that blends ancestral practices with speculative storytelling, offering narratives shaped by transformation, resistance, and connection. Her work weaves truth and imagination, often exploring the intersection of ritual, identity, and power.

ROBERT JEFFERY II: MONSTERS ON THE MOUNT'

Robert Jeffrey II is an award-winning/ nominated professional writer (comic books, video games, tabletop gaming, prose fiction, and journalism) with over 20 years of experience as a creative writer. He has worked with clients such as DC Comics, the Centers for Disease Control, Son of Oak Gaming, 133Art Publishing, RAE Comics, SUBSUME Media, New Agenda Publishing, MV Media, BlackSci-Fi.com, and Nitto Tires. He is a graduate of the 2017 DC Comics Writers Workshop Class and recently worked as a video game writer for developer Blowfish Studios on such projects as Shadowman: Darque Legacy and Phantom Galaxies. You can find him at www.robertkjeffrey.com and on IG at robertk.jeffrey.

ALAN JONES: RIGGAMARO

Alan Jones is an Atlanta Native birthed at Hugh Spalding (where black folks were treated and, in this case, birthed). He holds a BBA in Computer Science and MBA with concentration in Finance. Alan has worked exclusively in the FinTech space since 1996 (largely on Oracle platforms). but integrated client platform with 3rd parties. His clients include J.P. Morgan Chase (on Wall Street, NYC), Vanguard for a total of six years, U.S House or Representatives. Honda Motors (Torrance, CA), Savannah River Nuclear Site, CDW, and American Honda. Alan's writing credits include Technique (GA Sech), The Signal (GA State), and The Atlanta Tribune. He has contributed to numerous anthologies, including Terminus 1 and Terminus 2.

W. ALEXANDER LAWSON: UNCLAIMED

W. Alexander Lawson is a writer and educator from Broward County, Florida. Drawing from his personal experiences and familial history, he composes Black Speculative Fiction with an emphasis on the LGBTQIA+ community. Lawson holds an Associate of Arts from Broward College (BC), a Bachelor of Arts in English at Clark Atlanta University (CAU), and a Master of Arts in Professional Writing, with a concentration in creative writing and secondary concentrations in rhetoric & composition and applied writing from Kennesaw State University (KSU).

KYOKO M: THINGS THAT GO BUMP IN THE NIGHT

Kyoko M is a USA Today bestselling author and a fangirl. She is the author of The Black Parade urban fantasy series, the Of Cinder and Bone science-fiction series, and the Starlight Contingency space opera series with Falstaff Books. The Black Parade has been reviewed by Publishers Weekly and New York Times bestselling author Ilona Andrews. Of Cinder and Bone placed in the Top 30 Books in Hugh Howey's 2021 Self Published Science Fiction Contest. Kyoko M has appeared as a guest and panelist at such conventions as Geek Girl Con, DragonCon, Blacktasticon, Momocon, JordanCon, ConCarolinas, and MultiverseCon. She is also a contributor to Marvel Comics' Black Panther: Tales of Wakanda (2021) anthology as well as the Captain America: The Shield of Sam Wilson (2025) anthology. She has a Bachelor of Arts in English Lit degree from the University of Georgia, which gave her every valid excuse to devour book after book with a concentration in Greek mythology and Christian mythology.

VIOLETTE MEIER: DAPHINE

Atlanta native Violette Meier is a happily married mother, writer, and folk artist who earned her B.A. in English at Clark Atlanta University and a MDiv at the Interdenominational Theological Center. She is also a certified herbalist, chaplain, and educator.

The great-granddaughter of a dream interpreter, Violette is a lover of all things supernatural. Her eerie and unpredictable paranormal, fantasy, and horror stories recreate myths and legends and fashion new folklore. Violette is always working on something fresh.

Her books include: Out of Night, Angel Crush, Son of the Rock, Archfiend, Ruah the Immortal, Oracles, Tales of a Numinous

Nature, Hags, Haints and Hoodoo, Preternatural Haze, Loving and Living Life One Day at time, With All With My Being, Violette Ardor: A Volume of Poetry, This Sickness We Call Love: Poems of Love, Lust, and Lamentation, and two children's books. You can also find her work in various anthologies. To learn more about Violette and her eerie antics, visit her website **VioletteMeier.com.**

BALOGUN OJETADE: VANTABLACK

Balogun Ojetade is Master Instructor and Technical Director of the Afrikan Martial Arts Institute and The Founder and Owner of Roaring Lions Productions, which creates works of non-fiction, fiction, screenplays, audio plays and films.

He is the author of more than forty non-fiction and fiction books, contributing co-editor of three anthologies: Ki: Khanga: The Anthology, Steamfunk and Dieselfunk and contributing editor of the Rococoa anthology and Black Power: The Superhero Anthology.

He is creator of the Steamfunkateers Role Playing Game, the comedic martial arts role playing game, The Ice Cold RPG, the horror RPGs 4EV4 Friends and The Haunting of Truth High and the revolutionary role playing game Stick It to The Man! Finally, Balogun is the Director and Fight Choreographer of the feature film, A Single Link, and the short films, Forward Motion, Rite of Passage: Initiation and The Dentist of Westminster; co-author of the award winning screenplay, Ngolo; co-creator of Ki Khanga: The Sword and Soul Role-Playing Game, creator of the comic book series Jagunjagun Lewa and co-creator of the comic book series, Ngolo.

GLENN PARRIS: BAT OUT OF HELL

Born in Queens NY, graduate of The Bronx High School of Science, and Fordham University, Dr. Glenn Parris earned his medical degree at SUNY Buffalo, NY, and completed his residency and fellowship at Emory University in ATL. He owns and directs a private rheumatology practice in the northeast

Atlanta suburbs. He writes science fiction, fantasy, medical mystery, horror, and comic book fiction. Author of The Underside of Darkness for Marvel's Black Panther: Tales of Wakanda, The Renaissance of Aspirin, and the dark fantasy short stories, The Tooth Fairies, Quest for Tearhaven, Unbitten: A Vampire Dream, The Sleepwalking Dead, Red Rose Reign, and the speculative science fiction novel, Dragon's Heir, the first in a trilogy called The Efilu Saga. Coming soon; Raiders of the Middle Passage, Third World, The Gray Zone, Bat Out of Hell, and others. He has been a panel guest at the Planet ComiCon, ThrillerFest, TremediCon, DragonCon, BoucherCon, MultiverseCon, Creatures, Crimes and Creativity, and the World Fantasy Convention.

ALVIN JORDAN RICHARDSON: COLORS OF THE COSMOS

Jay Gervara (real name Alvin Jordan Richardson) is the visionary creator and founder of Kovi Entertainment Universe, the first of its kind, a Virgin Islands based comic book company bringing a bold, fictional superhero mythology to the Caribbean. With roots steeped in cultural pride and storytelling prowess, Jay has forged a new path in the comic book world, blending Caribbean heritage with the grandiosity of heroic fiction. His flagship character, Olu: The Punished Fox, a mercenary turned island king, has already made waves with two published issues now in stores & laying the foundation for a universe unlike any other. As he expands into the world of literature, Jay's first writing credit as a literary author will be in collaboration with the legendary Milton Davis in Terminus 3 with the story Colors of the Cosmos.

DEDREN SNEAD: PENNY CANDY LADY

Dedren Snead is a computer scientist, artist, and Ford Foundation Global Fellow whose work bridges technology and storytelling to create inclusive narratives that celebrate diverse cultural perspectives. As founder of SUBSUME Media and SUBSUME Studios—the world's first Afrofuturism technology studio in downtown Atlanta—he has been featured in CNN and Black Enterprise for his pioneering approach to combining traditional cultural wisdom with cutting-edge technology.

AZIZA SPHINX: RIVER GHOST

A techie by trade and writer by necessity, Aziza Sphinx is a hybrid author who has been writing and publishing professionally for over 20 years. The author of gown folks speculative fiction that blurs the lines between transpersonal psychology, fantasy, and sanity, many of her fairytale remakes, short stories, and speculative poems have been included in a wide range of anthologies and ezines. When not sharing her knowledge of overcoming 'writer's avoidance,' Aziza spends her nights playing in the shadows with her vampires, demons, wraiths, and reapers. She also occasionally plays in the light and entertains the living. To lean more of Aziza's literary exploits, visit https://penned-in-blue-llc.square.site/aziza-sphinx

KORTNEY WATKINS: SWING

Kortney Y. Watkins is an English professor, writer, and poet who resides in the Atlanta metro amongst loving kin and friends. You can find her other short stories as a previously featured author in the anthological series of Terminus: Tales of the Black Fantastic, books I and II. A quirky, geeky, dark romantic, she lives for the moods of the moon, waits for the roaring of the rain, and nestles snuggly in the high hopes that God's stars promise, should they be caught and deigned to be wished upon.

We hope you enjoyed this third edition of Terminus. For more fantastic tales of the ATL, visit MVmedia!
www.mvmediaatl.com